With her roots firmly planted in the South, #1 *New York Times* bestselling author **Sherryl Woods** has written many of her more than one hundred books in that distinctive setting, whether it's her home state of Virginia, her adopted state, Florida, or her much-adored South Carolina. Now she's added North Carolina's Outer Banks to her list of favorite spots. And she remains partial to small towns, wherever they may be.

Sherryl divides her time between her childhood summer home overlooking the Potomac River in Colonial Beach, Virginia, and her oceanfront home with its lighthouse view in Key Biscayne, Florida. "Wherever I am, if there's no water in sight, I get a little antsy," she says.

Sherryl loves to hear from readers. You can visit her on her website at www.sherrylwoods.com, link to her Facebook fan page from there or contact her directly at Sherryl703@gmail.com.

Despite a no-nonsense background as a West Point graduate and US Army officer, *USA TODAY* bestselling author **Caro Carson** has always treasured the happily-ever-after of a good romance novel. After reading romances no matter where in the world the army sent her, Caro began a career in the pharmaceutical industry. Little did she know the years she spent discussing science with physicians would provide excellent story material for her new career as a romance author. Now Caro is delighted to be living her own happily-ever-after with her husband and two children in the great state of Florida, a location that has saved the coaster-loving theme-park fanatic a fortune on plane tickets.

SHERRYL WOODS

MY DEAREST CAL

⬨HARLEQUIN® BESTSELLING AUTHOR COLLECTION

ISBN-13: 978-1-335-14398-3

My Dearest Cal

Copyright © 2017 by Harlequin Books S.A.

The publisher acknowledges the copyright holders of the individual works as follows:

My Dearest Cal
© 1991 by Sherryl Woods

A Texas Rescue Christmas
© 2014 by Caro Carson

Recycling programs
for this product may
not exist in your area.

H HARLEQUIN®
TM www.Harlequin.com

Printed in U.S.A.

CONTENTS

MY DEAREST CAL

Sherryl Woods

For Craig, Dianne, Michael and Kelly for all the holiday family dinners and for the insight into postal regulations. For Ken, Eddie, Matda, Fred and all the rest, who brighten the endless time an author seems to spend at the mailbox. And especially for Nona, with thanks for sharing your love of horses with me and in memory of your beloved and gallant Bolshoi.

Chapter One

April showers, Marilou thought with a disgusted sniff. She splashed through an ankle-deep puddle on her way to work. At this rate the poor May flowers would drown. She sneezed and shivered as a chilly Thursday morning wind scooped up the hem of her raincoat and lifted it just high enough to allow the rain to drench her new red skirt. Drown, hell. They'd probably freeze first.

It must be warm and sunny someplace right now, she thought longingly as she trudged across the parking lot toward her office. Wherever it was, she would give anything to be there. Tahiti. Hawaii. Even the Sahara. It didn't much matter as long as it was dry. And hot. The winter in Atlanta had been the pits. It was now one week into the dreariest, wettest April on record. Judging from the endless gray sky, spring obviously wasn't going to be much of an improvement.

A few minutes later, still sneezing and blowing her nose, Marilou settled into her cubbyhole in the U.S. Postal Service's Dead Letter Office and grimly faced the stacks of unopened mail that had gone astray in the

Southeast. Whole shelves around her held everything from lost keys to movie reels, all silent testimony to the carelessness of people in a hurry. A red bikini top dangled from a hook—the bottom had vanished. One of her coworkers had hung the provocative garment where he could see it as he worked. She had a hunch Matt thoroughly enjoyed imagining the woman who'd been wearing it and the no doubt fascinating story behind its loss and subsequent discovery in some corner mailbox.

Normally Marilou started the day with enthusiasm, liking the challenge of reuniting letters and parcels with the intended recipients. She'd only been at it a little more than a year and a half, but so far she'd never found it tedious. It was a little like she imagined detective work would be. Getting treasured photos or a favorite teddy bear back to its rightful owner required the same kind of ingenuity and persistence it took to track missing persons or lost heirs. It was also emotionally rewarding, even if the person never knew about her involvement. Once in a while, like the time she'd gotten several thousand dollars' worth of stock certificates back where they belonged, she'd received letters of praise and heartfelt thanks. This wasn't the adventurous life she'd once envisioned for herself, but it was good.

Usually, she amended with a sigh.

Today, however, with her shoes soaked again and her feet icy cold, she was in no mood to be sympathetic to the people who'd forgotten to put return addresses on their envelopes. She was tired of trying to decipher ink that had run after getting drenched by rain. She was out of patience with people who stuck their bills in backward so that the company address wasn't visible. And she'd had it up to her stuffed nose with idiots who figured they'd just send off their tax forms with no postage. As a protest against the IRS, it was useless. The forms went back to the sender, once she'd wasted half a day tracking them down. All in all, she felt like throwing the whole mess from her desk straight into the shredder, but she was too darned conscientious.

She shivered, then took one last sip of hot coffee before reaching for the one envelope that showed any promise. Addressed by a seemingly shaky hand to a Mr. Cal Rivers, it had been sent to an address in Florida that apparently didn't exist. "No such address" had been stamped emphatically across the front and again on the back.

Palm Tree Lane. Oh, how she liked the sound of that. Where there were palm trees, there was probably sunshine. Maybe even temperatures above the freeze-your-butt variety. Honest-to-gosh spring temperatures. She paused a minute to savor the very idea of lying on some sun-kissed stretch of sand, baking until she could actually breathe again.

When she finally got around to opening the letter, she was already feeling better just for having taken that brief mental vacation. But as she quickly scanned the thick vellum pages, filled with their crimped scrawl of words, her spirits sank once more. There was no return address anywhere. And although she wasn't supposed to read the contents, one or two phrases caught her eye— "Never forget that I love you…so sorry we've never had a chance to get to know each other… I'm dying now…"

Oh, my God. *Dying!* Knowing it was against every rule, Marilou went back to the beginning. "My dearest Cal…"

Now that she knew the ending, every word was so

poignant, it made her want to weep. It seemed to be a farewell letter from a grandmother to a grandson she'd never met. Filled with longing and regrets, it broke Marilou's heart. The terrible, unexpected loss of her own parents was still new and raw, even after nearly eighteen months. There had been so many things left unsaid between them, so many arguments that would never be resolved. She ached at the thought that some little boy might have family he didn't even know about. There had to be a way to see that this letter reached him, that the family was reunited before it was too late.

Filled with determination, she hunted through the pile of phone books from every state in the region until she found the one she wanted. Please, just this once, let it be easy, she thought as she flipped through the pages to the Rs. Let this kid be named after his father. Or at the very least, let there not be twenty-five listings for Rivers. Rivas. Rivero—at least fifty of them. Then she found it. Rivers, Cal. Two-twenty-nine Palm Lane. Not Palm *Tree* Lane. What was the big deal? she thought indignantly. Some fool mailman couldn't figure out what the dear old woman meant?

Marilou reached for the phone, punched in the area code and number, only to hear the dreaded sound that always preceded some recorded message. With a sinking sensation, she anticipated this one.

"…has been disconnected." Of course. No new number. Just disconnected.

She flipped back through the directory for the phone number of the local post office, called and asked if there was any record of a Cal Rivers leaving a forwarding address.

"It's not in the computer," the disinterested clerk told her eventually.

"Maybe it just expired. There should be a record..."

"I'm telling you it's not in here. For all I know it was never in here."

"Couldn't you..."

"Lady, I don't have all day to hunt for things that don't exist."

"What about the carrier for that route? Maybe he'd remember."

"That's probably Priscilla."

"Could I speak to her?"

"She's off today," the clerk said in a tone that ended any further discussion.

"Thanks for your help," Marilou said sarcastically into the already-dead connection. Apparently sunshine wasn't a guaranteed panacea for the ill tempers of the world.

She put the letter aside and went through the remaining stack of mail. One after another she was able to identify either sender or recipient and get the mail back on track. Those that were hopeless, actually the greatest percentage, went into the shredder. But even as she efficiently handled her usual hundreds of letters, that one brief note from Cal Rivers's grandmother began to haunt her.

According to regulations she was supposed to dispose of the letter since her search for sender and recipient had been unsuccessful. Only when there was something of value was the post office required to hold it for a year. In her mind, though, there really was something of value—a link to family, a cry for forgiveness. It might not have a dollar value, but to her way of thinking there was nothing more important. She couldn't bring herself to throw the letter away.

She understood that her obsession had everything to do with those last few days with her parents, days clouded with petty arguments and misunderstandings. When they'd left on their vacation, tensions had been running high. Marilou was their much-loved and overly protected only daughter. They hadn't wanted her to take off for Europe for a year without a job, without friends. Always skeptical that her photography was a sensible career choice, they'd been certain that she'd starve while trying to sell the pictures she shot on her travels. After a lifetime of secure government service, the concept of freelancing was beyond them. Nothing she'd said had been able to persuade them that the time was right for a few risks, for one glorious post-college adventure before settling down.

With the last bitter argument still fresh in her mind, Marilou had been devastated by the news that they'd been involved in a head-on collision with a stolen car filled with teenagers on a joyride. Her father had been killed outright. Her mother had lingered on for several horrifying weeks, never regaining consciousness.

In the emotional aftermath of the tragedy and in an attempt to cheat fate, she had resigned herself to staying as safe as her parents had wanted. The bribe hadn't worked; her mother had died anyway. When the family savings had been depleted by the exorbitant medical bills, and when the last of her energy was drained, the civil service job had been waiting for her, thanks to her father's career with the post office and his compassionate supervisor. She told herself she should be grateful to have it.

With an odd sort of lethargy, Marilou had settled down to a routine, but the longing for adventure, for a chance to use her photographic skills for more than holiday snapshots had never quite gone away. Every foreign stamp that crossed her desk stirred all of the old dreams of travel. Every letter gone astray reminded her of the mysteries that awaited. The plea for forgiveness from Cal Rivers's grandmother tapped into every one of her secret longings and regrets.

That night when a passing bus hit a giant puddle and soaked her from head to toe, she made up her mind. She had weeks of vacation coming. She had a healthy savings account again. She had a cold. And, most of all, she had those unfulfilled dreams.

So, she decided impulsively, she was going to Florida in search of Mr. Cal Rivers and his little boy. That child probably needed a grandmother as desperately as that poor dying lady needed to be in touch with him. Marilou might not be able to get her own family back, but maybe she could give him his. If she got a taste of adventure along the way, so much the better.

"Crazy, obstinate, mule-headed son of a bitch! Get in here. What kind of genes do you have anyway? Any other fool would be dancing and prancing to get a chance to be with that gorgeous lady in there. That little gal's folks paid a pretty penny for you to do your stuff, so get on with it."

"I think you're going about this all wrong," Cal Rivers said to the bowlegged man who barely reached to shoulder height next to his own six foot two. "How would you feel if some man came along and threw you into a cold, sterile room with a total stranger and told you to get to it, then stood by watching?"

Chaney dragged a bright red bandanna from his pocket and wiped the sweat off his leathery face. He grinned. "At my age, I'd be damned glad of the chance. 'Cept for the watching, of course. I don't go in for none of that kinky stuff."

Cal laughed. "Come to think of it, you probably would, you old reprobate. Your courting technique doesn't seem to appeal to your four-legged friend, though."

"Son, I know more about what appeals to horseflesh than you will if you stick around here for the next forty years. Devil's Magic is as ornery and cussed as they come. Ain't a danged thing I can do if this critter's got it into his head to take the day off."

He glared at the huge black horse in disgust. "Ain't a stallion in that barn I don't understand, 'cept for this one. If you ask me, winning all them races went to his head. Even that highfalutin stud you brought back from England ain't as difficult as he is."

A faintly critical *meow* sounded from the corner, where a fat marmalade cat regarded them haughtily. Wherever Devil's Magic went, that cat was sure to be close by. According to Chaney, the only way to get the horse into a trailer was to send the cat in ahead. At the sound of yet another meow, Devil's Magic's ears pricked up. As if he'd been waiting for a cue, he suddenly turned his attention to business. It appeared that the mare was just what he'd been looking for all his life, after all. With any luck, Mrs. Henry Robert Dolan's prized Thoroughbred mare would catch and eleven months from now would drop a foal sired by one of the biggest money winners in Florida racing history.

It went against Cal's grain to stand by and watch Chaney do most of the work, but owning a horse-breeding operation was still new to him. He'd been raised in Texas, but about as far from horses as a man could get. The lack of knowledge wasn't something that worried him, though. As he had with every business he'd ever bought he'd hired himself one of the best men he could find to run it with him. Chaney Jackson had a reputation as an intuitive, no-nonsense manager. He had set ideas about everything from feed to barn design, ideas his previous boss hadn't given him the rein or money to implement. Cal was giving him both, and they'd improved both the buildings and the paddocks so much within the first three months that owners had been quick to move horses into the new barns.

Once he'd taken care of the facilities, Cal had plunged into learning everything he could about Thoroughbred breeding and pedigrees, going straight back to the introduction of Arabian stock into England. *The General Stud Book* had become his bible. From the first, he was anticipating that day down the road when he'd have a string of the finest Thoroughbred stallions standing at stud. Devil's Magic was at the center of his plans. If everything came together as he expected, by then the business would be ripe for a takeover and he would be bored again.

It never took long for the restlessness to settle in. He was a quick learner and an instinctive entrepreneur. If he'd had more patience and more ambition, he'd be a billionaire by now, head of some international conglomerate and regularly quoted on the front page of the *Wall*

Street Journal. Instead he'd been willing to settle for knowing that he had a few million in the bank, give or take the money he'd set aside to get Silver River Stables on its feet. It was more than enough to give him his freedom whenever he chose to take it.

"Why'd you buy this place anyway?" Chaney asked later that night, when they'd settled down on the porch of the graceful farmhouse that sat amid acres of some of the most beautiful horse country in Ocala, Florida. The night air was cool and rich with the scent of grass and horses, faintly reminiscent of some of those special days in his youth when his father had let him go along with him on fruitless, humiliating job-hunting trips to ranches across Texas, ranches owned by men in the oil business who hadn't lost their shirts the way Cal's daddy had.

"You don't know a danged thing about horses, that's for sure," Chaney added with the bluntness Cal had come to admire. It was the first time, though, the older man had let himself ask a personal question, though Cal had no doubt at all the question had been nagging at him for months now. "All them books and magazines you read don't make up for doing. Did you ever see a horse up close before you signed the papers to take over here?"

Cal sipped on a beer and stared into the dwindling light as he considered the truth of Chaney's statement and his understandable bafflement. He supposed his decision to buy a Thoroughbred stud farm did seem odd to a man like Chaney, who'd spent his whole life around horses and understood that world the way Cal knew about investing and making money. Unfortunately he didn't have an answer that made much sense. He'd been drawn to this place the first time he'd seen it. He hadn't been able to explain it then and he still couldn't. He settled for evasion.

"I picked a winner once at Santa Anita," he said. "A real long shot. Paid pretty decent money. I guess I got hooked."

Chaney snorted with disgust. "Big deal. I've picked a bundle of surefire winners. Don't have to mean I know diddly about breeding."

"But you do," Cal noted matter-of-factly.

"I do, indeed."

"Which is why I need you."

"That's the danged truth. I still don't get it, though. This operation didn't come cheap, even the way they'd been lettin' it go. If you got enough money to buy this place and that new stallion you picked up over in England, you could do just about anything you wanted to. There's things a whole lot less risky than breeding race horses."

"And I've already done most of 'em," Cal said. "Every one of them required that I sit indoors all day long. No matter what the business, it was getting to be dull and predictable. I was driving around out here one day, thinking about the future, when I saw this place was for sale. I decided a good risk was just what I was looking for."

Even in the shadowy light, Cal could see Chaney's disbelieving expression. "Just like that? You bought a whole danged farm just like that?"

"Just like that." It hadn't been quite that simple, of course, but pretty darned close. It had taken days of cutthroat negotiations, and even then his accountant had very nearly had apoplexy. If Joshua hadn't been his closest friend, he'd have fired him. Instead he'd tolerated the nonstop arguments, then ignored them. Joshua still refused to set foot on the farm, preferring to mutter his comments about follies and muleheadedness via long-distance.

The ability to make decisions that seemed whimsical and impractical to others was one of the few real pleasures his wealth gave him. Maybe too much thinking would have made him overly cautious, would have kept him from the riskier ventures, which were often the ones that proved to be the most exciting challenges. He wasn't much into introspection, but one thing he knew about himself: he did dearly love a challenge. Once the challenge faded, he knew it was time to move on.

Chaney rocked, staring thoughtfully toward the horizon. Cal waited, rocking rhythmically beside him and wondering why he'd never realized before that endless peace and quiet didn't necessarily equate with boredom. If he'd had to analyze the way he felt right now, he would have said he was contented. It surprised him. Contentment wasn't a state of mind with which he was all that familiar.

"A man like you, impulsive and all," Chaney began, giving him a curious, sideways glance. "You must get yourself into a hell of a mess with women."

Cal chuckled at the understatement. Whole gossip columns from Dallas to New York had been devoted to *that* subject. "I've been known to, my friend. I've been known to." There wasn't a whit of regret in his tone, though sometimes in the darkest hours of the night he had a few.

The old man's gaze narrowed, and the rocking chair creaked to a stop. "You ain't gonna have some woman coming chasing after you here, are you? Not that it's any of my business, of course, but I'm not crazy about working at a place where some woman's fussin' and changin' everything. Old man Courtney and I, we did okay here the last few years. Can't say I was happy about the way he let business slide after his wife died, but we settled into our routine. I kinda got used to the way things were with just us menfolk around, you know what I mean?"

"I know, and that's definitely not something you need to worry about," Cal promised, thinking of just how good he was getting to be at severing ties. He was thirty-seven now, and he'd had twenty years of practice. There was no one looking for him and, sadly he supposed, no one he regretted leaving behind.

"When I move on," he assured Chaney, "I never leave a forwarding address. Keeps life a whole lot less complicated."

Chapter Two

It took Marilou Stockton exactly three days, four hours and twenty-seven minutes to trace Cal Rivers to the newly named and recently renovated Silver River Stables in Ocala. She would have found him sooner if she hadn't taken time out between phone calls to sit on the sand under a palm tree for the first two days of her month-long Florida vacation. Those few hours in the sun had slowed her investigation down, but they'd definitely been worth it.

For the first time ever, her fair skin was developing a nice golden glow and, best of all, she could breathe again. She actually felt healthy instead of waterlogged, which meant it was time to take care of business. Once that was done, she could really get into some serious relaxing. The anticipation of day after leisurely day under these clear tropical skies made her hurry.

She gulped down her large glass of fresh-squeezed Florida orange juice and toast, sacrificing her lazy walk on the beach in favor of studying her maps and the directions she'd been given by Cal Rivers's Palm Lane mail carrier. The carrier had turned out to be a woman in her twenties with a long memory and a talkative nature. She'd revealed that there'd been no forwarding address. Instead the mail was initially picked up weekly from the post office by a Mr. Joshua Ames, who'd had some sort of power of attorney. The mail had long since stopped coming, though, and so had this Mr. Ames.

"Too bad, too," Priscilla reported to Marilou. "He was a real hunk."

Since she didn't go to see him, Marilou couldn't attest to the man's physical attributes, but she could swear that he was about as talkative as one of those monks who'd taken a vow of silence. The instant she'd mentioned Cal Rivers on the phone, he'd clammed right up. She wondered what a man had to pay for that kind of loyalty. The only thing she'd managed to extract was an unwitting admission that Cal Rivers was still in Florida.

Which meant that he probably had a Florida driver's license.

Which meant that with a little resourcefulness— Priscilla had an old boyfriend who was a cop—Marilou was able to get his new address from the Division of Motor Vehicles. Once she had that, Priscilla had been more than happy to help her figure out the best route to take to Ocala.

By 9:00 a.m. on the fourth day of her vacation, with a renewed spirit of optimism, she was in her rental car and headed for Ocala. She figured it would take her three hours, four at the most, to actually meet Cal Rivers Sr. face-to-face, hand over the letter for Cal Rivers Jr. and be on her way back to the beach.

For the most part her calculations were accurate. The drive took exactly two and a half hours through ter-

rain that changed from sand and palm trees to fields of
green shaded by moss-draped oaks. She was so caught
up in the dramatic shift from beach resort clutter to open
spaces and Southern-style architecture that she missed
the entrance to Silver River Stables and wound up going
several fascinating miles out of her way. By the time she
figured it out, she'd wasted nearly half an hour. In retro-
spect, she realized it was probably an omen.

Armed with more precise directions from a chatty
gas station attendant, she finally found the discreetly
marked gate. As she drove through, she noted wryly
that the postal box was crammed so full of junk mail it
was spilling onto the ground. Apparently this Mr. Cal
Rivers had a thing about the mail. She ought to cart the
whole batch up to him and dump it in his lap.

Then again, *that* mail wasn't her worry. The letter in
her purse was the only one she was here to deliver, and
the sooner she did that and got on with the rest of her
vacation, the better she'd like it. If she hurried, she could
still be back under that palm tree with a piña colada by
midafternoon. With any luck, there was still time for
an adventure or two before she went back to her hum-
drum life in Atlanta.

Marilou parked her car in the vast shade of a sprawling live oak. As she walked toward the house, she noted
the fresh coat of paint, the geranium-red trim and the
sweeping veranda with a couple of well-used rockers facing west. There was something comfortable and cared-
for about the house that reassured her about Cal Rivers,
until she spotted the row of empty beer bottles lined up
along the railing. She hadn't considered the possibility
that the man might be an old drunk, an itinerant drift-
ing from town to town only one step ahead of the law.

Maybe that was why he'd vanished from Palm Lane and taken such care to cover his tracks. Her hand poised to knock, she hesitated for an instant, her gaze fastened on those bottles.

"Lady, this here's private property," growled a voice as rusty as an unoiled gate hinge. Marilou whirled around and found an old man dressed in dusty jeans and a well-worn Western-style shirt. He regarded her suspiciously. "Whatever you're selling we don't want any."

"I'm not selling anything. I'm looking for a Mr. Cal Rivers and his little boy." She smiled. He kept right on glaring.

"Ain't no little boys around here."

"What about Mr. Rivers? Is that you?"

"Nope."

"Is he here?"

His gaze narrowed. "What do you want with him?"

She could be every bit as discreet as Joshua Ames. She said primly, "My business with Mr. Rivers is personal."

The man's scowl deepened, carving ruts in his weathered complexion. Finally he muttered something about knowing it was too good to be true, shoved a battered cap back on his head and stomped off, stirring up a trail of dust. She had no idea if he was going to get Cal Rivers or simply abandoning her here. Just as she was about to go off after him, she heard his voice again.

"I'm telling you I don't know what she wants, boss. She wouldn't tell me a danged thing. Said it was *personal*." He mimicked her tone in a way that said he knew all too well that the word meant trouble.

"Okay, Chaney, I'll take care of it," a responding voice soothed. This voice, Marilou noted with a prompt and unexpected quickening of her pulse, was low and lazy and midnight seductive. This voice promised adventure and danger in spades. She instinctively grabbed the porch rail and held on.

The man who rounded the corner of the house suited that voice. He was tall and lean, the kind of man who wore jeans and faded plaid shirts and made them look more fashionable than Armani suits. His boots, however, appeared to be every bit as new as the paint on the house. The incongruity intrigued her. She studied him more closely, trying her best not to stare with her mouth agape. The man was gorgeous, especially to someone to whom the dark, brooding type appealed.

There was a faint hint of Indian ancestry in his coal-black hair and angled features, but it had been tempered along the way. His eyes were a startling, clear blue, and right now they were as cool and distant as a mountain lake hidden amid pine shadows. He would make a fascinating subject, she thought at once, longing for her camera.

"I understand you're looking for me," he said, stopping several yards shy of the porch steps. His expression was wary, his stance forbidding. A less determined woman than Marilou would have taken the hint and scooted right back down the steps and out of his life. Marilou squared her shoulders and smiled, relieved when his features softened ever so slightly. However slight, it was an improvement over the old man's wary antagonism.

"If you're Mr. Cal Rivers, I am," she said.

He nodded, but said nothing to invite further conversation. Southern hospitality, she thought, must stop at the Georgia border. Still, she plunged on.

"Do you have a son?"

"Nope."

The single word, confirming what she'd already been told, left absolutely no room for doubt. She supposed he certainly ought to know, but it took her aback. "Oh," she murmured, trying to readjust her thinking.

He grinned at her sudden confusion. "Am I supposed to?"

"Well, yes," she said, a little awed by the transformation of his harsh features that went with that slow, lazy grin. The devil in that smile could lure a saint to sin. With her inexperience, she'd be no match for it at all. Still, it would be a challenge to capture those quicksilver changes of mood on film. "At least, I thought you would have a son. Maybe the letter's meant for you instead."

"What letter?"

There was more wariness than curiosity behind the question, which made her increasingly nervous. She hadn't expected to feel as if she had to prove something, when she was just out to do a good deed. "The one I found," she began determinedly. "I work for the post office, you see. The dead letter office in Atlanta, actually. Well, it's a long story and—"

Suddenly her voice seemed to dry right up under his intense scrutiny. The full force of all that masculine attention was something new and decidedly disconcerting. She found herself rambling, despite her parched throat. "I'm very thirsty. The drive was longer than I expected and I didn't want to take the time to stop. Then I got lost. Do you suppose I could have a glass of water or something before I tell you the rest?"

"Chaney," Cal said curtly. The little man who'd been

hovering in the background stomped off toward the back of the house. He was muttering under his breath again.

"He doesn't seem to like visitors," she observed.

"Chaney is highly suspicious of women who have personal business with me. He figures it'll disrupt the routine around here. Judging from the last few minutes, I'd say he's very astute."

Marilou recognized a criticism when she heard it, but if he'd intended to chase her off with his sharp tongue and cool manner it was just too bad. When she didn't budge, he said grudgingly, "I suppose you might as well sit until Chaney gets back. You look as if you've spent too much time in the sun."

So much for her tan, she thought ruefully.

Taking his grudging offer at face value, Marilou chose the rocker that was farthest from the beer bottles. His gaze followed her, but he didn't say a word. The silence, coupled with the thoroughness of his scrutiny, was definitely unnerving. Men didn't usually look at her like that, as if she were mysterious and fascinating and dangerous. She supposed it made sense in this instance. After all, she had popped up here out of the blue and she still hadn't explained why she'd come. No wonder the man was staring. It probably wasn't a bit personal. That realization didn't stop the fluttering of her pulse, though. With his gaze steady on her, it felt personal. When Chaney came back with a tall glass of ice-cold lemonade, she clung to it, taking a deep swallow. Maybe she wasn't cut out for adventure after all, not if it involved blatantly masculine men like Cal Rivers.

"As I was saying," she began, rushing now, wanting this over with. "The other day I got this letter. It had been sent to the wrong address. Palm Tree Lane instead of Palm Lane. I suppose it was a simple enough mistake to make. I still think the mail carrier should have been able to figure it out, but Priscilla says it must have come through on her day off."

"Priscilla?"

"Your old mail carrier. Anyway, the letter wound up in Atlanta, because there wasn't any return address, either. That's what happens when a letter goes astray. It comes to me, or actually to my branch. I guess I should have thrown it out, but I just couldn't. She sounded so pitiful, you see. I…"

"Slow down," Cal advised, unexpected amusement again lurking in the depths of his eyes. "This isn't an emergency."

"But it could be," she insisted. "I mean the letter says she's dying."

Cal looked startled. Even Chaney seemed taken aback by her announcement. "Who's dying?" Cal demanded. "What the devil are you talking about, woman?"

"I'm sorry. I should have said right away. It's your grandmother."

The words had an incredible effect. His expression, which had been gently tolerant only an instant before, froze into icy disdain. "You have the wrong person," he said, turning his back on her. The muscles across his shoulders tensed visibly.

"No, I don't think so," she said stubbornly, ignoring his reaction. "You did live on Palm Lane, didn't you?"

When he didn't answer, she got up and moved until she was standing in his line of vision again. "Didn't you?" she demanded, catching the brief flash of confusion in his eyes before he shut off any evidence of emotion again.

"Yes," he said finally.

"Then, see," she coaxed reasonably, "it has to be you."

"I'm telling you that I am not the man you're looking for."

Marilou lost patience with him. How could anyone be so stubborn and ornery in the face of the evidence? "I don't know how you can say that, unless you figure that there was another Cal Rivers living in that very house."

"Lady, I do not have a grandmother." His voice rose to a defiant roar that carried on the still air.

"Of course you do," she said impatiently. "Everyone has grandparents."

"Mine are dead," he declared with absolutely no emotion. "Gone. I've never met any of them."

"But that's just it," she said excitedly. "Something happened a long time ago. I don't know what exactly, but she's sorry. Maybe everyone thought it would be better if you just thought she was dead. At any rate, she really wants to make it up to you, and she's dying. If you don't hurry, it might be too late."

"I'm very sorry that this lady, whoever she is, is dying, but it has nothing to do with me."

Sensing that she was losing, and desperate not to, Marilou took a few steps forward until she was practically toe-to-toe with him. He looked miserable and uncomfortable, but he didn't back up when she told him, "It has everything to do with you. Please, you have to see that."

Cal tried to stare her down, and when that didn't work, he demanded, "What is this woman's name?"

"I... I don't know. It wasn't on the letter."

"Then how can you possibly be so certain she's a relative of mine? Do you think you know more about my family than I do?"

"No, but the letter was addressed to you."

"Where does this woman live?"

"In Wyoming. I don't know exactly where. It was postmarked Cheyenne, but it could have come from anywhere around there, I suppose. Mail from a lot of small towns winds up being postmarked from the nearest big city. There wasn't any street address. That's why I couldn't send the letter back to her."

Even though his anger was daunting, Marilou was watching his face closely. She saw the faint flicker of recognition when she'd mentioned Wyoming. "I'm right, aren't I? You did have relatives in Wyoming, didn't you?"

He gazed off in the distance. "A long time ago, maybe. I don't know," he said, his tone distracted. Then his expression turned fierce again. "I think you'd better leave."

This wasn't going at all the way she'd anticipated. She felt tears beginning to well up in her eyes and realized she was going to make an even bigger fool of herself by crying. "I can't," she replied softly. "I have to see this through."

"You have seen it through," he countered impatiently. "You've done your job. I'm sure the post office will give you your bonus or whatever."

Marilou was thoroughly insulted that he thought that's what this was all about. "The post office doesn't even know I'm here. If they did, they'd probably fire me."

He stared at her. "What are you saying?"

"I took a vacation to find you."

"Well, I'll be," Chaney muttered, his expression totally agog.

Cal paced, shaking his head. Finally he turned. "Lady, are you nuts?" His tone was suddenly more bemused than furious.

"No, I am not nuts," she said defensively. "I just happen to care about this."

"Why? Is there some sort of reward for meddling in things that are none of your concern? I'll see that you get it."

"Dammit, this has nothing to do with any reward. It's about family. What's more important than that?"

"Money," he said so promptly it made her blood run cold. He meant it, too. She could tell that. Nothing she was saying about his grandmother seemed to be penetrating that thick skull of his. It was disappointing that a man this gorgeous had to be such an idiot.

Ignoring him, she sank back down in the rocker to think. What the dickens was she supposed to do now? She had thought it was going to be a simple matter of finding Cal Rivers, explaining about the letter and then walking away. Instead she was faced with a man who wouldn't even believe that he had a grandmother and, worse, didn't seem to care one way or the other.

No, she corrected. That wasn't quite true. There had been that one brief second when he'd revealed a hint of vulnerability, a moment of confusion. Maybe he was afraid for some reason. She studied the unyielding set of his shoulders, the angry scowl on his face. He didn't look like the sort to be scared of anything short of a raging stampede of horses. More likely, he was an insensitive, uncaring jerk. Not everyone had good in them, despite what she'd been taught.

She ought to leave and let him stay here and get snockered on beer every night. Maybe the beer helped him to live with whatever had made him the cold, un-caring man that he was. It certainly wasn't up to her to reform him. There probably weren't enough years left in her lifetime to accomplish that.

Then she thought of the letter in her purse. She owed it to that dear old lady to try harder. Cal Rivers might not be much by her standards, but he was family. And Mar-ilou was the only hope either of them had, the only link. There was an old saying about fools rushing in. Well, she'd already rushed. She might as well stick around for the consequences. If she sat her for a little while, surely something would come to her.

Besides, as she debated whether to go or stay, the clouds had begun building in the west. Fat drops of rain were already plopping into the dust. She regarded the sudden downpour with a sense of resignation. There was apparently no escape anywhere from these damn April showers.

"I don't think she's planning on leavin', boss," Chaney said, his baleful gaze resting on the pretty little redhead who'd plunked herself down in a chair on the porch and was rocking to beat the band.

Cal didn't think she was going anywhere either. He noted the stubborn set of her chin and the fire in her green eyes and decided he might have miscalculated just the tiniest bit about the pesky woman with her crazy story about a dying grandmother. It wouldn't be the first time some reporter or gold digger had used an outra-geous tale to get to him. This one was better than most. He'd give her that. She almost had him believing her.

She was also the most stubborn female he'd encoun-tered in some time. He'd attempted to brush her off with a chilly reception and a few intimidating words. Obviously, it was going to take more. He just wasn't quite sure what would work with a woman who was apparently so dead sure she was on a mission. Maybe he could cajole her into going with a promise or two. It wouldn't kill him to fib a little, if it meant dislodging her from that chair and his life.

"Okay," he said at last, willing himself to look cooperative. "I'm not saying I believe you, but I'm willing to look into it. Leave the letter with me and I'll check it out."

The expression she directed at him was very wary. "Check it out how?"

Her persistence almost cost him the tight rein on his temper. "I'll have to think about it. Maybe I'll hire a private investigator. Yes," he said, warming up to the notion. She ought to buy that. "I'll hire a detective."

She was shaking her head. "That's a waste of perfectly good money. I can find her for you in no time and I won't charge you a penny."

"Really," he protested desperately. "That's not necessary. I can afford it and I really can't take up any more of your time."

Her gaze narrowed suspiciously. "You're just trying to get rid of me, aren't you? You figure I'll give you the letter and walk out and you'll tear it up the minute my back is turned."

"Lady, if you're so dead-set sure that the letter is mine, then what I do with it is none of your business."

She frowned at him, her expression thoughtful. "I suppose you're right."

"Of course I am. You've done all you can do. You can go now and your conscience will be perfectly clear."

She nodded slowly and his mood brightened considerably. Then she turned one of those penetrating looks on him, a look that seemed to see straight into his lying heart. "Nope. I can't do that," she said, sounding downright sorrowful. "I feel responsible."

Cal lost his last thread of restraint. "Dammit, you are not responsible!"

"I can't help how I feel."

"Feel any way you want to, just do it someplace else."

"Let me just make a few calls for you, get the search started."

"No!"

"It'll relieve my mind."

"No!"

She nodded, her expression triumphant. "I knew you weren't really going to follow through."

Cal threw up his hands in a gesture of defeat. "That's it. I give up."

He was no more than half a dozen feet from the porch when Chaney stopped him. "What should I do about her?" he asked, gazing pointedly toward Marilou.

"Ignore her," Cal said finally, stalking off into the rain. "I'm going back to Lady Mary."

As an interim plan, it would have to do, but he had no doubt it wouldn't be the end of Miss Marilou Stockton. Oh, she looked like a frail little thing with her sunburned nose and too-big T-shirt. In fact, for an instant there he'd been drawn to her innocence and naiveté. It was a knee-jerk reaction to a woman who looked as if she needed protecting. Fortunately he'd learned long ago that those kind of women were the most dangerous of all. They usually had a streak of muleheadedness that drove a man nuts. So far, Marilou was running true to form. She'd be waiting whenever he decided to come back. He had no doubts about that.

"I'm going to strangle Joshua the next time I see him," he muttered. The accountant had to be behind this visit. No one else could have pointed the way from his last address to this place. Joshua was probably sitting in that fancy office of his chortling with glee this very minute. He no doubt considered it just revenge for Cal's failure to heed his advice.

Hell, for all he knew Joshua had made up the damned letter in the first place. He'd been making less than subtle noises about it being time for a family reunion for months now, preaching a lot of psychological hogwash about facing the past. The more Cal thought about it, the more sense it made. Joshua was definitely behind this visit.

Disgusted at the abrupt end to his newfound peace and quiet and unable to think of a single tactic to rid himself permanently of his unwanted visitor, Cal ignored the downpour and headed for the barn. He might not know much about horses, but he figured he had a better shot at understanding them than he ever would figuring out women or friends who meddled in things that were none of their business.

He'd left Zeke walking Lady Mary and the groom could probably use someone to spell him. From what Chaney'd taught him colic in a horse was nothing to fool around with. If the mare hadn't improved, he'd probably have the vet out before the night was over. Lady Mary's health was a helluva lot more important than listening to this woman's crazy tales.

Before he turned the corner toward the stables, though, he made the mistake of casting one last look over his shoulder. Marilou's rocker had gone perfectly still. She was staring after him, an expression of stunned indignation on her face. Even Chaney looked startled by the abrupt dismissal. He was staring worriedly from Cal to their unwanted guest and back again. Cal glared back at both of them. He had nothing to apologize for. If he didn't want anybody dredging up his past, that was his business, right? Damn right!

So why was there this incredibly guilty knot in his gut, a knot that was probably every bit as painful as Lady Mary's colic?

Chapter Three

Marilou did not consider herself to be either an especially assertive woman or a femme fatale type, but few men had ever had the audacity to flat-out ignore her. None that she could recall had ever walked off in the middle of an argument. It took her fully sixty seconds to recuperate from the shock of watching Cal Rivers deliver the last word then turn his back on her and go charging off to see this Lady Mary, whoever she was.

The image of rough and rowdy Cal Rivers with some elegant member of the British aristocracy seemed ludicrous to her. Now an Irish barmaid, that was something else. She could envision that all too clearly. Unexpected jealousy taunted her.

Startled by the absurdly out of place and purely feminine reaction, she looked up to find Chaney watching her. Fortunately he didn't appear to have picked up on her thoughts. Instead he seemed torn with indecision. Finally he shrugged half-apologetically and started off in the same direction Cal had taken. He was partway across the yard before he turned with obvious reluctance and came back.

"You might's well take off," he said. He sounded hopeful.

Unwilling to accept defeat, Marilou shook her head. "I don't think so. Not until he promises to follow up on his grandmother's letter."

Chaney squinted at her curiously, his action emphasizing the deep furrows in his tanned brow. "You ain't family, are you?"

"No."

"You ever met him before?"

"No."

"You one of them paid do-gooders? Like a social worker or some such?"

"I told you. I work for the post office and I'm not even here in an official capacity."

"Then I just don't get it. What difference does it make to you what he does?"

"His grandmother is dying," she repeated, incredulous at his lack of understanding. Was she the only one left in the world who cared about family?

"This might be their only chance to meet and reconcile. Doesn't that matter to you?" she demanded. "You could help, you know. Maybe he'd listen to you."

Chaney shuffled and looked uncomfortable. He slapped his hat against his thigh, then shoved it back on his head. Staring at his feet, he mumbled, "Ain't no reason I can see for me to get involved. The world would be a whole lot better off if more people just minded their own business. Hell, I don't even know the woman."

"But..."

He persisted. "Apparently he don't know her either."

"Then it's about time he did, before it's too late and he has to deal with a whole lot of guilt."

Chaney seemed to get a big kick out of that idea. "I ain't known him all that long, but I don't think Cal Rivers is the kind of man to be much troubled by guilt."

"More's the pity."

Chaney's mouth gaped at the sarcasm. Obviously he considered Cal Rivers's behavior to be above reproach. "Okay," he said finally, "so let's just say that you ain't going till he agrees to this." He regarded her now with open curiosity. "How you gonna talk him into it?"

Marilou frowned and admitted, "If I knew that, I'd be out there after him instead of wasting my vacation in this chair. I'll think of something, though. I can promise you that."

"Maybe you ought to go think on it someplace else. He sees you here later, he's likely to be madder than an old wet hen. He ain't the kind of man who likes to be pushed."

"What kind of man is he?" she asked, seizing the opening and hoping for clues that would help her plot a new strategy.

"One who wouldn't like me gossiping about him."

"It wouldn't be gossip," she said. At the lift of Chaney's bushy gray brows, she added, "Not exactly."

"You put whatever name you like on it, I ain't saying a thing. He owns this place, and I'd like to hang on to my job."

"So, he's tough."

"Listen here, missy, you didn't hear me say nothing like that."

She grinned innocently. "I could have sworn I did."

"Women!" He threw up his hands in disgust. "You

just go on and think what you like. I'll be getting back to work now."

"Thanks for the talk."

"We didn't have no talk. If you say we did, I'll call you a liar."

"I suspect your boss is already calling me far worse," she said, surprised by the odd little pang of regret that crept through her. Why should it bother her what a jerk thought?

Chaney muttered something unintelligible, then said grudgingly, "If you want any more of that lemonade, there's a pitcher full in the refrigerator. I suppose you might's well help yourself."

"Thanks." Surprised by the gesture, she nodded. She considered whether it would be wise to probe any more, then decided to risk the one question that had been nagging at her. She knew that the old hand could answer it, if he was of a mind to.

"Chaney?"

"Ma'am?"

"Who's Lady Mary? Would she have any influence with him?" She tried to inject the question with nothing more than innocent curiosity, but it seemed to reverberate with hidden meanings. Maybe a man wouldn't notice them, she thought hopefully.

Chaney obviously did. She caught the faint suggestion of a sly smile tugging at his usually sour, down-turned mouth. "Why, ma'am, I'm not so sure that's something I ought to be discussing with you," he said evasively. "I suppose if you get real curious, sooner or later you'll find out for yourself."

Marilou had a feeling that there was the tiniest suggestion of implied criticism in his comment, but there was also a dare. Somehow she knew that before the day was out, she'd take him up on it.

Once she'd been left on her own, Marilou decided that a little more lemonade might help her quench this odd, insatiable thirst that had developed the minute she had laid eyes on Cal Rivers with his gray-blue eyes, pitch-black hair and powerful masculine body that belonged astride a horse.

Or a woman.

Dear heavens, where had that wayward thought come from? Foolish question. The man's sex appeal was prac-tically branded on him. He radiated sexual energy the way Florida Power and Light sent out electricity. It was just what they did. That didn't mean she had to fall under his spell. She refused to behave that predictably.

She hurriedly poured herself another glass of the thirst-quenching lemonade, then wandered into the liv-ing room, looking around with blatant curiosity at the prissy furniture that didn't fit at all the man she'd just met. It must have come with the house, or else this Lady Mary had done the decorating with all the dark wood and old-fashioned brocades. She wandered on, poking her head into other rooms as she went. Snooping, her mother would have said disapprovingly. Marilou pre-ferred to think of it as reconnaissance. She needed to know everything she could about Cal Rivers if she was going to talk him into doing what was right.

"You know I'm right about this, Mama," she mur-mured aloud, just in case her mother was someplace where she could see her.

Admittedly she was finding her survey fascinating. Cal's office, when she discovered it, was more what she'd expected. With its worn leather furniture and fox hunt prints, it looked comfortable and well-used, exactly like the kind of place a single man would choose to spend a quiet evening. There was even an old stone-hearth fireplace that would be just right on one of Central Florida's chilly winter nights. There was another row of empty beer bottles on the window sill behind the huge oak desk. Magazines were scattered helter-skelter on the hardwood floor, an incongruous mix of business publications and farm magazines plus some days-old copies of the *Racing Form*. Shirts had been tossed over the backs of chairs… and forgotten, judging from the barnyard smell of them.

Psychologically incapable of remaining idle for long, Marilou stacked the magazines by topic, dumped the beer bottles into the trash can, then gathered up the shirts and carried them into the kitchen in search of a washing machine. It occurred to her as she tossed them into the brand-new automatic washer that she was overstepping Chaney's hospitality.

Overstepping, hell. These were giant strides, she thought with a twinge of conscience.

Still, maybe they'd both be so grateful to have clean shirts they wouldn't complain. Then she recalled the hard expression in Cal's eyes just before he'd stalked off. He'd label it meddling and she knew it. Gratitude would probably be the last thing on his mind. She'd be lucky if he didn't have her charged with breaking and entering and then hauled off to jail. Now that would be an adventure.

Even at the risk of incurring his wrath, though, she had to keep busy. She always thought better when her hands were occupied, and right now she needed to think of a compelling argument to convince Cal to go see his grandmother. Frankly, though, she couldn't imagine anything much more important than the woman's impending death. What kind of hard-hearted creature could ignore that?

She paused, the cup of detergent suspended over the washer, and recalled their conversation from start to finish. For just a heartbeat, she could have sworn she'd seen something vulnerable in those cool-as-gun-metal eyes of his. If only she could reach that part of him again, make him see that it was time to let bygones be bygones. He had a gentle, thoughtful side. She was sure of it.

"What the hell do you think you're doing?"

The furious voice whipped across her. She spun around, scattering blue powder in every direction, and met an icy glare. She would have given almost anything for a hint of that vulnerability now, but all she saw was steel and fury. He looked hard and deep-down angry and, try as she might, she couldn't really say she blamed him.

"I'm sorry," she said at once. "I was thinking and when I think I need to be doing something and it looked as if there was a lot around here that needed doing so I just... I just sort of did it. I'm sorry."

Cal poked his thumbs through the waistband of his jeans and swore softly. "Chaney was right. You're not going to give up, are you?"

Marilou gave the rhetorical question all the consideration he expected and answered right back, "Probably not."

His gaze narrowed. "Did Joshua send you here?"

"Joshua? Oh, you mean Mr. Ames." She grinned. "We talked."

"And he told you how to find me. I knew it!"

"Not exactly. If you're paying him to keep his mouth shut, he's living up to his end of the bargain."

"Then how?"

"I can be very resourceful when I have to be. He dropped a couple of clues, unwittingly by the way, and I ran with them. Don't go blaming him for my turning up here."

He raked his fingers through his hair. "Dammit all to hell, woman, what is it you want from me?"

"It's not all that complicated. I just want you to go see your grandmother. If you'd just read the letter, you'd see how important it is." She reached in her pocket for the envelope, but he was already backing away as if she were about to offer him a red-hot poker, fiery end first.

"It's just a letter, for goodness' sakes. It wouldn't kill you to read it."

"How do I even know she's mine?"

The look Marilou gave him when he said that would have withered a cactus. Cal muttered another oath under his breath and realized he'd done more swearing in the past few hours than he'd done in the past year. It was not a good sign. He only cussed when he couldn't think of anything sensible to say. This pint-size hellion did not inspire clear thinking. Between needling his conscience and triggering his hormones, she was more worrisome than a boardroom filled with outraged stockholders. He knew how to soothe them with bottom lines and profit margins. He didn't have a clue about what tactics might work on the woman whose big green eyes were fixed on him so steadily. He hated the disappointment that rose in them every time he denied this grandmother she claimed was his.

"Okay," he said finally. "You say she's mine. I asked

before and I'll say it again: How come nobody in my family ever mentioned her?"

"Did you ask?"

Cal squirmed under that direct, no-nonsense gaze. He wondered if this prickly woman had a husband. Despite her obvious physical attributes, he couldn't imagine any man in his right mind putting up with her. She'd be hell on a guilty conscience. She was playing havoc with his, and he didn't have a blasted thing to feel guilty about. He'd put his family ties, such as they were, behind him long ago to no one's regret.

"No, I never asked. I figured you either had grandparents or you didn't. If you didn't, most likely they were dead."

"Well, one of yours isn't. Yet," she amended significantly.

"Okay. Okay. You've made your point. I'll think about what you've said. Go on back to wherever you came from and I'll take care of it."

If he expected that to be the end of it, he quickly realized that he'd underestimated her determination. She regarded him with blatant skepticism. "That doesn't sound like much of a promise to me. How do I know you won't rip up the letter the minute I'm out the door?"

"You don't."

He knew it was the wrong answer the minute he'd said it. He cursed himself for a fool when she scowled, folded her arms across her chest and declared with open defiance, "Then I'm not going."

"Good Lord, woman, do you plan to move in?"

That took a little of the starch out of her. She struck him as the sort of woman who jumped in impetuously and then was too stubborn to back down. Once she saw the obvious implications of her crazy stance, she'd run. Never in a million years would she allow herself to be trapped into staying with a couple of men she'd never seen before today. She'd be on the road by sundown and glad to escape.

"No, of course not… I mean…"

There, he thought with satisfaction, grinning at her confusion. "Puts you in a bit of a quandary then, doesn't it?"

Her gaze narrowed at the ill-advised taunt, and her chin rose another notch. "Maybe I will, after all…if that's what it takes."

It was sheer bravado, but Cal had been in enough negotiating sessions in his time to recognize a tactical blunder when it smacked him between the eyes. He'd pushed too hard…again. He should have given her room to maneuver, to retreat gracefully. He found an out and offered it, a little desperately if the truth be known. "You're probably expected back at your hotel."

"No," she said, too quickly, then reconsidered. "I mean, not for hours yet."

He threw up his hands at her naïveté. A woman this innocent had no business being let loose on her own. "Don't you know how much trouble you could get yourself into telling a strange man that you're all alone down here?" he asked impatiently. "You don't know anything about me. I could be a second cousin to Jack the Ripper."

Surprisingly she grinned at his irritation. "I doubt that."

"You're too damned trusting."

"Not really. I just figure that the second cousin to Jack the Ripper would not go planting the idea in my mind, unless it was meant to scare me off."

"That's exactly what it's meant to do."

"But not because you're dangerous," she said with such absolute certainty that it gave him an odd little quiver in the region of his heart. "You just don't want to deal with this business about your grandmother."

"Fine. You caught me. I don't want to deal with it. I am not going to deal with it. So you might as well go."

She was shaking her head before he was done. She squared her shoulders and then she smiled. That smile had probably devastated tougher men than him. Cal fought its impact without much success. He could feel the warmth seeping into him, curling around his cold emotions.

"I don't think I'll leave just yet," she said softly.

Something that felt astonishingly like relief flooded through him. He suddenly realized that the prospect of having Miss Marilou Stockton around awhile longer wasn't quite as displeasing as it ought to have been. Maybe he wasn't nearly as keen on peace and quiet as he'd thought.

Or maybe he'd just noticed how seeing a woman in this big old homey kitchen felt right. He wondered what other rooms she'd suit. He doubted that the feisty little gal in front of him would be flattered if she knew the decidedly wicked direction his thoughts were taking. Nor would she feel quite so safe. It would be better in the long run for both of them if she went now.

"If you're staying, how about fixing dinner?" he baited, trying a new tactic and wondering exactly how far he'd have to push her before she'd bolt from this dare. Finding out could be fascinating. Nothing entertained him more than testing the mettle of a woman. He hadn't met one yet who could withstand his scrutiny.

Ignoring the dull flush creeping into her cheeks, he added, "Chaney and I are getting tired of steak, which is about the only thing we can cook without ruining it."

"If you'd weed that garden I saw out back, maybe you'd have some decent vegetables to have with your steak."

"I'm not looking for recipes. I'm after a cook. Are you willing?"

She stared at him incredulously, clearly stunned by this unexpected turnaround. "You...you *want* me to stay?"

He shrugged indifferently. "Suit yourself. All I'm saying is if you're going to hang around, you might as well make yourself useful. I've been thinking it was about time to hire on a housekeeper. I suppose you'd do as good as anyone."

"I would do? *Do?*" Indignation sparked in her eyes. "You're crazy, you know that? You are flat-out, ought-to-be-locked-up crazy if you think I'm going to play housekeeper for the pair of you."

"There's no playing to it. I'll pay good wages. Besides, it looks to me as if you've already got a good start on the job," he said, gazing pointedly in the direction of the washer, which was now well into its spin cycle and apparently without the benefit of detergent, since the powder was all over the floor. "Might's well plunge in whole hog."

Her gaze narrowed. "I thought you wanted me as far away from here as possible and the sooner the better."

He grinned. It was working. At last he'd found the way to make her turn tail and run. "Maybe I've reconsidered. I'm a pragmatic man. You're still here. It's getting dark and Chaney and I are getting hungry."

"I thought you'd be eating with Lady what's-her-name."

He almost burst out laughing at that, but managed to say with a straight face, "She's a little off her feed tonight."

"Too bad." She said it politely enough, but for a woman who'd gone all mushy about his grandmother, she didn't seem to him to be very sorry for Lady Mary.

"So, how about it?" he prodded. "The refrigerator's well stocked."

"Then use your imagination and fix your own damn meal," she suggested, but she didn't bolt for the door as he'd intended. Nor did she make a move toward the stove. As a matter of fact, she pulled out a chair and plunked herself down on it, then stared up at him expectantly, those big green eyes flashing fire again. The responding heat that flamed through him took him by surprise. He suddenly realized that this latest miscalculation was likely to cost him dearly. It took her about ten seconds to confirm it.

She smiled up at him with saucy arrogance and said sweetly, "As long as you're cooking, I'll take my steak rare."

Chapter Four

Marilou was fully aware that she had just boxed herself into an impossible corner. Even as the words had tumbled across her lips, she'd been astonished at her impulsive declaration. Moving in, for heaven's sakes? Was she out of her mind or simply out of her depth?

Well, she was definitely the latter and quite possibly the former. Matching wits with a man like Cal Rivers was no game for a woman like her. She didn't have the slightest idea of the rules or how to play by them.

At some point, she had vaguely recognized the subtle shift from mental to sensual challenge, and still she'd been helpless to abandon the fray. In fact, to her shock, she'd been invigorated by it, compelled to take his dares simply because he'd made them and because she knew that he'd expected her to refuse. She'd enjoyed watching his expression go from wary to amused to stunned in a matter of seconds. It was the most exciting, reckless thing she'd done in all of her twenty-five years.

Now, with second thoughts popping up like weeds, it appeared she was stuck. She couldn't very well say thanks for the steak, then wave and wander off once dinner was done. He'd be laughing at her from now till Sunday. No, her pride wouldn't permit that. Nor would her determined commitment to Cal's grandmother, a woman she was never even likely to meet but for whom she felt an odd, special kinship. Besides, she countered the rising doubts, this might very well be the closest she ever came to a longed-for adventure. She wasn't about to walk away from it just when it was getting interesting.

Actually, it was getting downright fascinating, she decided as she gazed out the back door and watched the subtle bunching of the muscles across Cal's broad shoulders as he hunkered down to start the grill, a puny little hibachi meant for picnics, not full-scale dinners at home. He'd stuffed a package of frozen vegetables into the microwave, along with three potatoes, and turned it on for twenty minutes. Marilou shuddered. The minute he wasn't looking she retrieved the vegetables and waited expectantly for the potatoes to explode, since he hadn't bothered to pierce the skins.

Directing a glare at her as he entered, he stomped past, grabbed a package of steaks from the freezer and headed for the still-cold grill. Marilou couldn't bear to watch.

"Cal?" she said finally.

"What?" he growled.

"Don't you think you ought to defrost those first in the microwave?"

"They'll defrost on the grill."

"Not in this lifetime."

"Either you cook or you shut up. I don't need any coaching from the sidelines."

She groaned as he plunked the solid steaks onto the

grill. "No. You do need a housekeeper. I can see that now. Maybe we could strike a deal after all."

He gazed at her distrustfully. "Oh?"

"Just short-term. I'll help out around here tonight, if you'll think about going to see your grandmother." She discovered that she was not above a little bribery. It was not a discovery that especially pleased her.

He regarded the icy beef, frowned, then met her gaze. "No steaks?"

She hurriedly improvised a menu. "Spaghetti with the best sauce this side of Italy."

His expression brightened hopefully, like a kid promised chocolate chip cookies. "No kidding?"

"I never kid about my sauce."

"No more nagging, at least through dinner?"

"No nagging," she conceded reluctantly.

"You don't expect any promises?"

"No promises, except that you'll do some honest soul-searching."

"You drive a hard bargain for such a little thing, but for a decent meal I think I just might promise you the moon."

"We'll save that, in case you haven't made up your mind by breakfast."

A killer grin spread across his face, the kind of grin that made female knees go weak and hearts pound. Her body responded with disgusting predictability as he warned, "Be careful, lady. You tell me you can make pancakes and easy-over eggs and it could take me months to give this problem the thoughtful consideration it deserves."

"Oh, no," she said, laughing. "This offer has an expiration date, and it could change at any second if I suspect you're not keeping your end of the deal."

"Are you married, Marilou Stockton?"

She was startled by the question and by the fact that he'd leaned in close to ask it. She could smell the heady masculine scent of him and feel the tug of his body heat. "No," she said, her voice suddenly whisper soft.

He nodded in satisfaction, then grinned. "I didn't think so."

"Why?"

"Because you've got a tongue that's sharp enough to cut out a man's heart."

"That's a dangerous thing to say to a woman you're expecting to cook your dinner."

"You won't lace the food with arsenic."

"What makes you so sure?"

"Then you'd never get me to Wyoming." He was whistling cheerfully as he left the room, so cheerfully in fact that Marilou wondered if she hadn't just played right into his hand. The amazing thing was that she didn't seem to care if she had. She was beginning to enjoy the unexpected and thoroughly outrageous twists and turns the day had taken.

If Chaney was stunned to find Marilou in the kitchen and spaghetti with homemade sauce on the table, he kept it to himself, casting sly glances from her to his taciturn boss and back again. He attacked the dinner like a man who'd been starved, and whatever questions he had about the turn of events, he bit back, while Marilou was left with a whole string of questions herself.

Why had Cal gone to such pains to vanish from his Palm Lane home? Why did he clam up so whenever the talk turned to family? What sort of secrets had his family kept from him? Or had he been abandoned? Maybe that was why this whole discussion about a long-lost grandmother made him prickly as an old bear startled out of its winter slumber.

Whatever the case, she apparently wasn't going to be allowed to satisfy her curiosity tonight. She'd promised to cut him some slack and she would. Not that he gave her much choice. His good humor had vanished sometime between her offer to cook and his return to the table. Aside from a few surreptitious glances in her direction, he ate silently, apparently lost in his own thoughts. She could only hope they were about his grandmother. If his troubled expression was any indication, they had to be.

The minute the meal was over, Cal muttered a grudging thanks and stalked off into the night again. Chaney, with one last speculative look at Marilou, traipsed after him. Marilou was left with a huge stack of dirty dishes. And when they were done and neither of the men had reappeared, she was left with figuring out where she might sleep.

She found sheets that smelled of sunshine stacked in a closet in the upstairs hall. She grabbed a couple and began making up the bed in what appeared to be a vacant bedroom, as far from the master bedroom as she could get.

She'd seen the size of the bed in his room. Just the sight of it had done funny things to her insides. She'd made things worse by daring to test its feather softness before retreating guiltily. At the memory of the way that bed had made her feel, she felt a blush creeping into her cheeks.

Just then she heard the flick of a match and caught

the scent of sulphur. Until that second she hadn't even realized that Cal had come up the stairs. A faint puff of smoke from his cigarette drifted into the room.

"You look like you're settling in," he said, his voice dropping to a lazy, seductive tone that brought goose bumps to her flesh and set off a whole new flurry of doubts about her decision to stay. Visions of that bed down the hall stirred up a storm of sensations.

"This room seemed to be empty," she said, keeping her back to him as she smoothed the pillow. "I hope it's okay."

"It's fine, though there's one down the hall you might enjoy more," he said. "I'd be happy to keep you company."

Her skin burned at the deliberately provocative invitation. "Thanks, but you probably snore."

"You'll never know till you spend the night with me."

"I could always bug your room."

He chuckled at the quick retort. "You know, most women would have been scared off by now," he said. She thought she detected a very faint and very reluctant note of admiration in his voice.

"I've told you before that you don't scare me," she responded lightly, ignoring the rapid thudding of her heart, which contradicted her words. She turned to stare directly at him just to prove the point. "You're all bluff."

There was a quick flash of amusement in his eyes before they began a low, deliberate inspection. Her pulse hammered and heat rose through her before she finally shifted her gaze away. No man's look had ever been so blatantly seductive. She would have picked up a magazine and fanned herself if he hadn't been watching. Of course, if he hadn't been watching, she wouldn't have

needed to. It was just more of his game and she knew
it. Her body apparently didn't.

"I wouldn't call my bluff if I were you," he warned,
still not taking his eyes off her. "You just might get
more than you bargained for, Miss Marilou Stockton.
A lot more."

After one last, lingering glance that made her knees
wobble, he walked on down the hall. Marilou sank down
on the edge of the bed and fanned herself so hard that the
magazine she was using almost came apart in her hands.
She had a feeling Cal's touch would have the exact same
effect on her senses. If she let this man get any closer,
she'd never be whole again unless he were around to
see to it. The prospect tempted, even as it unsettled her.

In the end it was the longest, most nerve-racking night
of Marilou's life. She heard the groan of Cal's bed, the
thump of his boots hitting the floor, then more creak-
ing as he settled onto that feather mattress for the night.
As the cool night breeze ruffled the curtains, she could
swear she heard him breathing…but not snoring.

She eventually drifted into a restless sleep, but at 4:00
a.m. she was awakened by some faint noise. She listened,
but all she heard now was absolute silence. Finally she
abandoned any hope of sleeping, pulled on her clothes
from the day before and crept barefoot downstairs. After
an instant's guilty hesitation in front of the automatic
coffeepot, she gave in to her need for caffeine. She supposed for the moment she could make a case that she
was still playing housekeeper, at least for the next few
hours until she had Cal's answer.

She wondered if his response, even a positive one,
was likely to be enough for her now. Always readily
hooked by mysteries, was she going to be able to walk

away from this one without knowing the ending or the secrets still hidden from her? Would she be able to forget so easily the man whose pain ran so deep that he'd chosen to shut out the world and let Joshua Ames run interference for him?

She sighed. Coffee cup in hand, she wandered outside. The air was chilly and the grass glistened with dew in the light from a full moon. She breathed deeply, entranced by the unfamiliar earthy scents. There was something raw and basic, something untouched by all the manufactured perfumes and air-conditioned sterility of the city. She stepped onto the cool carpet of lawn, feeling a childlike exhilaration as her bare feet met the dampness. Suddenly she remembered other mornings, creeping barefooted out of the house to get the paper without waking her parents, feeling as if the world was hers and hers alone at that silent hour before even the birds began to greet the dawn.

She went back inside for her shoes, then set out to explore, taking the path that Cal had taken the day before. As she turned the corner of the house, she was surprised to discover him on the track beyond the stables. Obviously the sound of his leaving had been what had awakened her. She started toward him, then stopped in the shadows to watch in wonder. All the gentleness she had suspected and that he normally worked so hard to hide was in full view now.

He was walking a horse, one hand on the lead, the other in constant motion, caressing in slow, calming strokes as they went round and round the oval track. She could hear his low crooning, the soothing tone but not the words, and realized that she envied both words and touch.

Concern washed through her as she noted that his shoulders were slumped with exhaustion, his clothes haphazard as if he'd grabbed them hurriedly. She moved closer, saying nothing until he looked up and spotted her leaning against the split rail fence.

"Is everything okay?" she asked, sensing that this was not part of the daily routine. She slipped through the fence and began to walk alongside.

He directed a worried look at the horse. "She has colic. If she's not better by dawn, I'm going to have to get the vet out here for her. Last night I thought she was through the worst of it, but Zeke called up at the house about an hour ago and said she was bad again. I just wish to hell I knew what caused it. It's times like these I realize how damned little I know. Chaney says it could be anything, but I feel responsible."

"Is it dangerous?"

"Horses die from it," he said bluntly, his growing concern etched on his harsh features.

With a sense of dismay Marilou looked at the mare, whose coat gleamed silver-gray in the moonlight. "She's so beautiful."

"One of the best. I've got a gorgeous stud picked out for her. If I'm right, her foal could be a stakes winner on the turf. If I can't get her through this, though, it's something I'll never know."

She could feel his frustration along with his compassion. "You don't like not knowing things, do you?"

He shrugged, one hand automatically soothing the mare. "Who does?"

"I'm not talking curiosity. I mean control. That's what's bothering you now. This is a situation you can't control."

He grinned ruefully. "To tell you the truth, I never imagined I'd even be trying to control a situation like this. You should hear Chaney on the subject. He thinks I'm in over my head. Joshua thinks I've gone round the bend. He doesn't comprehend anything that doesn't involve software."

"What about you? What do you think?"

"I think I'd be a damned fool if I didn't admit that Chaney is absolutely right. Right now you couldn't fill the first page of a diary with what I really know about horses. The only reason Chaney gave in and went to bed for a couple of hours was that he knows this morning could be worse and I promised to wake him if she developed a temperature."

"In many ways you seem like an odd pair, but you have a lot of respect for him, don't you?"

"Chaney managed this farm for years before I came along. Some of Florida's top Thoroughbreds were bred here when it was in its heyday. There's not much about horses and breeding he doesn't know. I'm lucky to have him."

"What did you do before?"

He grinned ruefully. "Which year?"

"Can't hold a job, huh?" she teased, knowing instinctively that was far from the truth.

"Can't settle down. I've bought and sold half a dozen businesses in the past twenty years. Making money gets to be a bore."

"I suppose that depends on how easily you do it. I've never had that problem."

"Why'd you pick the post office?"

"I had an 'in.' My dad had worked there all his life. It's steady work."

"Could you walk away from it?"

"What do you mean?"

"Is it something you care about passionately?"

"Passionately, no. But I like it."

"Then why not leave? Try something you do care about."

The thought of her camera equipment stored in a closet in her Atlanta apartment teased at her. He couldn't know about that, and she wasn't ready to talk about it. Not yet. "Like what?"

"I don't know. Maybe a housekeeping job in Ocala."

Her heart caught, even as she knew deep down that he'd meant the question only hypothetically. She lifted her gaze to meet his and saw him studying her with that same intensity that had so unnerved her the night before. "What are the fringe benefits?" she asked, matching his light, bantering tone.

His lips curved in a faint smile. "A cautious woman. There's a lot to be said for that."

If he'd labeled her lazy or indifferent, she would have been no more irritated. "I didn't set out to be cautious," she said with an edge. "It just happened."

"Hey, why so touchy? There's nothing wrong with caution. Most folks say it's the sensible way to live."

"My parents certainly thought so."

His gaze rested on her consideringly. "Why does that make you so angry?"

"I'm not angry," she snapped. She hadn't realized that her voice had climbed until the horse nickered nervously and pranced away.

Cal turned his attention to the mare, settling her down, then observed, "You don't seem like a lady who'd be happy all shut up inside. I saw you out on the lawn earlier. You liked the way the grass felt under your feet, didn't you?"

She shrugged, feigning indifference. "That doesn't mean I want to spend my life barefoot."

"You're getting all prickly again, Marilou. I wonder why? Am I hitting too close to home?"

"Maybe so," she conceded grudgingly. "Once, a long time ago, I had other plans."

"What plans?"

"Oh, travel mainly," she said, admitting to only part of the truth. "I wanted to see the world. When I finished college, I was going to take off and explore, try different things."

"Why didn't you?"

"Things didn't work out."

"It's been my experience that you can either make things work out or not. Blaming it on fate or whatever is just an excuse."

She glared up at him, aware that her eyes were filling with tears. "You don't know anything about it, Cal Rivers. You obviously just run from responsibility. I couldn't."

He ignored her charge and asked pointedly, "Responsibility to whom?"

"My parents."

"Were they sick? Did they need your help?"

"They died."

Refusing to look at him, she heard his sharp intake of breath, the low curse, then, "I'm sorry."

His compassion surrounded her and, after all this time of having no one to lean on, made her want to move into his arms and draw on his strength. Instead she said simply, "It's been a couple of years now. I should be over it, but sometimes it sneaks up on me and I realize I'm not."

"Life can deal some pretty lousy blows. There's no set timetable for recovery that I know about. How come you didn't follow through on your plans after they died?"

"Because they had hated the idea. We'd been arguing about it the night of their car accident. It just seemed like the wrong thing to do once they were gone. Disrespectful, somehow. I guess in a way I envy you, being able to walk away without looking back. That's what you do, isn't it? You just take off whenever the mood strikes you?"

"That's about right. Just so you know, though, I never turn my back on my responsibilities. When I sell a business, I make sure my people are taken care of. I owe them that. Most of them wind up better off than they were before I came."

"Do you think security is all you owe them? What about explanations, loyalty?"

"The best loyalty comes in the form of a steady paycheck. That's the beginning and end of what I owe them."

"You can just cut everyone off like that? You certainly vanished from Palm Lane like a man who didn't want anyone following. I had the devil's own time trying to track you down."

"I believe in making clean breaks and starting fresh."

"Breaks are never clean, not unless you make it a point to keep a real distance between you and the people around you. I'm not saying my way's better, but it seems to me that yours is a stupid way to live."

"Maybe so, but I've had a long time to get used to it."

Marilou shuddered and then was filled with a deep sadness. "I'd never get used to it."

"Do you have a man waiting for you back in Atlanta?"

"No, no man," she said to Cal. "Not the way you mean."

"Friends?"

"A few, though a lot of them have left Atlanta the past couple of years."

"Then why go back? Start your adventure now, this minute."

"And do what?"

"Stay here with us. The housekeeping job is yours for as long as you want it. When you're ready to move on, you can."

The idea tempted in a way he'd probably never intended. Not that Cal Rivers wasn't very aware of the impact he'd have on a woman, any woman, but he probably figured he'd warned her adequately about the kind of no-strings man he was.

"How long do you expect to stick around here yourself?" she asked.

"It's hard to say. Right now it's all new. I want to make this stud farm one of the best. That takes time. A few good stallions were part of the original deal, but I want more. In some cases that'll mean buying them as yearlings, training them and giving them time to be tested on the track. I suppose I'd like to have a Kentucky Derby winner just once."

Marilou was surprised by his level of enthusiasm and apparent commitment to such a long-range plan. "Why did you pick this, anyway? It's a far cry from the computer business you had in Daytona."

"You know about that?"

"I discovered it when I was trying to track you down."

"Maybe you've missed your calling. Maybe you ought to be a private eye."

"In some ways I already am. You still haven't answered me. Why a stud farm?"

"It looked like fun," he said with a touch of irony as they took yet another turn around the quarter-mile training track.

"Then you must not have known about these 4:00 a.m. strolls."

"Maybe I just wanted to get into practice for fatherhood."

Marilou swallowed the sudden lump in her throat. "Are you and Lady Mary planning a large family?"

At that the horse pricked up its ears and turned its head toward Marilou. She nickered softly. Cal chuckled. "I think Lady Mary has her own family plans and they don't include me."

Marilou looked from him to the horse and back again. "Lady Mary?"

"Lady Mary," he confirmed.

She felt laughter bubbling up from deep inside, relieved laughter. "Why didn't you tell me last night?"

"It was too much fun watching you jump to conclusions."

Just then Chaney joined them, nodding at Marilou, then looking at the horse. "She doing any better?"

"I think so. She seems to have settled down quite a bit."

"Want me to take over?"

"Let's take her back to the barn and see how it goes," Cal suggested.

"I'll go back and get breakfast on the table," Marilou volunteered.

They both shot her a surprised look. Cal nodded. "We'll be in soon."

As she walked away, she heard Chaney demand, "Is she staying?"

"At least through breakfast, it seems," Cal said. "After that, I guess we'll see."

Marilou couldn't tell from his tone if it mattered to him one way or the other. The apparent indifference set her teeth on edge. She worked out her frustration by cooking the biggest, heartiest breakfast she could think of. By the time Cal and Chaney came back in, she had the food on the table.

"Well, boss, will you look at this," Chaney said with glee, digging into the stack of pancakes she'd kept warm in the oven. Apparently he was willing to overlook his objections about her presence as long as she kept his stomach filled.

Cal grunted. He might be unwilling to acknowledge her new attitude, but she noticed that it didn't keep him from taking five pancakes for himself. "You surprise me," he said, swallowing the last of them. "For a minute there last night, I figured you for one of those types who can't cook a lick."

"Oh, I can cook. I just don't like men making assumptions about the role I should play."

His gaze narrowed. "Sounds like the usual rhetoric to me."

Unintimidated by his fierce look, Marilou scowled right back. He laughed then and shook his head. "Lady, you really are a piece of work. So, tell me, what do you plan to do about clothes? I never met a woman yet who was satisfied to wear the same outfit day after day."

That, of course, was a quandary that had crossed

her mind already. She supposed there was no help for it. She was going to have to leave and drive back to her hotel, unless…

"I don't suppose you're ready to discuss this visit to your grandmother yet?"

He pushed back from the table and tilted his chair onto its back legs. Long fingers intertwined and rested on his belt buckle. "Nope."

She sighed. "I was afraid of that."

"You decided about taking me up on my offer?"

"What offer's that?" Chaney asked.

"I thought maybe she'd like to hire on as our housekeeper."

Chaney choked on his coffee, then settled into a sullen pout.

"Hey, you liked the pancakes, didn't you?" Cal teased. "And what about the spaghetti?"

"We wasn't starving before she came."

"The next thing to it. I was ready to start ordering pizza deliveries. What about it, Marilou? You gonna stick around?"

She suddenly realized that she wanted very much to stay, and it had very little to do with the letter anymore. She took a deep breath. "What about a trial run?"

"How long?"

"A month. That's how long my vacation lasts."

He stuck out his hand, enveloping hers. The currents that raced along her arm headed straight for her abdomen, spawning desire and confusion in equal measures. Oh, yes, she thought, she was definitely in over her head, definitely out of her mind.

"I guess I'll go and get my things," she said, lifting her gaze to his. "If you're sure."

"I'm sure." He kept his gaze on her as she cleaned up the kitchen and got her purse.

"I shouldn't be more than a few hours," she said finally, still struggling to determine the wisdom of her decision.

Apparently he read her doubts and misinterpreted them. Frowning, he said, "And here I thought we'd been making progress. I was sure you trusted me to be here when you got back."

"I don't trust you a bit, but I'm going anyway," she said, glad that he couldn't read her so easily. "And don't get your hopes up, because I will be back and I haven't forgotten about the letter, either."

He laughed at that, the first unrestrained emotion she'd seen. "I never doubted that for a minute, sweetheart."

She hesitated at the door, then teased, "Don't change the locks."

"I wouldn't dream of it," he countered with a wink.

If he meant the devilish wink to be a warning of some sort, it failed. Marilou found the challenge of it flat-out irresistible.

Chapter Five

Cal stayed clear of the house until nearly supper time. It was one of the hardest struggles of his life. Oh, he had plenty to do to keep occupied, but all of his thoughts seemed centered on Marilou Stockton. He couldn't imagine a more troubling turn of events. He'd made it a practice not to let any woman get too close. He hadn't lived with a woman for the past ten years, not since he'd realized and accepted that he was the kind of man who simply couldn't settle down and make the kind of commitment any decent woman deserved.

Now he had gone and broken his own rule. He'd invited a woman who was dead set on reforming him to stick around and give it her best shot. Even if he hadn't been convinced of his own lunacy, Chaney would have been more than happy to point it out. His scowling disapproval spoke volumes. As a result of that silent condemnation, Cal flatly refused to be caught looking to see if Marilou had returned, although Chaney was giving him regular reports.

Squinting toward the horizon at midafternoon,

Chaney announced obliquely, "Not yet." Obviously he figured that Cal would know perfectly well what he meant.

"Not yet," he said again an hour later and again the hour after that, until Cal felt like strangling him. All of the men were giving him a wide berth as his temper grew shorter with each passing minute.

What if she didn't come back? The prospect nagged at him worse than her presence had. God knew, he couldn't blame her for running scared. There was a contradictory blend of recklessness and caution in her that fascinated him. Maybe the caution had won out. After all, he'd warned her about his lifestyle in one breath, then with the next he'd taunted her to share it. Even though the invitation to stay had been couched as a job offer, only a totally naive woman would believe that the two of them could keep it that way for long. The air had crackled with sexual tension from the minute they'd laid eyes on each other. He realized with a sudden guilty pang that Marilou might just be too innocent, too hell-bent on proving something to herself to recognize all the snapping and sparring for what it was, a prelude to passion of a different sort entirely. Well, heaven help the two of them if she'd misunderstood!

Cal prided himself on being an analytical man. Some even described him as coolly calculating. He never ever let his emotions get in the way of a business decision. That made this impulsive move all the more disconcerting. There was an emotional tug here that was not only totally out of character, but went against every commonsense instinct he possessed.

Maybe it was her long red hair pulled back in that braid that his fingers itched to undo.

Maybe it was her green eyes, which met his with such a total lack of guile.

More likely—and most dangerous—it was the depth of caring that radiated from her. That compassion had made her travel several hundred miles to find a long-lost grandson for a woman she didn't even know. The part of him that was accustomed to burying family ties wanted to know what sort of woman was driven to do something like that. He wanted that warmth and generosity of spirit directed at him, even as he distrusted it.

It was nearly dusk when he finally spotted the dust flying up on the long driveway to the house. He caught himself grinning as he watched. She drove at a damn-the-consequences speed with which she apparently did everything else regarding him. Relief, so profound it astonished him, flooded through him. Perversely it kept him hiding out down in the stables until long after Chaney had gone to his quarters to clean up for supper.

If Cal had hoped that the defiant gesture would prove his indifference, he was very much mistaken. He had only to walk into the kitchen and see her there to feel the unfamiliar swell of emotion that had plagued him throughout the day.

Marilou was dressed in a flowered sundress that showed off shoulders lightly dusted with freckles and emphasized a tiny waist. He had to fight an almost ir-resistible urge to circle that waist with his hands and kiss every one of those faint marks left by the sun. As he passed by, he caught the scent of roses, sweet and all too alluring. Strappy little sandals that had no business on a farm showed off her ankles. She had fine ankles, he observed with a catch in his heartbeat. When he saw

Chaney regarding them appreciatively, he had to restrain the primitive, proprietary impulse to slug him.

Keeping his purely masculine response under control might have been more difficult if he hadn't been drawn toward the pots simmering on the stove. Chili, thick with meat and beans and spices, bubbled in one. In another, ears of sweet corn tumbled in the boiling water. In the last, greens simmered with a ham hock. As he drew in a deep, satisfying breath, he realized that it had been twenty years since he'd had a real home-cooked meal. Hell, maybe longer. His mother hadn't been much of a cook. She'd grown up in a house filled with servants. His daddy's income, once the oil business crashed, hadn't even been enough to support a cleaning woman once a week. After that his mother tended to serve complaints instead of decent meals. The fancy restaurants that had eventually taken the place of frozen dinners as his own career took off were more likely to serve beef Wellington than chili.

"Smells good," he said, recalling the last time he'd eaten real Texas chili. It had been in a diner near the bus station an hour before he'd left home for good. Joshua had been sitting on the stool next to him, talking a mile a minute, coming up with every reason he could think of to keep Cal from running. Not a one of those reasons had been worth a tinker's damn once he'd made up his mind to go. He wondered what Joshua would have to say when he heard about his new, temporary housekeeper.

Marilou turned at the sound of his voice and greeted him with a radiant, unhesitating smile that almost took his breath away. Any sane man would fly home from work for a welcome like that.

"I hope you like chili," she said, a hint of nervousness

in her eyes. "I made enough for an army. This kitchen looks as if it were built for the entire crew. I wasn't sure if you'd want some for the other men."

"Not tonight. They're used to going out on their own or cooking out in the bunkhouse. If it looks like you're going to stick around, we'll see if they want to change that."

"They might want to sample my cooking before they make up their minds."

"If that corn bread that's baking tastes half as good as it smells, I can almost guarantee they'll want to join us," he said.

"Amen to that," Chaney agreed, walking in just then and eyeing the big golden squares she was cutting and putting into a basket lined with a bright red-and-white-checked napkin. He was reaching for a piece before she could get the corn bread on the table.

"I think you may have found a way to his heart, after all," Cal observed wryly as he sat at the big round table that she'd set with a red-checked cloth and the sturdy white everyday dishes. It occurred to him again that she had an instinct for making things homey instead of fancy. She'd left the previous owner's fine English bone china and expensive Irish crystal in the cupboard where they belonged.

Marilou grinned back at him. "Cooking is a tried and true method. My mother swears she got my father to marry her by baking him mouth-watering lemon meringue pies."

Chaney coughed and shot a warning glance at Cal. "Did you hear that, boss? I guess she's put you on notice. There's a lot to be said for a woman who don't play games."

Marilou blushed prettily at the taunt, but met Chaney's gaze evenly. "Who says it's not you I'm after, you handsome devil?"

Chaney's eyes went wide as half dollars, and he gobbled down the rest of his meal as if he had to get to a fire. Cal and Marilou both burst into laughter as he muttered his excuses and scrambled away from the table, leaving them to their coconut cake and coffee.

Cal tilted his chair back and watched Marilou grow increasingly nervous. She fussed with her napkin and avoided his gaze as if she'd just realized the new intimacy of their relationship.

"Settle down, girl," he said gently. "I'm not out to ravish you." Yet, he amended silently. He'd never taken a skittish woman yet, and the past few months on the farm had taught him a lot about patience and calming nerves. Unfortunately it had also been a time of celibacy, and a woman as pretty as Marilou could make a man in that condition a little crazy.

"Maybe that's what's bothering me," she said, clearly emboldened by his disclaimer.

His whole body tensed at the unexpected taunt. That flash of daring in her nature was far more dangerous than she realized. "Careful, Marilou. I could change my mind real easy."

She smiled knowingly. "I'm not worried."

"You ought to be, sweetheart. I'm no saint."

"Oh, I know that," she said breezily. "But I also know you're not about to take a chance on involvement, not with a woman who's already underfoot."

"Meaning?"

"That your type of woman probably has one foot on a plane before you dare to kiss her."

The tart observation was so close to the mark, it astounded him. It also worried him a little that she could read him so well, while he couldn't figure her out a bit. She was like a diamond, showing off new facets depending on which way it faced the light. That made her a challenge, and he knew himself well enough to recognize that made her the most dangerous woman he'd met in a long time. Still, instead of keeping his distance, he asked, "What about you? What's kept you single all this time?"

"I'm only twenty-five."

"I'm still surprised some man hasn't snapped you up."

"I'm not running, if that's what you mean. I suppose, if anything, I've just been waiting for the right man to come along."

"What would he be like?"

"Intelligent, adventurous, maybe even a little wild," she said with a grin that reminded him of a teenager sharing secret confidences. "Know anyone who fits those qualifications?"

"What does a woman who bakes corn bread and coconut cake want with a man who's wild?"

"You know what they say, opposites attract."

"Maybe so, but do they last?"

"You're asking the wrong person. I haven't met a man like that yet, much less tried to make the relationship work."

"You could always practice with me," he offered.

He watched as she swallowed hard, then worked to hide her sudden nervousness. "I'm not so sure you're as wild and daring as you'd like me to believe. In fact, I think you might be surprised at just how domesticated you could become if you gave yourself half a chance."

He found himself grinning. "So, based on your analysis, we're not opposites at all?"

"Not deep down."

"Then, according to the theory, there should be no attraction."

"That's right," she said with that devilish gleam reappearing in her eyes.

That glint, like moonlight on emeralds, was yet another challenge he couldn't refuse. He reached out, hooked his hand around a rung of the ladder-back chair and dragged her to him. Before she could recover from the sudden movement, his lips were on hers, catching her soft gasp of surprise. His fingers curved around her bare shoulders, savoring the smooth texture that was like silk against the sandpaper roughness of his calluses. Her hands were pressed against his chest. After one startled push, a faint flutter of protest, they gentled against him. Her tongue, shy and hesitant, touched his lips, then retreated, as if she were afraid to dare more. It was the touch of an angel with the impact of Satan.

No more experienced kiss had ever awakened such wonder, such desperate wanting in him. No sweet touch of innocence had ever stirred such terror. With an anguished moan, he tore himself away and stood up. He couldn't even bring himself to look at her, fearing what he'd see. If there were tears of dismay in her eyes, if he'd frightened her, he'd never forgive himself.

"Go on up to bed," he said gruffly.

"The dishes…"

"Leave 'em. It won't be the first time they sat here overnight."

"You're paying me to do them," she insisted, stacking them by the sink and avoiding his gaze. "And I have no intention of spending an extra hour in the morning scrubbing off dried food."

"I'll put them in the damned dishwasher. Now go on, before I do something we'll both regret."

She sighed then and walked slowly to the door. Only when her back was to him did he risk really looking at her. Her spine was straight and proud. There was no way he could tell how deeply he'd hurt her, until she turned and looked back. To his surprise, there was no condemnation in her eyes, only something that looked faintly like sorrow.

"I think maybe you already have," she told him softly. Then she was gone, leaving the scent of roses trailing behind her and a heavy ache in his heart.

For a man who'd lived his whole life without regrets, Cal realized he'd just filled a whole day with a passel of them.

Cal's kiss had had more force than a tornado sweeping through Georgia. It took three days for Marilou to feel comfortable looking him in the eye again, though she did so with determined regularity. She refused to let him see that he'd shaken her. It was small comfort that he didn't seem to be much easier around her. When he could, he avoided her and left it to Chaney to tell her what time to have meals on the table, where to go for supplies and to write out the checks for household needs.

Marilou was a patient woman, but she was beginning to worry that she was wasting precious time. By now Cal's grandmother could be much worse, and Marilou hadn't even succeeded in getting him to look at the letter. She'd planned on mentioning it at dinner the night before, but he hadn't come in. Chaney had offered no explanations. He'd just silently eaten his own meal, thanked her in his gruff manner and gone out, leaving Marilou alone with her thoughts and a whole lot of confusing emotions.

It seemed to her that she had two choices. She could wait Cal out, hoping that sooner or later he'd get past this stubbornness on his own. Or she could push him and risk having him toss her and the letter all the way back to Georgia. She finally opted for waiting, at least for a few more days. And since this was supposed to be an adventure, she decided she might as well make the most of it. That night at dinner she asked Chaney if he thought Cal would mind if she did some work in the garden.

"It's a disgrace," she said. "You should see the way the weeds have taken over. You'd have plenty of fresh vegetables if somebody just put in a little effort. I saw some tomatoes and some zucchini. Possibly some green beans. What do you think?"

"Ain't up to me."

"Well, the ground's wasted the way it is. I think I'll just go ahead."

The next day she picked up a half dozen tomato plants, along with seedlings for several other vegetables. She spent an extra half hour getting directions on exactly how to prepare the ground and plant them. She could hardly wait to get started.

As soon as she'd put away the groceries, she put on a pair of shorts and a halter top, then went to the barn for a shovel, a rake and a hoe. Zeke, Roddy and Chaney took one hard look at her and simply stared until she flushed with embarrassment.

"I'll get what you need," Cal growled as he returned to the barn leading Devil's Magic. He handed the horse

over to Chaney and shot a stern glance that had Zeke
and Roddy scurrying back to work. "If you're going to
parade around down here, put some damned clothes on."

She looked down at the shorts and knit top. "For
heaven's sakes, people wear less than this at the beach."

"If you were at the beach, you'd fit right in. Around
here the only females wearing fewer clothes are the fil-
lies and, believe me, they're not much competition."

She supposed he had a point, though she doubted any
of the men in that barn were likely to be stirred to passion by one look at her in this outfit. "Sorry," she apologized anyway. "I didn't think."

His eyes met hers. She noticed he was careful to keep
his glance from dropping below her chin. "Next time
you will," he said, handing her the gardening equipment. "Don't stay out in that sun too long. It's overcast
today. It'll fool you."

She nodded as he vanished. While she worked in the
garden she was aware that Cal paused to stare at her
every time he returned to the barn, but he never waved
or acknowledged her presence in any way. In fact, for
all the attention he paid to her, she might have been invisible.

It took her two days to get the garden into shape. The
work was far harder than she'd anticipated, but when
she was done, when the ground had been turned and
watered and the plants were in nice, even rows, she felt
a rare sense of accomplishment. There had been something soothing about the task. When it was over, though,
she immediately began looking around for something
new to try. The Thoroughbreds were the obvious choice.

The next morning, dressed in jeans, a T-shirt and

tennis shoes, she presented herself to Chaney. "I want to learn about horses," she announced.

He shoved his hat back on his head and regarded her skeptically. "There's books in the house."

"The horses are here. I figure I'll learn a lot more by doing than I will by reading, don't you?"

"You know anything at all?"

"Nope."

At his disgusted expression, she added, "Just think of me as fresh clay. You get to mold me. I'll do whatever you say."

"I ain't so sure the boss is gonna like this. He hired you to keep house."

"You have any complaints about the food?"

"No."

"When you do, I'll give this up. Come on, Chaney. I really want to learn, and Cal says you're the best."

She could practically see his chest swell with pride. "He's got a point." He stared thoughtfully across the paddock, watching the way Lady Mary was bobbing her head when she caught sight of them. The horse's ears pricked up and she trotted across to them, nuzzling against Chaney's jacket, apparently looking for the sugar cubes Marilou suspected he hid there for all the horses.

Finally, after he'd given Lady Mary the sugar, he turned back to Marilou. "I suppose if you've got your head set on this, you might's well learn things right. I'll start you out at the bottom, though. No favoritism."

"Absolutely. So, what should I do?"

"You can start by mucking out stalls."

"What's that?"

"It ain't anything like baking pies, I can tell you that,"

he said with a gleeful expression. "Roddy, come on over here and meet Marilou. She wants to learn about horses."

Roddy, who looked to be no more than eighteen or nineteen, gazed at her shyly. He rubbed his hands on his jeans, then held one out to her. "Morning, ma'am," he said in a whisper as she shook his callused hand.

"You let her help you this morning, son. I don't mean watchin', either. Put her to work."

Roddy's cheeks burned and his eyes widened in dismay. "But, Chaney, that ain't no work for a lady."

"No," Marilou said quickly, judging from his reaction that Chaney truly was starting her at the bottom. "It's okay, Roddy. You just show me. I'm not afraid of a little hard work."

He still looked uncertain, but apparently sensed her determination. He nodded at last. "Okay, ma'am. If you say so."

Although she'd begun to figure out just what she'd gotten herself into even before they reached the stable, she was not fully prepared for the overpowering scents that greeted her as Roddy led her into the first stall to be mucked out. He showed her how to rake out the filthy straw and replace it with clean, while the horses were either in the paddock or being worked on the track. Though in many ways the barn was a lot cleaner than she would have imagined, there was no way to keep it spotless. The work was hot, smelly and tiring. The worst of it was that she didn't seem to be learning anything about horses. They weren't even around. She knew better than to complain, though. If Chaney was testing her mettle, she was determined to pass.

By the time he came in to check her work, she had

blisters on her hands, straw in her hair and dirt and dust from head to toe.

"She did great," Roddy told the manager. He pointed out the stalls she'd done entirely on her own, and Marilou found herself holding her breath as Chaney inspected them.

"Not bad," he finally said grudgingly.

Marilou felt as if she'd been given a letter of commendation. "Thanks. What about tomorrow?"

He actually came close to smiling at that. "You ain't scared off yet?"

She grinned back at him. "Not a chance."

"Then I'll think on it tonight and we'll figure out a plan."

"Thanks, Chaney."

If nothing else, the hard work had kept her from thinking too hard about Cal. He'd barely crossed her mind all morning. But once she was back at the house, she began to wonder just what he was going to think when he found out what she'd done. Chaney had been right about one thing: Cal was paying her to keep house, not to muck out stalls or even to plant a kitchen garden, for that matter.

She didn't have long to wait. Cal stormed into the kitchen with a scowl she could read from across the room. She immediately turned back to the sink. He came up behind her and reached for one of the blistered hands she was holding under the cool tap water.

At the sight of the raw, broken skin, he muttered an oath. "Sit. Let me get some ointment."

"They'll be fine," she said without moving.

"Not if they get infected," he countered as he reached into a cupboard for a jar of cream. He nudged her toward a chair, then took her hands and soothed on the cool, white ointment. His touch was gentle, but the expression in his eyes was fierce, and Marilou knew he was only holding his anger in check temporarily. The instant he'd treated both hands, those cool gray eyes met hers and there was no doubt about the storm brewing.

"What the devil did you think you were doing?" he demanded roughly. "I kept my mouth shut about the damned garden, but this has gone too far. You're not cut out for this kind of work."

"I won't die from a few blisters."

"Maybe not, but did you ever consider the disruption to my staff? I've got a lovesick groom out there and a manager who's still hooting over the sight of you with straw and horse dung from head to toe."

Marilou did not believe for one minute that Roddy was lovesick or that Chaney had been making fun of her. Cal was making excuses for his own reaction. He didn't like the way she'd wheedled her way into another part of his life.

"I had time on my hands."

"Then clean the damned closets. That's what you're being paid to do."

"The closets are cleaned, and don't forget that this housekeeping game can end just as quickly as it began. You don't take it seriously and neither do I."

"Then why don't you just quit and go home?"

"You know why."

"The letter," he said.

"That's right. The letter. You haven't even asked to see it."

"Fine. What the hell. Show it to me. Then maybe things can get back to normal around here."

"You mean where you're the boss and the rest of us just bow and scrape?"

"No, I mean when I don't have some damned fool woman interfering in my life."

"You read that letter and call your grandmother, and I'll be out of here so fast it'll make your head spin."

"Get the letter," he snapped.

Marilou ran up to her room and retrieved the letter from her purse. Oddly, though, as she took it downstairs, she realized that instead of gloating with satisfaction, what she was feeling felt a whole lot more like pain.

Chapter Six

Cal had no idea why he'd been so infuriated when Chaney had told him about Marilou's working in the barn. All he knew was that the admiring comments from Roddy and the other grooms had made him see red. Then when he'd walked into the kitchen and seen her rinsing her blistered hands at the sink, he'd lost it. Marilou wasn't some fragile little flower needing his protection, but by God he was not going to let her wear herself out while she was working for him.

It wasn't until he was already in the midst of yelling that he had recognized the spark in her eyes for what it was—pride and excitement. She had actually loved spending the day in all that filth. That made him all the madder, because he hadn't been the one to share with her an experience that obviously meant so much.

Talk about perversity! He was getting to be a real genius at it. Now, as payment for his stupidity, he was going to have to read that damned letter.

Read it, hell. If he knew Marilou, that wasn't going to be the end of it. She was going to expect action, and he wasn't ready for a confrontation with his past. The memories had been coming back the past few days, not all of them bad, but enough of them that he wished this so-called grandmother had never tried to track him down.

He was pacing the length of the porch and back again when Marilou returned. Silently she handed him the letter, then retreated to one of the rockers and sat down. The thick vellum paper couldn't have weighed over an ounce or two, but it felt like a ton in his hands. He didn't want to open the envelope, didn't want to know its contents, didn't want to believe that it was really meant for him.

If Marilou had pushed, it would have been easier to rip the letter up right then and there in a gesture of defiance. Or at the very least, he could have blamed her for the way he was feeling. Instead she just rocked and waited, all patience and serenity and expectation.

Finally, itching for a fight, he went over and sat in the chair next to her, still regarding the letter warily.

"What are you afraid of?" she said quietly. "It's just a letter."

"It's the past," he corrected grimly. "And I'm not so sure I want to be reminded of it."

"Why?"

It was something he'd never talked about, not even to Joshua. He figured his friend had seen enough and guessed the rest. Even if that hadn't been the case, Cal wasn't the kind of man who liked baring his soul. A man dealt with his problems; he didn't share them. He stiffened instinctively at Marilou's question, but then he looked into her eyes and there was that tenderness again, that genuine caring. He sighed and, to his amazement, the words just began to come.

Keeping his gaze riveted on the horizon, he said slowly, "From the day I was born about the only thing I can remember about my parents is the fights. Nothing was ever good enough for my mother. Nothing. My father tried and tried, but no matter what he said or did, she was always looking for more." He turned to her. "Do you see? A man can be destroyed by that kind of self-ishness and greed."

"Was your father destroyed by it?"

He shrugged. "No," he admitted, still bemused by that. "For some reason he never seemed to blame her. It was like he believed she had a right to be angry and hateful."

"Did they ever explain?"

"I never asked. I just got out as soon as I could and swore I'd never let any woman do to me what my mother did to my father."

"But maybe she had her reasons. Don't you at least want to understand what they were?"

"There's nothing that could make what she did right. Maybe things didn't turn out exactly the way she'd expected, but she had no call to treat him the way she did."

"I'm not trying to make excuses for her. I just think maybe the letter will help you to understand. She may have felt very much alone."

The certainty in her tone made him ask, "Did you read it?"

She nodded, her expression at once full of guilt and apology. "I wasn't supposed to, except to look for an address, but then I saw that your grandmother was dying and I had to read it all. I could see how important it was to her to try to find you. Read it, Cal. Maybe it'll make up a little for what you lost."

He tried once more to convince her—and himself—
that he was beyond the reach of the past. "I didn't lose
so much, just a harridan of a mother and a spineless father. I gained a lot more: success, satisfaction, power."

She regarded him doubtfully, obviously unimpressed
by his accomplishments. "I suppose that is a lot by some
standards, but in my book it doesn't make up for family.
Seems to me all the money in the world can't compen-
sate for loneliness."

"Don't kid yourself, Marilou. I am rarely lonely."

"Maybe," she said, but he could tell she wasn't buying it. Still the truth of the matter was, he'd never known
what loneliness meant until he'd forced himself to spend
the past few days staying clear of her. Even now he was
drawn to her in a way that warned him to run, to flee
the hurt that always, always came with caring.

And yet he stayed, weighing the letter in his hand, trying not to see the expectancy in her eyes as she waited.
Finally, with a sigh of resignation, he opened the envelope and withdrew the pages with their crimped scrawl.

My dearest Cal…
I know you'll be surprised to hear from me after all
these years. For all I know you didn't even know I
existed. I can't really blame your mother for that. It
was my fault for being so pigheaded. If you inherited anything from our side of the family, I hope
it wasn't that. Stubbornness can be a blessing and
a curse. In my case, it cost me everything I held
dear, and I believe if your mother is at all honest
with herself, she'd have to say the same.

  You see, I thought your mother was making a
dreadful mistake when she married your father.

I had nothing against him, though she was too young and rebellious to realize that. I just knew that I'd spoiled her. She'd been raised to expect so much, things I suspected your father would never be able to provide. Asking a man to give what's beyond him is a terrible thing. No marriage can survive it. I ought to know. I did the same thing to your grandfather and he left me. I could see all the same problems coming with Sissy and your father and it broke my heart.

Still, I should never have caused a rift so deep it could last a lifetime. And once done, I should have had the will to fix it, but I kept waiting for her to come back. I guess she couldn't bear to admit I was right, and I know I was. The people I hired to keep an eye on her whereabouts told me that much. Later, when you were born, I wanted so much to mend fences, but when I wrote, she ignored my letters. I guess after waiting so long, I can't really blame her.

Never forget that I love you, boy. I'm so sorry that we've never had a chance to get to know each other. I'm dying now, so I don't know if we'll ever meet. Just know that not a day goes by when I don't think of you with all my love. Be happy, Cal, and forgive an old woman for her mistakes.
Your grandmother.

Cal's eyes were blurred with tears as he came to the end. He'd never thought of himself as sentimental, but he found that his heart was filled with anguish over all the pain his grandmother must have suffered for that one strong-willed mistake. He knew all about digging in his heels and then learning to live with the consequences. She'd been right, but as she said, at what cost? So much bitterness. So many years of loneliness and regrets. To his surprise he found he was incapable of placing blame, not with her anyway. At last he had a few of the answers to questions that had always plagued him. The relief this brought him was not nearly as complete as he'd hoped. Anger didn't fade that quickly, and nothing she'd said absolved his parents.

He lifted his head and saw that Marilou was studying him closely.

"You believe me now, don't you?" she said softly. "You know she's your grandmother."

"I can't deny that it all fits," he admitted reluctantly.

"Then you'll go see her?"

Not really surprised by the question, he shook his head. "No. There's no need."

"Cal, she's dying. She needs to see you."

"Seeing me won't relieve her guilty conscience. The only one who could do that is my mother, and I doubt she'd feel so inclined."

"You could call her. She should know about this, too."

He stared at her incredulously. "You've got to be kidding. I haven't seen or spoken to my mother for twenty years, not since the day I walked out."

"Then it's about time you did."

"You read the letter. My grandmother knows where to find my mother. It's between the two of them."

"And you can just leave it at that?" she said furiously. "What kind of man are you? Do you have so many people in your life that you can afford to throw away a woman who loves you as much as she obviously does?"

"Grow up, Marilou," he said fiercely, then muttered

a curse as he saw her wince. He softened his tone, but not his message. "This isn't some romantic story with a guaranteed happy ending. Pieces of paper and pretty sentiments don't make up for years of anger."

"They aren't just pretty sentiments. She means it, Cal. She's sorry. You have to go. You have to let her die in peace. If you don't, especially now that you know, the guilt will eat away at you for the rest of your life."

"What do you know about guilt, my little innocent?" He couldn't hide the edge of sarcasm that crept into his thoughts. He was tired as hell of her pious attitude about what was right for him.

Her rocking chair stilled and she stared up at him, her expression bleak except for the furious sparks in her eyes.

"You think I don't know anything about guilt?" she began quietly. "Believe me, Cal Rivers, you don't hold an exclusive on it. I've been living with it since the day my parents died in that accident. I've blamed myself for every bitter word. I've lain awake nights wondering whether they might have avoided the crash if they hadn't been so upset and worried about our argument."

Huge tears were welling up in her eyes, shimmering on her lashes. For the second time in minutes, Cal felt his own eyes grow misty with the unfamiliar sting of salt. Sorrow and guilt over his harsh accusation lay heavily in his chest as her voice fell to a broken whisper. "I never had the chance to tell them I was sorry. I never told them how much I loved them. Now I'll never get to say the words or to hug them or even to say good—"

With the break in her voice came tears, spilling down her cheeks as she gazed at him helplessly. "Oh, Cal, I miss them so much."

Without thought for the consequences, he lifted her up and gathered her close, sheltering her in his embrace. If he was inexperienced at being comforted, he was even more so at offering it. He murmured nonsense at first, then searched for more, for words that could ease her pain. "I know, babe. I know," he soothed. "They knew how much you loved them, even if you never said the words."

"How?" she asked, clinging to him, watching him with so much hope in her eyes, needing forgiveness he had no right to give. "You can never assume that people know what's in your heart."

"With you, it's possible," he promised. "You're the kind of woman who radiates love. Anyone who knows you would have to feel it. Your parents would be proud of you, Marilou. They taught you to love and to fight for what you believe in. Even though you argued on that last day, I'll bet they were proud to see you standing up for what you wanted in life. Hell, even though your nagging drives me crazy sometimes, I have to admire your conviction. It's who you are."

She wiped away her tears with the back of her hand, the gesture reminding him of a child trying to salvage pride after an outburst. A sad smile tugged at her lips. "Then I guess you won't mind that I'm not going to let up about this. I may not be able to convince you today, but I will sooner or later."

He laughed ruefully. "You are almost as stubborn as I am."

"Let that be a warning to you. I never give up. In my job that's a requirement."

Something about her words stung his pride. He broke free and took a step away, distancing himself from the inexplicable hurt. "So that's why you've been hanging around? You just can't walk away until you've done your job?"

Obviously she heard the tension and irritation in his tone. She frowned as she met his gaze, then looked even more unsettled. She poked her hands in her pockets and glanced down at the ground.

"What else could it be?" she asked in a voice barely above a whisper. That shy question lured like the rustle of satin sheets.

"Maybe this," he said, dragging her back into his arms. He fastened his gaze on hers and murmured again, "Maybe this."

When his mouth claimed hers, the kiss was fueled by anger. He was deliberately rough, taking possession in a way that left no room for doubts about his intentions. It was time she recognized what was happening between them. This was between grown-ups now, the wild flaring of desire as hot and intense as any he had ever known. If he'd thought about it, he would have labeled it branding, but he was beyond thought. His body was hard and aching and needy. Marilou was soft and sweet and every bit as needy. She met spark with flame and made no apologies for it. Perhaps if she had, if she'd shown only the tiniest hint of reservation, he would have been able to stop with that one deep, drugging, mistaken kiss.

Instead, with her willing in his arms, he wanted more. He wanted to taste the sweet skin at the nape of her neck, to feel the weight of her breasts against his palm, to touch and excite and possess. Her whimpers of pleasure, the flaring of excitement in her green eyes, the way she fit herself against the hard contours of his body, all were the gestures of a woman who wanted claiming, a woman who felt the same passion, the same need that he did. The emotions that rioted deep within him suddenly made him angry and as scared as he'd ever been in his life. He wouldn't let this woman touch him, wouldn't allow her to reach the places in his soul that were still raw from past hurts.

He smoothed away the wisps of hair that framed her face, studying the lush lips that were still parted and moist from his kisses. He rubbed the pad of his thumb over the silk of her cheek, then across a bottom lip that quivered at his touch. It all felt so good, so right, which made it vital that he prove to himself and to her how wrong it was.

"This is why you stayed, isn't it?" he whispered, moving his hands over her, shaping the curve of her hip, cupping her bottom until she was tight against him. The look in his eyes and his words were deliberately provocative, just one phrase shy of crude. He'd show her where things stood, then watch her run. With his touch bold and his voice low and thick with innuendo, he murmured, "When it comes right down to it, this is what it's all about between a man and a woman. You want me as much as I want you."

She met his gaze then with a look that began as longing, then quickly turned to reproach as his meaning settled in. If he'd forced her upstairs and into his bed, she could have looked no more injured. He waited for satisfaction to come. Instead regret slammed into him, and he backed away as if he'd been burned and she were the flame.

"Damn," he muttered, suddenly confused and blaming her for it. "You're better at making a man feel guilty with one look than somebody else could with a whole dictionary full of words."

She reached up and touched his face. "I'm not trying to make you feel guilty. At least not about this. You're right. I do want you every bit as much as you want me. I'm not liar enough to even try to deny what's plain as day to both of us. But not like this, Cal. Not when the motivations are all tangled up."

"Hell, honey, when it comes to sex, motivations pretty much stay tangled."

"Then I guess that's something we'll just have to work on along with all the rest."

Amazed by her calm acceptance of what had very nearly happened between them and the way he'd tried to make it into something primitive and sordid rather than beautiful, he regarded her warily. "You're not going to run like a scared rabbit?"

She grinned at him then, a wobbly smile that was sheer bravado. His heart lurched unsteadily. She was so beautiful, so incredibly desirable and so damned gullible and innocent. She was no match for a man who'd always had few scruples when it came to women.

"So," she teased, "that's what you were hoping. It's going to take more than an offer of your manly charms to scare me off, Cal Rivers, so you might as well get used to having me around."

He shook his head in genuine bewilderment. "It occurs to me that you actually enjoy testing a man's patience," he said, delighted laughter suddenly threading through his voice.

"I'm beginning to think maybe I do," she admitted. "And you're such an easy subject."

"Careful, sweetheart. I'm dangerous when I'm provoked."

"So you keep warning me. But like I said, I don't scare easy."

His whole body pulsing with awareness and frustration, Cal conceded the round. "Maybe I do," he muttered, leaving before the temptation to kiss her again grew overwhelming.

Several hours and several drinks later he was on the phone to Joshua, the one person in the world who knew just about everything there was to know about him.

"Cal, do you know what time it is?" his friend grumbled sleepily.

"Sometime after one, I suppose," Cal said unapologetically. "I haven't checked the clock since midnight."

"Hasn't anyone ever explained the concept of business hours to you?"

"On occasion. I'm not calling to discuss business."

That seemed to wake Joshua right up. "Oh?"

"What do you know about Marilou Stockton?"

"Who?"

"Don't play games. I know she called you."

"Oh, wait," he said thoughtfully. "I remember now. She was looking for you a couple of weeks back. Are you telling me she found you?"

"She found me all right. You must have sent her straight to me."

"I didn't tell her a damn thing. You know me better than that. What's she after? She's not some woman you ran out on, is she? Her name didn't sound familiar."

Cal caught himself grinning ruefully. "Where did you ever get the idea that I've told you about every woman in my life?"

"Good Lord! You mean there are more?"

"Very funny."

"Cal, as fascinating as this conversation is, I have a 7:00 a.m. breakfast meeting. Could we cut to the chase?"

"She's here."

"Now? At one in the morning?"

"She's been here."

"Since when?"

"Since two weeks ago."

Joshua, damn him, chuckled. "Well, well. How did that come about?"

"I hired her," he admitted miserably. "Stop laughing, dammit."

"Sorry. I can't help it. Maybe you'd better explain. Exactly what did you hire her to do? I didn't have the impression she was even looking for a job."

"She wasn't. It was just temporarily, as a housekeeper. At least that's the way it started, but now I'm not sure how to go about getting rid of her."

"Why do you want to? Is she stealing the silver?" Joshua inquired, too cheerfully, it seemed to Cal.

"No," he said, aware that a bleak note had crept into his voice. "Why doesn't matter. I just think she ought to go."

"Then fire her. You used to be pretty good at that, as I recall."

"I only fired you once, and even then I couldn't make it stick. I think you'd better take care of this for me."

"Me? Since when did I ever get involved in your personnel problems?"

"Since I just made it part of your job description."

"Is there something more here that I should know about?"

"Nothing," Cal denied emphatically.

"Which means there's something. Why don't you drive over tomorrow and we can talk about it?"

"I'm leaving town in the morning. Take care of this before I get back," he said, and hung up before Joshua could argue with him. The phone rang within seconds. It rang again five minutes later. When it started ringing again ten minutes after that, he picked it up reluctantly.

"No," Joshua said in response to his growled greeting. "But I think maybe I will drive out to see what this is all about. She must really be something if she's got you running scared."

"I am not running scared," he said emphatically, something the last two shots of Scotch made difficult to pull off.

"And I'm Secretariat," Joshua said, chuckling again. "You sure lead an interesting life, old friend. Just watching you keeps me young."

"Oh, go to hell," Cal grumbled, figuring that was where he was going to end up after tonight anyway. He might as well have company.

Chapter Seven

Marilou wasn't all that surprised by Cal's disappearance after that searing kiss and their conversation about the desire that was growing between them. Running seemed to be his way of dealing with unwanted emotions. She knew that and yet, with her whole body still aching with longing, she'd listened until well after midnight for the reassuring sound of his footsteps on the porch. If he'd come in, though, it had been after she'd fallen asleep.

Now, edgy with anticipation, she was putting dishes on the table for breakfast and fixing the ham, eggs and cheese grits she'd discovered were his favorite breakfast. Chaney came in, nodded, then stuck a napkin in the open throat of his blue chambray work shirt and silently began to eat. Marilou sat down across from him and began picking at her breakfast, her gaze going constantly to the screen door.

"He's gone," Chaney said finally in a flat tone that told her he wasn't too happy about it.

Startled, she stared at him. "Gone? You mean he's out with the horses already?"

"I mean gone. Took the trailer and a couple of the men and headed up to Kentucky. Dang fool thing, if you ask me. Should have flown and saved all that time. The men could have taken the trailer up. Tried to tell him that, but no, he was dead set on getting out of here this morning. Left here at five." He regarded her knowingly. "Any idea why he was in such a blamed hurry?"

She swallowed hard, sensing the undercurrent of disapproval in Chaney's tone. "He didn't say anything to me," she responded defensively. "Why did he go? He must have said."

"Said he wanted to get up there early for the spring horse sales. He's hoping to pick up a couple of good yearlings."

Though she hadn't known when the sales were scheduled, she knew how important they were. Cal and Chaney had been discussing them practically since the day she'd arrived. "You let him go alone for that?"

Chaney hooted at that. "I don't *let* the boss do nothing. He does what he dang well pleases. You might do well to remember that yourself, missy. Can't hog-tie a man that's spent his whole life independent."

She glared at him, filled with indignation at Chaney's interpretation of events since her arrival. "I have no desire to hog-tie anyone, and you know perfectly well what I meant. You both agree that you know more about horses than he does. Why didn't you go? Was it because he left earlier than you'd planned?"

Chaney shrugged. "I wasn't planning to go in the first place. I studied the catalog with him. We talked about which horses he should take a look at. He's got to get his feet wet some time. Man like him operates best when he makes his own mistakes. That's one way to learn real fast."

"But what can you tell from a picture? Don't you have to look at the horse? What if it can't move?"

"I've been teaching him all about conformation. They have photographers trained to shoot the horse just to show off the way he's made. The boss'll recognize good conformation when he sees it. And if the danged horse can't move, don't you think he'll notice? The man may be a greenhorn, but he ain't blind."

"I suppose," she said as she settled into a funk.

Her month's vacation was nearly half over. Even after yesterday's apparent breakthrough, she still hadn't gotten Cal to agree to an actual visit with his grandmother. How was she supposed to work on convincing him when he was hundreds of miles away for who knows how long? How was she supposed to decide about going or staying herself without him around to let her know what he was really thinking? What did she even want with a man who could dismiss family ties so easily? He'd probably forget her just as readily, locking her away in the past with all the other memories he considered too painful to deal with.

In fact, if she were to go by yesterday alone, he'd probably say goodbye and good riddance. He'd be pleased to be rid of her nagging. Even so, he might not be quite so pleased to be robbed of her kisses, no matter how hard he'd worked to make them into something ugly and demeaning. She wasn't so naive that she couldn't recognize wanting when it was pressed square against her. A tiny sigh of longing escaped before she could restrain it.

Chaney regarded her with something that almost

looked like sympathy. He muttered his thanks for break-fast, then headed for the door. Twisting his hat in his hand, he stood in the doorway. "In case you was wondering, it'd be my guess that he'll be back by Monday."

"I wasn't wondering," she lied.

"Well, like I said, just in case." He hesitated, still fiddling uncomfortably with his hat.

"Is there something else?"

"I don't suppose you'd want to help out again today."

"I'm probably just in the way," she said morosely.

If she'd hoped for a denial, she'd picked the wrong man. There wasn't a diplomatic bone in Chaney's body, no matter how much pity he was feeling toward her. "Let's face it," he pointed out. "You still got a lot to learn."

"I know that."

"Even so, your help would still be welcome while Zeke and Pedro are on the road with Cal."

Her mood brightened a little. "You mean it?"

"Hell, gal, I don't say things I don't mean. You should know that much by now. See Roddy when you're ready. He'll tell you what to do."

"Thanks, Chaney. I'll be there as soon as I get these dishes scrubbed up."

He nodded curtly, slid his hat on his head and left. His gruff invitation pleased her as nothing else could have. She knew better than to believe that she was more help than hindrance, but the fact that he'd asked at all told her volumes about the fact that he was beginning to accept her.

As soon as she'd straightened up the kitchen and run the vacuum, she put on her work jeans and a long-sleeved shirt, tying the shirttail in a knot at her waist. Anticipating the next few hours of hot, sweaty work with surprising enthusiasm, she started toward the stables, then paused at the sight of dust swirling on the long, winding driveway. Her pulse kicked into high speed.

Maybe it was Cal coming back, she thought as she walked back toward the house. But when the car rounded the final curve in the driveway, she saw that it was an unfamiliar Lincoln, long and black and impressive despite its layer of fresh dust.

The man who stepped out was equally impressive with his broad shoulders, impeccable navy-blue suit, Italian loafers and a face that had been lovingly chiseled into angles similar to Cal's. The perfection might have been too much were it not for the slight bend in his nose, indicating that at one time at least this man had played hard and gotten his nose bloodied in the process. Right now there was curiosity written all over that handsome face, so much so that it had Marilou blushing as she went to greet him. Even before he introduced himself, she guessed that this was Priscilla's hunk, Joshua Ames. Cal could not possibly know two men of calendar caliber.

"You must be Marilou Stockton," he said, holding out his hand.

"How did you know?"

"Cal mentioned you were here. I must say I was impressed with your resourcefulness in tracking him down."

"Were you?" she said doubtfully. "He probably gave you hell for it."

"Actually, he did, but I swore I didn't give anything away."

She grinned. "Oh, but you did. Not much, mind you, but enough for me to figure out the rest."

"But all I said was…" His voice trailed off in genuine bewilderment. "I didn't say anything. I know I didn't."

"You admitted he was still in Florida."

He blinked and rubbed a hand across his eyes. "I must be spending too much time at my computer. How did you get from that piece of information to a farm in Ocala?"

"That's my secret, Mr. Ames."

"Call me Joshua. All my friends do."

"And are we going to be friends?" she inquired bluntly.

His blue eyes searched her face for several impossibly long minutes before he nodded. "Yes, I think we are. Where's Cal?"

"On his way to Kentucky."

His face registered astonishment, which rapidly gave way to amusement. "Well, well, the coward ran after all."

Something about his comment told Marilou that Joshua had a pretty good idea of what had gone on between the two of them. "I'm surprised you didn't know about the trip," she said with feigned innocence. "When did you speak to him last?"

"About one o'clock this morning," he said, confirming her suspicions.

"Well, well," she said, mimicking him.

He caught the amusement in her eyes, and suddenly the two of them were laughing. "I'm sorry you wasted a trip," she said finally.

"Believe me, I don't consider it a waste, though why anyone would want to live out here is beyond me, especially a man like Cal."

"Meaning?"

"He's a city boy with an incredible head for business. He belongs in boardrooms, not out here mowing grass."

"I don't think he mows much grass, actually. He spends most of his time with the horses or studying up on breeding. Believe me, he takes this seriously as a business. Come with me. I'll show you around. There are some gorgeous horses in his stables already."

Joshua actually shuddered. "No, thank you. If you have a glass of iced tea, I'd be grateful for it. Then I'll be on my way back into town. I think I've seen enough."

"Meaning me," she said, amusement in her voice. "Did I live up to your expectations?"

"I had no expectations," he contradicted. It was a half-hearted denial. He didn't seem to feel especially guilty about being so obvious. When Marilou regarded him skeptically, he admitted, "Okay, I was a little worried you might be some sort of gold digger. It wouldn't be the first time some woman has gone after Cal for his money."

"I don't want his money, Joshua. I don't even want him. I just want to see him reunited with his family."

Shock registered on Joshua's face. "Good Lord! Does he know that?"

"Oh, he knows it." Her gaze narrowed. "Have you known Cal a long time?"

"Most of his life."

"What can you tell me about his relationship with his family?"

"You'll have to ask Cal. I don't gossip about my clients or my friends. Cal is both."

She nodded. "He made a good choice, then, in trusting you."

"I will say one thing, though. I wish you luck. It's past time for him to be making peace with his past."

Joshua quickly changed the subject then, asking Marilou personal questions about her own background in a way that told her anyone dealing with Joshua Ames would always have to be on their toes. As they finished their iced tea, she realized that she'd given away far more than she'd learned during the brief visit. Still, she had genuinely liked and trusted him.

Walking him back to his car, she said sincerely, "I'm glad we had a chance to meet, but I am sorry you didn't get to see Cal."

"Forget it. You're much prettier than he is," he said.

"Will you come to dinner when Cal gets back?" she asked.

"I'm not so sure I can stand this much fresh air again. Get Cal to bring you over to Daytona."

She grinned at him. "Is this your way of telling me you've decided he's safe out here with me?"

"I guess that's one way of looking at it. Mind if I give you one piece of advice?" he asked, his expression suddenly sober.

"Of course not."

"I still don't know exactly what business about his family brought you here, but Cal is a man who's had his heart broken one too many times. I think whatever your reason for coming, he's far more attracted to you than he's admitted even to me. If he doesn't mean anything to you, you might want to think about going before he gets back."

Marilou nodded.

He touched her cheek. "No offense?"

"No. I'm glad you care enough about him to speak your mind. I'll be honest with you. I don't know how things will end up between the two of us, but I care enough to stick around and find out." She sighed ruefully. "Judging from today's escape, I'm not so sure Cal is equally open to the possibilities."

"He'll come around once he sees that you're not playing games with him. Just be sure that's what you want."

"I'll think it through. I promise."

"Then that's good enough for me."

Over the next few days, Joshua's advice was constantly on her mind. She reveled in the backbreaking work that Chaney assigned, because it made it easier to get through the lonely nights when her thoughts strayed invariably to Cal and the relationship that was blossoming so unexpectedly between them, a relationship fraught with complications. Despite the difficulties, she'd felt a greater sense of fulfillment here than she had in all the months she'd worked for the post office.

The work got easier day by day. She was a quick learner, Roddy told her, blushing. Chaney nodded his agreement. When she asked, he told her which of the books in Cal's office she ought to read first, and that was how she spent the evenings. She curled up in Cal's big leather chair, which still carried the lingering scent of him, and read about the world of Thoroughbreds and the science—or mere theory, according to some—of breeding the best.

More nights than not that's where she fell asleep, the books and magazines tumbling from her lap as she shifted to find a comfortable position. That's where she was when Roddy pounded on the door, shouting her name at three in the morning. She scrambled from the chair and ran.

"Roddy, what is it?"

"It's Winning Pride. She's about to have her foal. You said you wanted to watch. Chaney sent me to get you."

Excitement raced through her. Pulling on Cal's denim jacket as she ran, they reached the barn just in time to see the beautiful mare drop a foal the exact same ebony as its sire, Devil's Magic. From its mother, it had inherited a white blaze on its head.

"We've got us a beauty, a little filly," Chaney announced.

A deep sense of awe filled Marilou as the mother cleaned up the foal, then moved away. Finally on legs that seemed skinny as matchsticks and twice as wobbly, the foal struggled to stand upright. Winning Pride nickered softly and her offspring took one tentative step and then another until she was close enough to tuck her head and suckle as her mother stood patiently. Marilou longed for her camera, wishing once again that she hadn't been so determined to leave photography locked away in the past. Maybe someday Cal would let her come back during foaling season to take pictures of the miraculous moments.

Roddy went to work cleaning up after the birth, and Chaney ran his hands swiftly and knowingly over the newborn, finally pronouncing her fit. The whole thing had taken no more than an hour.

"You going back up to the house?" Chaney asked.

Marilou shook her head, her gaze still fastened on the mare and filly as if she could memorize the image as indelibly as she could have captured it on film. "I want to stay awhile longer."

"Can't say as I blame you," he admitted. "It's an awesome thing to see the first time."

"Can you tell if she'll be a runner?"

"Some say you can. I always like to see 'em on a track before I make a prediction like that." He grinned. "Then again, ain't no sure thing even then."

"Does she have a name yet?"

"The boss had a couple in mind, but he'll have to register them with the Jockey Club and make sure they're okay. I suppose he'll be wanting to do that before he settles on one."

"Do you know what they were?"

"Can't say as I recall."

"Then I'm going to call her Dawn's Magic."

"That's a right pretty name. Fits her, too."

Marilou grinned. "Think I can make it stick?"

"I ain't a betting man anymore, but I'd guess you could get just about anything you wanted out of the boss."

Marilou looked at him in amazement. "Why would you think that?"

"You're still here, ain't you," he said, chuckling as he walked off and left her to think about what he'd said.

Chilled by the cool night air, she found a blanket and wrapped it around her shoulders, then settled into a corner to watch Winning Pride and her foal. That bonding, as natural an instinct as breathing, was something she longed to experience. She wasn't so old yet that she felt the ticking of her biological clock, but age didn't seem to have much to do with the desire to become a mother. Maybe it was just that she'd spent these past few months so absorbed with the idea of family. She fell asleep wondering idly—and dangerously—what a child of hers and Cal's would be like. Stubborn and willful were the two characteristics that came to mind.

* * *

The sight that greeted Cal when he stepped into the barn almost took his breath away. Pale golden rays of sun slanted through the windows and turned Marilou's hair into a radiant halo. The loose strands were tangled with the straw of her impromptu bed. Her lips were curved into the beginning of a smile, suggesting pleasant dreams or the faint memory of whatever had been on her mind when she fell asleep. She was wearing his denim jacket, which was several sizes too big for her. It had fallen open, and the thin cotton of her blouse was stretched taut across her breasts. Princess, the fat marmalade cat, had deserted Devil's Magic and was curled against Marilou's side. He hoped the desertion wasn't permanent. Otherwise, he'd have one nasty stallion on his hands.

He stood perfectly still, afraid of waking her, afraid of going any closer. He'd lived the past few days in a torment of desire and doubts. Getting close to her while those thoughts still raged, and with her looking so damned vulnerable and seductive, was courting disaster.

He sighed and took a reluctant step back, but not in time. Winning Pride sensed his presence and whinnied softly, as if to draw his attention to the new filly Chaney had told him about the minute he'd pulled into the yard. Unable to walk away, he crept closer and whispered, "She's a beauty, all right." Even as the words crossed his lips, he knew they could be applied equally to the foal and to Marilou, who shifted restlessly on her bed of straw. Princess meowed indignantly at being disturbed.

Suddenly Marilou's eyes blinked wide and she scrambled into a sitting position, dragging her fingers through the tangles of her hair. "Cal, you're back."

"Miss me?" he said lightly, not really expecting her to admit to it, not even willing to admit how much he wanted her to.

She nodded sleepily, too groggy to hide her instinctive reaction. His breath caught at the innocent admission. His gaze fastened on hers and he felt the familiar heat rising, that first soft stir of yearning. He'd been so sure that a few days of distance would calm his frayed nerves, would plant all the warnings clearly in his brain. Instead his blood ran every bit as hot and wild as it had before he left.

"There are more comfortable beds in the house," he noted, then regretted even the reference to a bed when she was all sleep-tousled and desirable.

"But none this close to the action."

He found himself grinning at her excitement. "There's something to be said for being a farm girl, isn't there?"

"If you'd told me a few weeks ago that I'd be helping out at the birth of a foal, I'd have sworn you were crazy. The idea would have scared me to death, but the reality, my God, Cal, it's like nothing I've ever experienced before. Not that I did all that much. Winning Pride did all of the work. Still, I don't think I'll ever forget it."

"Chaney says you have a name all picked out."

She blushed. "I know I don't have the right. You have a name all ready for submission, but I couldn't help it."

"What's your choice?"

"Dawn's Magic, for when she was born, for her sire and for what she meant to me."

Winning Pride pricked up her ears and bobbed her head. Cal laughed. "Seems like the mama approves."

Marilou grinned. "Is it up to her?"

"Seems like her right. I'll pass it by the Jockey Club and see if anyone else has a claim on it."

"Thank you." She held his gaze for far too long, long enough to make his heart thunder and his thoughts rove again into dangerous territory. As if she sensed the shift in mood, she blinked and said hurriedly, "My heavens, Cal, you must be starved. Why didn't you say something? I'll go up right now and fix breakfast."

"There's no need to hurry. I want to see the new horses settled before I come up."

"The trip was successful?"

"I thought so," he said, then grinned ruefully. "We'll see what Chaney has to say when he sees what I've brought home."

She laughed. "There's something to be said for a man who values honesty above tact."

"It can be a little rough on the ego, though."

"I can certainly vouch for that."

"He says you've been doing a good job."

"He likes my blueberry muffins."

"I mean with the horses."

Her eyes widened with pleasant surprise. "He said that?"

"And more," he teased. "But I think I'll keep the rest to myself."

She blushed and started back to the house.

"Marilou."

"Yes?"

"I'm glad you stayed."

"I hired on for a month. I didn't want to go back on my word."

"I would have understood if you had," he said. Left unsaid was how terrified he'd been that she would go, scared off by his nasty temper and blatant advances. He'd realized while he was gone that he wasn't going to shake off his feelings for her quite as easily as he'd hoped. That figured out, he had only to decide how best to understand them. The only way to do that, it seemed to him, was to get this issue of that damned letter settled once and for all. With that out of the way, maybe then they could figure out what there really was between them. Maybe they'd discover that the letter was the only glue holding them together at all. It was what a part of him hoped…and what the rest of him somehow dreaded.

It was nearly an hour before he finally made his way back to the house. Chaney came out just as he reached the back door.

"I put the horses in the barn by the new paddock," Cal told him. "As soon as I eat, I'll be back down to see what you think of them. You were right about that Seattle Slew colt. The price went too high. It just about killed me to do it, but I finally backed out of the bidding."

"Ain't no sense going into hock for an untried horse. There's plenty of potential with some of the others if you know what to look for. You're gonna have to start looking for a trainer now. Whether you want to hire one here or send the horses out, it's time."

"My inclination is to hire our own. Think about it, Chaney. See if any names come to mind. When I come back out, we'll talk about it. I don't want to do anything on this without your say-so."

Chaney nodded. "I've got some ideas. A lot depends on how much you're willing to spend."

"I told you when we started up that I would spend what it took to make this place the best. That hasn't changed."

"Glad to hear it."

Cal studied his manager closely, convinced that there was something on the old man's mind. "You got something else to say?"

"Nothing that can't wait until you've had your breakfast."

"Come on. You might's well spit it out before you choke on it."

A frown creased Chaney's brow and his eyes grew serious. "What're you gonna do about her?"

"Marilou?"

Chaney looked disgusted at his deliberate obtuseness. "You know any other females around here?"

"Okay. What do you want me to say?"

"Is she going or staying?"

"That's up to her."

"You ain't got no opinion on the matter?"

"None I care to discuss."

"I ain't asking you to discuss 'em with me, so long as you discuss 'em with her. Seems to me she's got a right to know where she stands around here."

Cal nodded. "I'll keep that in mind."

Chaney's expression turned even more sour. *"I'll keep that in mind,"* he mimicked under his breath. Glaring at Cal, he added, "If you ask me, that ain't no way to treat a lady. Not that you asked me, of course."

Cal grinned at the unexpected championing of Marilou. "You must really like her blueberry muffins."

"I don't know what they've got to do with anything." He threw up his hands. "You just go on and do whatever you dang well please. Suppose you will anyway. Just know that she's been fitting in real good around here.

I'd hate to see her run off because the two of you can't settle your differences."

Cal watched his retreating form and shook his head. What the devil had gone on around here while he'd been gone? Had sweet Marilou spun her web of magic around Chaney's tough old heart, too?

He walked into the kitchen and found the woman in question seated at the table, her hair back in its tidy braid, her face scrubbed and glowing, her eyes closed. At the sound of the screen door slamming, she jumped, startled awake.

"Sorry," he apologized. "Why don't you go up to bed? You can't have gotten much sleep last night."

"I'll be fine. I have work to do today. The garden needs weeding. I haven't had a chance to get to it the past couple of days." As she talked, she went to the oven. She withdrew a plate stacked high with pancakes, ham and eggs and put it on the table.

"I hope it's not ruined," she said, studying it worriedly. "Maybe I should make more."

"This will be just fine," he said, his voice gruffer than he intended, thanks to the lecture he'd just had from Chaney.

When she'd poured him a cup of coffee, he watched her standing indecisively between table and sink. "Sit back down," he said impatiently.

She lifted startled eyes to meet his. "Is anything wrong?"

"We need to talk."

Apparently she didn't like his tone, because she stiffened defensively. "About what?"

"When is this vacation of yours over?"

"The end of next week."

"What are your plans?"

"Plans?"

"Are you going or staying?"

She blinked once, revealing a flicker of hurt, before carefully shuttering her emotions. "I'm not sure there's any reason for me to stay."

"What if I asked you to."

"Why would you do that?" she asked bluntly.

"You're making yourself useful around here."

Her mouth curved ruefully. "Just doing what I'm paid to do."

"You're doing more than that and you know it. I don't want to take advantage, though. If you're planning on staying, we need to think seriously about what you'd do and what your pay would be."

"Cal, you don't need me here," she said with what sounded to him like a trace of wistfulness.

"I never said that."

"I'm not blind. Anybody could do the cooking and cleaning. As for the work I do down in the barn, you could hire a groom in no time. I'm just a rank beginner."

"Do you enjoy it?" he asked, genuinely curious.

The smile that spread across her face was answer enough, but she said, "I'm learning so much. I love being around the horses. I can't wait to see them run. And I've been reading your books. Chaney didn't think you'd mind. Breeding is all so complicated, I mean if you do it right and don't just let nature take its course. And the business side of it, I haven't begun to figure that out yet. What makes a yearling a good investment? It seems to me that it's awfully risky. I saw the story about the spring sales and what you paid for those horses. That's more than I'll earn in my entire lifetime. I had no idea."

Her eyes were shining like polished gemstones. "Do you know what I was reading just last night before Winning Pride had her foal? I think it was in the *General Stud Book* or maybe it was the *Thoroughbred Record*..."

"Hey, slow down," he said, laughing.

"Sorry," she said, grinning apologetically. "I get carried away. I guess I've just been storing all this up, waiting for the right audience. Chaney lets me talk, but I'm not so sure he really listens."

"Oh, I think he's been hearing you loud and clear. I get the feeling he'd like to see you stay on, though he'd never flat-out admit it. What do you really want to do, Marilou?"

"It's not just up to me."

"If it was?"

She hesitated. Finally she lifted her gaze to his. "I don't think it's possible for me to stay on here as an employee, not after the other day. We couldn't go on sleeping down the hall from each other and just ignore the rest. At least I couldn't," she admitted, an embarrassed pink creeping into her cheeks.

Even though he recognized the truth in what she was saying, Cal's heart sank. "There's a lot between us," he agreed. "There's no avoiding that, and I can't promise to keep away from you."

"Then I guess that's our answer." She'd locked her hands together in front of her on the table and sat staring at them. Finally she asked, "What about your grandmother, Cal? I don't want to go home without knowing that's resolved."

"Find her, then," he said softly, overcoming his deep-seated reluctance. "I owe you that much, I guess."

"This is for you, Cal, not me."

Angrily he shoved his chair back from the table. "Don't give me a bunch of psychological babble. Can't you ever leave well enough alone? You're coming out the winner. I've agreed to let you look for her."

"You won't regret it," she vowed, beaming at him in spite of his nasty tone.

"I already do," he said with a heavy sigh. He took one last look at her, then walked out the door.

Chapter Eight

Though she had Cal's blessing to begin the hunt for his grandmother, Marilou recognized that his heart wasn't in the search. Oddly enough, neither was hers. To her surprise, she let the whole day pass without making any attempt to track the old woman down. She blamed her actions on the fact that she had a lot of catching up to do around the house. She'd been so busy helping out with the horses that she'd gotten behind with the gardening and cleaning.

Since the morning air was still cool, she went outside to get the weeding done first. She was kneeling down staring at all the little green shoots in the ground, a frown on her face, when Cal came up behind her.

"Whatever it is, it can't be that serious," he said.

"I'm afraid it is."

"Bugs?"

She shook her head.

"What then?"

"You're going to laugh at me."

He grinned at that. "Actually I could use a good

laugh." He hunkered down beside her and stared at the ground. "I don't see the problem." He crumbled a clump of earth between his fingers. "Ground feels good. Everything looks healthy."

"Too healthy," she grumbled.

"Huh?"

"I'm weeding," she said, as if that explained everything. Judging from his blank expression, he still didn't get it. "Cal, I can't tell the weeds from what I planted."

He managed to keep from hooting, but he couldn't suppress the smile that stole across his face. "That's a problem, all right. Haven't you ever done any gardening before?"

She shook her head. "I just figured you'd look at what was coming up and know if it was a good guy or bad one. I mean I planted all these nice, tidy rows, but now it's not so clear to me exactly where they are."

"Maybe you should just let it all run wild and see how it turns out."

She scowled at him. "You are not taking this seriously. And you'd better, because I'm going to leave it in your hands when I go."

He frowned at that, but kept his tone light. "Then we're both in trouble, because I don't know any more about it than you do."

"Well, we're just going to have to learn," she said decisively. "I'll go to the library later and get a book. Or maybe I'll call the nursery and have them send someone over. Do you suppose they make house calls?"

"For the right price, they'll probably talk to the damned plants for you. Call them, if it will make you happy."

He couldn't seem to take his eyes off her face. Finally

he reached over and brushed the tip of her nose. "You have a smudge," he explained, his voice dropping. But then his finger moved on to her lips, tracing the curve of her mouth and sending waves of heat through her. She had the most compelling urge to draw that finger deeply into her mouth.

"What am I going to do about you, Marilou?" he said, and she could hear the helplessness and frustration in his tone.

"Kiss me?" she suggested, her breath catching at the instantaneous flaring of desire in his eyes. Maybe if they made love right here in the middle of the garden she could stop worrying about the damned weeds...

He shook his head, ending that fantasy. "Can't do that, sweetheart."

"Why?"

"Because I don't think I could stop with a kiss anymore. I want you too damned much." He caressed her cheek, then swept the pad of his thumb across her lips one last time. Anticipation turned her insides to warm honey, but he was already standing up, already stepping away.

"Cal," she whispered, wishing he didn't have quite such a strong sense of integrity.

"I have to get back to work," he said, looking around desperately as if he hoped Chaney would materialize to rescue him.

"Cal," she said again, but he had already started away and he never looked back.

Marilou blinked back tears of frustration as she turned back to the garden. She still couldn't tell weeds from vegetables, but she yanked up a few sprouts just for the satisfaction of it.

"Oh, hell," she finally muttered. Then she went inside and called the nursery for help.

While she was waiting, she began to clean, spending most of her time in Cal's office. As she was straightening the closet, she came across an old camera, a 35 millimeter that had seen better days. Still, she held it lovingly, focusing it, testing its weight in her hands. Suddenly she desperately wanted to take photographs of everything, especially of Cal. Once she was gone, she would at least have something to remember the adventure by.

Abandoning her chores and forgetting all about the impending arrival of the man from the nursery, she borrowed Chaney's truck and sped into town for film. She spent the rest of the afternoon roaming the farm, shooting pictures of the horses, even capturing Chaney at work, when he wasn't aware of her presence. Roddy, sporting a blush and a shy smile, posed with Devil's Magic. Even Zeke and Pedro paused long enough in their chores for her to get a picture. The only person she missed was Cal. Maybe she was going to have to make do with her memories after all.

That night at dinner, she finally had to admit to herself that she'd spent the day delaying the inevitable. Somehow she had recognized that she and Cal had reached a real turning point. Whatever happened next with his grandmother was going to alter things between them forever. She put the letter in plain view on the kitchen table, then waited for a reaction. Cal's glance kept straying toward the pale blue envelope. His lips settled into a frown and stayed that way.

Finally, when Chaney had gone out after making a snippy remark about escaping the kitchen's icy atmosphere, Cal scowled at her and mumbled, "So?"

Stubbornly Marilou wanted him to say the words. She lifted her gaze to meet his. "I beg your pardon?"

"Don't play games. Did you find her?"

"I haven't started looking," she admitted.

His eyes widened. "Why the hell not?"

"I'm not sure. I didn't get to it." She couldn't bring herself to admit that all day long she'd been depressed by the fact that once Cal's grandmother was found and the two of them were reunited, her role in Cal's life would be at an end.

"Look, I told you it's what I wanted, if that's what's worrying you."

"Maybe I'm still not convinced."

"Sweetheart, I'm not ever going to jump up and down in excitement and plead with you to do this. If that's what you're waiting for, hell will freeze over first."

Marilou sighed. That was exactly what she was hoping for, though she knew better than to admit it. It was entirely likely that Cal would never have—or even want—the sort of warm, loving family relationships that she missed so desperately. Maybe she was the one who was foolish and unrealistic for wanting that for him. He seemed to be perfectly content with the life he'd carved out for himself. Who was she to come along and insist that his quiet, solitary existence needed to be crowded with a grandmother and maybe even the mother and father he'd held in contempt for so long now?

As she debated her right to go on interfering, Cal picked up the letter and studied it, turning it over and over in his hands as if just touching it would reveal something to him. "How're you going to go about finding her?" he asked eventually. "Doesn't seem as if there's a lot to go on. We don't even know her name."

She took his mild curiosity as a good sign, about the most encouragement she was likely to get. "She's your maternal grandmother. We know that much. What was your mother's maiden name?"

"McDonald, I think."

She frowned. Cal apparently caught her disappointment. He said with a rare touch of wry humor, "You were hoping for something a little more unusual like maybe Capriatti or Janovich?"

Marilou chuckled. "Well, those names probably would be easier to locate in Wyoming, but that's okay. We can still manage."

"What city will you look in?"

"I'll start in Cheyenne, since that's the postmark. Then, if I don't come up with anything, I'll widen the search to the surrounding area. The library probably has phone books. I'll drive over tomorrow and take a look. If worse comes to worst, I'll get a map and just start calling information. The population of the whole state isn't that big."

"That could take forever."

"Be thankful the letter didn't come from New York," she said. "*That* could take forever. This will be a snap. It may cost a little in long-distance call charges, though."

"I don't give a damn about the money. Do what you have to do. What makes you so certain she wants to be found? If she'd really wanted me to find her, wouldn't she have put a phone number or at least an address on the letter?"

"She's old and sick. Remember, she even got your address wrong, and you know some detective probably tracked that down for her. You'd be surprised at how many people are careless about little details. That's why I have a job."

He tossed the letter back onto the table. "Speaking of that, you're probably getting anxious to get back," he said, watching her intently.

"In some ways, I suppose," she said evasively, surprised that there was really very little she missed about the place that had been her home all her life. Already Cal's image was the one that filled her dreams, and his home was beginning to feel like someplace she wanted to belong. That, she reminded herself, was dangerous. Hurriedly she got to her feet and began doing dishes. Suddenly Cal was beside her, dish towel in hand, his heat and scent tempting her.

"I'll dry," he offered.

"There's no need," she said, anxious for him to go, hungry for him to stay.

"I want to."

She shrugged, feigning an indifference that was far from the electric awareness she was actually feeling.

They worked in companionable silence for the next few minutes, though Marilou was aware of an increasing tension in the air. She sensed that it had nothing to do with the letter or Cal's family. She put the last plate in the drainer, rinsed out the sink and started to turn around, only to find herself sandwiched between Cal and the counter. Her gaze shot up to his. Eyes that had darkened to a stormy gray pinned her in place. Warm breath whispered against her cheek.

"Damn, I missed you," he said, the reluctant words sounding as if they'd been wrenched from deep inside him. He brushed a tender kiss across her forehead, then another on her cheek. Marilou felt as if she were sus-

pended in time, holding her breath, anticipating the instant when his lips would finally claim hers with the
hunger that she'd never known with anyone but Cal.

"Did you miss me?" he inquired lazily, letting her
wait, apparently all too sure that the kiss he withheld
was one she wanted all too much. "You said you did this
morning. Did you mean it?"

She nodded, feeling too weak and shy and breathless
to get the actual words out.

He grinned and sprinkled light, teasing kisses across
her shoulder. The sweet torment was every bit as arous-
ing as he'd meant it to be. She swallowed hard as he
taunted, "Not good enough, sweetheart. Not nearly good
enough."

Something told her that admitting the truth would
give Cal an advantage she wasn't nearly ready for him
to have. Summoning up a bold and sassy smile, she said
sweetly, "Sorry. It's the best I can do on short notice."

As his surprised laughter echoed in the kitchen, she
ducked out of his loose embrace and darted for the back
door. She made it into the yard before he caught up with
her and swung her back into his arms.

"Scaredy-cat," he said softly, holding her close, his
hands looped behind her waist, their thighs touching
provocatively.

"I'm not the one who ran away to Kentucky," she
retorted.

"That was a business trip."

"Of course it was."

"Well, it was."

"Oh, I know that. I also know that it wasn't scheduled
to begin until a couple of days later."

"You think that's enough evidence to hang a man on?"

She grinned. "First off, I'm not trying to hang you. And second, that's not my only evidence. I have additional testimony from a very reliable source."

"What source?"

"Joshua Ames. You do consider him reliable, don't you? He is the man you turn to in a crisis?"

A dull red crept into his cheeks, and he avoided her eyes. "What the devil does Joshua have to do with anything?" he grumbled.

"It seems he received some sort of desperation phone call at one in the morning and decided he'd better pay an emergency visit. You'd already fled the danger."

"Joshua was here?"

"You've got it. A nice man, by the way."

"Well, I'll be damned."

"You sound surprised."

"I am. Joshua hasn't set foot on this place since I bought it. He keeps thinking I'll come to my senses and buy a company that actually has offices and skyscrapers or at the very least a secretarial pool."

"I gathered he's not much on wide open spaces."

"Joshua prefers his environment to be regulated by air conditioners and dehumidifiers. If a business can't be computed with a calculator and run by statistics, he figures it isn't worth knowing about. This place is totally beyond him. Every time I send him a bill for hay and oats, he gets heart palpitations. When I told him I wanted to modernize the breeding shed, he thought I'd gone over the edge."

"How did the two of you get to be such friends?"

He looked at her finally, amusement twinkling in his eyes. "He moved in down the block, way back when we were kids. He was frail and sickly then. He wore glasses and liked to study. You can just imagine how the other kids bullied him."

"So you went to his rescue."

"No more than he came to mine in his own way. His house provided a safe haven from the instability at home."

"When he showed up here the other day, he was the one running to the rescue. Judging from the looks of him, he outgrew his need for protection rather dramatically."

Cal drew her closer, regarding her intently. "You thought he was good-looking?" he inquired with a dangerous edge in his voice.

"A hunk, as a matter of fact," she said deliberately.

"And no doubt he thought you were beautiful."

"I believe he did mention finding me attractive," she conceded, then added modestly, "He was probably just being polite."

Cal's fingers tangled in her hair and tightened as his mouth came down on hers. "You won't get polite from me," he murmured just before the hungry demand of his kiss stole their breath away. There was nothing teasing about the hot, moist possessiveness of his mouth covering hers, nothing reluctant about the bold forays of his tongue. Days of wanting and need exploded in that single urgent kiss.

They were both gasping when he finally broke away, and there was a bemused expression in his eyes that she was sure was matched in her own. "God, Marilou," he said raggedly. "What the hell do you do to me?"

"Irritate you?" she suggested, trying for a teasing tone that would deny the thudding of her heart.

He grinned. "Besides that."

"Whatever it is, you seem to have the same effect on me."

"What are we going to do about it?" he asked, sounding surprisingly confused and helpless.

"Give it time, Cal. That's all we can do."

"How much time can we give it if you're going running back to Atlanta in another week or so?"

She leveled a serious look at him and said quietly, "Maybe that's time enough."

He nodded thoughtfully, then that killer smile of his broke across his face. "Who knows? Maybe it is." He took her hand. "Come on."

Startled and still reeling from the implications of their conversation, she gazed at him. "Where?"

"To the barn, my sweet. Where did you think?"

Marilou felt a blush steal over her skin. Cal's smile broadened. "Don't you want to say good-night to Dawn's Magic?"

"Absolutely," she said at once, but she found she had to work very hard to keep the disappointment out of her voice.

It took Marilou the better part of two days to find Mrs. Caroline Whitfield McDonald. The significance of Cal apparently being named for his grandmother was not lost on her. She began to wonder if his own mother might not be more amenable to a reconciliation than Cal thought.

As she sat daydreaming at the kitchen table, she envisioned a time when this whole house would ring with the sound of laughter and family gossip. Then, daring to take the fantasy one step further, she imagined children underfoot. Hers and Cal's. Those stubborn, willful little devils, who would charm and torment, just like their father. She sighed. It was a wonderful dream, but that's all it was. If she doubted that for an instant, Cal's reaction to her news proved just how wide the gap between fantasy and reality really was.

She found him standing by the rail at the training track, watching as one of the new two-year-olds worked out. His gaze was so intent, he didn't even notice when she came up alongside him. He held a stopwatch in his hand and kept his eyes glued to the horse as it moved around the near turn. When the new chestnut colt flew by, he nodded in satisfaction.

"A good workout?" she asked.

He turned then without surprise and she realized he had known she was there after all. "Better than good. That horse could be on the track in Miami or New York before the end of the summer. He'll certainly be ready for the Derby prep races next spring."

He waved the jockey over and questioned him extensively about the way the horse had run. Marilou listened closely, anxious to learn everything she could about the training process. Her fascination with the business was growing daily, as was her desire to capture more of the excitement on film. After that one day, she'd put Cal's camera back where she'd found it and tucked the film in her suitcase. She hadn't dared to take it out again. It had stirred too many longings, reminded her of too many plans long since abandoned.

Cal turned back to her just then and apparently some of her wistfulness was written on her face. "What's wrong?" he asked at once.

"I was just wishing I'd brought my camera down here."

"Good heavens," he teased. "What's a tourist without a camera?"

When she didn't smile at his lighthearted banter, he sobered at once. "What am I missing here?"

"Nothing."

He touched her cheek, the stroke of his finger gentle. "Marilou?"

"It's just that photography was once very important to me."

"That's the career you gave up?"

She nodded. "If you call it a career when I never did a day's work in it."

"You studied it in college, though?"

"Yes. I even won a couple of contests. My portfolio was very impressive, according to some of the professors I had."

"What had you planned to do? Studio work? Photojournalism?"

"I hadn't really decided. That was one of the reasons I wanted so badly to go to Europe. I thought maybe I'd be able to figure out over there whether I had the talent to do photographic essays, gallery showings." She grinned ruefully. "I guess you can see why my parents thought it was risky. My ambition was to do the extraordinary. I'm not sure whether the talent lived up to the dream. Even if it had, there were no guarantees I could turn it into a paying career."

"And your folks didn't want you to be a starving artist?"

"Especially not way off in Europe all alone."

"Couldn't you find a compromise?"

"Maybe if we hadn't gotten so angry we could have. As it turned out, we never had the chance to try."

Cal touched her cheek. "I'm sorry."

"Thanks."

"If you miss it so much, why don't you start over now? You're hardly too old to be launching a new career."

She shrugged. "Maybe I'm just too scared. I hadn't touched a camera in years until I borrowed yours the other day. I've gotten used to playing it safe. You can't fail if you don't try."

"I know all about playing it safe," he said gently. "And as someone very wise reminded me recently, it may not be the best way to live your life, not if you expect to find real happiness."

Uncomfortable with the still-sensitive topic, she was glad for the opening to change the subject. "Speaking of risks and moving forward, I found your grandmother."

Cal's expression altered at once, as if he'd automatically slammed the door on his emotions, which only seconds before had been laid bare. "Where?" he said, his voice tight.

"She lives on a cattle ranch about seventy-five miles north of Cheyenne. Seems she's pretty well-known around those parts. I spoke to the editor of the weekly paper in the closest town, and he says she's been sick for months now, but she's still running that ranch—essentially by herself. I guess that stubborn streak is definitely a family trait, just like she said."

"I guess you're relieved, knowing that she's still alive, that we're not too late."

"Aren't you?"

"I suppose."

She had to fight the desire to snap at him for his callousness. She said only, "I've got the phone number up at the house. With the time difference, it's still too early to call, but maybe when you come in for lunch?"

He shoved his hands in his pockets and stared at her, his expression as forbidding as she'd ever seen it. "I'm not calling," he said emphatically.

"I don't understand," Marilou said, her voice faltering as she studied his implacable expression. "You promised, Cal."

"I said to find her. I never once said what I would do once you had."

Marilou felt disappointment and fury stirring inside her. She was tired of playing games when she couldn't begin to understand the tough, insensitive rules. She shoved her hands in her pockets and faced Cal squarely. "You know something, Cal Rivers, Joshua was right about you. You are nothing but a lily-livered coward."

"What?" he demanded, obviously stunned by the angry charge.

"You heard me. You are so flat-out terrified of being hurt that you don't give a flying fig how much you hurt other people. Your parents. Your grandmother. Me. Not a one of us matters to you as long as you can go on living the way you want to. You like being alone so you don't have to be responsible for anyone but yourself. Talk about safe! You're so safe shut away out here that you might as well be locked up in some jail cell. If you ask me, it's a hell of a way to live."

"It suits me," he said stonily.

"I guess it does, but it doesn't suit me. I've done my part. I tried to help you. I've found your grandmother. I'll pack my things and be out of here in the morning."

Even as the angry words tumbled out of her mouth, she realized that saying goodbye would be the hardest thing she'd ever done. With unexpected clarity, she saw what had happened the past few weeks. Like some silly schoolgirl, she'd gone and fallen in love with Cal Rivers, the most impossible, contrary man on the face of the earth. On the one hand, he represented the kind of bold, self-confident adventurer she'd always dreamed about; on the other, he was the antithesis of the family man she needed to feel whole.

Well, maybe she couldn't undo what she was feeling, but she could sure as hell walk away from it before she got her heart broken. She'd get over him eventually. All she would have to do would be to keep reminding herself what a self-centered coward he was. No woman with a brain left in her head could love a man like that for long.

She looked into his face one last time and tried to interpret the riot of emotions in his eyes. Whatever he was thinking, though, he was staying silent. That silence, confirming all of her most damning thoughts, was enough finally to send her packing.

She whirled around and ran back to the house, desperate to escape, even more desperate to keep Cal from seeing the hot, bitter tears that spilled down her cheeks.

Chapter Nine

Cal didn't go near the house the rest of the afternoon. He didn't think he could stand to see that awful, defeated look in Marilou's eyes again. He'd seen her bitter disappointment, but he'd been unable to say the words that would make it go away. Every time he'd tried, they'd stuck in his throat. A simple yes would have done it, but even that was beyond him.

Besides, nothing about this was simple. Feelings buried for so long weren't easy to put into words. Maybe he was a fool or a coward or both, but he wouldn't be a hypocrite to boot. He couldn't feign enthusiasm just to please Marilou. Though he credited her with being intuitive about most things, she didn't understand this. She couldn't possibly realize what she was asking of him. He didn't want to go back, didn't want to dredge up all of the old hurts. What possible difference could it make at this late date for him to go barging into the life of a woman he'd never met?

It was past supper time when he finally got up the courage to walk into the house. With a sense of resignation, he saw that Marilou wasn't in the kitchen, where he'd grown used to finding her. There were no dishes on the table, no pots simmering on the stove, no wonderful aromas coming from the oven.

Not that he was hungry. He doubted if he could get food past the lump that was lodged in his throat. He just wanted her to be there, waiting for him with that gentle, trusting, caring smile. Instead the room felt cold and empty without her. He was getting a taste of what his life would be like without her.

Logic told him he could make everything right in a heartbeat. All he had to do was admit he was wrong and say he'd make the stupid phone call. Maybe he wouldn't even have to make it. Maybe the promise would be enough to buy a few more days.

A few more days to do what? Convince her that family wasn't all that important? Not likely. To Marilou, who'd lost her only relatives so tragically, it was obviously the only thing that did matter. It was the one blind spot in her otherwise open-minded nature.

Still, even knowing this was something that would always put them at loggerheads, he couldn't let her go. He knew that as surely as he'd always known when it was time to move on, time to hunt for a new challenge. Right now he felt settled, and he intended to keep it that way. Marilou, he'd come to realize, was a major part of that feeling of contentment that had swept over him so unexpectedly when he'd bought Silver River Stables. The feeling of finally finding his niche had grown stronger day by day ever since. One thing life had taught him was that when something was good, you reached for it and held on for as long as the ride lasted. Well, this was one ride that was a long way from over.

There was one way he could buy himself some time, he decided, though he felt a twinge of regret at the duplicity of it. She couldn't leave without his say-so. She'd returned her rental car after the first week. Since then she'd borrowed his car or Chaney's old pickup to run errands. She actually seemed to prefer that dented, rusty four-by-four. He'd watched her speeding up the drive, noisily shifting gears with more enthusiasm than skill, the brim of her Atlanta Braves baseball cap shading her eyes, which he knew instinctively were flashing with excitement.

Her pure, full-throttle way of attacking life, which he had a feeling she'd been holding in check for too long now, was one of the things he'd come to like most about her. She tackled new projects with the same determination that he brought to learning a new business. He'd never known a woman to get so much enjoyment out of the craziest things. Mucking out the damned stalls, for instance. Weeding the vegetable garden she'd planted outside the kitchen door. Getting up at the crack of dawn to make homemade biscuits and laughing when the first batch turned out to be as hard and heavy as bricks. Damn, he was going to miss her genuine zest for life. How could he possibly let her go?

The fact was he couldn't, not unless he was the worst sort of fool. And if he refused to give her a lift into town or to let Chaney take her, she'd have to stick around so they could work things out. In his desperation, he refused to consider how unlikely it would be that a woman essentially being held hostage would bargain with the man doing the kidnapping. He simply went to bed with his strategy set and his mind made up.

* * *

He wasn't expecting his plan to be foiled, but he stayed awake the whole night, just in case she took it into her head to sneak out. He was already in the kitchen drinking coffee—lousy coffee, now that he'd gotten used to hers—when she came downstairs at daybreak, lugging her suitcase. The sight of that bag made his heart ache, so he concentrated on her instead.

She was dressed for travel, as neat and tidy as the day she'd arrived in that beguiling oversize T-shirt and jeans that fit snugly over a fanny that was beginning to drive him crazy. She'd swept her hair up in a top knot and jammed her baseball cap over it. Stray wisps teased at her cheeks. When one strand fell into her eyes, she blew it away with lips tinted a tantalizing shade of strawberry pink. He felt his heart turn over in his chest and the now-familiar lump formed swiftly in his throat. His blood turned hot and sizzled with uncompromised lust.

Without saying a word, without even looking at him, she poured herself a cup of coffee and stood at the counter. Her gaze was directed out the window. Everything about her stance spelled angry distance, feisty determination and hurry. It was evident she couldn't wait to get away.

"You can at least sit at the table with me," he grumbled, his whole body screaming for some slight contact, one fleeting brush of flesh against flesh.

"I'd rather not," she said primly.

"Oh, for heaven's sake, Marilou—"

She whipped her head around and her expression stopped the remainder of his explosion. "I'll be leaving as soon as Chaney's free to take me."

"Chaney won't be free," he said, and his chin jutted just as defiantly as hers.

She blinked and for just a second looked uncertain. "What...what do you mean? I spoke with him last night."

"And I spoke to him after that. I sent him to Miami to talk to a trainer down there."

She traded uncertainty for immediate indignation. "You what?" she demanded, her coffee cup hovering midway between her mouth and the counter. "How am I supposed to leave?"

He tilted his chair back and smiled complacently. "I guess you'll just have to wait until he gets back. Could be tomorrow. Could be next week. It's hard to tell."

The complacency was obviously a mistake. Her cup hit the counter so hard the coffee splattered every which way. "In a pig's eye," she said, planting hands on hips. "I said I was leaving today and I am."

"It's a long walk to town."

"Roddy will take me."

"Not if he hopes to keep his job."

Fresh indignation brought a flush to her cheeks. "You wouldn't."

The front legs of his chair hit the floor emphatically. "I would," he said grimly.

"But that's rotten. In fact, that's blackmail."

"That's management. With Chaney away, we all have extra work to do around here. You could help out, in fact."

"Go to hell," she snapped furiously. "You know that has nothing to do with it. You don't need me and you could spare Roddy for the half hour or so it would take to get me to town."

"I've been to hell," he said evenly. "I prefer it here.

As for my reasoning, you can accept it or not. It won't change anything."

"You are the most arrogant, maddening man it has ever been my misfortune to meet. If it weren't for the fact that your grandmother wants so badly to meet you, I'd say she's better off not knowing what you're really like."

"Thanks," he said. "Now, if you'll excuse me, I have work to do."

He was chuckling when he walked out the door. He was not laughing an hour later when he happened to glance up and see Marilou walking down the driveway, struggling with her suitcase. Another two or three minutes and she'd be at the highway. In her present mood, she probably wouldn't hesitate to hitch a ride.

"Dammit," he muttered and took off at a run. Chaney's pickup was closest. Fortunately the keys were above the visor. He cranked up the reluctant engine and took off down the drive, slamming on the brakes in a cloud of dust when he came alongside her.

"Get in," he shouted over the rumble of the engine.

She didn't even spare him a glance. He could see her lips moving as she muttered something that sounded like, "Not on your life."

"Marilou, get in this truck." His voice was no doubt loud enough by now to be heard in the far paddocks.

"Who died and made you king of the road?"

He counted to ten, as the truck heaved and sputtered, reluctantly keeping pace with her slow steps. "Marilou, please. You can't walk all the way to town," he reasoned. "It's miles, and there's a storm threatening."

"I'm sure someone will come along and give me a lift."

"If they don't rape or murder you."

"I can protect myself."

"Can you really?" he countered with a weary smile. He drew in a deep breath then and said what he probably should have said the day before. "Okay, sweetheart," he said with a certain sense of inevitability. "You win."

"Win?"

"Yes, win, dammit. You might as well stick around for the grand finale of all your meddling."

That brought her to a stop at last. She dropped her suitcase, turned and looked at him. "What grand finale?" she inquired, her voice still thick with skepticism.

"You and I are going to fly to Wyoming," he said, improvising. He figured such drastic measures were the only way to convince her of his sincerity. He could tell that right now she wasn't much in the mood to trust any promise that fell short of total capitulation.

Her eyes widened at the announcement. "Wyoming?" she repeated as if it were on the moon and getting there was nigh on to impossible.

When she added weakly, "Together," he knew he had her hooked. He had also landed himself in one helluva mess. A trip to Wyoming held about as much appeal to him as falling into a bed of nettles.

"Together," he confirmed wearily, wondering what it would take to bribe the pilot to land them in some remote stretch of Montana and abandon them there. Maybe after he'd made wild, passionate love to her for a week or so, she'd forget all about his grandmother. Maybe he'd forget that the fact that she cared was why he needed her in his life.

"Why are you changing your mind? What made you decide to go to Wyoming?"

To get you to stay in my life, he wanted to say, but

stubborn pride silenced him. Instead he said, "If I call the woman out of the blue the way you want me to, she'd probably die of shock. The more I think about it, the more I see that going out there is the only thing to do. We might as well get it over with."

"Together?" Marilou said again.

Her expression, caught between excitement and panic, made Cal smile despite his many misgivings. "What's the matter, Marilou? Scared of flying?"

"No, of course not," she denied hotly.

"Then it must be me, after all."

She shot him a determined look. "Not a chance."

"Then you'll come along?"

A smile broke across her face, and Cal felt the dread that had filled him for the past twenty-four hours finally begin to abate. "I wouldn't miss it for the world," she said, clambering awkwardly into the truck. "When do we leave?"

"As long as your bags are already packed," he said dryly, "I suppose we might as well try to get my plane fueled and ready by this afternoon."

As soon as he'd uttered the words, his own desperate panic set in, but he had only to look at the radiance of Marilou's expression to see that he'd done the only thing he could possibly do.

Though she wanted to follow Cal upstairs to make sure he actually packed a bag and didn't sneak off to Timbuktu, Marilou settled down at the kitchen table to wait. She drank another cup of the awful coffee that Cal had made that morning. It left her already-jangled nerves even more frayed. It finally got so bad she couldn't make herself sit still. She began to pace. Then she began throwing a load of laundry into the washer. Then she wiped off the countertops again.

How had her life become so complicated? She was about to go chasing off across the country to the Wild West with a man who was as close as she was ever likely to come to a free-spirited cowboy, a man she wanted so badly her whole body ached with longing.

"Good grief," she murmured. She felt Cal's touch at the nape of her neck, setting off sparks low in her abdomen.

"Are you okay?" he asked worriedly.

"Fine."

"We don't have to go," he volunteered so quickly that she smiled.

"Oh, no, you don't. I'm not letting you off the hook that easily."

He grinned ruefully. "It was worth a try."

"And a noble try it was. Where's the plane?"

"At the airport. The pilot's having it refueled. Chaney will take us. He should be here any minute."

"Chaney?" she said, her eyes widening incredulously. "I thought he was in Miami."

"Don't look at me like that. He was. He came back with the plane just now. I can't go off and leave this place without someone being in charge."

"If you say so," she said doubtfully.

"I swear to you that I did not have him hidden in the barn."

"If he arrives here smelling like manure, you're going to have a lot of explaining to do, Cal Rivers."

"If he shows up smelling like anything else, *he's* going to have a lot of explaining to do. He was supposed to be down there hanging around the Gulfstream backstretch talking to trainers."

A few minutes later when Chaney pulled up in front of the house, Cal took their bags out.

"How'd the trip go?"

"The plane ride was just great. I wasn't on the ground long enough to get much business done, though. I'd barely made it to the track when you called and said to get home. What the devil's the danged emergency?"

"I'm going to Wyoming."

"What's out there?"

"Family business."

Chaney seemed to take count of the bags. "She going, too?"

"Yes. We shouldn't be gone more than a day or two."

The old man got a speculative gleam in his eyes. "You stay as long as you want," he said slyly. "The boys and I can manage around here."

"A couple of days," Cal repeated adamantly. "This isn't a vacation."

"Maybe it ought to be," Chaney countered, casting a pointed look at Marilou. "If a man's got any sense at all, he ought to take advantage of the opportunities that come his way."

"Thanks for the advice," Cal said dryly, avoiding Marilou's gaze.

It was only later, when the plane was in the air, that she dared to meet Cal's eye. "Opportunity, huh?"

"I don't think he meant that the way it sounded," he said, but he was watching her speculatively. The hungry longing in his eyes turned her blood to liquid fire. Her heart pounded with sweet anticipation.

"I think he did," she said, her voice husky. "When did Chaney turn matchmaker?"

"You said it yourself. He's hooked on those blueberry muffins you've been baking for him. He's not above any sneaky tactic in the book that'll get you to stick around."

Deep in her gut she felt the first stirring of real hope. Chaney's approval meant a lot. If she could win over a crusty old dyed-in-the-wool bachelor like him, surely she had a chance to gain Cal's trust and love. She had no doubts at all that he was attracted to her. The frequent flaring of desire in his eyes was plain as day. Even his most casual touches were meant to inflame and entice. And they were effective. Half the time she felt as if her heart was hammering so hard it would burst right through her chest.

She looked up and realized he was watching her with that familiar look in his eyes. He held out his hand and she placed hers in it.

"Scared?" he asked.

She shook her head. "Excited. I can't believe I'm doing this. I've never done anything this impulsively in my life."

"You came to Florida."

"True."

"And you moved in with me."

"I didn't actually move in with you."

"Oh?"

"I mean I moved into your house, temporarily, but that's different from moving in with you the way you mean."

"How did I mean it?"

"Stop it, Cal. You're deliberately teasing me."

He grinned. "I suppose. I was hoping I was doing more than that."

She eyed him warily. "Did you lure me out here to try to seduce me?"

"Sweetheart, I could have done that back in Florida," he said with irritating but all too accurate arrogance.

"Says who?"

He grinned and rubbed his thumb in erotic circles in her palm. His gaze held hers and he said softly, "Says me."

She swallowed hard. "Okay, so maybe you could," she said breezily. "The point is that we are going to Wyoming so that you can meet your grandmother. There won't be enough time for dalliance."

He hooted at that. "Dalliance?"

"Cal Rivers, if you keep laughing at me, any prospect for kisses now or at any time in the future is seriously jeopardized."

"Is that so?"

"Yes, that's so," she began, but her breath caught as he lowered his lips to hers. The kiss began before she could think to stop it. It went on because she didn't want to end the glorious sensations that swept through her as his mouth moved against hers.

"Damn you," she murmured, when he deliberately lifted his head for one taunting instant. The victory was clearly his. She caught Cal's triumphant laughter as she covered his lips with her own. She was unprepared for the sheer exhilaration of those kisses, for the deliciously wicked freedom she felt even as he was binding her heart to his. Even after they were on the ground in Cheyenne, Marilou's heart was still somewhere in the clouds.

When Cal registered them in a one-bedroom suite at

an old hotel in Cheyenne, she was fully aware of the implications. When he ordered champagne with their dinner from room service, her pulse soared. And when he slid his arms around her, neither of them gave a thought to the meal that was being ruined while they discovered the sensual adventure of being together.

Chapter Ten

"Do you have any idea how incredible I feel?" Marilou said, freeing herself from Cal's embrace and spinning around in the wonderful, old-fashioned suite with its Victorian furniture and red brocade draperies. It was luxurious and slightly decadent, sending her imagination off on a delicious fantasy. She'd had no idea her thoughts could turn so wicked. It was clear that Cal brought out this deeply feminine and sensual side of her.

Oh, my, how she intended to enjoy it! She was here in a new and exciting place with a man she loved, a man who just might be coming to care for her. All of the pieces of her life—the longing for adventure, the search for romance, the need for family—all of it seemed to be suddenly falling into place. It was as if she'd waited her whole life for this man, for this moment. The sweet throb of anticipation made her giddy.

Then the thought of Cal's grandmother stole in and sobered her at once.

"Cal, shouldn't we go to your grandmother's ranch?"

"Not tonight. It's already late. Besides, we deserve this time just for us."

"You're not just putting off the inevitable, are you?"

"No. I want you, sweetheart, and I can't wait any longer to have you. I intend to do a little long-delayed romancing before we get side-tracked."

"Champagne. Chateaubriand for two. That's definitely romantic. Isn't that outrageously expensive?" she asked.

"You're worth it," he murmured, reaching for her, his gaze still smoky with desire. "Do you have any idea how beautiful you are?"

"Beautiful? Me?"

Cal laughed and drew her close. The musky scent of his after-shave enticed her and the last guilty thoughts of Cal's grandmother fled.

"Don't play coy. You know you're gorgeous, especially the way you look now with your red hair spilling loose over your shoulders and your cheeks all flushed." He ran his fingers through the silky tangles. "You look like a woman who was made for loving."

The huskiness of his voice and the gleam in his eyes made her knees go weak. This was the way love was supposed to feel, terrific and scary all at once. It was supposed to set free all your wildest dreams. It allowed you to dare, to take impossible risks, trusting that love would keep you safe.

"Cal," she said tentatively, her imagination flying again.

"Hmm?"

She stood on tiptoe and whispered in his ear, "I have this fantasy."

For an instant, he appeared stunned. Then he immediately sat down, crossed his legs and assumed a look of total fascination. "Yeah? What sort of fantasy does an innocent young lady from Atlanta have?"

"You won't laugh?"

"Sweetheart," he said fervently. "If this is leading where I think it's leading, I definitely will not laugh."

She grinned, thoroughly emboldened by his enthusiasm and maybe just a little by the champagne. "I think maybe it came from watching too many Westerns. You know, the cowboy was always coming into some bar, hot and dusty from the trail. And this woman was always dressed up real fancy and the room always looked a little like this."

"Like a bordello?"

"You're catching on."

"My, my. I never would have guessed where your thoughts would roam. In this fantasy of yours, is the woman, shall we say, an employee? Or is she a lady who's just arrived from back east?"

"I think she'd better be a lady," she said, blushing furiously as Cal's gaze lingered on her meaningfully. If he'd actually stripped away her clothes, she could have felt no more exposed or wanted or vulnerable. "I don't have the experience for the other."

"In this game, imagination is almost as important as skill. So far, believe me, you're at the top of the class. Tell me, in this fantasy does the cowboy offer to buy the lady a drink?"

She nodded. "Champagne, of course."

"Of course. Fortunately this cowboy happens to have a bottle handy." He poured a refill of the sparkling liquid into a crystal flute and handed it to her, their fingers grazing. His eyes caught hers and held until her pulse bucked, then raced faster than any Thoroughbred in his stables. He poured a glass for himself, then touched his glass to hers. Even the ping of crystal meeting crystal made her senses sing.

"To fantasy," he said.

"To fantasy," she murmured, thinking that the reality was already surpassing the excitement of the dream.

"Marilou," he whispered, his voice a low command that drew her gaze back to his.

Eyes wide with anticipation, she waited.

"I think we need to pick up the pace of this fantasy, before I go crazy here."

"What happens next in your version?" she said.

"I thought this was your fantasy."

"Actually, I sort of run out of steam when they get to the top of the steps," she admitted regretfully.

He swallowed hard and stared at her. "Are you…"

"Yep. Afraid so."

"I guess I knew that. Are you sure this is what you want, then?"

She nodded slowly, her gaze never leaving his. "More than anything. But you're going to have to take over from here. I'm out of lines."

A lazy, provocative smile spread across his face. "I think I can manage. It seems to me that the next scene definitely calls for a kiss."

"A chaste kiss?"

"Absolutely," he said, drawing her down on his lap and brushing his lips across her forehead. She sighed and settled in his arms, her fingers stroking the faint stubble on his cheeks. He went absolutely still at her touch, his gaze leveled on her face.

"And then?" she whispered.

"And then a not so chaste kiss," he said, his voice rough as sandpaper and so low she had to lean close to hear it. The scent of warm musk enveloped her.

The first kiss with its merest whisper of danger brought her to the edge of a precipice. The second pushed her over the edge into a riot of glorious new sensations. He gently brushed aside her hair and caressed the exposed sweep of sensitive skin, murmuring endearments all the while, intent on easing fears she'd long since overcome. When he unfastened the first button of her blouse, she felt daring. When he undid the rest, she felt a rush of heat and the slow, sweet tug of longing.

"Touch me," he pleaded, and she skimmed cautious fingers over skin that was already on fire to her touch. The textures, so different from her own, fascinated her, and with his encouragement she became increasingly bold, stripping away his shirt, anxiously tugging off the T-shirt beneath. Back in Florida she'd seen him in no more, seen him with his bronzed shoulders bared to the sun, but there she hadn't been able to touch. Now she couldn't seem to satisfy herself with one caress. She wanted to stroke, to savor, to taste. She wanted to stare until she'd memorized every fascinating, masculine inch of him.

The cowboy of her fantasy was even sexier in flesh and blood. And he was willing. Even an innocent virgin could tell the man was hot and bothered. Her fingers toyed with his belt buckle and she could feel his stomach muscles rippling and tensing. His sharp intake of breath stilled her hands when they dared to roam lower still.

"I like touching you," she admitted, suddenly shy and all too aware of the sensual power the man held over her. No gentleman would take advantage of that power. Besides, this was Cal and, for all his flaws, she loved him. She'd been telling him exactly what was on her mind from the day they'd met. There was no sane reason to stop now. When she dared to look at him, she saw that he was far from shocked by her statement. If anything, the tenderness in his eyes was deeper than before.

"No more than I like looking at you," he said. "And holding you. And touching you." His hand gently cupped her breast. The sight of tanned flesh against cream skin was erotic enough, but his thumb deliberately taunted her nipple until jolts of excitement shot through her. She gasped at the intensity of sensation.

"Scared?" he inquired with gentle concern.

"Only of not living up to your expectations."

"There's no chance in hell of that. The only way you could disappoint me now would be to call this off."

"I don't think I could do that if I wanted to," she said as the tension mounted to an unbearable level. Whether the timing was right or not, she wanted this, and she sensed that Cal needed it. He needed to know that she trusted him, that he could count on her no matter how the next few days turned out. She wanted desperately to be there for him, in every way that a woman supported a man she loved.

"Don't make me wait any longer, Marilou. Let me love you."

"I want that, Cal. I really want that," she whispered as he swept her up and carried her into the bedroom.

After that, fantasy and reality became a glorious blur. Sensations she'd only read about soared through her, leaving her body trembling and her heart filled with joy. Cal was gentle and passionate and demanding, branding her as his own forever. No matter what happened from this moment on, she would be his, body and soul. She had given him an emotional part of herself that she could never reclaim, and she had given it without regret.

As ecstasy faded, though, and Cal lay by her side, she was less certain whether he had shared himself as fully with her as it had seemed. Though he had withheld nothing in terms of tenderness or explosive passion, he had distanced himself almost at once. Even though he continued to hold her close, his expression was shuttered now, his mood increasingly withdrawn, his silence almost palpable. It was as if a chill had crept into the room, a chill that no amount of body heat could warm. To her dismay, Marilou felt far lonelier than she had before they'd made love. Instead of binding them together as she'd hoped, the act of love seemed to have set them adrift.

Cal felt as if he'd been poleaxed.

No woman had ever affected him as deeply, had ever loved him as unselfishly as Marilou had. Her willingness to give scared the dickens out of him. He should have known better. His life was complicated enough without getting entangled with an inexperienced woman who was bound to make more of this than she should. How the hell could he explain *that* to her, though? Just about anything honest he could think of to say would devastate her. He couldn't bring himself to lie.

So he stayed silent, holding her, knowing that with each passing minute she was getting more confused, more hurt.

Finally she shivered and sat up, pulling the blankets around her.

"Cold?" Cal asked. "Want me to turn up the heat?"

Marilou shook her head. "I'd rather you told me what's wrong."

He felt ice, where only moments ago there had been fire. He searched for glib words and found only evasions. "Wrong?" he said, feeling like a damned fool. "I don't know what you mean."

His hand continued to caress her thigh in an attempt to reassure her in some way. She brushed it aside and slid away from him. The movement put inches between them. It might as well have been a mile.

"Cal, less than five minutes ago you and I were as close as two people can possibly be. Now I feel as if we're on different planets."

"It was great sex," he blurted. The crude words were out before he could censor them, the damage done.

She stared at him in shock for no longer than a heartbeat. Then her temper kicked in. "Great sex!" she repeated furiously, getting out of bed and dragging the blankets with her. She kicked the surplus out of the way as if it were the train of an elegant gown. It was an impressive performance. If it hadn't been for the welling of tears in her eyes, she might have convinced him that she was more angry than hurt, more furious than confused. She did try, though. Oh, how she tried!

"Great sex! You have one helluva nerve."

Cal knew that his cheeks had turned a dull red. He used her anger to increase the distance until he felt safer. It didn't seem to matter that he also felt like slime. "What were you expecting?" he mocked, deliberately undercutting the very real ties he couldn't bear to acknowledge. "Undying commitment? You know how I feel about commitment. I've never lied to you about that."

"No. I'll give you that. You've been honest. You've

always made it plain that you don't ever intend to think about anybody other than yourself. I guess I just fooled myself into thinking that you might be changing. This trip…" She waved her hand at the bed. "This… I thought it meant something."

"It does," he said in a voice that had gone whisper soft, desperate.

"What?" When he remained stoically silent, she said, "Answer me, dammit. What does this mean? Maybe 'great sex' says it all. If so, just say it."

"I don't know," he exploded. "Okay? I don't know what it means. You've taken me by surprise."

She stared at him, clearly stunned. "I've taken you by surprise? Cal, as naive as I may be, even I have seen this coming for weeks."

"I'm not just talking about the sex. I'm talking about all of it, whatever all of it is. Don't push, Marilou. Too much is happening right now and I need time to think about it."

She drew herself up proudly. He gave her credit for withstanding his cruel assault with dignity. She'd never looked more beautiful than she did as she wrapped the blanket more tightly around her and grabbed a pillow from the bed. "Well, when you figure it out," she said softly, "I'll be in the other room."

"Fine."

"Fine."

But it wasn't fine, Marilou thought miserably as she tried to find a comfortable position on the hard, cramped Victorian-style sofa. Cal had betrayed her trust in the most devastating way possible. He'd lured her out here under false pretenses: he'd only come to pacify her. For

all she knew he didn't have any intention of going to
see his grandmother in the morning. The sex had probably just been a delaying tactic. He was such a skilled
and imaginative lover, he'd probably figured he could
keep her occupied until she forgot all about the reason
for the trip.

Well, the delays were over. It was time to fish or cut
bait. This wasn't something he needed to do for her. It
was something he had to do for himself. If only she could
make him see that. She spent the rest of the night trying to come up with some way to get through that im-
penetrable defensive shield of his. Not one single bright
idea occurred to her. Not even one *lousy* idea presented
itself. The only thing she got for her sleepless night on
the sofa was a stiff neck.

She had already ordered coffee and toast from room
service by the time he ventured out of the bedroom in
the morning. She felt some satisfaction when she noted
that he looked just about as rotten as she felt.

"Sleep well?" he inquired, regarding her warily as he
poured himself a cup of coffee.

"Well enough. You?"

"Terrific. Like a baby, in fact."

"There's toast if you want it."

"I'll go down for breakfast as soon as I've showered."

"Fine."

"You're welcome to come along."

"That's all right. The toast is plenty."

"Fine."

"Cal…"

"Marilou…"

"You first."

"I'm sorry about last night," he said roughly. "I suppose I managed to make the whole thing sound cheap, and that's not the way I felt about it at all."

"I'm sorry if I assumed too much." She had to force the words out. It hurt to admit she'd been wrong. It hurt to accept that they would never be more deeply involved than they had been last night. Casual lovers. The phrase, about as contradictory as any two words she could imagine, made her want to throw up.

"I guess we're just going to have to slow down," Cal said, looking nervous as a teenager trying to explain his way out of a first sexual encounter. "We don't seem to operate on the same wavelength when it comes to this. I thought you were ready, but obviously I was wrong."

"After today it won't really matter," she said stiffly. "Once you've seen your grandmother, I'll be going back to Atlanta. I'll be out of your hair and you can go on with your life any way that suits you."

His expression hardened at her matter-of-fact tone. "Right."

For one fleeting second, she thought she detected a chink in his armor, a hint of longing. "That is what you want, isn't it?"

He hid whatever he was really feeling behind a wall of stubborn pride. "That's exactly what I want. And you can't wait to get back to Atlanta, right?"

She sighed in resignation and said what he wanted to hear. "Right."

Wrong, Marilou thought dejectedly as he slammed out of the room. It was all turning out wrong.

Except for the visit to Cal's grandmother. At least that would be a happy ending. He hadn't backed out of it. She found him downstairs in the coffee shop, sipping black coffee and puffing on a cigarette. It was the first time she'd caught him smoking since she'd first arrived at his house in Florida. She scowled at the number of half-smoked butts he had already ground out in the ashtray. When he spotted her, he put out the one he'd been holding and regarded her balefully.

"No comment?"

She shook her head. "You're a grown man. If you want to ruin your lungs, it's up to you."

"It's hard to believe there's something about my life about which you don't hold a strong opinion."

"Don't kid yourself. I have an opinion. I just see no point in sharing it."

"Damn," he muttered, crumpling up the remainder of the pack and tossing it on the table. He scowled at her fiercely. "I knew you were trouble the day I met you."

She swallowed hard at the anger she heard in his voice. "I never meant to be, Cal. I came because of the letter. I thought it was the right thing to do. Now I just want what's best for you."

"And you've got it all figured out what that is? It must be nice to go through life being so sure of things."

"This morning I'm not sure about much."

"See, there you go again."

"All I said…"

"I know what you said, and I know what you meant," he snapped irritably. "Oh, for heaven's sake, sit down."

"What a pleasant invitation," she retorted, but she sat. "What time are you planning to drive out to your grandmother's?"

"We might as well go now," he said with such sullen indifference that she wanted to pour his steaming hot coffee straight into his miserable lap.

"I thought you wanted breakfast," she said instead.

"I'd rather get this over with."

"You make it sound like some sort of torture."

"That's exactly what it feels like."

Cal's black mood didn't lift on the long drive to his grandmother's ranch, despite the fact that the sky was a brilliant blue and the scenery was spectacular. Even though Marilou longed once more for her camera so she could record the uncommonly desolate beauty, she found that the setting was only a minor distraction from the tension in the air. Cal made no attempt at small talk, and Marilou's own feeble tries were greeted with stony silence.

How could he be like this, when he was about to meet his grandmother? she wondered. She would have been on pins and needles with excitement instead of wallowing in this miserable attitude of dread. This difference between them was something so basic she should have accepted long ago how unsuited they were. It was possible for two people in love to overcome differences in life-styles, but not conflicting values that went to the very core of their personalities. How could she have been blind enough to fall in love with a man who didn't treasure family the way she did?

It was nearly noon when Cal turned onto the long road leading from the highway to his grandmother's ranch. Despite his glowering expression, she was almost certain she saw a glimmer of interest in his eyes as he scanned the property. Though the holdings seemed to be vast, there were signs of disrepair. His frown deepened as they passed a crumbling fence post.

"I suppose it's difficult for her to stay on top of everything if she's been ill," Marilou ventured.

"I suppose."

"How big do you think the ranch is?"

"How would I know?"

She shrugged. "The house looks like it's been taken care of," she said as the long, low structure finally came into view. It had fresh white paint and black trim. Huge planters of pink and purple flowers bordered the front steps. The lawn had been recently cut, and the air was filled with the scent of just-mown grass.

Cal stopped the car about fifty yards from the house, even though there was room in the driveway right behind the fifteen-year-old Cadillac that had been polished to a glossy, almost-new finish. It was several minutes before he finally released his death grip on the steering wheel and turned off the engine.

"I guess she's home," he said, glancing at the huge black car.

"Do you want to see her alone?"

For just an instant, she caught the hint of panic in his eyes. "I think you have a right to be in on it."

"Not really."

"I want you there," he said gruffly, his tone partway between order and desperation.

Marilou reached over and squeezed his hand. "Cal, you're going to make an old woman very happy. Can that be so terrible?"

"If only it were that simple."

"It's only as complicated as you make it."

"Then it's damned complicated." He regarded the house warily before finally sighing heavily. "Come on, then. Let's go."

He clung to her hand as they crossed the yard. It was impossible to tell if he was holding on for moral support or simply because he feared she'd turn tail at the last minute and leave him alone to face his grandmother. His footsteps slowed as they neared the porch. At the steps, though, he squared his shoulders, gave her a smile that was sheer bravado and crossed the porch. When he rang the bell, they could hear the chimes sounding throughout the house.

It seemed to take forever before they heard any movement from within. The curtain over the leaded glass in the door was pushed aside, then fluttered back into place and the door swung open.

Marilou had expected some tiny, frail woman only barely able to leave her deathbed, but the woman who faced them was anything but tiny or frail. Stern-faced, her hair still thick and black and laced with threads of gray, she carried herself with incredible dignity. There was no way of telling from her expression what emotions were raging inside. Only her hand, curved around a carved, ivory-handled walking stick, gave away any hint of infirmity or distress. It trembled visibly as her gaze swept swiftly and indifferently over Marilou and settled avidly on her grandson.

"Cal," she said at once, without the slightest evidence of surprise or doubt. "You've come home."

Chapter Eleven

Cal faced the tall, reed-thin woman in the doorway and felt years of his life slide away. There was no doubt at all that this was his grandmother. From the almost coal-black hair and exotic features to the snapping blue eyes and imperious bearing, she looked exactly like his mother. For one lightning-swift instant, she'd appeared taken aback to find two strangers on her doorstep, but she recovered quickly.

When she spoke his name, he couldn't mistake the note of certainty and triumph in her voice. It was as if she'd been expecting him. The tension that had been coiled inside him wound tighter. Every finely honed instinct told him this had been a setup. She had stacked the deck, dealt the cards, then waited to come out a winner.

"Come in, boy," she ordered, still ignoring Marilou as if she were no more than a pesky nuisance. Her attitude annoyed the dickens out of him, but Marilou was apparently far too caught up in observing the byplay to be insulted.

"Don't just stand there," his grandmother badgered. "We're wasting heat."

Cal felt caught between furious indignation and admiration for her audacity. He wasn't sure exactly what sort of reception he'd expected, but this definitely wasn't it. He had been fooled by the frail handwriting and conciliatory tone, just as she'd expected him to be. Caroline Whitfield McDonald was obviously still very much in command, not only of all her faculties, but apparently— to her mind, anyway—of all she surveyed.

Something continued to puzzle him, though. How had she recognized him so readily? Had those detectives she'd hired sent her pictures? The possibility of such an invasion of his privacy unnerved him. Only a woman whose heart was made of steel would resort to such tactics. Now, as she stood aside, proud and dignified, waiting for them to enter, he remained rooted to the spot on the porch, leery of taking another step until he had some answers.

"What is it, boy?" she demanded.

"How did you know?" he said finally.

As his cool, curious gaze raked over her, a glimmer of a smile touched her thin lips. "There's nothing uncanny about it, boy. Come. I'll show you."

She ushered them into a parlor, where a fire blazed. She waved Marilou toward a chair. Then, after crossing to the grand piano that filled an incredibly large bay window, she picked up a silver-framed photograph and wordlessly handed it to him.

Cal's fingers trembled as he touched the cool metal frame. Aware of his grandmother and Marilou watching him expectantly, it took everything in him to actually look at the picture. When he did, he realized at once what she had seen in his face: his grandfather's features, the same dusky complexion, black hair and unexpectedly clear blue eyes. In the wedding picture in which his grandmother wore pristine satin and lace that flowed to the ground in luxurious folds, his grandfather looked uncomfortable in a tuxedo, the stern angles of his face softened as he stared lovingly at his beautiful bride.

Despite his wariness, Cal couldn't help smiling as he carefully placed the picture back among the dozens that were arranged haphazardly on the piano. "Yeah," he said thoughtfully, beginning to relax his guard ever so slightly. "I see what you mean."

"Look at the others, if you like."

He shook his head, deliberately not lingering on the snapshots and portraits of his mother. He couldn't help noticing, though, that there was no picture from his parents' wedding. Had they been forced to elope? How odd that he'd never known that, that he'd apparently never asked the questions most children did about how their parents met, about family ties and wedding albums.

"Sit, then," his grandmother insisted, grabbing a bell and ringing it as she settled herself in an antique rocker beside the fire. An old Mexican woman, her face a road map of wrinkles, appeared at once. Her sharp, brown-eyed gaze studied Cal and Marilou, and her face at once broke into a delighted smile.

"Por fin," she murmured fervently. "At last."

"Indeed," his grandmother said. Then, "Tea, Elena." She looked Marilou up and down. "And cake. She looks as though she could do with a little meat on her bones."

Marilou flushed, but remained silent, obviously intent on doing her part to make sure this reunion ran smoothly. His grandmother was staring hard at him. "You'd probably rather have a drink," she said, "but I don't keep the stuff, not after the way your grandfather drank himself into an early grave."

"I thought you said you'd driven him away."

"There's more than one way for a man to run. He hid in a bottle. Maybe he figured that way he'd make life hell for both of us."

Though regret flashed briefly in her eyes, her tone was all self-righteous indignation and harsh judgment. He wondered fleetingly if she'd always been this hard, this uncompromising.

"Tea will be fine," he said at last, unable to take his eyes off the woman who reminded him so much of his mother. Unwanted memories were flooding back, along with all of the pain. Right this instant he resented the hell out of Marilou for having forced him to come, and he hated his grandmother and all she stood for.

"What're you staring at, boy?" she demanded, when Elena had retreated. "Were you expecting to find me with one foot in my grave?"

"Your letter did say you were dying," he retorted calmly, unwilling to admit the direction in which his thoughts had actually strayed.

"We all do."

Instantly suspicious, he felt Marilou stiffen beside him, as well. "But you're not ill?" he said, his glance toward Marilou meant to convey I-told-you-so.

His grandmother thumped her cane impatiently. "Of course I'm ill. I'm eighty years old. I'm tired. I can't keep up with things the way I used to. My bones ache from autumn right through spring. The doctor says my heart's failing. The old fool. What else would it be doing at my age?" Her gaze narrowed. "Is that why you're here?

Did you come to pay your last respects? Don't expect to dance on my grave too soon."

Cal realized then that despite his natural caution, he had been touched by Marilou's eternal optimism. In some secret part of himself he had dared to harbor one scant hope for a real relationship. It withered irrevocably under her cutting tone and the admission that she'd deliberately tricked him into coming. Stunned to discover how much it hurt, he got to his feet and grabbed his coat. "We're out of here. This was a mistake. Come on, Marilou."

"No," she said softly, her gaze fastened on his grandmother.

He stood where he was and regarded her incredulously. "What is wrong with you? You can see for yourself that the letter was some damned ruse to drag me here. This isn't *Little House on the Prairie,* dammit. Not every family melodrama has a happy ending. Can't you see that yet?"

He glowered at his grandmother, who sat rigidly, listening to his tirade with no hint of emotion. Her apparent indifference kept him going. "She's just a scheming old woman who's used to getting her way, and we've played straight into her hands."

Marilou shook her head. "That's not the way it is, is it?" she said pointedly to his grandmother.

"I don't know what you're talking about, girl," the old woman said, but her shoulders suddenly weren't quite as stiff as they had been, and her tone lacked starch. Cal saw that her gnarled hands were knotted together tensely in her lap.

Marilou shook her head impatiently. "You two! I have never met two people more obviously cut from the same cloth. You're both stubborn as mules. Can't either one of you just admit that you need each other?"

"What makes you think that?" his grandmother demanded. "I've gotten along for all these years…"

"So have I," Cal insisted.

"Terrific," Marilou said, obviously beginning to warm up to the fight. Her words dripped sarcasm. "You've gotten along. Is that enough?" She turned to his grandmother. "If so, why did you write that letter?"

"I needed to get some things off my chest. That's all."

"You wanted him to come," Marilou contradicted.

"No, she *expected* me to come," Cal muttered in disgust. "There's a difference."

"I've learned not to expect anything," his grandmother retorted, glaring at him. "Not from family."

"Ditto." Cal scowled right back at her.

"Oh, for heaven's sake," Marilou said. "I am going into the kitchen to help Elena with the tea. When I come back, I expect you two to be behaving like civilized adults instead of a couple of spoiled brats."

When she'd stalked out of the room, Cal felt suddenly bereft. Though she seemed to take some perverse pleasure in needling him, Marilou had at least served as a buffer. Now he was left with his grandmother all alone. He would have preferred facing something easy, like a firing squad.

She simply sat there waiting, dressed all in black as if she were all ready for a funeral. He wondered how many years she'd worn the drab mourning outfits. Had it begun when his grandfather died? Had she settled permanently into the role of bereaved widow out of some sense of guilt, guilt that had only been compounded

when his mother ran off? He was still trying to figure
out what made her tick when he realized she'd spoken.

"What?"

"She's an outspoken little thing, isn't she?" his grandmother said with grudging admiration. "Where'd you
find her?"

"Actually she found me. Your letter went astray. She
saw that I got it."

"I suppose I ought to thank her, then."

"Frankly I'd prefer to strangle her."

"You sleeping with her?"

He flushed angrily and began to pace. "That's none
of your business, old woman."

"It is if you're going to be staying under my roof.
There is certain behavior I don't tolerate. I don't care
how old-fashioned that makes me."

"Who the hell said anything about staying here?"

"Well, where else would you stay?"

"We have a room in Cheyenne."

"That's too far away."

"So, you're actually admitting that you wanted me
here," he said, managing a wry grin.

She waved a bejeweled hand dismissively. "Oh, for
pity's sake, of course I did."

"Then why couldn't you just say that?"

"For the same reason you didn't want to come, I expect. For all that we're family, we don't know each other.
I find it difficult enough to trust folks I do know."

"Same here," he admitted reluctantly.

Piercing eyes regarded him intently. "You planning
on sticking around long enough for us to get to know
each other?"

"I don't know," he said honestly. "Everything in me tells me to take off."

"Whitfields are not cowards."

"My name is Rivers, grandmother. Have you conveniently forgotten my father?"

"You're still a Whitfield, through and through. You might move on a bit too readily, but you've got gumption that your daddy never had."

"How the hell would you know that? You said in your letter you ran him off before you ever had a chance to know him."

"He chose to go, and he talked your mother into running with him. A real man would have stayed right here and proved me wrong."

"A real man would never have let you dominate him, and I doubt you'd have tolerated that for very long. You're a bully, Grandmother. I've known you less than an hour and I can see that."

"Because you know all about bullying and getting your own way. I'd say we're evenly matched. You have to admit that makes the prospect of sticking around into an almost irresistible challenge for a man like you."

Cal suddenly caught the glint of amusement in her eyes and found yet more of the tension sliding away. He chuckled. "I do like a challenge," he admitted.

His grandmother nodded toward the kitchen. "That one's a challenge, too, isn't she?"

"You could say that," he admitted ruefully.

It would have been wrong to describe the sound she made as flat-out laughter, but it was probably the closest the sour old thing had come in years. "Then I'd say you have your hands full, boy. You can't let a couple of women get the best of you now, can you?"

He laughed at that. "No, I don't suppose I can."

"Good. You'll take the room at the end of the hall. She can have the one next to me."

"Then you'd damn well better be a heavy sleeper," he taunted.

"We'll just see about that. Now go on in the kitchen and drink your tea, then go get your things. I'll see you at dinner." She struggled to her feet. "I think I'd better have a nap now."

For the first time he detected a slight unsteadiness before she determinedly straightened her back and marched off, leaving him to ponder how she'd managed to shanghai him into doing exactly what she'd wanted him to do. He wondered how Marilou was going to react to the news that they were moving in.

Why wonder, he thought disgustedly, he knew exactly how she was going to react. Even as furious as she was with him, he could have staked money that she'd be thrilled by this outcome. When it came to family, she was entirely predictable.

"Why aren't you in there with your grandmother?" she demanded when he ventured into the cozy kitchen that was filled with the scent of apple pie and cinnamon. She and Elena were sitting at the table contentedly sipping tea and eating thick, fudgy brownies.

"I can see that you were in a real rush to get back to us," he observed, pouring himself a cup of tea and grabbing one of the brownies.

"The *señorita* and I, we agree you need time to get reacquainted," Elena said.

"Believe me, we already know everything we need to know about each other," he said. "She's an aggressive, manipulative, calculating woman."

Marilou shook her head. "Interesting how you choose to use those words to denigrate her, when you'd find them essential in a business opponent."

"I came here looking for a grandmother, not a tycoon."

"Sounds sexist to me," Marilou said.

"Okay, okay, we're all agreed that this is going to be a fair fight among equals. Notice," he said, dropping an impulsive kiss on her cheek, "that I included you among the combatants."

"Not me. I'm just an innocent bystander."

"Not anymore. If I'm moving in here, you're coming along, which puts you smack in the middle of the fray."

Marilou nearly choked at that. "We're moving here?"

"Under this very roof, though with a very discreet distance from your bedroom to mine."

He watched for some sign of disappointment but she simply stilled, and that flash of pain he'd put in her eyes last night returned to haunt him. He glanced sideways at Elena, who had busied herself at the stove, then finally shrugged. This was not the time to have a discussion about last night.

"I think maybe this is a bad idea," Marilou said finally.

He stared at her. "What are you talking about? I thought this was exactly what you wanted."

"For you and your grandmother, yes. I don't belong here now. I should go back to Atlanta."

"Absolutely not," he said, immediately resorting to blackmail to get her to stay. "If you go, I go."

"Cal," she protested.

"No. That's it. We stay together or we go together. I'm only doing this for you."

"Dammit, Cal, I don't want you to do this for me. This is your life, your family."

"Right now, you are a part of that life."

"Right now," she repeated wistfully, staring determinedly into her cup. He wondered if she was aware of the salty tears that splashed into the tea.

Damn, why couldn't he give her more than that? She was a woman who deserved happily-ever-afters, if anyone did. He should let her go so that she could find them. Instead, though, he knew that he'd never make it through the next couple of days without her there to badger him on.

"Please stay," he said finally.

She gazed up at him then, her expression as close to helpless as he was ever likely to see it. It wrenched his heart to see her torn in two like that and to know that he was responsible. "I'll stay," she said finally.

In that instant Cal realized that he was, in fact, every bit as manipulative as his grandmother. Of all the damned things to inherit.

Chapter Twelve

Settling into the McDonald ranch life was a mixed blessing for Marilou. Though she loved watching the nonstop sparring between Cal and his grandmother, for the most part she had absolutely nothing to do. Though Cal invited her along when he toured the place with the old woman, Marilou always made her excuses and declined. She was determined that the two of them get to know each other without her around as the buffer Cal intended her to be. She offered to help Elena, but the energetic housekeeper flatly refused.

"You are a houseguest, *señorita*. It would not be right," Elena said. "There are books in the library, if you wish to read. Or you could ride. One of the men would be glad to saddle a horse for you."

"Maybe I'll just go for a walk," she said finally, grabbing a bright red jacket to ward off the bone-chilling wind that felt very little like spring.

Despite the brisk breeze, the sky was clear, and wildflowers were beginning to bloom. In no time at all, her lonely, depressed mood began to lift. After more than an hour of wandering, she came to an old tree that had apparently been toppled by lightning and never cleared. Drawing her jacket more snugly around her, she climbed onto the weathered tree trunk and stared at the sparse, magnificent scenery, thinking about how much had happened to her in the month since she had made the impulsive decision to go after Cal.

She'd been to places she'd only dreamed about, experienced things she'd only read about and, most amazing of all, she had fallen deeply, irrevocably, head over heels in love. Unfortunately the man happened to be a pig-headed idiot who was clinging to his self-imposed emotional isolation with the tenacity of a pit bull. Sooner or later she was going to have to accept the fact that while Cal might come to love her, he might very well never trust her…or any woman, for that matter.

As if she'd conjured him, he suddenly slid his arms around her waist from behind. He smelled of woodsmoke and fresh air with the faintest hint of the after-shave he'd used hours earlier. He nuzzled the back of her neck, sending warmth catapulting through her.

"You look far too serious for such a beautiful day," he accused gently. "What were you thinking about?"

"Oh, cabbages and kings."

"Hmm, must have been me."

She turned and grinned at him, rubbing her hand against his cheek. "Which are you, a cabbage or a king?"

"That's probably a matter of opinion. Want to come for a ride with me? It'll dust the cobwebs from your mind."

She shook her head.

"How come?"

"I don't ride," she admitted reluctantly.

Cal stared at her, clearly astonished. "But you spent all that time around the horses in Florida."

"Around them, not on them. Do you think Chaney was about to let me on one of your precious Thorough-breds?"

"We have stable ponies, too. All you had to do was ask."

"I guess the right time just never presented itself."

He reached for her hand. "Then that's about to change. Let's go, sweetheart."

"Cal," she protested weakly, though her pulse had already kicked in with excitement at the prospect of one more adventure. Life with Cal would always...

Life with Cal couldn't be, she reminded herself sternly. There was only now, these next few days, and the adventure would be over for her. Maybe, though, when she got home and she would get out her camera equipment again. Maybe she would try to pick up where she had left off. The prospect gave her something to look forward to besides the loneliness.

"Let's go," she said, jumping to the ground. "I'll race you back to the barn."

She took off at a run, knowing she would be beat, laughing anyway at the sheer exhilaration of the race, delighted when Cal passed her, then turned and caught her in an exuberant embrace. His lips on hers were cold as ice, but they held the power of fire. His hands slid inside her jacket and found her breasts, the nipples already tightened into hard buds from the brisk air and already sensitive in anticipation of his touch.

"Have you forgiven me?" he said, his eyes riveted to hers.

"For what?"

"For hurting you the other night?"

"You were honest with me, Cal. It's always better to know the truth, even if you don't like it."

"I wish…"

Her heart in her throat and tears threatening, she pressed a finger against his lips. "Shh. No matter what happens, I will always remember this time in my life. You've made these weeks special for me."

"You are an incredible woman, Marilou Stockton."

She wasn't sure she could bear to hear another word. "And you are a man who promised to teach me to ride. Are you welshing on that promise?"

"Never."

"Then show me how to get on one of these beasts. Who knows, maybe I'll decide I want to become a jockey."

"Sweetheart, as much as I adore your cute little figure, as perfect as I think you are, you are about five inches too tall and ten pounds too heavy to be a jockey."

She frowned. "That is a problem. I could probably lose the weight, but there's not much I can do about the height. I guess I'll just have to settle for riding the range or something."

"First, let's just see how you do riding around this paddock."

"Is that a note of skepticism I hear?"

He laughed. "You won't catch me with that. No comment."

"Wise man."

Though it would have taken torture to pry the admission out of her, Marilou had to concede that Cal had been fairly close to the mark in analyzing her skill. She hurt in places that no lady ever discussed. For once, since the visit to Mrs. McDonald began, she was very glad that she and Cal had been banished to separate bedrooms. She would have hated like crazy to moan with pain the minute he tried to touch her. Not that he remained entirely aloof, but fortunately her lips seemed to be one of the few places not battered and bruised by this latest adventure. And Cal was a very inventive kisser.

The days took on an easy rhythm. The three of them had breakfast together, then Cal and his grandmother huddled together to discuss the ranch. Occasionally Marilou sat in on the conversations, liking them best when they veered into family history. Though listening at times emphasized her place as an outsider, she was still delighted that Cal was slowly beginning to acknowledge his place as a McDonald heir.

"Your books are a shambles," he announced late one morning, rubbing his temples after hours of staring at page after page of figures written in his grandmother's cramped handwriting. Marilou had long since given up trying to decipher it and sat sipping yet another cup of English breakfast tea. She was becoming addicted to the stuff. Cal's grandmother provided a different variety of tea for practically every hour of the day.

"You need to get a computer," Cal said, not for the first time. To Marilou it was beginning to be like background music. Her thoughts wandered, then refocused as he added, "Or at the very least an accountant."

"I'm too old to learn all that technical nonsense," his grandmother insisted predictably, glowering at him. "And if I've learned one thing about money, it's that no one will watch over it as well as you do it yourself."

"If that isn't the most old-fashioned, set-in-your-ways

thinking I've ever heard," he grumbled. "I could never run a business if I didn't share some of the responsibilities."

"I have men to run the cattle," his grandmother offered.

"I'm surprised," he retorted.

Marilou chuckled. She'd been listening to Cal and his grandmother bickering like this since breakfast. They'd had the exact same argument the past three mornings. As far as she was concerned, it was heavenly. Only strangers maintained a polite facade. Families fought and nagged and loved in equal measures. Apparently Elena agreed. She'd stopped hovering over Mrs. McDonald and now bustled around with an approving smile on her face, content that the uproar in the house was a happy one.

"Why should I hire an accountant when I have you to figure it out for me?" his grandmother finally said slyly.

Cal threw down his pencil. "Because I won't be around."

"Hmph!"

"Grandmother, I have told you repeatedly that I have to go back to Florida by the beginning of the week. I have my own business to run and I've been away too long already."

"Race horses," she said with a derisive sniff. "Cattle, that's the thing. Been good enough for the Whitfields for all these generations. Don't see why it's not good enough for you."

"I'm only one-quarter Whitfield."

"Must be the stubborn quarter," Marilou offered.

Two pairs of blue eyes glowered at her. She grinned happily. "I don't suppose I could talk the two of you into going for a drive instead of sitting around sniping at each other. It's a lovely day. The air is balmy at last. Elena said she'd pack us a picnic—fried chicken, deviled eggs, the works."

A spark of longing flared in Mrs. McDonald's eyes, then she shook her head. "The ground's too cold for these old bones, but you two run along."

"We'll take a blanket," Marilou promised. "You'll be fine."

A smile played about the old lady's lips, and for an instant she seemed lost in reminiscence. "It would be pleasant, I suppose. Your grandfather and I..." She sighed. "Well, that was a long time ago."

"Please come," Marilou begged. "You can tell us more about the family."

She knew that was a surefire lure. Mrs. McDonald had been using every opportunity to seduce Cal with those fascinating tales of his ancestors, men who'd pioneered in the West, surviving droughts and natural disasters, forging what had become something of a cattle empire. Apparently she hoped to convince him that he would be abandoning his heritage if he didn't stay and claim the ranch as his own. Periodically Marilou had dared to add her own subtle hints along the same lines.

"If you two are planning to gang up on me again, I'll pass and stay here," he said now, but Marilou caught the tolerant amusement in his eyes. He was beginning to care for the old woman. She could hear the tenderness in his voice more and more frequently.

"You aren't afraid of a couple of women, are you?" she inquired innocently.

"Damned right I am. When it comes to the two of you, any man would be a fool if he didn't watch his backside all the time. Last night some crumbling old diary turned up under my pillow. I don't suppose either of you knows how it got there."

"Not me," Marilou said cheerfully. "I've been banned from that end of the hall."

"And you?" he inquired, directing his gaze at his grandmother.

"I might have mentioned something to Elena…"

"Lord, you mean she's in on it, too? I haven't got a prayer."

"I like a man who recognizes a worthy opponent," Mrs. McDonald said approvingly. "Now stop dillydallying, boy. If we're going, let's go. Elena will be furious if we ruin her lunch."

As soon as they were all in the car, Cal turned to Marilou. "I suppose you know exactly where you want to go."

She grinned. "Well, your grandmother did mention that there was a creek along the eastern edge of the property."

He sighed. "How far?"

Marilou exchanged a conspiratorial glance with Mrs. McDonald. "Not far," they said in unison.

It took a little over an hour to get there. Cal was muttering under his breath by the time they finally came to the creek that wound its way through the distant pastures. Even he had to admit, though, that the setting was spectacular. Wildflowers had painted the spring landscape in shades of purple, yellow and red. Sunlight glinted off the shallow creek bed. Cattle roamed in the distance. And on the far edge of the horizon were the faint purple shadows of the mountains.

From the back seat of the car, Marilou heard Mrs.

McDonald sigh. "It's every bit as beautiful this time of year as I remember," she said.

Cal turned to study her, a worried frown on his brow. "How long has it been since you were out here?"

"A while," she evaded.

"Grandmother?"

"Last spring."

"Why so long?"

Marilou already knew the answer to that. Elena had confided that over the past year Mrs. McDonald had found it increasingly difficult to get around. The doctors blamed it on osteoporosis and arthritis. There were days, the housekeeper lamented, when the old woman wasn't able to get out of bed at all. Even now she was in far more pain than she'd been letting on to the two of them, but she'd apparently been determined that Cal would never see it. Marilou felt it wasn't her secret to share, but she hoped that soon Mrs. McDonald would tell Cal the whole truth about her rapidly deteriorating condition. She also knew that the old woman didn't want him staying on out of pity.

Even now she didn't so much as hint at the truth. She merely said, "I was busy. Besides, I pay that lazy manager to see to things for me."

"If you don't trust your books to anyone, how can you entrust responsibility for the rest to someone you've repeatedly described to me as lazy and inept?"

"What choice do I have? I can't ride a horse anymore. The men don't take orders well from an old lady. Even Garrett's got more command over them than I would."

"Maybe I should have a talk with him."

Mrs. McDonald smiled contentedly. "Yes, dear, why don't you do that? I expect Garrett back any day now."

"If you think this Garrett's reliable, maybe you should try giving him more authority. I suspect he's chafing at the bit to really take charge of this place."

"That chance will come along soon enough. When I can't draw breath enough to make a few decisions, I'll just lay down and die. Then, since you keep insisting that you will be nothing more than an absentee landlord, Garrett can take over."

Marilou caught Cal's agitation. He was practically grinding his teeth. "Grandmother, how many times do I have to tell you that I do not want you to leave this place to me?"

She waved off his comment, as she had each of the other times. "And just who should I leave it to, if not to family?"

He didn't answer right away. Finally he suggested quietly, "You could leave it to Mother."

"She turned her back on it."

"You sent her away."

"She could have come back."

"Hat in hand, I suppose?"

"Don't be ridiculous. I never wanted her to beg. It would have been better for everyone if I'd been wrong about the marriage. I wasn't."

"You told me you're sorry. Why can't you tell her?"

"I told her. She didn't want to hear it."

"That was years ago. Try again."

Marilou was startled by Cal's vehemence. He'd made a lot of strides in his relationship with his grandmother, but she hadn't expected him to suddenly take his mother's side this way. Maybe everything was going to fall into place just the way she'd imagined it. Sitting out here in the warm spring air, the sun bright in the clear-

est blue sky she'd ever seen, it was possible once again
to believe in miracles and happy endings.

"Maybe you could call her," she suggested hesitantly.
The last time she'd suggested he work for a reconciliation between his mother and grandmother, he'd bitten
her head off. Today he seemed mellow enough to listen.

"It's not my fight," he said, staring pointedly at his
grandmother.

"That doesn't mean…"

Mrs. McDonald touched Marilou's hand. "No, girl,
he's right. This is something I should do…if anyone
does it."

"Will you, then?" Marilou asked with surprising urgency. In her heart she knew that this was the final step
if any real healing was ever to take place.

Mrs. McDonald stared at her. "My dear, why does
this matter so much to you?"

She shrugged. "I know it's none of my business."

"That isn't what I said. Why do you feel so strongly
about it?"

"I just think families ought to stick together. You've
been talking about family history ever since we got here.
Don't you have some responsibility to see that the tradi-
tion goes on?" she challenged.

The old woman's gaze faltered at that. Then she
sighed. "I'll give it some thought. Now why don't you
two go take a walk together? I'm sure you'd like some
time alone."

Cal's eyes met Marilou's and he winked.

"How do you know we haven't been sneaking off to
be together at night?"

"Because the floorboards in that hall creak under a

mouse's step. You two have been staying put, just like I told you to."

"That's no way to get great-grandchildren," Cal challenged, sending Marilou's pulse caroming wildly.

His grandmother waved her cane at him. "There will be no illegitimate great-grandbabies in this family. Not if I have anything to say about it. You make an honest woman of this girl and I'll build you a whole private suite."

Marilou's breath caught in her throat as she watched for Cal's reaction. His expression sobered at once, all too quickly it seemed to her. Suddenly she wanted to run, to feel the warm breeze against her cheeks, the grass against her bare feet. She wanted to get away from Cal and his insensitive teasing, and from all the things that could never be.

Cal was already standing over her, though, his hand extended. "Come on. It seems we're not needed around here."

Marilou was slow to get up, unwilling to be lured into Cal's spell so easily. Stalling for time, she turned to Mrs. McDonald worriedly. "What will you do?"

"I'll do some thinking, maybe a little remembering. I'll be just fine. Run along and enjoy yourselves."

They were barely out of sight before Cal slid his arms around Marilou's waist and pulled her tight against him. His lips met hers, lightly at first, then with more demand. She tried to hold back, tried not to let his warmth flood through her, his mouth persuade her, but it was useless. She would have forever to miss being in his arms. She wouldn't give up the spine-tingling sensations—couldn't give them up—before she had to.

Chapter Thirteen

Keeping his defenses securely in place was getting to be increasingly difficult for Cal. As a hardheaded businessman himself, his admiration for his grandmother's gritty determination and amazing spirit grew day by day, though he wasn't about to tell her that. She was too damned sure of herself as it was. Admittedly, though, the thriving ranch was a testament to her intelligence and feistiness. It couldn't have been easy for a woman in her position to take on such a vast empire back during the Depression and keep it going during decades when others had been turning their property over to oil exploration or sheep ranching.

"Once a cattleman, always a cattleman," she said staunchly when he asked how she had withstood the pressures to change.

"Sometimes being a stubborn, willful woman has served you well," he noted wryly.

"It has always served me well," she corrected with a smile.

"You really must do something about those books,

though. And I'd like to see you diversifying your investments. Why don't I bring Joshua out for a few days to help you out?"

His grandmother regarded him suspiciously. "Who is this Joshua person?"

"My accountant and my friend. I've known him almost all my life. He's the most trustworthy, honorable man I know. I'll have him fly out tomorrow, in fact," he said decisively. Once he knew his grandmother's finances were under control, he'd feel free to go back to Florida. This was definitely the best course of action, he thought, though Marilou was staring at him, her expression horrified.

"What's wrong?" he demanded, though he suspected he knew.

"Don't you think you ought to speak with Joshua first, before making that kind of commitment for him?"

That was the last thing he'd been expecting. He'd anticipated another lecture on running away. "Why?"

"Cal, you've said it yourself. He hates isolation. This place would make him crazy. Isn't there someone else you could hire?"

"I'm not asking him to move here, just to spend a couple of days."

"He'll consider it a lifetime. He got nervous the minute he set foot outside his car that day he drove over to Ocala."

Somehow he found it irritating that Marilou had zeroed in so readily on Joshua's idiosyncrasies and now felt compelled to jump to his defense.

"He'll survive," he grumbled. "In fact, the change will do him good. He's too stuffy for his own good. He could use a little adventure in his life."

"Garrett might make it a little more palatable for him," his grandmother said slyly.

Cal and Marilou whirled on her. "What?" they said in unison.

"She's a real beauty, though there's not a sign that she's aware of it."

"Garrett is a woman?" Cal said incredulously.

His grandmother stared at him with masterful innocence. "Of course, she is."

"*Of course?* You never said."

"You never asked."

"That seems to be a problem of his," Marilou piped in cheerfully. Cal glared at her.

"Why does it bother you so much that my foreman is a woman?"

"It doesn't bother me. It just surprises me."

"And you don't like surprises," Marilou inserted. "Any more than Joshua would. You can't drag him into this without warning him, Cal."

"About what, Garrett?"

"Oh, stop being impossible. I suspect Joshua knows how to handle most women."

"I repeat," his grandmother said, "he hasn't met Garrett."

"Did someone mention my name?" a slender blonde asked from the doorway.

Marilou was gaping. With her long legs and tiny waist, Garrett belonged on the cover of a magazine, something definitely more upscale than a farm journal. Her hair fell nearly to her hips, her features were fragile, but there was a lean athleticism about her that no doubt came from years of handling heavy chores. Men's chores.

"You're Garrett?" Cal said, knowing Marilou was watching Garrett speculatively, clearly sizing her up with her finely honed woman's intuition. From the grin that was slowly spreading across Marilou's face, he forgot all about jealousy and decided that Joshua's bachelor days were seriously numbered. He noticed that she didn't voice another objection to calling his friend.

"I'm surprised," he said finally, grasping the hand that was held out to him.

Garrett turned a chiding gaze on his grandmother. "She loves to do that to people. My real name is Tracy Garrett. If I hadn't gotten hooked on using my last name years ago, she wouldn't be able to get away with it. Sorry I was away when you arrived. Mrs. Mac sent me over to Montana to take a look at some stock."

"What did you think?" his grandmother asked, suddenly all business. "Did you spend a bundle of my money?"

"I left you pocket change," Garrett retorted, then gave a concise but obviously knowledgeable report, including the amount she'd spent for the cattle. He listened closely, impressed not only with her acumen, but with the way his grandmother deferred to her judgment. She didn't bat an eye at a dollar figure that had Marilou gasping and even left him a little startled. Apparently even at eighty there was nothing conservative about his grandmother's approach to business.

Dinner turned into a lively affair. Garrett had a knack for keeping everyone off guard with her insightful comments and wry wit. There was absolutely no pretense about her, not in the way she dressed or the straightforward way she talked. And Casey, her twelve-year-old daughter, was a real hellion. She and his grandmother had a rapport that made Cal oddly envious.

He felt ridiculous being jealous of a precocious child, but he couldn't help wondering how much different his life might have been if he'd grown up around here, instead of turning up years later as an interloper. He was feeling easier here by the day, more at home. Not that he intended for one second to stay, but at least he wasn't on pins and needles with the anxious need to run. He was glad, after all, that he'd had this chance to meet the old woman, and he owed Marilou for that.

He glanced across the table and saw that she was thoroughly engrossed in the lively conversation between his grandmother and Garrett. One of the things he loved the most about Marilou was the way she fit in without needing to be the center of attention. Few women could do that happily, but she seemed to thrive on staying in the background and seeing that everyone else had a wonderful time. It was a knack that he was increasingly coming to treasure.

She looked up just then, caught him watching her and smiled. Her green eyes shimmered in the candlelight in a way that made his heart skid wildly. Suddenly he needed her, wanted her more than he'd ever wanted another woman. Regret over the distance they'd been forced to keep between them the past few days slammed into him.

He leaned closer. "Feel like a walk?" he whispered under his breath, reaching for her hand beneath the table. He captured it in her lap, watching with delight as fire crept into her cheeks.

"Shouldn't we stay?" she said, her rapt gaze never leaving his face.

He glanced toward his grandmother, who nodded subtly. "Oh, I think we'd be forgiven," he said.

"Can I come?" Garrett's daughter chimed in, already partway out of her chair, confident of her welcome.

Cal had barely restrained a groan, when Garrett said, "No, you may not. It's almost your bedtime and you have studying to do."

"School's almost out. What's the point?" she grumbled, casting an appealing glance around the table. Help was not forthcoming.

"The point is that I expect you to do as you're told, young lady."

Casey grinned at Mrs. McDonald. "What's that word you told me the other day?"

"Martinet," she said, her lips twitching. Cal chuckled at the obvious conspiracy between the two of them.

"Yeah, mom. That's what you are, an old martinet."

"I may be a rigid disciplinarian, but I am hardly old," Garrett responded, her eyes flashing. "If you doubt that, I'll race you to our cottage. The loser will do dishes for the entire summer."

"You're on," Casey said, scrambling up with a whoop. Her mother rolled her eyes at Cal's grandmother. "Sorry, Mrs. Mac. She was locked up in the car too long today."

"Seems to me that might be true for both of you," Mrs. McDonald said. "Run along, dear. We'll talk more in the morning."

She peered at Cal when they'd gone. "I thought you were going for a walk."

"In a minute," he said, settling back into his place at the table. He still had a firm grip on Marilou's hand, which she kept trying without success to move to less volatile territory. "Why on earth did you tell me that your manager was lazy and inept? It's obvious to me that Garrett is neither and that you wouldn't tolerate it if she were."

"Yes, well…" Her voice trailed off guiltily.

"Come on, grandmother," he prodded. "What's the real story?"

"You can't blame an old woman for trying."

"Trying what?" he asked, completely bemused. Then in a flash it came to him. "Of course. You figured if I felt the whole business was about to come apart, I'd stick around to help save it."

"Okay, yes," she confessed without flinching. "It occurred to me, if it was something you could get your teeth into, you'd see the need for staying."

"And the books? Did you prepare that awful set just for me?"

His grandmother smiled faintly. "No. I guarantee that they are every bit the shambles you found them to be. Garrett has no more interest in bookkeeping than I do."

"Does that mean you won't object to my bringing Joshua out here?"

"Seems to me, from what Marilou has said, that Joshua's the one most likely to object."

"Don't worry about that. I pay him well enough to justify some occasional discomfort on his part."

"Then bring him on. I'm fresh out of ammunition to keep you around."

He was just about to leave the table and take that much-delayed walk, when he heard the note of resignation in her voice. It wavered pitifully. She could have been faking it, but he couldn't bring himself to risk it. "Grandmother, this doesn't mean I'll never come back."

She sighed heavily. "We'll see."

"I promise."

Despite his promise, though, he couldn't shake the image of the way she looked as they left the dining room, her shoulders slumped and her face etched with sadness.

"So, what did you think of Garrett?" Marilou asked, when she and Cal were outside. Stars were scattered across the sky by the zillions, tiny sparks of fairy dust that enchanted her. She shivered in the cool night air, and Cal draped his jacket around her.

"I think hiring her was probably the smartest thing my grandmother ever did. They seem to get along well, don't you think?"

"I suppose."

Cal paused, and she sensed his sudden confusion over her disinterested tone. He touched two fingers to her chin and tilted it up until their eyes met. "Why the lack of enthusiasm? I thought you liked her."

"I do. I really do. It's just that she's not..."

"She's not family," Cal completed wearily. "Marilou, I can't stay here. I don't want to stay here. Getting to know my grandmother has changed my life in a lot of ways. There's a lot to be said for knowing that you have solid roots somewhere, but she and I are too much alike to ever live peacefully in the same county, much less the same house. If that's what you were hoping for, I'm sorry."

She sighed. "Deep down I know you're right. But the past couple of days here, I've felt something I'd really missed."

"That sense of belonging," he said, surprising her with his understanding. "I know. I've seen it on your face. You do fit in, every bit as much as I do."

She shook her head. "No. When you get right down

to it, even though your grandmother and Elena have been wonderful, I'm still an outsider. I always will be."

"You'll always be welcome here. You know that."

"I suppose," she agreed.

She heard the catch in Cal's breath, felt the uneasy silence that fell between them and cursed herself for spoiling such a lovely, romantic spring evening. Still, if a clock had ticked loudly and symbolically in the background, she would have been no more aware that their time together was slipping away.

It hurt. And if Cal didn't kiss her very soon and very hard, she was going to start bawling like a baby, and that would really mess things up. She wanted to leave with a brave front so that he would always remember her as a tough lady. If there was one thing she knew that Cal Rivers respected, it was a woman with grit.

Since she needed his arms around her more than she feared rejection, she turned and slid hers around his waist. "Hold me," she said softly. "Please."

When she was crushed against him, when she could hear the steady rhythm of his heart, when she could feel the tensing of his muscles and his heat under her fingertips, she finally felt safe. He stood there rocking with her for the longest time, before both hands slid up to frame her face.

"What's this?" he murmured, brushing away tears with the pad of his thumbs. "Why so sad?"

"I don't know," she denied.

"Liar. Come on. Don't you know you can tell me anything?"

She nodded. "I'm just being silly."

"About what?"

"I just realized that I'll never get to see Dawn's Magic

on the track or get to muck out the stalls or see how my tomatoes turned out." She forced a wobbly grin. "That is if I even left any tomato plants in the ground when I weeded."

Cal seemed taken aback by what she said, or maybe by the desolation in her tone. Then he got this faraway look in his eyes. "I never really thought that far ahead," he said finally, his voice flat.

"It's okay," she said at once, drawing on sheer bravado. "I mean, this is the way things were supposed to turn out. I did my job. You're back with your grandmother. I should be happy."

"Then why does it feel like we're getting ready to go to a funeral around here?" he said, humor teasing at his lips but not quite tilting the corners into a smile.

"Beats me," she said jauntily. "I can't explain it."

His arms tightened around her. He drew in a deep breath, then said firmly, "Well, I can. We're both behaving like a couple of idiots when there's an obvious solution here."

"I sure don't see one."

"Of course there is. You'll just come back to Florida with me."

Marilou's pulse kicked in like a filly's at the sight of a racetrack.

"I mean, it makes perfect sense," he went on, his enthusiasm clearly mounting. "You want to be there. Chaney's missing your blueberry muffins. I… I care for you. Why not, Marilou? You're not all that anxious to go back to your old job. Pack up your things and move down to live with us. I promise you that you'd never regret it."

After her first initial, dazed reaction, Marilou actually listened to Cal's words. Maybe if he hadn't stumbled over that one hurried phrase summing up his feelings, she could have bought the act. Instead his pretty speech simply didn't add up to a proposal, no matter how desperately she tried to shape it into one.

"What exactly are you offering?" she said finally, taking a step away so she could see his face more clearly.

"A place to live, a job." He appeared to hesitate for an instant before adding cautiously, "Me, if you'll have me."

"You?"

He frowned. "Look, I know it's not exactly conventional, but we'd be good together. You know that. These past few weeks are the happiest I've ever had. We don't fight. Well, not much anyway."

"What about love?" she said grimly. "What about those great-grandbabies you were talking to your grandmother about?"

He looked as if she'd leveled a two-by-four straight at his stomach. This time he was the one stepping back, so quickly that it made her heart ache.

"You know that's not possible," he said, his voice low and tight, maybe with anger, maybe with pain.

"Why isn't it possible?" she said, deliberately provoking him into an argument. She was spoiling for a fight now, a really good one. Maybe it would help her to forget about how much it hurt. "Are you telling me I'm good enough to live with, attractive enough to sleep with, but not special enough to marry?"

"This has nothing to do with you."

"How can you say that?"

"Because *I'm* the problem. I'll never marry. You've known that from the first."

"But I have never understood why. I'm not even sure you do. Your words are an automatic response. It's as if you've told that to yourself for so many years now that you've convinced yourself it's the way your life has to be."

"I told myself that, because it was the truth. I'm sorry I can't give you what you'd hoped for, but you'd never regret being with me, Marilou. You'd have everything you ever dreamed of, including the freedom to leave anytime you wanted to. I'd never hold you."

"Do you honestly expect that to please me?" She stared at him in amazement. "You do, don't you? Cal, I'll admit that love is giving someone the freedom to go or stay, but it's also trust and commitment. It's sharing the good times and the bad, not running off whenever it's convenient or whenever things get a little sticky. You can't build a relationship on any less, whether there's a marriage license attached to it or not."

He heard her out, his hands stuffed in his pockets, his shoulders squared. "Since I can't offer what you want, I guess you'll be going then."

She wondered if he even heard the raw anguish in his voice. "I don't see that I have any choice. I can't be happy with the terms you're offering." She dared one last touch, her fingers lingering on his cheek. "The hell of it is, I don't think you can be, either."

As soon as the words were out of her mouth, she turned and walked away. She wanted to run, as far and as fast as she could, but she wouldn't, not with him watching.

Marilou spent the endless night packing and pacing. Mrs. McDonald was right, the floorboards did squeak. She was probably keeping the entire household awake.

She knew that was exactly what she'd done, when she

went for a cup of tea at dawn and found Mrs. McDonald already seated at the dining room table.

"You're leaving," she said, her expression surprisingly compassionate.

Marilou didn't even bother to ask how she knew. "If someone could drive me into Cheyenne, yes."

"If you're sure it's what you want, I'll have one of the men take you." She watched Marilou for several minutes before she finally set her cup on the table and leaned closer. "You're doing exactly what he expected you to do, you know. You're walking out on him."

Startled by the assessment, Marilou stared at her. "He all but told me to go."

"I don't think so. I think he let you see every one of his fears, showed you his vulnerabilities and then waited for you to hurt him, just the way the rest of us have. You're going to do it, too."

As the gently spoken accusation ripped into her, Marilou buried her face in her hands. Was that what she had done? Had she been so dead set on not compromising her own principles that she'd failed to see that Cal was simply testing her? Would her leaving mean she'd failed him?

"I have to risk it," she said miserably. "Unless he honestly recognizes our love, unless he allows himself to trust in it, there will always be tests, and he'll always set them up so that I'll fail. He has to admit first that he really loves me. Then, maybe, we'll have a chance."

"You do really love him, then?"

"More than anything," she said. "Enough to leave him."

Mrs. McDonald shook her head. "How did you get

to be so stubborn when you're not even a Whitfield or a McDonald?" she asked with a rueful grin.

"Years of practice and spending a month around Cal. He seems to have that effect on me."

"You'll be good for him. I trust he'll wake up before long and see that."

"I'm trying very hard to count on that, too," Marilou said, blinking back a fresh batch of tears. "I'd better go now."

"God bless you for bringing him to me, my child. I owe you everything for doing that."

"Your thanks is more than enough." She held tightly to the old woman's gnarled hand. "Love him for me."

"Always, my dear. Always."

Chapter Fourteen

Once Marilou had gone, Cal felt as if the sky had turned a sullen gray. With her soft-spoken accusations and tearful, brave farewell kisses, she'd left him with a lot to think about, none of it pleasant.

Except for the kisses, of course. The memory of those last kisses made him ache with a sweet longing he'd never expected to feel for any woman. Her sensuality, with its delightful mix of shyness and daring, left him hot and needy. Her caring and warmth had stirred a tender side in him and made him hunger for the full-blown joy of her uncompromising love. He was gut-deep lonely for the first time in his life. He could have sworn he'd known loneliness before, but it had been nothing like this.

Maybe, he thought as he prowled the house restlessly, maybe it was time to take the same risk on love that he had always gambled on business.

Maybe, if he hadn't already sent for Joshua, he would have gone running after her, but he felt duty-bound now to wait for his friend's arrival. Joshua's mood was going to be foul enough when he discovered what Cal had in mind for him. He clung to the excuse with the desperation of a drowning man. It kept him from making an impulsive decision that was probably based more on hormones than some sudden shift in his psyche.

What he needed, he decided, was a good, hard ride. That ought to use up some of this misdirected energy. He saddled up a stallion with a wild, anxious glint in its eye. He figured their moods matched. With very little prodding, the horse took off at a gallop, racing the wind, racing thoughts that pricked Cal's conscience like barbed wire.

Despite the chase of memories, exhilaration eventually began to replace moodiness. By the time he'd reached the creek where they'd picnicked with his grandmother, he was hot, dusty and tired. As his horse drank thirstily from the creek, Cal sat astride him and surveyed the land that his grandmother continued to insist on deeding to him.

The palette of colors was harsher than those of Florida, the land less lush. Yet he felt an affinity for the barren, wide-open scenery. Maybe there was something to genetics beyond looks and heart disease and the like. Maybe he'd inherited his love of the land from generations of Whitfields after all. It would explain why he'd felt so at home the minute he'd set foot on the land at Silver River Stables, why he'd been drawn to try something so totally alien to his previous business choices.

Even recognizing that his Florida Thoroughbred operation had been an instinctive and wise choice didn't mean it would be equally smart to take over here, as well. For one thing, his grandmother was a tough old bird. No matter what she'd said about giving him free rein, chances were good that she'd want to have her say about the decisions. As strong-willed as they both were, they'd be butting heads constantly. He caught himself smiling at the prospect. She'd be a worthy opponent, better than many of the men he'd encountered in board-rooms. It could be fascinating.

Still, he could be setting himself up for heartbreak. He'd spent years thinking of no one except himself. He wouldn't be able to do that if he agreed to his grand-mother's terms. They'd be tied together by more than balance sheets and beef prices. She wouldn't tolerate halfway measures. She'd want his soul, his total com-mitment. Why hadn't Marilou been able to see how in-tolerable that would be to a man who'd depended only on himself for all these years? Even his grandmother recognized what she was asking. That didn't keep her from making the demand, but unlike Marilou, at least she wasn't blind to the implications.

Still no closer to a decision about that or the woman who'd walked out of his life, he heard the pounding of hooves and looked up to see Garrett riding toward him, her hair tangled and her cheeks flushed from the ride.

"Your grandmother's looking for you."

"I figured she would be. It's been all of an hour since I last checked in."

She cast a reproving glance at him. "Your attitude stinks, mister. No wonder Marilou dumped you," she said bluntly.

"Marilou didn't dump me," he felt compelled to say, clinging to some small shred of pride. "She had to get back to work."

"Right."

Her sarcastic dig, which was closer to the mark than

he cared to admit, nagged at him. "You've passed along my grandmother's message like a good employee. You can take off now."

She studied him without moving, unfazed by his nasty mood. "You don't like her much, do you?" she said, seemingly baffled.

Cal was taken aback by her assessment. "Actually, I do," he confessed. "We're a lot alike, maybe too much so."

"Then why don't you treat her with the respect she deserves? Not many men or women could have done what she's done all these years." Her eyes sparked, and she leaned forward as she tried to share her own obviously intense feelings about his grandmother's accomplishments. "Talk to some of the other ranchers around these parts and you'll see what I mean. She has an indomitable spirit, but she's lonely. All I've heard her talk about since I first came here two years ago was what it would be like if she could just find you. Now that you're here, it seems to me like you're breaking her heart."

"I don't mean to," he said candidly. "I'm just not sure I can do what she wants. Your position will certainly be strengthened if I relinquish my rights to this place. Isn't that what you want?"

"Maybe what you or I want isn't so important," she said quietly, then started off. Before he could recover from her final barb, she added, "By the way, your greenhorn friend is here."

"Joshua? I wasn't expecting him until tomorrow."

"Apparently your employees jump to do your bidding, just like we do around here at your grandmother's. I think maybe you should have warned him about this place. He seemed to go into shock when one of the cows wandered over to check him out."

Cal laughed. "Joshua could do with a few surprises in his life."

Suddenly she was chuckling with him. "Judging from the horrified expression in his eyes, I'm not sure he'd agree."

"I'm sure he wouldn't."

She seemed to relax in the saddle. "Are you coming back now?"

"I'm inclined to let him get better acquainted with the cows first."

"He may quit on you," she warned.

"He might at that. Then again, if he's gotten a good look at the fringe benefits, I'm sure he'll stick around." With a wink, he spurred his horse and took off across the fields, Garrett in hot and furious pursuit.

"I am not a fringe benefit," she shouted, the complaint merging with his laughter as both were carried away on the wind.

Joshua was, indeed, looking a little grim. Cal found him pacing in the parlor, his expression murderous. Since he had deliberately provoked Garrett into running off, he was left to face his friend alone. Not even his grandmother was around to serve as a buffer.

"Are you out of your mind?" Joshua demanded as he came into the room. He ignored Cal's outstretched hand.

"What's the problem?" Cal inquired innocently.

"Just for starters, there are no nonstop flights between Orlando and this godforsaken hellhole."

"I offered to send my plane for you."

"Right. The one with the pilot who thinks he's still flying Medevac helicopters in Vietnam."

"Who better to get you to a hellhole? Any other complaints?"

"Dozens, and that doesn't include the ones I'm anticipating. Why am I here?"

"My grandmother could use a little help with the books."

"I'm quite sure there are adequate accountants in this part of the world."

"None with your expertise or loyalty."

Joshua wagged a warning finger at him. "Don't count too heavily on the latter."

"Oh, but I do, my friend."

"How has your grandmother gotten along all these years without an accountant?"

"By her wits, I suspect. Certainly not by any understanding of accounting procedures as you and I know them. Will you help, Joshua? I can guarantee it will be a challenge, even for a man with your skills."

Joshua sank down in a chair. "Do you realize there is not a drop of Scotch in this house?"

"Play your cards right and I'll sneak some in for you. Will you help?"

He threw up his hands in a gesture of resignation. "Oh, what the hell. As long as I'm here, I might as well give it a shot. What's your stake in this?"

"She wants to leave the place to me."

Joshua's eyes widened. "Good Lord, as if your Florida place weren't enough of a headache. How do you feel about that?"

"I'm not sure yet. At first I was adamantly opposed

to the idea, but Marilou managed to get in a few good zingers about my cowardice before she left…"

"She's gone?"

He nodded glumly. "Back to Atlanta."

"For good?"

"Based on the things she said as she flew out here, I'd say the move is permanent."

"How do you feel about that?"

"It was her choice."

"You sound as if you expected her to make it."

"I saw it coming, yes."

Silence fell as Joshua studied him consideringly. "Are you so sure you didn't back her into a corner until it was the only choice she could make?"

"Meaning?"

"You're not stupid, Cal, even if you do choose to live in the oddest places. I'm sure if you think about it, you can figure it out."

After several more uncomfortable days of self-examination, he eventually realized what Joshua meant. He'd been so terrified of losing Marilou that he'd been the one to force her to break it off. That idiotic speech he'd made about living together without commitment had been guaranteed to drive her away. Her departure had only confirmed his general opinion that women always ran when things got tough.

Now that she was gone, he was already restless and bored with trying to make sense of his grandmother's cattle operation. Even with the haphazard bookkeeping and his lack of expertise in the beef market, it wasn't much of a challenge. He hadn't given a thought to Silver River Stables in days, despite repeated calls from

Chaney. He'd been reading the *Wall Street Journal* with an eye toward finding something new.

But Joshua's pointed remark had underscored what he'd been thinking earlier that very day: he would always be quick to run unless he finally took the biggest risk of all and admitted to Marilou that he was in love with her.

She had brought excitement to every minute he'd spent with her. Her innocence and enthusiasm had made every day unique, jammed every hour with special moments. He didn't need another new business. He needed the one woman who could make him look at life in a new way, who could teach him the real meaning of family and love and commitment.

And he'd waited far too long to tell her that.

"I'm leaving tomorrow," he told his grandmother and Joshua at dinner that night.

"Leaving?" Joshua repeated, his expression horrified. "Without me?"

"You'll survive."

"Where are you going?" his grandmother asked, her demeanor instantly stiff.

"Atlanta."

At that her disapproval vanished. "It's about time. For a while there I was worried you weren't going to see what's plain as day."

He shook his head and sighed. "I'm surprised you didn't point it out."

She patted his hand. "Some things a man has to figure out for himself."

Marilou was flat-out miserable. In the month she'd been away from Atlanta the rain had finally quit and the skies were a clear blue, but she felt every bit as depressed as she had before she'd gone away. She couldn't get Cal out of her mind. She'd even planted a damned vegetable garden on the balcony of her apartment. The tomatoes were taking over. At least, she thought they were tomatoes. Maybe it was the zucchini that was going nuts.

She'd taken to scouring the sports pages for stories on racing. She'd even picked up *The Daily Racing Form*, which had aroused all sorts of curious stares at work, since the nearest track was in Alabama. She hadn't found one single word about Silver River Stables or Devil's Magic or any of the other horses. There were rumors that a well-respected trainer was in negotiations with an Ocala Thoroughbred breeder, but the reports were so vague that she couldn't be sure Cal was involved.

Half a dozen times she'd picked up the phone to call Florida or Wyoming. Each time, she'd cradled the receiver without dialing. Each time she'd told herself she had to wait for Cal to make the first move.

Telling him goodbye that night had very nearly killed her and, judging from the pallor of his complexion and the set of his lips as he'd heard her out, it had been no easier on him. Still, he had let her go. As his grandmother had warned her, he'd probably told himself a hundred times since then that he was better off without a woman who found it so easy to cut the ties between them.

With her mind only half on her job, she was sorting through the endless stacks of mail in search of something that would engage her interest, when Helen came over, a bemused expression on her face.

"Where'd you go on your vacation? Weren't you in Wyoming?"

"Part of the time."

"I think this letter's for you, then. What kind of crazy guy would take a chance on getting it to you this way? Must be a real romantic."

Puzzled, Marilou held out her hand. As soon as she saw the pale blue vellum envelope, her heart began to thud. The stationery wasn't all that uncommon, but coupled with Helen's remarks, there was little doubt about who had sent it. The last time she'd seen this paper, postmarked from Cheyenne, her whole life had taken an incredible new turn. She turned it over and over, almost afraid to open it.

On the front of the envelope, written not in the shaky hand of Mrs. McDonald but in Cal's bold strokes, were simply her name and Atlanta, Georgia. It was an address so incomplete that it virtually guaranteed it would wind up here in the dead letter office.

The message inside would have provided few clues about the sender to any clerk other than Marilou: I love you. Marry me. Cal.

She felt her pulse soar. Beaming at Helen, she rushed to her supervisor and pleaded for a break. "I have to make a call. It's important."

"Ten minutes," he growled. "And don't expect another one in an hour."

"I promise."

She practically ran to the pay phone down the hall and punched in Cal's Wyoming number. "Elena, it's Marilou. Could I speak to Cal, please?"

"No está aqui, señorita. He go away."

Her spirits plummeted. "Away?"

"Si. You wish to speak to *la señora?"*

"No. Just give her my love." The minute she'd hung

up, she redialed, this time to the farm in Ocala. "Chaney, it's Marilou."

"Hey, gal, we miss you down here. You still in Wyoming with Cal?"

Her spirits nose-dived. Cal must not be there, either. "No, I'm back in Atlanta. Cal's apparently left Wyoming, too. Isn't he there?"

"Nope, we ain't seen hide nor hair of him since the two of you took off. Don't know how he expects me to run this place when he don't even call in or take the calls I make."

"I'm sure he trusts your decisions, Chaney. Do whatever you think is right. How's Dawn's Magic?"

"Growing like a danged weed. You coming back to see her?"

"Maybe," she said wistfully, clinging more tightly to the letter.

"You want me to give the boss a message if he does finally take it into his head to call?" he asked grumpily.

"No," she said. "No message."

Thoroughly dispirited, she replaced the receiver and turned to go back to work.

"You looking for me by any chance?"

She whirled around at the sound of Cal's voice and found him lounging against the wall, dressed like she'd never seen him before. His suit was boardroom gray, his shirt a pristine white, his tie a vibrant and daring red. The man looked like business, but the gleam in his eyes was something else entirely. Something dangerous. Something wicked.

Something vaguely vulnerable.

"You're here," she said, breathless with amazement and excitement. Her heart skittered crazily, and she jammed her hands in her pockets to keep from grabbing the man right here in the hall.

He straightened up and took a step toward her. "Seemed to me that a man ought to be in the vicinity when he proposes, just in case the woman decides to say yes."

She ran her tongue over lips gone suddenly dry. Cal's eyes were locked on the tantalizing gesture. He swallowed hard and took one more step. Marilou felt the wall against her back and Cal's heat less than a heartbeat away.

"I do like a man who anticipates all the possibilities," she said, breathless.

"Enough to marry me?" he said, and that whisper of vulnerability came back.

"Certainly enough to give it some thought," she said, her expression all tease and challenge.

The expression on Cal's face then told her he was past playing games. "It took me a long time to get to this point, Marilou."

"Some might say too long," she agreed.

"Don't go playing coy with me. My heart can't take it."

"Neither can mine," she admitted, moving away from cool tile and into the warm circle of his embrace.

"Is that a yes?"

Her arms went around his neck. "Yes, yes, yes."

She was lost in Cal's kisses when she heard the shocked voice of her supervisor. "Miss Stockton, is this any way to conduct yourself on government time?"

She promptly and dutifully tried to wriggle free, but Cal's arms held tight. "Miss Stockton is no longer on government time," he said. "From now on she's on mine." Apparently he heard her quick intake of breath, because he met her eyes. "That okay with you, Miss Stockton?"

After barely an instant's hesitation, she threw the last trace of caution to the winds. "That is very much okay with me."

Before her boss could react, Cal had scooped her up in his arms and carried her out of the building. "I know that carrying the bride across the threshold is supposed to come after the wedding, but I'm anticipating. You don't suppose we could get married yet today, do you?"

"Are you afraid if we wait you'll change your mind?"

"I'm more worried that you'll come to your senses."

"Not a chance. I love you, Cal Rivers. I always will."

"Don't promise always," he pleaded. "Just today."

She touched a silencing finger to his lips. "No, my dearest Cal, always." She sealed the promise with yet another bone-melting, breath-stealing kiss. "By the way, in case it's of any interest, that man you just insulted back there was a notary."

Cal looked dismayed. "Think he'd forgive me long enough to perform a wedding ceremony?"

"He might be more inclined to forgive you if you let me finish working today."

"I'm afraid his price is way too high. We'll just have to wait. Besides, I think it might be nice to have a real family wedding in Wyoming. How would you feel about that?"

"I can't imagine any place I'd rather have a wedding. What about you?"

"I think I'd feel as if I'd finally come home."

"Do you mean that?"

"I've learned one thing over the past couple of weeks.

Wherever *you* are will always be home to me. Besides, I think my grandmother ordered the cake the day I flew off to get you. She'll be horribly disappointed if we don't show up so she can make a fuss over you."

"How long do you suppose this fuss will take?"

Cal grinned at her. "No more than twenty-four hours, if I have anything to say about it."

"That sounds just about right to me, too," she agreed. "What shall we do in the meantime?"

"I have a few ideas," he said, and whispered several in her ear.

"I do like your ideas."

"I thought you might," he said, as he tucked her into the back of a limousine. He assured her he'd chosen the vehicle specifically for its very dark tinted windows. "I wasn't sure I could wait to get you home."

She smiled slowly and reached for his tie. "Tell the driver just to keep going until he hears from you again."

"That could be days," Cal said.

"Then tell him he might as well aim this thing toward Wyoming."

Epilogue

It was not yet dawn when Cal pulled into the stable area at Churchill Downs. Mist still hovered in the air, creating an eerie ambiance. There was something almost mystical about this time of day at any backstretch in the country, but on the day of the Kentucky Derby an indefinable stir of excitement was added. Even the horses seemed aware of it, their ears pricked, their prancing steps livelier. The stable boys and grooms moved just a little faster to complete their chores. The hot walkers and exercise riders talked odds. The trainers definitely paced more nervously. Only the owners, most of them far more jaded than Cal, were still sound asleep in their fancy Louisville hotel suites, recovering from the previous night's Derby festivities.

Cal hadn't slept a wink. Neither had Marilou. They had passed the night making love, making promises, perhaps even making the baby that would be the start of their family. It was barely four thirty when Cal rolled out of bed and headed for the shower. Marilou had joined him, but for once they were too excited about the rest of the day to lose track of time in each other's arms yet again.

In denims and boots, they left the car and went to the stall where Dawn's Magic was dining on a special blend of grains in lieu of her normal early-morning workout. The filly whinnied when she saw Marilou, bobbing her head until Marilou held out a hand filled with chunks of carrot, her favorite treat.

"You are spoiling that horse outrageously," Cal said.

"How do you know these carrots don't provide the precise incentive she needs to win these big races? Are you willing to tamper with a successful formula?"

"I know I'm not," Reeve Bennett said, joining them. The trainer had been hired by Chaney and Cal after an illustrious career in California. Dawn's Magic was their first Triple Crown contender, though by no means the first major stakes horse Cal had bred. "Morning, you two. Couldn't you sleep?"

"You have to be kidding," Marilou said. "I didn't want to miss a second of this."

"Which reminds me," Cal said. "I have something in the car for you." He returned in minutes with a large package tied with a big red bow. Dawn's Magic seemed to feel the ribbon was for her. She kept stretching her long neck in an attempt to nab it.

"Oh, no, you don't," Marilou said with a chuckle. "This is *my* treat. You've already had yours." She tugged the ribbons loose and opened the box. Nestled amid the foam chips and tissue paper was a new camera, a top-of-the-line professional model. Her gaze rose to meet

Cal's. Again she caught that wavering uncertainty that came far less frequently now.

"I called all over the place to find out the best model. If it's not what you want, you can trade it in."

"It's wonderful," she reassured him. "Thank you."

"I thought today might be a good day for you to finally begin that career you've put off. I'm having a darkroom built on the back of the house while you're gone. You could do conformation photography. Goodness knows there are plenty of horses around. Or you could do studio work. If you want that, we'll put on another room. Do you really like it?"

Tears sprang to her eyes. If she hadn't been holding such an incredible piece of equipment, she would have dumped it on the ground in favor of throwing her arms around her husband. "You couldn't have given me anything I would like more."

"There's film in it already. You'd better get started if you want to catch all of Dawn's Magic's big day. I don't think Reeve is likely to wait around for you to get ready."

Marilou spent the next two hours getting a feel for the camera. Cal had obviously anticipated her fascination. He'd bought rolls and rolls of extra film. By the time they left to change for the race, she had already shot close to a hundred pictures and couldn't stop talking about every one of them.

When they returned to the suite, though, she put the camera on the dresser and went to Cal, sliding her arms around his neck. She molded her lips over his, teasing his mouth with her tongue until she heard the soft moan low in his throat and felt his whole body shudder.

"Some thank-you," he murmured huskily.

"There's more where that came from," she said, nudging him toward the bed.

"Marilou..."

"Hmm," she said, as she tipped him backward until he was sprawling across the still-rumpled sheets. She reached for his boots.

"Sweetheart..."

"Yes, love?"

"We don't have time..."

"You have to change," she reminded him innocently. "I'm just helping."

Her hand reached just a little high before she slid it slowly down his thigh, then on down to the other boot.

"You are not helping."

"Of course I am," she said, tugging off the boot. Her fingers slipped inside the cuff of his jeans as she reached for his socks. Her nails raked gently down his calves, before she bared his feet, then kissed each toe.

Cal's protests seemed to have lost steam. The heat in the room had gone up by several degrees. She reached for the buckle on his belt. Cal cleared his throat.

"I think maybe I ought to get that."

"No, dear. You just rest."

"Marilou, I am not resting. Resting is a body's natural quiet state. My nerves are on full alert."

"Really? That's nice."

"You have turned into an incredible tease."

"Are you complaining?"

"Not about the teasing. Your timing could do with a little work. We need to be back at the track in exactly one hour."

"We'll be there."

"But in what condition?"

"If you'll be a little cooperative here, I'll have us out of here in no time."

Cal's body bucked as she very, very slowly pulled down the zipper on his pants. "Holy... Okay, wench, enough," he said, grabbing her wrist and pulling her down on top of him. In less than a heartbeat, she was flat on her back, her hands pinned above her head, Cal, half-dressed, looming over her.

"Let's see if I understand this technique," he said, freeing her hands long enough to run his knuckles along the open throat of her blouse. When the caress slowed at the first button, he followed up with a kiss. One at her throat. Then another fraction of an inch lower. Then another, peppering them across her chest until she was writhing beneath him.

"How am I doing?" he inquired with lazy good humor.

"Like a pro," she said, working on the buttons of his shirt and fanning her hands across his bare chest until she could reach every square inch of burning flesh with hungry kisses.

The game flew out of control with his first, hot claiming of her breast. Suddenly slow became needy, then need turned to urgency. Their remaining clothes were nudged just far enough out of the way to allow Cal to drive into her with a white-hot fervor that sent Marilou quickly into a shattering, earth-moving climax. Still in the throes of passion, she arched her hips up, giving back to Cal all the love, all the commitment he had dared to give her.

Slowly their breath returned to normal, their hearts beat in a gentler rhythm, their skin cooled. But still they didn't move, Cal's weight crushing her into the bed, his legs tangled with hers.

"I'm getting far too old for this," he said at last, levering himself up and trying to figure out where her clothes ended and his own began.

Marilou chuckled. "Lordy, I hope not. I'm not even thirty yet and I have no intention of stopping with just one baby."

"Then you'd better hope you're pregnant now. I figure I've got another year, maybe two before you exhaust me. Maybe you could manage twins. That would save a little on the wear and tear."

"Say that when they both start teething at the same time," she teased. "Get moving, love. We now have exactly twenty-seven minutes to get back to the track. I don't want to miss one single second of Derby Day."

"You should have thought of that before you decided to have your way with me," he grumbled just as the phone rang. Marilou reached for it, but he beat her to it then waved her toward the shower.

They were only ten minutes late to the track. Chaney was waiting for them, looking uncomfortable in a suit. He kept running a finger around the collar of his shirt and tugging on his tie.

"You look very handsome," Marilou told him.

"Don't see why I had to get dressed up like this. Only time I ever wear this suit is for funerals and weddings."

"Well, today you're going to be wearing it in the winner's circle," Marilou declared. "What are the odds on our baby?"

"She's a long shot, just like you knew she would be. Thirty-to-one in the morning line."

"That's okay," Marilou said confidently. "That just means we'll make more money betting her."

"You know, missy, I wouldn't go getting your hopes too high. She's a danged good horse, but it's a tough race for a filly to win."

Marilou kissed his leathery cheek. "Care to go for a little side wager?"

He shook his head. "No way. You have a way of getting what you want out of life."

"I haven't got you fixed up with a good woman yet," she said, deliberately taunting him.

He scowled at her. "And you ain't going to, either. You just stay out of my love life and I'll keep out of yours. Go take your pictures, girl. Maybe it'll keep you out of mischief."

Cal rejoined her then and linked his fingers through hers. "Ready to go to the box?"

She could feel the restrained excitement that practically vibrated through him. She squeezed his hand. "Let's do it."

As they walked into the clubhouse, they were met by noise. Thousands were jammed into the stands and filled the infield. Mint juleps seemed to be the drink of the day, though Marilou was far too nervous to consider putting alcohol on a stomach that was already rolling. As they cut a path through the crowd to the box Cal had taken, Marilou's gaze suddenly shot ahead and found the tall, staid form of his grandmother. Though the older woman tried hard to maintain a disapproving frown, excitement snapped in her eyes as she drew Cal into an embrace.

"Thank you for coming," he said.

"I figured if this was something you insist on doing,

I'd better know why," she said. "You say this horse of yours is good?"

"The best," Marilou told her.

"Then if I put two dollars on her to show, I won't be wasting my money?"

Cal grinned. "That kind of bet won't make you rich, Grandmother, but it should be safe enough. Where's Joshua? I thought he was bringing you."

"He dropped me off. Said he had an errand to run. I expect he'll be back before too long."

Just then they heard his voice. "I'm here," he said, edging his way toward them.

Marilou turned around, a smile on her face. Then she caught Cal's expression. He appeared stunned. His grandmother turned pale, then sank into her seat.

"What is it?" Marilou said, taking an instinctively protective step closer to Cal.

He swallowed hard, his gaze never shifting away from Joshua and the two people behind him. Marilou hadn't even realized they were all together until she'd seen Cal's expression.

The woman wore a floppy white hat, a lovely silk dress and shoes that had probably come from the designer salon at Neiman-Marcus. She exuded money and self-confidence. The man, who stood shoulder to shoulder to her in height, was gray-haired and hesitant, though he had a glint of sharp intelligence in his eyes that age hadn't dimmed.

"Hello, Mother, Father," Cal said, his voice tight as he directed a forbidding look at Joshua.

"Your parents," Marilou breathed. When Cal remained stiffly silent, she introduced herself, then stepped aside so they could enter the box. There was another flaring of tension when they spotted Mrs. Mc-Donald.

Joshua caught Marilou's elbow and pulled her back when she moved to join them. "Cal's probably going to have my hide for this, but I thought it was time."

She grinned at him. "You weren't thinking of running out on us now, were you?"

He grinned back. "Actually, I planned to do exactly that. You'll need the seats. Cal intended them for me and my date. All things considered, I think I'll be safer down at the rail."

Marilou let him go, then went to her seat at Cal's side. She tried to make small talk, but everyone was too tense to respond. It was only when the bugle blew to announce that the horses were coming onto the track for the Derby that they began to relax. Cal's father asked about Dawn's Magic. Marilou told about watching the horse being born. Cal talked about his breeding. Marilou took bets for all of them into the clubhouse windows and placed them. By the time she came back, some sort of uneasy truce seemed to reign.

"She looks good," Marilou exclaimed when Dawn's Magic stepped onto the track as the strains of "My Old Kentucky Home" wafted through the air. "Don't you think she looks wonderful?"

Cal managed a grin. "The fact that she's here at all is an honor," he reminded her.

"I don't want to hear that garbage. You sound like Chaney. She's going to win the race." She smiled at him impishly. "And I'll beat you down to the winner's circle."

His arm circled her waist. "That's a bet."

While Cal focused his binoculars on the post parade, Marilou attached her telephoto lens and snapped pictures. It seemed to take only seconds before the horses were in the gate.

"They're off!" the track announcer said, and a roar went up from the crowd.

Dawn's Magic broke well from her gate on the outside and moved quickly to a slot just off the lead. It was exactly where Reeve had wanted her. The track was fast, not muddy, but the filly wasn't used to having dirt kicked in her face. He'd worried what she would do if she fell back too far. She was in third and only three-quarters of a length off the pace as they rounded the first turn.

"She's going to do it," Marilou said confidently.

"Sweetheart, it's a long race," Cal warned.

"But she's like me. We're both the kind who go the distance."

"If she has your heart, then she'll definitely take it," he said, giving her a quick squeeze before returning his attention to the backstretch, where two of the favorites were beginning to make their moves. His grandmother's gaze was riveted on the pack of horses speeding for the next turn. As they came flying around the far side of the oval track, Dawn's Magic was almost neck and neck with the leader.

"Come on, baby," Marilou whispered, her camera forgotten. "You can do it."

Cal went absolutely still as the horses turned for home. Dawn's Magic's fell back to third, and Marilou's heart sank. That usually spelled the beginning of the end. Horses often gave up after falling behind.

"Come on," she pleaded, her hands clenched. Cal took one of them and massaged the tension away, until she folded her hand around his. Dawn's Magic's jockey showed her his whip then, flicking her lightly on the neck. The gallant horse dug deep into some inner reserve and began to move, a thousand pounds of incredible muscle supported by frail ankles and driven by heart.

With less than a length to go, she had caught up with the favorite and the crowd was going wild. Marilou strained but couldn't hear the final call as they tore across the finish line. Her gaze shot to Cal's, as did everyone else's in the box. The tote board flashed Photo in giant letters to indicate that it was too close to call. The stewards would review films again and again, checking for the fraction of an inch between victory and defeat.

As if he couldn't bear the waiting, Cal focused his binoculars again on the horses as they were riding out around the far side of the track.

"Is she okay?" Marilou asked him, her heart in her throat.

He grinned and shook his head. "Looks to me like she'd like to go for another quarter mile or so."

"I told you," she said. "I told you she had it in her."

He hugged her. "So you did."

Just at that instant, Dawn's Magic's number twelve went into the first place spot on the tote board. The stands exploded with sound—cheers from those with winning tickets and even appreciative applause from those who'd recognized that Dawn's Magic had the makings of a Triple Crown champion.

Cal grabbed Marilou's hand and started from the box. Marilou held her breath and sent him a silent message. After just an instant's hesitation, he turned to his family.

"Come with us," he said, his voice choked. "This should be a family celebration."

Marilou reached for his grandmother's arm and helped her up, but then his mother slipped into place on her other side. "Let me walk with you, Mother," she said hesitantly. "We have a lot to talk about."

A slow smile spread across Mrs. McDonald's face, and she winked at Cal. "Maybe we'll talk about me buying into that Thoroughbred operation of yours," she said slyly.

Cal linked his arm through hers. "The only way you're getting a piece of that action, Grandmother, is at the two-dollar window."

Marilou listened to the start of the familiar bickering, felt the slow easing of twenty years of tension, and kept her eyes on the love that was finally flowering again. It would need a lot of tending, a lot of nurturing, but it would grow. She would do her best to see to it.

Family, she thought with a tug of real longing. Then Cal reached for her hand and the longing fled, chased away forever by the strong, loving man at her side.

For years afterward, that moment would be captured for her with one snap of the track photographer's shutter. Five people, eyes brimming with tears, smiling and holding hands while Dawn's Magic nuzzled Marilou's pocket for the carrot that was hidden there.

* * * * *

Also by *USA TODAY* bestselling author Caro Carson

Harlequin Special Edition

Visit the Author Profile page
at Harlequin.com for more titles.

A TEXAS RESCUE
CHRISTMAS

Caro Carson

For William Edward,
a brave and brilliant boy.

Chapter One

James Waterson III left his family's ranch at the glorious age of eighteen, ready to exceed the already high expectations of his friends and family, teachers and coaches. James the third, better known as Trey among the ranch hands and football fans, the recruiters and reporters, was going to conquer college football as the star of Oklahoma Tech University. He'd so easily conquered high school football, the NFL was already aware of his name.

At the age of twenty, Trey was washed up.

What's wrong with that boy? He blew his big chance.

What's wrong with him? He was so bright when I had him in class.

What's wrong with the Waterson kid? He must've gotten into drugs.

What a waste, what a shame, why, why, why?

His parents, of course, had left the family ranch in Texas to visit him in Oklahoma numerous times. They'd consulted with his coaches and met with his professors, and no one could understand why Trey Waterson, the promising freshman recruit, could no longer remem-

ber the play calls and passing routes now that he was a
sophomore.

*Well, Mr. Waterson, I'm not saying your son can't
handle stress, but we've seen kids freeze up when they
get in a big stadium. We're talking about a crowd of one
hundred thousand.*

No one could deny that Trey's test grades were no
longer easy As, but struggling Ds and failing Fs.

*To be honest, Mrs. Waterson, he was supposed to
come to my office for tutoring directly after class, but
he never showed. As I told the athletic director, I can't
help a kid who refuses to be helped.*

Trey's parents had believed him. He wasn't trying to
skip class. He was not experimenting with drugs. They
remembered the hit he'd taken in the last quarter of a
home game, and worried that he was somehow suffering, months later.

*We take good care of our players. Your son had a CT
scan and passed a neurological exam that very week.
Everything looks completely normal. No damage from
that game, and no brain tumors or anything else that
would explain the changes in his behavior.*

That had been the most disheartening news of all.
Trey was healthy, according to the doctors. An MRI was
ordered, anyway; Trey was told it was "unremarkable."
He could balance on each foot. He could touch his nose
with his index finger and stick out his tongue straight
and name the current President of the United States.

When he finally found his professor's office and
correctly described how to calculate the area within
the shape created by rotating a parabola around the
z-axis, Trey believed the doctors, too. There was noth-

ing wrong with him. He was just having a hard time, somehow. Not sleeping well, for some reason.

After their conversation, the professor gave him the exam, letting him make up the missed test just because Trey was the future of the Oklahoma Tech football program.

Trey failed the math test.

He understood the mathematical theory, but he couldn't calculate three times six. Five plus twelve. He sat in the professor's office and sweated clean through his shirt. He thought he was going to vomit from the fear, the sheer terror, of not being certain if he was counting on his fingers correctly. Seventeen times four? Not enough fingers, he knew that much.

We're sorry, Mr. and Mrs. Waterson. I know your son passed the drug screen, but these boys get pretty clever about hiding substances in urine samples. Now, now, hold up. We're not accusing him of taking drugs, but he has been cut from the football team. He has until May to bring his grade point average up to the school standard.

Trey came home for spring break, in time to help with the annual calf branding. As coordinated as ever, he threw lassoes and branded calves, day after day. He felt so damned normal, he wondered why he'd fallen apart. After spring break, he'd go back. He'd make up all the work he'd missed. He'd survive his nineteenth year. Then he picked up the branding iron, held it over the calf's hide and forgot which way was up. He was on the James Hill Ranch. The brand was a straightforward three initials: JHR. The iron didn't look right.

Trey had spun the brand the other way, but it looked just as wrong as it had at first glance.

Hurry up, the iron's cooling.

He must be holding the iron correctly, then, if they were telling him to hurry. James Waterson III permanently branded a calf on his own family's ranch with the symbol upside down.

He returned to Oklahoma Tech, failed all his courses, turned twenty years old and never returned home again.

It was much easier to lie to his parents on the phone. He had a good apartment, a good job, a good life. No, he wasn't going to go back to school next year, but that was okay, because he'd rather work with his hands. That became his big excuse: he'd rather work with his hands. His parents didn't need to know that he was spreading mulch for a landscaping firm.

His mother was worried sick, but he could fool her once a year when his parents came to visit. Before their arrival, he would practice driving from his one-bedroom apartment to their hotel and back, daily, until he could do it without getting lost. He'd preplan the restaurants they'd go to, and rehearse those routes, too. He'd smile and drop names as if he had lots of friends, and then his parents would leave after four or five days, and Trey would go back to his life of isolation and safe routine.

But now he had to go back to the James Hill Ranch.

Trey looked at the wedding invitation in his hand, at its classic ivory vellum and deep black engraving. It contained little squares of tissue paper and extra envelopes, a confusing piece of correspondence until he'd laid all the parts out on his kitchen counter.

Miss Patricia Ann Cargill
and
Mr. Luke Edward Waterson
request the honor of your presence
at their marriage.

The groom was his younger brother. His one and only brother. The wedding would be held on the ranch, one third of which Trey owned as his birthright. There was no acceptable excuse to miss his brother's wedding.

Ready or not, after ten years away from home, Trey Waterson had to return to the James Hill Ranch.

It was enough to make a grown man break out in a cold sweat.

Becky Cargill perched in her first-class seat, ice water in her hand, and sweated unladylike buckets. She'd never been so nervous in her life. Then again, she'd never tried to run away from home before.

The flight attendants were extra solicitous, even by the standards of the first-class cabin, but Becky didn't know if that meant she looked as ill as she felt, or if they'd simply seen her name on the passenger manifest. *Becky* meant nothing, but her last name, Cargill…well, that meant money. Of course, not everyone named Cargill was a relative of the Texas Cargill oil barons, just as not every Rockefeller or DuPont was one of *those* Rockefellers or DuPonts, but Becky's mother had indeed been married to one of *those* Cargills, and she made sure no one ever forgot.

Becky's birth father was not a Cargill, but when the man known to one and all as Daddy Cargill had been her stepfather, when he'd been in the first weeks of passionate fascination with Becky's mother, he'd let his new stepdaughter use his last name. Her mother wouldn't let her drop it now. Not ever.

Becky was her mother's little trophy, always dressed like a doll, the picture of sweetness and innocence. Her mother would turn on the charm for the Right Kind of

People. *I'm Charlene Maynard*—or Lexington, whichever of her subsequent husbands' names was most in
vogue, and then she'd gesture toward Becky—*and this,
of course, is my sweet little girl, Becky Cargill.* By having a different last name from her mother, Becky was
a useful sort of calling card, proof her mother had been
accepted into more than one dynasty as a wife for the
Right Kind of Man.

It was only recently that Becky had started to see
that she'd been part of the reason men proposed to her
mother. Mr. Lexington, for example, had enjoyed being
photographed as the doting stepfather of a Cargill. In
society page photos, it implied an alliance between the
Lexingtons and the Cargills existed. For the Maynards,
the appeal had been slightly different. That family had
several young sons. Wouldn't Becky Cargill someday
grow into just the Right Kind of Girl for one of their
many boys?

Until she did, Becky was to be seen but not heard.
She was to smile and not cry. She was to be pure and virginal and obedient at all times. Becky fingered the pearl
button that kept her Peter Pan collar demurely fastened
at her throat. Her style had not changed much since her
mother had divorced Daddy Cargill. Becky had been
nine years old at the time.

Now she was twenty-four.

No one ever guessed her age. Her mother made certain of that, too. Becky had been shocked this summer
when her mother had started dropping delicate hints to
the Right Kind of Men that although Becky was indeed
young, she was approaching a certain *desirable* age.

Shock had turned to devastation this winter weekend when her mother had, rather viciously, told her it

was time for her to show her appreciation for the lifestyle she'd been privileged to enjoy. Hector Ferrique, old enough to be Becky's grandfather, was the owner of the Cape Cod vacation home in which they'd been living this year. Apparently, it was time to thank Hector for the free use of his spare mansion, and for the first time in her pure and virginal life, Becky was expected to do the thanking.

Hector will arrive this evening, and we're all flying to the Caribbean to spend the Christmas holiday. I've packed your things.

The flight attendants noticed when Becky fished in the seat pocket for the air-sickness bag. "Can I get you anything else? Perhaps a ginger ale or some crackers?"

Why don't you line up about five of those little bottles of scotch on my tray table?

But, no. She'd never had five shots of any kind of alcohol. She was on her own for the first time, and she was going to need all her wits about her. Besides, she'd probably get carded, as usual, and that would be the straw that broke the camel's back. She might possibly cry. Or get angry.

"The ice water is just fine, thank you. Can you tell me why the plane hasn't left the gate yet?"

"They are waiting on the weather forecast for Austin. They won't let us take off if the destination airport is going to close due to ice and snow."

Becky looked out the window at the snow-covered Boston airport. "It snows every day."

"Yes, but it's unusual in Texas." The flight attendant tapped her wristwatch in a cheerful, apologetic manner. "They'll update the airport status on the hour, and then we'll know if we're cleared for take-off. Don't worry,

Miss Cargill, we've got agents standing by to help you make alternate transportation arrangements if the flight is cancelled. You'll have first priority, of course. We'll get you home for the holidays."

Of course, since her last name was Cargill, the flight attendant had assumed Texas was home. Becky simply smiled, a display of pink lip-glossed sweetness, and the attendant moved on to the businessman in the next row, tapping her wristwatch, repeating her apology.

Becky dabbed at her upper lip with her napkin, mortified at the nervous sweat she couldn't control. She could feel a single bead of moisture rolling slowly down her chest, between her breasts, but, of course, she would not dab there.

Mother must have noticed my absence by now. She'll call the airport, and I'll be taken right off the plane, like a child. They won't card me first, not when she calls and says her daughter is on the plane without her permission.

Miraculously, the pilot came over the speakers and announced that they were going to take off. Becky's stomach went from fearful nausea to desperately hopeful butterflies. Within minutes, they began taxiing down the runway. She was leaving Boston, and her mother, and the horrible man to whom Becky was expected to sacrifice her virginity.

The pilot's voice was female, and somehow, that made Becky feel better. The only person Becky knew who could possibly defend her against Hector Ferrique was also a female, and a female pilot was going to get her there safely in an ice storm. With any luck at all, the snow and ice would arrive immediately after they landed, and it would become impossible for her mother to chase her down.

The plane lifted off. Becky had gotten away. Now she needed to stay away. Even if the Austin airport closed after Becky arrived, her mother could and would find her and drag her back, unless Becky could find some-one strong enough to stand up to her. There was only one person in her life who'd ever seemed stronger than Mother, and that was Daddy Cargill's real daughter, Pa-tricia.

The year that Becky was nine, the year that her mother had married Daddy Cargill, was the year that Becky had worshipped her new stepsister, Patricia. Eight years older than she, Patricia had swept home from board-ing school on weekends and vacations to keep Becky's mother in check. Heavens, she'd kept her own father in check. Becky had watched in wide-eyed wonder as Pa-tricia had plucked the key to the innermost vault of the wine cellar right out of Mother's hand. *I do think there are plenty of other vintages for you to enjoy. Let's save the Cote de Nuits for an appropriate occasion, shall we?*

Then Patricia had given Becky a whole can of Dr Pepper and let her drink it in her bedroom. Sitting at Patricia's tri-fold vanity mirror, Becky had played with real, red lipstick.

The divorce was inevitable between their parents, of course, and one day, while Patricia was away at her boarding school, Becky and her mother had moved out. Becky had cried and said she wanted to be a Cargill. Her mother had agreed that keeping the name would be wise, which wasn't what Becky had meant at all.

This morning, as Becky's mother had announced that Hector Ferrique would be coming to visit his own beach house, the newspaper had announced that Patricia Cargill was getting married in Austin.

Becky had seized on those lines of newsprint, using them as her excuse to get to the airport. How easy to finally use that Cargill name, the one she'd been borrowing since fourth grade, to change the chauffeur's schedule. "No, my flight leaves this morning. Mother's will be later this afternoon. My sister, Patricia Cargill, is getting married in Austin this weekend. I'll be at the wedding while Mother and Hector are in Bimini. No, just the three blue bags are mine. The rest are Mother's. Thank you."

Becky was hoping the Cargill name would let her crash a wedding she hadn't been invited to. If her mother came to drag her away, Becky hoped the bride would kick her former stepmother out of the reception—but let her former stepsister stay. Indefinitely. As plans went, it was weak, but it was all a pure and virginal and obedient person like herself had been able to come up with on a moment's notice.

Please, Patricia, don't kick me out. I'm still just little Becky Cargill, and I've got nowhere else to go.

Chapter Two

Becky peered through the gray haze of winter weather at the endless county road. She spotted another gate for a ranch up ahead. Two posts and a crossbeam in the air, that was the standard ranch entrance in Texas. She'd already turned her rental car into two properties that weren't the James Hill Ranch. At the first, she'd gotten flustered and made the tiny car's engine produce horrid sounds as she put it in Reverse. After she'd driven through the second wrong gate, which had clearly been labeled the River Mack Ranch, making her feel like an idiot, she'd tried to make a U-turn to avoid the reverse gear. The U-turn had worked, but all her belongings had been thrown around as the car bounced over rough ground before making it back onto the road.

Becky could make out a letter J on the fence beside the upcoming gate. If the J stood for James, then she hadn't gotten lost after all, although the clunky GPS system, emblazoned with the rental car company's logo and bolted onto the car's dash, had gone silent many miles ago. She was officially out in the middle of nowhere on

a two-lane road that had no name, only numerical dig-
its the GPS voice had rattled off before losing its satel-
lite connection.

Her phone, however, still had a signal. It rang again,
shrill after being jarred out of the leather purse Becky
had stuffed it in. Her mother was calling. She should
answer.

Becky gripped the steering wheel. She couldn't answer the phone. She rarely drove anywhere, and she'd
never driven this kind of car, so she had to concentrate.
Snow had been falling, rare enough in December, apparently, to make it the sole topic of conversation in the
Austin airport. The snow was beginning to look more
wet, like sleet.

She would not panic. She'd just keep two hands on the
wheel, and she would not answer the phone. *I'm twenty-
four years old. I can drive a car in bad weather.*

She hadn't wanted to. At the airport, her request for a
taxi to the James Hill Ranch had been met with so many
chuckles and "you're not from around here, are you?"
responses, she'd given up and gotten in line for the first
rental car desk she saw.

Too late, she realized that her mother would be able
to use the credit card transaction to find her. Becky had
never seen a credit card bill, but she knew her mother
could check it, somehow, almost immediately. She hadn't
dared to use her credit card without permission since she
was twenty-one. That year, her mother had placed her
in a ski school in Aspen with teenagers who belonged
to the Right Kind of Families. When her fellow students
had learned Becky was actually of legal drinking age,
they'd convinced her to buy the booze to go with their
energy drinks. The next morning, her mother had asked

her to produce the liter of vodka that she'd purchased in town at precisely 8:19 p.m. the evening before. Becky had been confined to her hotel room the rest of the trip—and she'd learned a valuable lesson about credit cards.

The phone rang once more. Her mother had probably tracked her credit card already. *Why did you rent such a low-budget car? Look at you, arriving at the Cargills in a rental car like a poor relation. You could have at least taken a limo, for God's sake.*

Becky hadn't gone to Daddy Cargill's mansion. She read more sections of the newspaper than her mother did. Outside of the society pages, there'd been a featured real estate listing for the infamous mansion. Photos of the outrageously tacky decor had accompanied the article. Patricia no longer lived there, and obviously had not for years.

Patricia was getting married at the James Hill Ranch. That was Becky's destination. Her best hope for sanctuary.

"Shoot!" Becky realized she was driving right past the gate. She hit the brakes and turned the wheel, but the snowfall had become ice, and the car spun wildly. Her seat belt held her in place, but her head thunked against the side window before the car came to a halt, facing the wrong way.

I will not cry.

The car's engine made that awful sound as she put it into Reverse.

I will not cry.

Everything in the car—up to and including her teeth—rattled as she traveled over a cattle guard on her way through a second, more elegant gate of wrough iron and limestone pillars.

I will not cry.

She presented herself at the door. She'd never before seen a housekeeper who answered a door while wearing jeans. She'd never been greeted by a staff member with "howdy" instead of "good morning, miss." Becky requested that Miss Cargill be notified that her sister, Miss Cargill, had arrived.

"Sure, uh-huh," said the older woman in jeans. "Come in, sweetheart. It's freezing out there."

Too late, Becky surmised that this was not a housekeeper. She'd probably just given orders to a relative of the groom. The woman did not introduce herself, however. She just launched right into a conversation as if they were acquainted.

"If you're here for the wedding, I've got some bad news. It's been cancelled. Didn't you get a message from your sister? I swear, she called a hundred people yesterday herself.

"The pastor was afraid to drive, and the caterers were in a tizzy. Luke and Patricia, they decided they didn't want to miss their honeymoon, what with the airports closing and all. They're taking some gigantic sailboat from Galveston all the way around Florida to the Bahamas. Anyway, they took their license to a justice of the peace first thing this morning and got married. Now Luke's parents are driving them all the way to the port to make their boat on time. But we're supposed to cut into their cake and send them a video of us doing it, so stick around, honey."

Patricia was gone.

Becky's cell phone rang, shrill.

"May I use your powder room?" Becky asked, smiling sweetly, although her pink lip gloss had faded away hours ago.

She locked herself in the bathroom, and she cried.

"Why, it's James Waterson the third, as I live and breathe! Aren't you a sight for sore eyes? I swear, you are even taller than your brother. What are you now? Six-three? Six-four?"

Trey steeled himself against the onslaught. He hadn't had a chance to scrutinize the woman's face, yet she was hugging him and patting him on the cheek, treating him like he was a growing boy when he'd just passed his thirty-first birthday. Clearly, she knew him, but he did not know her. If she'd just hold still and let him look at her face for a moment—but she chatted away, turned and dragged him from the door.

He hadn't had a chance to look about as he'd come in. He preferred to pause and get his bearings when he entered a new building, but this stranger gave him no chance. Trey looked around, consciously choosing to focus on what his eyes could see and deliberately ignoring the sounds hitting his ear. He was tired from the strain of travel, and he could only take in so much.

The woman pulled him into the high-raftered great room, and Trey, still concentrating on visual information, immediately focused on the fireplace. It was decorated for a wedding with a swag of fluffy white material and silver Texas stars, but he knew what it would look like without all that. He knew that fireplace.

Massive, its limestone edifice rose from floor to ceiling in a severe rectangle that would have been boring if the limestone variations hadn't been unique from stone to stone. Trey had lain before roaring fires, staring up at

the limestone, idly noting which were white and beige
and yellow, which were solid, which were veined. From
infancy, he'd done so, he supposed. He last remembered
doing it with a girl while in high school, drinking his
mother's hot chocolate before sneaking his sweetheart
out to the barn for some unchaperoned time.

Yes, he knew that fireplace.

Suddenly, the whole room fell into place. Hell, the
whole house made sense. Trey knew where he was. It
was effortless. The kitchen was through there. The mudroom beyond that. His bedroom was down the hall. The
dogs needed to be fed outside that door, every morning,
before school.

There was nothing confusing about it.

God, he knew where he was. Not just how to navi-
gate from here to there. Not just enough to keep from
looking like a fool. He really and truly knew where in
the world he was.

"Can you believe they ran off like that? I mean, you
can't blame them with the storm coming and everything,
but..." The woman squeezed his arm conspiratorially.
"Okay, I blame them a little. I think most women would
want the wedding. You could always take a trip some
other time. I mean, it's the bride's big show with the
white gown, being the center of attention, the flowers,
the cake, you know? But Patricia, she's some kind of sailboat nut. I don't even know what you call those people.
Instead of horse crazy, are they boat crazy? Anyhow,
you would have thought your brother had never wanted
anything more in his entire life than to get on a sailboat
and go visitin' islands."

With a woman? Someone he loved enough to pledge
his life to? Trey didn't find that so hard to understand. It

sounded as if Luke had made the choice between wearing a tux for one day or spending a month on tropical seas with the woman he wanted the most. His little brother had never been stupid.

Then again, once upon a time, Trey hadn't been stupid, either. Now, he didn't recognize the person he was talking to. He tried to place the woman's face as she chattered on.

"Luke's always been a cattle rancher, not a sailor. I guess people do crazy things when they're in love. I hope it lasts. Lord knows, none of my marriages have. I don't blame you for not coming to any of them."

Trey had been invited to her weddings? That sick, sweaty feeling started between his shoulder blades.

The sound of the mudroom door slamming centered him once more. It was a sound Trey hadn't heard in ten years, yet it sounded utterly familiar, instantly recognizable without any effort.

The man's voice that followed was new to him. "No luck, sugar," it boomed.

"Oh, dear. Trey, come meet your new uncle."

Uncle. That meant this woman was his aunt. Trey looked at her, and suddenly it was so incredibly obvious. She was his mother's sister, his aunt June. How could he have forgotten that he had an aunt June?

He felt stupid.

The kitchen, however, he remembered. He hadn't stepped fully into the room, hadn't put both boots on the black-and-white-checkered floor, when he felt that utterly certain feeling once more. His brain worked for once. He didn't just recognize the kitchen, he knew every inch. This drawer held the silverware, that cupboard held the big pots, and the cold cereal was on the bottom shelf of the pantry. He knew all that without trying, and it made him realize how little he usually knew about other rooms. He'd been adrift in every room he'd been in for the past ten years.

His new uncle shook hands, then shook his head at Aunt June. "No sign of her, sugar."

Another woman, younger than Aunt June, came in from outside. He could see her through the doorway to the mudroom, stamping her boots and smacking icy droplets off her jacket sleeves. "It's turning into sleet out there, bad."

He didn't know her.

She knew him. "Ohmigod, Trey! I haven't seen you in ages." She dumped her coat on the mudroom floor and came rushing at him, arms open. They closed about him in a hug, unfamiliar in every way.

Don't panic. Think. Aunt June has daughters. Think of their names.

Aunt June patted his arm and started laughing. "I don't think he recognizes you, Emily. It's been ten years, at least. You were in pigtails and braces last time he saw you."

He had a cousin named Emily, of course.

Stupid, stupid, stupid.

Just to prove that he knew *something*, he opened the correct cabinet to pull out coffee mugs. His brother hadn't moved their mother's traditional coffee machine. It sat on the same counter it had always sat on. Trey knew the filters would be in the cupboard above it.

"Can I make y'all some coffee?" he said, his voice sounding gruff to his own ears. He owned a third of the house, and he had company. He ought to make some attempt to be a host.

"That's a good idea," Emily said. "I need to warm up before I keep looking."

And…he was lost again. The emotions of these three people were hard for him to keep track of. Everyone was happy one moment, worried the next.

"What are you looking for?" he asked, determined to make sense of the world. He started counting scoops of coffee into the filter basket. *One, two, three, four—*

"This girl named Becky disappeared."

Six, seven—crap. He'd lost count. Trey decided the amount of coffee looked about right, shoved it into place and hit the power button.

"You gonna put some water in there, sugar?" Aunt June asked, laughing.

Damn it.

But everyone was happy again for a moment, chuckling about old age and forgetfulness.

Then, they weren't happy. As Trey filled the carafe with water, his aunt started explaining who was missing. A young lady had arrived for the wedding, Patricia's sister, or so she'd said. They hadn't known Patricia had a sister.

"Just as sweet as can be," his aunt said.

"Pretty as a picture," his uncle said.

"She seemed nervous to me," Emily said. "Then she stood in a corner, and I saw her listening to something on her cell phone. She just put on her coat and mittens and hat, and walked out the door. I thought she was going to her car to get something, but she never came back."

Aunt June looked out the picture window above the kitchen sink, angling her head so she could cast worried looks at the sky. "It's been hours."

The coffeepot was brewing perfectly, making soothing noises. The scent of fresh coffee filled the kitchen. Trey knew where he was. He knew who everyone was around him. He ought to be content, but apparently, the part of him who'd been born a cowboy wasn't dead. Someone on the ranch was unaccounted for, and that meant trouble.

"No one has seen her for hours?" he asked, and he looked at the sky with a rancher's eye. The storm, as bad as it was, looked like it was just getting started. "You're sure she didn't leave for a hotel in town? Maybe hitch a ride with some other guest?"

"This is hers." Emily held up a lady's purse. Even Trey knew a woman wouldn't leave without her purse. Emily handed him a Massachusetts driver's license. "Here's what she looks like."

Her signature was neat and legible. *Rebecca Cargill.* A pretty woman. Brown hair, with thick, straight bangs. As Trey took a moment to let the image settle into his brain, something about the expression on her face resonated with him. There was strain beneath that smile, a brave smile for the camera. *I know how you feel, darlin'. I was afraid I wouldn't pass the damned exam, either.*

She could have been stressed over any number of things, of course. It was fanciful of him to imagine he knew what the look on her face meant.

"I'm sure she's found shelter by now," Aunt Jane said.

Trey looked up from the driver's license in his hand. "If she hasn't, she'll die tonight. It's too cold to survive without shelter."

Aunt Jane made a horrified little sound, and Trey cursed himself. He hadn't always been so blunt. Hell, people had called him charming in high school and college. Now he had to work not to blurt out every thought that passed through his thick head.

His new uncle put a protective arm around his wife. "She's probably fallen asleep in the hayloft in the barn, and she just hasn't heard us calling for her. She'll be fine."

Emily darted a look at her mother, then pressed a cell phone into Trey's hand. "Here's her phone. It's not password protected. I didn't want to be nosy, but I thought there'd be more photos of her."

Trey started sliding his thumb over the screen, skimming through the photos stored on the phone. They weren't very personal. Seascapes of some rocky shoreline that looked nothing like the Texas coast. Distant children wading in the surf, silhouetted against a sunrise. A couple walking away from the camera, holding hands.

Finally, he saw a more typical snapshot of a woman holding a mutt. Trey was able to mentally compare this woman with the one in the driver's license. Not Rebecca Cargill.

He slid his thumb across the screen once more. The next shot was also of the mutt, but this time, it was held by the woman on the driver's license. Same pretty face. Same brown bangs. Same strain beneath the smile.

"She looks so young," his aunt said, looking over his shoulder. "I can't believe her license says she's twenty-four, can you?"

Emily was looking over his other shoulder. "I thought we could use that photo if we needed to call the sheriff."

That snapped Trey into action. He handed Emily the phone as he addressed his aunt and uncle. "You haven't called the sheriff? Dark's coming. There isn't much time to get a search party out here."

"Your foreman, Gus, he's got the ranch hands doing the searching. They've been stomping all over the grounds. She couldn't have gone that far on foot."

His foreman? Trey didn't have a foreman. Luke did. Trey hadn't set foot on the ranch in a decade. With his parents traveling ten months out of the year as retirees, Luke was the Waterson who ran the James Hill Ranch. Luke had decided to promote their longtime ranch hand, Gus, to foreman. Trey had only agreed over the phone. He supposed it was just by virtue of being a Waterson that Aunt June addressed him as if he were still part of the James Hill.

Trey turned to Emily. "The sheriff's got helicopters. We don't. Call them."

She ran to the house phone, the one that still hung on the kitchen wall as it had for the past twenty years or more.

His aunt patted his arm. "Honey, even the big Austin airport has been closed for hours now. They aren't puttin' anything up in the sky while ice is coming down out of it."

"That may be true, but we'll let the sheriff's office make that decision. I'm not a pilot. I'm just—"

He stopped himself, then turned on his heel and headed back to the front door, past his father's arm chair, past his mother's lamp, the one he and his brother had broken and glued back together. He picked up his sheepskin coat where he'd left it and shrugged it on.

Aunt Jane followed him. "You're just what?"

He chose a Stetson from the few hanging on pegs by the door. Whether his father's or his brother's, it didn't matter. The men in the family were all built the same. It would fit.

"I'm the only Waterson around here right now, and I'll be damned if a young woman is going to die on this ranch on my brother's wedding day."

He crammed the hat on his head, and headed out the door.

Chapter Three

I am not going to die today.

Becky forced herself to stop sliding down the tree trunk.

Stand up, Becky. Straight. At least pretend you've got some confidence, for God's sake.

The landscape of central Texas all looked the same. As far as she could see, stretches of scraggly brown grasses were broken up by scraggly waist-high bushes. The only color she saw was her own pastel-pink ski parka, chosen by her mother for appearance, not survival.

Who am I going to impress with this fake Cargill confidence, Mama? But she stayed on her feet.

She spotted an occasional cactus, which proved that Hollywood didn't lie when it put a cactus in a cowboy movie. But there was no shelter. As she'd driven the ATV four-wheeler away from the barn, ice had crunched under her wheels. Although the exposed skin of her face had been stung by the wind almost immediately, she'd kept driving, feeling like the control she had over the loud engine was the last bit of control she had in the world.

She'd turned up her collar and buried her chin in her jacket, and kept going. Somewhere. Away from the house that her mother would find. Far from the house and the barn and the sheds, she'd crossed acres of ground that shined in the afternoon sun, for they were completely covered in a thick but beautifully reflective sheet of ice. By the time the next bank of storm clouds had rolled in, hiding the sun and killing the enchantment of her ice world, she'd been low on gas.

She'd turned around—a U-turn that was easy in the right kind of ranch vehicle—and started heading back, but she hadn't made it far before the engine had run out of fuel.

That had been hours ago. Literally, hours ago. Forced to seek shelter as the wind picked up and fresh sleet started to fall, she'd left the bright blue ATV out in plain sight—as if she'd had a choice—and she'd headed for a line of trees. Gnarled oaks had seemed not too far away, and clusters of shockingly green cedar trees were interspersed among them. They weren't much, but they were more shelter than the ATV provided.

They weren't close, either. She'd begun sweating as she crunched her way across the uneven land, so she'd unzipped her coat to let any moisture evaporate. One thing she'd learned while skiing in Aspen was that getting wet when it was freezing outside led to intolerable cold. Even the most devil-may-care snowboarders would have to get off the mountain and change into dry clothes when they worked up a sweat.

The Aspen ski school had included some lessons on building emergency shelters. Too bad Becky didn't have ski poles and skis with her, because they'd been used to build every kind. Too bad there was no snow. In Aspen, the snow had been so deep, they'd dug a trench that they could sit in to escape from the wind.

Actually, the instructors had dug the trench. The rich kids and Becky had just sat in it. Some survival training. Maybe she would have learned more if her mother hadn't tracked her credit card so closely.

I'm going to die because some teenagers convinced me to buy them vodka. I missed the rest of the survival lessons because of vodka. And Mother.

She wouldn't cry. The tears would freeze on her cheeks.

She huddled against the trunk of the largest oak. It provided a little protection from the wind, at least, but the bare branches blocked nothing from above. Ice was falling from the sky, and it was falling on her.

She was so cold. She could just slide down this tree, take a little nap...and never wake up.

Stand up. Straight. For God's sake, Becky, your shoes can't hurt that badly. You will stay in this receiving line and shake hands with the club president before I give you permission to leave.

Becky stomped her boots to stay awake. With each thump of the ground, she heard the thud and she felt the jarring impact, but she realized, in an almost emotionless acknowledgment of fact, that she could no longer feel her feet.

I could possibly die today.

It would be so unfair if she died. Damsels in distress were supposed to be rewarded for trying to avoid a fate worse than death.

Well, she'd avoided going to the Bahamas with Hector Ferrique, all right, but she couldn't say if that fate really would have been worse than this one. For starters, although it sounded repulsive, she didn't know how difficult it was to have sex with a man one didn't like. She didn't know how difficult it was to have sex at all.

I'm going to die a frozen, twenty-four-year-old virgin. Out here, no one will find my body for months. Maybe years.

Terror made her colder. She would not give in to terror.

She needed to find some way to cover her head, because the snow or rain or sleet or whatever it was had started soaking through her ski hat. Its high-tech material was water-resistant, but apparently not waterproof. It could only repel the sleet for so many hours.

Becky looked around for smaller, broken branches on the ground and gathered them up, clomping her way from one to the other on her numb feet like a frozen Frankenstein. Her arms were growing numb, too, so she stuffed the twigs and thin branches haphazardly into a fork in the tree's lowest branch.

The bare sticks weren't going to block many drops of icy rain. Becky looked at the green cypress trees. She remembered them from her elementary school days. They were tall and narrow, green from ground to the top, and when she was a little girl, she'd been very aware that adults complained about them incessantly. She stumbled her way toward one now, thinking its evergreen branches would be useful stacked on top of her bare sticks.

The cypress tree disagreed. Becky got as good a grip as she could manage, but the flat, fan-like greenery slipped through her gloves like it was coated with wax or oil. Frustration made her eyes sting with more tears she couldn't shed. The exertion of tugging and pulling was making her too warm in her coat, yet her feet weren't warming up at all with the activity.

She tried a new approach, stomping on the lowest branches with her clumsy Frankenstein feet. She lost her balance several times and grabbed at the slick greenery to stay upright, but she succeeded in breaking a few branches off at the trunk.

In triumph, she carried them back to her twig roof and layered them on top. Then she hunkered underneath her little roof, hugged the oak tree's trunk to keep the wind from whirling around her, and she waited.

For what?

There was nothing to wait for. Help was not coming. No one knew her at that ranch house. Her mother had left her a message about how she'd tracked her to the Austin airport, but it would take her time to get here and more time to figure out that Becky had gone to the groom's ranch, not the Cargill mansion. It was getting dark already. Mother would not find her tonight.

I left the ATV out where anyone could see it overhead.

There was nothing flying overhead, however. No planes. No helicopters. Nothing would come searching for her by air, not while this storm raged. It could be another day or more before anyone at this ranch realized an ATV was even missing. When the storm was over, when they could search for her, it would be too late.

Sweet little Becky Cargill, the good and obedient child, had defied everyone's expectations and run away.

Now sweet little Becky was going to die.

* * *

Trey could find Rebecca Cargill. Of that, he had no doubt. The only question was, would he find her before she succumbed to the cold?

Hang in there, miss. I'll be there soon.

All he needed to do was guess where *there* was.

Had she left the house on foot, Gus and the ranch hands would have found her by now. Trey checked the barn as a formality, but he knew she hadn't taken a horse. The cowboys would have noticed one was missing, and the horse itself would have had the sense to buck her off and run back to the warmth of the barn.

That left the ATVs. Trey walked out the other side of the barn, turned up his collar against the biting cold and crossed the yard in long, rapid strides to the outbuilding where they'd always kept two ATVs. Sure enough, one was missing.

She'd left the spare two-gallon gas can on the floor. The sight of that gas can sitting on the concrete slab, forgotten, chilled Trey in a way the weather could not. If the gasoline was here, then she'd run out of gas *there*. The only way she'd make it back to the ranch was if he went and got her.

He'd known that, too, standing in the black-and-white kitchen.

He shut the shed door against the howl of the storm and started tying supplies onto the back of the second ATV. It only took him minutes, thanks to the miracle of having his memories of the ranch. He'd gone camping with his brother, when his brother had wanted to learn how to build a campfire. Gone fishing with his father, when his biggest problem had been deciding if he liked baseball or football better. Gone riding the fence line after his last football game as a high school senior, checking all seventy-five thousand acres of the main section of the ranch with the foreman. He knew how to survive outdoors on the James Hill Ranch.

Trey rolled the ATV out of the shed, shut the door as Miss Rebecca Cargill had, sat on the ATV as she had and started the engine. Tracks led in every direction from the shed, and with the ground hard with ice, none of them look fresher than any other. Instead, he looked to the horizon and tried to view the ranch through her eyes, so he could guess which way she'd decided to go.

The strained girl in the driver's license photo had needed to get away. She'd shown up to a wedding where no one knew she existed, and a phone call had sent her right back out the door. He couldn't imagine what from, but she'd run. He didn't know why, but she'd wanted to be alone. Badly. Immediately.

Straight. She wouldn't have headed to any of the scenic spots like a visitor would, nor had she gone to check the water level in the creek like a ranch hand. She'd only needed to get away from some kind of situation that had no other solution, so she'd left her phone and her purse and her life, pointed the ATV away from the house and gone.

She'd driven as fast as she could, eating up the gas. She'd wanted space. Freedom. So as Trey drove, he chose the most obvious routes and the most level ground, keeping the last signs of civilization at his back. At every decision point, he chose the easiest path, the one that would allow him to get as far away as quickly as he could. And when his gas tank was on empty, he saw the bright blue ATV parked in the middle of one of the most remote pastures on his land.

He'd found Rebecca Cargill, because he'd known that she'd been running from a fate she couldn't control. He understood that emotion.

The year that he'd turned nineteen, he had done the same.

Chapter Four

The storm was getting worse. Becky's time was getting shorter, her body getting colder, her lungs struggling as the air temperature dropped lower and lower. She wanted to sleep, oh, so very badly. Staying conscious in the constant, inescapable cold had worn her out in a way she'd never experienced. If only she could sink down among the oak's roots and sleep…

She would die. When she finally closed her eyes today, they would not open again.

She wasn't ready for that.

There was so much she hadn't experienced. Her entire life, she'd been waiting to start living. Wrapped in her demure cashmere sweaters, standing still by her mother's side, she'd been waiting for permission.

Waiting to meet a wonderful man. Waiting to have her own home, a permanent home, the kind that children would return to every Christmas, even when they were grown with families of their own. Waiting to live a life Becky knew existed for other people, one full of ups and downs, one she wanted to experience for herself.

Now she was waiting for a miracle.

She curled her arms around herself a little tighter and slid down the tree trunk. She looked up at the little roof that had kept the worst of the sleet off her head and shoulders. She was afraid her meager attempt at shelter had only delayed the inevitable. Really afraid.

She couldn't stay on her feet any longer, but she kept her eyes open, because she did not want to die yet. One little miracle, that was all she needed.

"Rebecca Cargill!"

She shuddered in misery as she imagined an angry male voice shouting her name. When the brain froze, did one suffer delusions before dying?

"Rebecca!"

Goodness, that sounded so real.

"Where are you, darlin'?"

It was a miracle. Somewhere close by, an angry man was her miracle.

Here, I'm here, she tried to call. Her jaw had been so tightly clenched against the cold, she couldn't force the muscles to relax so she could speak.

I'm here, I'm here, don't leave me. Please, don't leave.

She hugged the tree trunk instead of herself. Using her arms as much as her legs, she hauled herself back to her feet.

"Rebecca. Good God."

Before she could turn around, she was swept off her feet, wrenched away from her tree and held against a man's chest instead. She wanted to throw her arms around his neck, not because it felt like he might drop her, but because she was so grateful he was here. But her whole body was so stiff, her arms wouldn't obey her brain.

"Stay with me, darlin'. We'll get you warmed up. Just stay with me."

Did he think she'd rather stay with that tree? That tree had not cared that she was there. Now that she was not alone, she realized how very lonely she'd been. Hour after hour, she'd been the only living creature. Even the birds and insects had disappeared into their own shelters. It had been Becky and a tree. And ice.

His boots crunched over the ground as he carried her, and he seemed to take very long strides and move very quickly. It was disorienting, to suddenly be with another human being. She was no longer alone. Thank God, she was not alone.

"Okay, Rebecca? Are you with me?"

I'm trying to answer you. Give me a minute. Her jaw didn't want to unclench, but she nodded.

He looked down at her then, and over the scarf that covered the lower half of his face, under the brim of his cowboy hat, she tried to make eye contact, but he wore wide ski goggles.

Goggles. The concept burst into her brain like they were a new invention. How convenient goggles would have been while riding in the cold wind. Every inch of his face was covered, which made him seem incredibly smart to her. And beautiful. The mere fact that he was here made him the most beautiful person on earth.

"Was that a nod," he asked, "or just a shiver?"

She tried to smile at her beautiful rescuer, and she thought she'd succeeded in making her frozen facial muscles move, but he only looked away again, and kept walking.

He can't see my face, either.

She hadn't been smart enough to prepare for this

weather, so she'd had to make do. She'd pulled her ski hat down low and her collar up high, but her eyes had been exposed, so a few hours ago, she'd taken the long strings of her ski cap and wrapped them across her eyes and tied them behind her head. She could see out through the slit in between them.

They'd reached an ATV, a black one, and the man set her on the seat. "Let me get you a blanket— Hey!"

She had no balance. She'd tried to grab for the handlebar, but her disobedient body hadn't responded and she'd started to do a face-plant into the ground. The man had reflexes like some kind of ninja, because he caught her. Keeping one hand on her, he tugged at some gear behind the seat and produced a blanket. It looked like a giant sheet of aluminum foil, but Becky knew it was a thermal blanket.

Despite the term "thermal," it didn't look warm, and when the man sat behind her on the ATV and started tucking it around her shoulders, it didn't feel warm, either. He positioned her in his lap, moving her so that she sat sideways. He pulled her arms, one by one, over his shoulders, and she tried to hold on to his neck as she pressed her face into his icy coat.

He started the engine. "Just a few more minutes. Stay with me a little longer, Rebecca."

I'm not going anywhere, she tried to say. It sounded more like, "Nnn...ing...anywhere," but her rescuer chuckled and she felt the wonderful rise and fall of his chest through his coat. He tucked the top of her head under his chin and started the engine.

At the first bump, she found her arms were too weak to hold on, but he kept her from falling. With one arm wrapped tightly around her, he steered the vehicle one-handed. The metallic blanket kept some of the wind off her, but she was not warm, and it would take hours of this driving to get back to the ranch house. She wouldn't last.

She couldn't fight the cold any longer, but at least she would not die alone. A strange sort of contentment filled her.

I got my miracle. I was found.

Rebecca closed her eyes. Secure in her rescuer's arms, she drifted into black oblivion.

Trey felt the woman's arms slip, limp, from his neck.

He kept driving, keeping a sharp eye out for the landmarks that had not changed. There was an old cabin a half mile away, built near the banks of a creek. It had been abandoned for the past hundred years, except for the ranch hands who'd found it better shelter than none when caught in a sudden rain, and the rancher's sons who'd found it to be a handy hideout. The creek had not moved, of course, so Trey felt absolutely certain of where he was, where everything was around him.

Thank God. If there was ever a time he couldn't afford to get lost, now was it.

"Rebecca. Keep breathing." He gave her a little shake. "Breathe, damn it. That's all you gotta do, honey. Breathe."

The cabin was situated within a trio of the largest mesquite trees Trey had come across in either Texas or Oklahoma. Someone had added a corrugated metal roof decades ago, for which Trey was grateful. It probably wouldn't leak. The fireplace was stone, and it looked to be standing fairly straight after all these years. Trey parked the ATV under a mesquite, knowing it would still become coated in ice, but the need to care for equipment as well as one could had been ingrained in him since birth.

He held Rebecca in his arms and stepped warily onto the narrow porch. Nearly half the boards were missing, but the ones that remained held his weight as he lifted the simple wooden crossbeam and opened the door. Setting Rebecca on the floor on top of the silver blanket was like laying down a rag doll. Hypothermia could be deadly and quick. He had no time. He ran back to the ATV, grabbed everything with both arms and ran back into the cabin.

He shouted her name and ordered her to breathe as he unpacked the single sleeping bag and laid it on top of a second metallic thermal blanket. Then he started to strip. Basic survival rules required skin-to-skin contact to stay warm. There was no time to gather wood and build a fire. Traveling farther was out of the question.

He shed layers, starting at the bottom. His boots, her boots. Socks. Pants. Any cloth in direct contact with skin held moisture, so their underwear had to go, too. Modesty meant nothing when death was threatening.

The air was freezing in the cabin, but he didn't dare slip her into the sleeping bag until every last stitch of clothing was off. If he slid her legs into the bag while her coat was still on, the coat could drip water onto the bag, and then they'd never get warm in a damp cocoon.

"C'mon, Rebecca. Wake up. Help me out."

She responded to his voice by stirring on the silver blanket, but that looked like it was all he was going to get from her. Still, it was something. She wasn't deeply unconscious. Maybe she was just exhausted, if he was lucky.

He took off the last of his clothing and went to work on hers. Damn it all to hell, it was cold, and he started to shiver, although he'd taken off her hat, gloves and coat in seconds. He would've had a hard time getting all the tiny pearl buttons of her sweater undone in any circumstances—it was a garment guaranteed to make a man think a girl was off-limits—but with the shivering and the cold and the seconds ticking by, he quit on the second button and ripped the shirt down the front.

It took two shaking hands to undo her bra clasp and toss the damp elastic to the side. Immediately, in a move that was more about speed than gentleness, he rolled her into the sleeping bag, yanked the zipper closed from her feet to her waist, then jumped in beside her and yanked the zipper shut the rest of the way. The one-man bag was designed to cover the head and left only a circle for the face. Although there were two of them sharing the circle, he pulled the opening's drawstring, making that circle even smaller, keeping just that extra bit of cold out.

He'd just zipped his naked self in with an ice cube. He'd once had a girlfriend whose feet were always so cold, she slept in wool socks. This woman was cold like that all over. It scared him, honestly, to feel skin so cold over an entire body.

"Time to warm up," he said, and he started moving his hands over that icy skin, trying to stimulate her circulation without damaging any skin that might have gotten frostbite.

She didn't move. He kept at it. She would warm up, because he wouldn't let her do otherwise. This was the most effective method possible. The cabin protected them from the worst of the weather, although the chinks in between the log walls were plentiful. They shared a sleeping bag that was undoubtedly rated for far colder conditions than this. They would survive, even without a fire.

And without their clothes. Trey hated himself for thinking about such a thing in the circumstances, but as he pulled Rebecca tightly against himself, he was quite aware that she was a woman. He'd heard a soldier in Oklahoma complain over a glass of beer about survival training with men. His instructor had required everyone to go through the hypothermia drill, the entire hypothermia drill, to force the men to overcome their aversion to sharing body heat like this.

Trey tucked Rebecca's legs between his. She was an ice cube, but she was a smooth and feminine ice cube. Frankly, if he had to share some "full frontal" with a stranger, he couldn't deny that a young woman was a highly preferable hypothermia partner. Still, they'd probably be embarrassed as hell about this someday—which was better than being dead.

"Come on, wake up and share this awkward moment with me. Rebecca, wake up and talk to me."

They were on their sides, facing each other, nearly nose to nose. As he stroked up her back to the nape of her neck, he drew his head away a little bit to take a look at her face, now that it wasn't hidden under hat and strings and collar.

His hand stopped. She was almost unnaturally beautiful. Her face was heart-shaped, framed by bangs. Her brows and long lashes were a rich brown. But the hypothermia made her skin appear to be white porcelain, and her lips were blue with cold. The effect was startling, like holding a life-size version of the porcelain angel that his mother put on their Christmas tree.

Acting on instinct, Trey pressed his mouth to hers, keeping his eyes open, staying for a long moment to allow the heat of his mouth to warm hers. He didn't want this beautiful woman to have blue lips.

When he felt her lips softening under his, he lifted his head and brushed her hair behind her ear. Her lips looked a little less blue in her perfect, heart-shaped face. He wondered what color her eyes were.

"Come on, sleeping beauty. It's time to wake up. Let me see if your eyes are as beautiful as the rest of you."

Trey closed his eyes when he kissed her this time, as though it were a real kiss.

Rebecca woke up.

Chapter Five

When Becky had closed her eyes, she hadn't expected to ever open them again, yet here she was, awake. She was alive, but she was still cold. Shivering, and sick of it.

The first millisecond of opening her eyes was spent on realizing she was alive. The second millisecond was much more interesting. She was looking right at the jaw of a man, a real man with a five-o'clock shadow and a firm mouth. But as she stared at that mouth, the man kissed her.

Her eyes fluttered shut once more. His lips were soft, but the greatest miracle of all was that they were warm. Oh, so warm—and she craved heat right now.

She loved that mouth, so she kissed it tenderly, then opened to taste his upper lip, his lower. If his lips were warm, than his tongue was warmer, and she lost herself in a good, hot French kiss.

He pulled away, and she opened her eyes once more to focus on his mouth as he spoke.

"Okay, then. I'd say you're awake."

She looked into eyes as blue as the summer sky.

But she was still cold, and it felt as though she would never stop shivering again. His warm hand stroked down her back, stilling her momentarily as it passed, and then she shivered again.

Her breasts brushed against the warm skin of his chest. His warm skin was just that. Just skin. Nothing else. Awareness came swiftly. Her breasts were bare. Startled, she made a sudden movement, her legs sliding against his, smooth against rough. She was bare everywhere.

"Oh, dear. We're—we're—"

"Kind of awkward, isn't it? But we won't freeze to death."

She looked away from his blue eyes to focus on her surroundings. They were hiding in some kind of cocoon, but she could see through the opening. Somehow, he'd magically surrounded them with a log cabin while she'd been sleeping.

"Where are we?"

Gosh, that was such a cowardly question for her to ask. She should have addressed the fact that they were utterly naked, but she went with the log cabin. She was like Mother, after all, ignoring the difficult and unpleasant issues, even if they were more important. When her mother had heard that her latest paramour was already married, she'd pointed to a purse and asked about its designer. Becky was nude and so was this man, but she was asking about location.

"We're in the old Tate cabin. It was built more than a century ago. Lucky for us, they built them to last back then."

She could see outside through some of the spaces between the logs. She could *feel* outside, gusts of damp cold. She burrowed into the sleeping bag, which meant she tucked herself more tightly against his naked body.

"The wind can come right through this cabin," she said against the warmth of his throat.

"Some of it does. We'd be worse off if we didn't have these walls. That storm is getting bad outside."

Well, that was blunt. "How are we going to get back to the ranch?"

"You mean the house? We're not. We're going to stay right here, and stay warm."

"And naked?" There, she'd addressed the elephant in the room. She wasn't a total coward.

"It's the best way for us to stay warm."

Becky cared about being warm more than anything else. "I'm so tired of shivering. It hurts."

"I imagine it would. Hadn't thought about it before. Having your muscles clench like that would wear you out. Don't worry, you'll stop shivering. You're no longer unconscious, so that's an improvement. I'm glad you're awake."

His large hands roamed all over her body, as she realized they'd been doing this entire time.

"Are you really glad I'm awake?" she muttered. "Because it seems while I was asleep, you got me naked."

"Strictly survival, Miss Cargill. When I undress a woman for fun, I like her to be awake and fully participating."

Undressing for fun. She knew people got naked to have sex, of course, but she'd never considered that the actual taking off of clothes was one of the fun parts. He made it sound worth trying.

"And kissing me? That was strictly survival, too?"

"Your lips were blue."

The way his gaze dropped to her lips when he said it made her stop shivering for a second. He was a darned good-looking man, in that outdoorsy, cowboy kind of way. And he'd found her. He was her miracle.

"What's your name?" she asked, watching him as he watched her lips.

"Trey Waterson."

"Tell me, Trey, are my lips still blue?" It was the single most provocative thing she'd ever said in her life, and she'd said it to a naked man. She bit her lip, wishing the words back.

He drew his palm up her spine and over her shoulder, to rest on her neck. With his thumb, he caressed her jaw as he frowned at her mouth, taking her question seriously.

"They're more pink, but still too pale."

He bent his head, and kissed her again, softly, slowly, and without the openmouthed hunger she'd had. It was a lovely kiss, all the same, and she felt rewarded for having been daring.

Then he rested his head next to hers, so they simply looked at one another in the last of the winter twilight. They could have been friends sharing the same pillow, settling in for a long slumber-party chat. The corners of his mouth curved upward in a bit of a smile. "You're going to make it, you know."

She was still shivering, but at his words, she realized the waves of shivers were coming and going, their intensity diminishing with each return. Her jaw wasn't clenched to prevent her teeth from chattering. Her arm was wrapped around his warm body instead of clinging to the bark of a tree.

"Thank you." How terribly inadequate that sounded.

"I mean, thank you for my life. Not 'thank you' like you just passed the mashed potatoes. There ought to be a better word to say. Thank you so much, because I really didn't want to die."

"I know you didn't."

"It was practically suicidal, the way I left. I can see that now, but I wasn't trying to kill myself, honest."

"You were just running away. People don't think real hard when they do that."

She shivered, and pressed her entire body closer to him for shelter. For protection. She hid her face between his warm neck and the sleeping bag.

His hand swept down her back, firmly over her backside, too, to the back of her thigh. He lifted her thigh just a tiny bit, adjusted the position of her leg. "Can you feel your feet? Your toes?"

She flexed her ankle and tried to wiggle her toes. They didn't exactly respond with individual wiggles, but she felt them pressing into his calf muscle. "They're still there. I'll never take my feet for granted again. You should have seen me out there, clomping around like I had cement boots. It's so hard to walk when you can't feel your feet."

"I wouldn't have let you stay out there long enough to clomp anywhere."

She almost smiled at that, remembering how he'd scooped her off her feet before she'd seen him coming. Her shivers subsided, and she moved to be able to see his face once more. Night had come, but their eyes had been adjusting all along, and moonlight poured through the cracks along with the cold air.

"Thank you," she repeated.

His soothing hand had just traveled over her shoulder. He stopped and squeezed her upper arm. "You don't have to keep saying that."

"I need to. I'm so grateful, you can't imagine."

With a sigh, he turned a bit so he was laying more on his back. "All right, then. Get it out of your system."

He looked like he was waiting patiently for something. "Thank you?" she said tentatively.

He nodded, solemn. "You're welcome, Rebecca."

She stared at him in the moonlight.

After a minute, he raised an eyebrow. "Is that it? Are we done?"

She gasped, a tiny sound of indignation. "Are you joking about this?"

He started to laugh.

She gave his shoulder a little shove. "If it weren't for you, I would have died."

"I'm glad you didn't." As if that was the end of it, he started maneuvering around in the bag. "I'm going to unzip this for a second—"

"No! I'm not warm enough."

"Just far enough to get my hand out. You need to drink this water before it freezes solid. Your body is working hard to warm up. It needs water." He grabbed for a canteen that was in a pile of other stuff, jostling them both. She felt her breasts bounce a little against his arm. She was embarrassed, but he didn't seem to notice as he brought the canteen back inside and zipped the bag.

"I think we'll have to sit up so you can drink," he said. "Ready? One, two, three."

Of course, they had to move at the same time. One person couldn't sit up in the sleeping bag if the other was laying down. She tried, but curling up into a sitting position was more than her body was ready to do yet.

"It's okay. Let's try that again." Trey put his arm underneath her and lifted her with him as he sat up.

"Thank you," she said.

"I knew there were more thank-yous in there. Drink up."

She felt those blue eyes on her as she chugged, suddenly realizing how terribly thirsty she was. When she finished, he wasn't looking at her any longer. Instead, he was frowning at the night sky beyond the cracks in the log wall.

"The wind has stopped, but the clouds have cleared up," he said. "We're in for a cold one."

"It looks nicer than this afternoon."

He made a negative movement of his head and hand. She felt every bit of it, sitting so close to him. "Cloud cover keeps some of the earth's heat in. Today's clouds dumped their sleet and left, so now there's nothing to stop the temperatures from falling." He took the canteen from her and unzipped the bag, efficiently setting it outside again.

"Falling? It's going to get colder than it already is?" She could feel the fear crawling up her throat.

He looked at her with concern. After a long second, he kissed her forehead. "Listen to me. Outside, the temperature may fall, but you are not going to get colder. You and I are going to stay right here, safe and sound and warm."

He laid her back gently, following her down and settling her body against his again. *Safe and sound and warm.* As a seduction, no man could have had her more completely in his thrall. There was something about him that made her feel restless inside, reckless. They were alive, the only two people in the world, and she couldn't get enough of his deep voice and his soothing hands.

She set her hand on the back of his neck and tilted her face to his. She wanted to be *kissed and held and warm.* She let her eyes drift shut, anticipating the feel of his mouth.

"It's not us I'm worried about," he said. "It's the cattle."

"Oh." She blinked, feeling a little sheepish. Cows had never crossed her mind, but apparently, even if virginal little Becky Cargill was naked, a man's thoughts didn't stay on her. Hopefully, he hadn't noticed that she'd been about to kiss him. "What—um, what do cows do when it's this cold?"

"The foreman knew this weather was coming. He probably got a good portion into the calving sheds. The rest would've been driven into one of the pastures that has a deep gully. The cattle huddle in there to get out of the wind and basically do what we're doing."

"Nice to know I don't have the common sense of a cow. I drove into a wide-open space. I was so stupid. It would have served me right if—"

His finger pressed her lips, cutting her off. "Don't say that. Ever. Do you hear me?"

She was so surprised at his ferocity, she couldn't even nod. She just stared at him, his face a shadow in the night.

"You got yourself out of the wind as much as possible. You built yourself a shelter. You stayed alive. Give yourself some credit, Rebecca. You've got common sense and you must have a giant heap of willpower, because you were still alive when I found you. Thank you for staying alive until I could get there."

He moved his finger away from her lips only to cup her head in his hand. He angled her so he could kiss her, not so softly this time.

"Thank you," he said against her mouth, "for staying alive. This works both ways. You didn't want to die, and I didn't want to find you dead. I feel this insane relief that you are with me. You did a phenomenal job of staying alive. Thank you."

He was kissing her again almost before he was done speaking, and this time, she felt the sweep of his tongue. They were tasting, kissing, and she wanted to absorb all the intensity of him, all that heat, into her body. For the first time, she realized he wanted to feel her heat, too, finally greedy as she was.

I feel this insane relief that you are here with me. That was it, exactly. To hear him say what she was feeling was like another miracle.

He ended the kiss first, still cupping the back of her head in his hand, now panting slightly over her lips. "Rebecca, I—"

She waited, but words seemed to fail him, and he rolled a little bit away, onto his back. He exhaled, a sound that she feared sounded like he was disgusted with himself. Perhaps he thought she was too fragile for kissing? Perhaps he didn't know that she shared his feelings.

Perhaps she ought to be brave enough to stop waiting for her life to begin. If she wanted to kiss this man, perhaps she ought to tell him.

"You're welcome," she said quietly.

"What?"

"You said 'thank you,' so I'm saying 'you're welcome.' I want you to know that if kissing is your particular way of saying thanks, then I hope you have a whole lot of it to get out of your system. You are one great kisser."

The night was utterly, completely silent in the remote cabin. She heard her own heart beating, too loud because she'd been too bold.

He started to chuckle. Then he gave her a tight, friendly squeeze, and let her go. He planted a kiss on top of her head, like they were pals.

Swell.

"I've got to step out for a minute." He started unzipping the bag.

He was leaving her. Alarm made her turn abruptly and push up onto her elbow as he slipped out. "You can't go. You'll freeze to death."

He'd pulled a Navajo-style blanket out of the gear and thrown it around his shoulders like a cape before she could catch more than a glimpse of his nude, male backside in a stripe of moonlight.

He stomped on one boot. "I'm not going to relieve myself in front of you, darlin'. I'll be back in a minute. Stay warm."

He stomped on the second boot, and left.

Rebecca flopped back down, and shivered. So much for her first attempt to grab life by the horns. She'd told a man he was welcome to kiss her, and he'd left to go find a tree.

I will not cry.

That never would have happened to her mother. Rebecca had never wanted to be like her mother, until tonight. In this one thing, she now wished she were. She wished she had the power to make Trey Waterson crazy about her.

Rebecca, he'd called her, and she hadn't corrected

him. Rebecca sounded like a woman who was confident. A woman whom men would want to kiss. She was still sweet Becky Cargill, and she felt like she always would be.

Very quietly, and only for one minute, Becky turned her face into the material of the sleeping bag, and gave herself permission to cry.

Chapter Six

You are one great kisser.

She'd said that, looking at him with those doe eyes in that heart-shaped face, porcelain perfection brought to life. Rebecca had told him he was a great kisser, and Trey had very nearly blurted out every thought that passed through his stupid brain. *You're beautiful. We're alive. Let's have sex.*

Thank God, he'd controlled it. He was grateful for every trial he'd failed in the past ten years, because those situations had taught him the hard way to relearn how to think before he spoke. He knew he was often too blunt despite his best efforts, but at least tonight, when faced with the greatest challenge of all, he hadn't made an idiot of himself in front of Rebecca Cargill.

You are one great kisser.

I want to do a hell of a lot more than kiss you.

That would have scared her. She would have been on guard and anxious no matter how hard he tried to explain that he didn't mean those outbursts. It didn't mean they weren't true—it meant that he did know better than to say such things. He just seemed to know it after the words had come out.

When he'd first been kicked out of Oklahoma Tech, sex had been the one, sweet oblivion where he didn't have to *think*. He didn't need to monitor himself. *That lingerie looks sexy as hell. Come here, so I can take it off you.* The unfiltered truths that came out in bed seemed to make women happier, and for that, he was grateful.

But the girlfriends had been fewer and farther between over the years. It was difficult to date a woman when you couldn't reliably find her house, and he was tired of the strain. Relationships that did last a little while had to end before anyone got too serious about moving in, settling down, having children. Trey had cared about each girlfriend, enough that he wouldn't have saddled any one of them with a husband who couldn't count the change at the grocery store.

A relationship with Rebecca Cargill was out of the question. She was something special. It would be impossible to keep things purely physical with a woman whose emotions were so vulnerable, but whose personality was turning more playful with each passing moment.

She'd impressed him just by surviving. She'd impressed him again with how well she'd taken it in stride when she'd woken up, stark naked, with a man she didn't know. He'd tried to set a casual tone about the situation, and he was doing his best to keep his private parts private, shifting out of the way so she wouldn't be pressed against parts of a stranger's body that she wouldn't want to know so intimately.

She was recovering quickly, and the more she revived, the harder it got. There were times she seemed almost innocently unaware of the position of their bodies. Didn't she realize that she was sometimes cuddling into a position that would have allowed him to enter her easily, if they'd been making love?

No, at least twice now it hadn't seemed to occur to her, so he'd been the one who'd moved, who'd shifted, who'd tried to keep things polite, naked as they were in a sleeping bag.

Keep things polite. That's all he had to do. He had to lie down with a beautiful woman who thought he was a good kisser, and not touch her nude body while they kept each other warm by touching.

Hell. He didn't think a man with a good brain could make sense out of that one.

He had no choice. It was a waste of time to freeze out here, when there was no way to avoid another round of innocent, sensual torture with Rebecca. It was time for this landscaper to cowboy up.

He lifted the crossbar and went back to her dangerous warmth.

Rebecca's one-minute crying jag did not go unpunished. They never did. She should have known better than to think that without Mother around, it was safe to cry.

Her tears had ended with a shiver, right between the shoulder blades. Too late, she realized she should have been zipping up the bag when she'd been indulging in her tears. Trey hadn't left her uncovered, of course, but even the slit left by the open zipper let in too much cold for her system to handle. She zipped the bag with fingers that shook. She huddled, her arms crossed over her chest as they had been all afternoon.

The first time her teeth clacked together with one of those convulsive reactions to being cold, she panicked.

"Trey!" she cried into the darkness.

The door had opened the same moment as her teeth had chattered, but she'd called his name, cold and fear making her desperate, although he was coming back to her already.

He dropped to his knee beside her, Navajo blanket spreading over them both. "What happened? Talk to me." He started running his hands over the sleeping bag. "You're shivering again."

"Come back, p-please."

He was already hauling off his boots. He fumbled for the zipper a moment, then climbed in beside her.

His skin was not as warm as it had been before, not after his time outside. Rebecca squeezed herself to him, anyway, hanging on for dear life.

His hands began their familiar journey, over her shoulder, down her spine, over her backside and to her thigh. The motion was steady, unrushed, when she was frantic to get warm. He used his voice like he used his hands, speaking calmly and evenly.

"I'm sorry, baby. You're going to be okay. It won't take long this time. Those shivers are going away."

The mantra repeated as his hand smoothed its way back up her body. "I'm sorry, baby. You're going to be okay. It won't take long."

"What took you so long?" she said against his shoulder.

"I was only gone a few minutes."

"It was an eternity."

"I'm sorry. I didn't realize you were that vulnerable. You're dehydrated, and you need food, so I guess your body is just not going to be able to handle much cold for a while, not until we get you watered and fed."

"Watered and fed like a good little cow." She had to laugh at his cowboy talk.

"That's right." She could hear the smile in his voice as he kept stroking her, soothing her, caressing her.

Petting her. *He's probably petting me like I'm a horse.* Even that thought made her smile. He was a cowboy, so she couldn't expect anything less. She didn't want anything less. This felt perfect.

"We'll warm up for a while, then we're going to eat and you're going to drink more water, okay?"

"I wish the warming part went faster. I swear, I want to sink my teeth into your shoulder. You know, to keep them from chattering."

"Yeah, well… God." He cleared his throat. "We'll talk to keep your teeth from chattering. Where do you live?"

"Boston, this season. Cape Cod. I'm a city slicker. Isn't that what you cowboys call us?"

His hand stopped. Changed course. "I'm not a cowboy."

She felt, instinctively, that was not true. "How do you know this ranch so well?"

"I was raised here, but I live in Oklahoma now. I've got a landscaping business, nothing large."

Feeling warmer, she cuddled into him, sliding her knee up the outside of his thigh. His hand stopped her knee when it reached the top of his thigh. He smoothed his way down her calf and ankle, then held the arch of her foot in his warm hand for a moment. It felt nice, but it kept her from positioning her knee in a more comfortable way.

"What do you do for a living?" he asked, his voice low and deliciously husky.

"My mother likes me to accompany her to her engagements."

He was quiet. She imagined a cowboy or a landscaper wouldn't know what to say to that.

The tip of her nose was cold, so she nuzzled it into the dip above his collarbone. "I don't have a real job. It would be nice, but my mother thinks it would make her look bad. She respects old money, the kind where someone's ancestors earned it a few generations back. She likes people who don't have to work."

"But you think it would be nice to have a job? Most people would think that not working was nice, if they could get away with it."

"It's a lot of work, to keep an income flowing so that you don't need to work."

Her mother was always on alert, always aware of who was hot on the social scene. Clothes and hair and body were in a constant state of updating for Mother. For Becky, they never changed. The right events had to be attended, so that invitations would be extended to others. Events were where Mother met men, men with old money. It was a full-time job, and Becky was her best accessory.

"Do you mean investments?" Trey asked. "Interest?"

"Something like that." Rebecca thought of Hector Ferrique, lending them one of his vacation homes. He wouldn't have lived in it this winter, anyway, but nothing was free.

"So, how are you related to the groom?" she asked, changing the subject just like Mother had taught her. "You have the same last name."

"Brother. You're the bride's sister?"

"Same last name, but no. Stepsister. Not even that. Our parents divorced fifteen years ago." She kept it light. Matter-of-fact.

"It's nice that you two are still close. That makes you a better sister than I am a brother."

Take the compliment, Becky. When someone has a good impression of you, for God's sake, don't correct them.

Mother was right. Mother was always right. Except, when Becky had been about to die, alone by a tree, she'd thought her life with Mother was all wrong, wrong, wrong.

She took a long, slow breath, in through the nose, out through the mouth. She breathed in cold Texas air and warm male skin. She breathed out...so much that she'd been holding inside.

"I'm not a good sister at all."

His hand squeezed her instep. "I'm sure that's not true."

"I crashed the wedding. I hadn't seen Patricia in years, not until Mother had the chance to take a little trip a few months ago and needed somewhere for me to go. She dropped me off at the Cargill place."

"You needed a babysitter?"

"We were between houses. She was kind of between men. She's kind of a professional wife."

"That's a lot of 'kind of.'"

"She's been married four times, to really wealthy men. Five, if you count my father."

"You don't count Daddy Cargill? How rich are the other men when an oil baron doesn't make the top four?"

"I'm Patricia's stepsister, remember?"

He was silent a moment. "Yeah, you told me that, Rebecca."

"It's Becky. Just Becky. I'm not even a Cargill. My father is some lazy son of a bitch bastard who didn't know his right from his left."

"Your mother's words?"

"Correct. It is the only time swearing is acceptable."

"Your mother's rules?"

"Correct again. But she was married to him, so she's been married five times."

"Going on six?" He was holding her instep tightly.

"I don't think so. She's only forty-five years old, and she looks smashing, to be honest. But I think those men put her in the bedmate category now. They like to take her on vacations. She looks good, and she can be a great conversationalist over dinner, a good travel partner. But when it comes to marriage, those men expect someone who is child-bearing age. You've seen the gray-haired guys who marry a supermodel who has their baby. The guy can be sixty years old, with some pregnant wife his daughter's age. I think it proves their virility, and all that."

Trey didn't speak for the longest time. Becky realized she had stopped shivering and felt warm again, but she missed the soothing stroke of his hand, although the way he held her instep was very…nice. Strangely intimate, to have her feet warmed by a man.

She set her hand on the rounded shaped of his shoulder. He remained still, so she drew her hand down his arm. It had to be twice as big as her arm, fascinating in all its hills and valleys. She followed it all the way to his hand, made a little U-turn on the back of his hand with her fingertips and started sliding back up again. Stroking him was as soothing as being stroked by him.

"That is the life you know?" he said, with that husky note back in his voice. "Old men who expect young women to marry them for their money?"

"And prove their virility by walking around with a pregnant belly in the latest designer's maternity wear. Don't forget that part."

"But you left, and crashed a wedding."

Her hand rounded his shoulder. She could press hard into his muscle; there was so much of it. With a deeper touch, she traveled down his biceps. "Mother wanted to go on another vacation. Christmas in the Caribbean. Who wants to spend Christmas in the Bahamas?"

"Apparently, my brother and your sister do."

His dry humor surprised her. "One, she's really not my sister, remember? And two, it's their honeymoon. That's different. A regular Christmas should be cozy at home. I want a big Christmas tree with a family all around it, opening gifts and drinking hot chocolate, like you see on TV."

"You haven't had that, not even as a child?"

"Kind of. When my mother married into the Lexingtons, they put on the big family Christmas. I always kind of felt sorry for the staff, though. It was like we were supposed to enjoy a big Christmas, but they weren't. They made all our beds while we opened the presents. We ate the big meal while they stood in the dining room, wearing the black-and-white uniforms to serve the turkey and mashed potatoes. I tried to help clean up the wrapping paper one year, but that was a big no-no. My mother said they were paid time and a half on holidays, and not to do their jobs."

He kissed the top of her head. She was used to being treated like a child, but with him, she didn't like it.

"You don't have to feel sorry for me," she said. "I'm not a child anymore."

"I know. That kiss was for the little girl you used to be. You tell her I think she's a sweetheart for being sympathetic toward people who have to work on Christmas."

He made her heart hurt, saying that. She wanted to cry, but crying never turned out well. She lapsed into silence, determined to close off that little piece of her heart. She could think about it some other time.

He let the silence last a long while before he spoke. "You listened to a message on your cell phone before you took off. That's what my cousin said."

Becky only nodded in reply. It was easier to ignore that little ache in her heart if she concentrated on his body. She kept pressing her fingers into him, sliding down his forearm.

"Rebecca, why did you run away? What were you so afraid of?"

When she reached his hand, she slid her foot away, and interlocked her fingers with his. It was as if her hand wanted intimacy, but her voice stayed light, joking, impersonal, even though she spoke the truth. "It was simply awful. I handled it so badly."

She tried to laugh at herself, a society laugh like her mother would have used. *Oh, kids these days. They can be so crazy. What can you do about it except wait for them to outgrow those teen years?*

"I ran away because I didn't want to be forced to

spend the week naked in bed with a stranger. Ironic, isn't it?"

She laughed as if she had a martini in her hand and diamonds around her throat, but Trey, he didn't laugh at all.

Chapter Seven

"So your mother is a—" Trey swallowed the only food he'd thrown into the survival gear. It was beef jerky, which took forever to chew, and which gave him a chance to search his lame mind for the right term. "Your mother is a call girl?"

"Oh, my goodness. Not at all. She would never consent to a one-night stand. Men court her. They woo her. They buy her diamonds and take her to the Riviera."

"Here, finish this water bottle. They take her to the Riviera without sleeping with her?" He knew he sounded as skeptical as he was.

"She always insists on separate rooms. It makes them all the more eager to take her on trips. They're hoping she'll consent to sleep with them, I'm sure. Until the past few years, though, she held out for marriage, every time. She's a big believer that men won't buy the cow if they get the milk for free. Now she holds out for the long-term affair. A house. Vacations. You've got to show her you mean to keep her around for a while."

As if Rebecca hadn't just told him about a way of

life that violated everything he'd been raised with, she took a hearty bite out of the beef jerky. "This is the best beef jerky, ever, and I'm not just saying that because I'm starving."

Trey scrubbed his hand over his face. He was having a hard time being sure he'd heard what he thought he'd heard. She reported it all so factually, without seeming to be involved herself, yet she was telling him about her life. A real life. She really lived with a woman who'd made a career of marrying rich men.

"Where do you fit in the picture? You said your mother likes you to accompany her to what, exactly?"

The thought was there, of course, of sick bastards who would sleep with a mother and move on to the daughter. It happened. That it could happen to Rebecca made him feel ill. Angry. Willing to fight.

"It's taken me a long time to figure it out, but I'm her proof that she's fertile. Men want to prove their virility with the young wife, right? Well, as long as she has little Becky around, I make her look younger than she is."

"Little Becky? You're twenty-four."

She seemed startled by this, sitting up even straighter in his arms.

They were sitting up in the sleeping bag to eat and drink, but the bag wasn't wide enough for them to sit side by side, hip to hip, without stretching the fabric. Instead, Rebecca was a little in front of him. Trey had managed to jerk some of the sleeping bag's material up between his legs, covering his crotch a bit, so she could sit between his thighs without her backside pressing directly against— Well, that would have taken awkward to a whole new level.

"How'd you know I was twenty-four?"

He bit off another chunk of the beef jerky. It bore zero resemblance to the garbage one could purchase at an Oklahoma gas station, because it was made here on the ranch. He handed it back to her. "I saw your driver's license. Eat some more."

She obeyed, and knowing more of her life story, it almost bothered Trey that she was so compliant. She needed the food more than he did, however, so he couldn't complain that she was obediently eating it.

"My driver's license," she repeated, sounding disappointed. "No one ever guesses my age. For years now, I've been passing as eighteen. Mother encourages it."

"You don't have the body of a teenager."

She stopped chewing.

Trey cursed himself, and the stupid way he blurted things out without thinking.

"I don't?" she asked, and damn if she didn't sound hopeful.

He ran his hand down her thigh as he had a hundred times tonight. "Not that I'm trying to—but it's pretty obvious—yes, you're built like a woman." He scrubbed his face once more. "This is a hell of a conversation."

"If you'd seen me with my clothes on, you wouldn't think I was all grown up."

He remembered the cashmere and its little-girl collar. All those damned buttons. "By the way, I ruined your sweater."

She waved a hand dismissively. He couldn't see it, of course, but he could feel the movement in the sleeping bag. "There's more where that came from. She dresses me very demurely."

"Why don't you buy your own clothes, then?"

"She tracks my credit card."

The final piece of the puzzle fell in place. *It would be nice to have a real job,* she'd said. She was ready to be free of her mother's life, but she had no way to do it on her own. He'd crashed at a teammate's house when he'd first left college. He'd slept on a friend's couch for a couple of months when he started working for a landscaper, so he could save up enough for that first month's and last month's rent on an apartment.

Rebecca's mother made sure she had no money of her own. When she'd been backed into a corner, Rebecca had run to a former stepsister for help. It hurt Trey to know that her closest relation, her only hope for an ally, was a former stepsister. Poor, isolated Rebecca.

"I'd assumed you were running away—"

"—from a fate worse than death," she finished for him.

It wasn't what he'd been about to say.

"When I was hugging that tree and waiting for a miracle, I had a lot of time to think. I realized that I've been too patient. All this time, I've been waiting for permission to leave."

They'd eaten all the food and drunk all the water they wanted. There was nothing left to do but sleep or talk. Rebecca leaned against him, like he was her support, and she seemed to settle in for a long chat.

Grateful for the material that kept his awareness of her body from being too obvious, he listened. He caressed her, because it had become a habit. And he dropped an occasional kiss on her shoulder, because she was in his arms and she didn't object and her skin felt smooth beneath his lips.

"I read a newspaper article about the foster care system," she said, as though talking in the dark like this was something they routinely did. "It focused on foster kids who were aging out of the system. That was the term they used, aging out. I realized that was what I'd been doing with my life, waiting to age out. Eventually, I'd have to get too old for my mother to keep pretending I was eighteen. I thought she'd release me, and I'd finally get to go to college or get an apartment, or something exciting like that."

Caress. Kiss. Listen.

"But I found out at six this morning what aging out meant. She'd told Hector Ferrique that I was twenty-one. He likes his women young, she said, but he doesn't want to risk any messy legal troubles. To be told I was twenty-one when he'd assumed I was younger…it was a little Christmas present from her to him."

Rebecca crossed her arms over her chest in that self-preserving way she had. He crossed his arms over hers, and held her tightly.

No one will hurt you while I'm around. But he didn't say it out loud.

"We were to fly out at four this afternoon. His home in Bimini had a marvelous location, she assured me, but only two bedrooms. It would be best if I stayed in the master suite with Hector. Mr. Ferrique. I should continue addressing him as Mr. Ferrique, unless he asked me to do otherwise. It makes me seem younger, you see. I'm already on the pill, of course. She's had me take that for years, just in case. I'm not to bother Hector about any other precautions."

Trey knew every inch of her skin, every shiver of every muscle. He knew exactly when her first tears fell. He kissed her shoulder, and kept her wrapped tightly in his arms, and swore to himself that Hector Ferrique would never touch her.

"At four this afternoon, I was nearly dead. You think sleeping with a man in Bimini is the worst thing in the world, but then you freeze, slowly, and you start to think that maybe it wouldn't have been that bad. Maybe your life was worth screwing some old guy."

She was crying in earnest now, and Trey thought his heart would break with hers.

"I was waiting for permission to grow up. I didn't deserve it. I was acting like a child when I ran away."

"It was a jail break. Rebecca, you were trying to get out of a kind of prison."

"When she called, she said I hadn't fooled anyone, and she knew I was in Austin. 'That bitch Patricia didn't invite you to her wedding.' I hung up the phone, and I had to go. Just go, anywhere. I wasn't thinking straight. It was crazy."

"You're allowed to have moments of craziness. Everyone does." God knew he had. Stupid, stupid moments that could have gotten him killed. Hanging out with other kids who knew they were flunking out. Drinking moonshine. Walking down the center line of a highway.

Rebecca hadn't been thinking straight, but she hadn't intended to run out of gas with an ice storm on the horizon. He'd practically dared the universe to kill him.

"You've lived to tell the tale, Rebecca. You've got a chance now to live your life, your way. I know you'll grab that with both hands."

It was more than he'd done. He'd stayed in one spot. Scared every time his brain let him down, he'd stuck to the undemanding life he'd stumbled into. Spreading mulch. Pulling weeds. Eating instant soup from the convenience store that he could see from his apartment, the one he couldn't get lost walking to.

Ten years later, he owned his own trucks and employed a dozen men, but he was still that same guy, stuck where life had dropped him.

But Rebecca Cargill, she was special. Ten years from now, she would be living her own life, free from her mother's demands. That life was starting here. He was witnessing a new beginning, her independence emerging as he sheltered her in his arms.

God, how he wanted her. He, who never left his safety zone, wanted her, a woman who could choose to go anywhere and be anything she wanted, after they survived this storm.

After they spent this night together.

He could seduce her. When she'd first regained consciousness, she'd kissed him with a hunger that could burn them both up. It would be a pleasure to change the tone of these caresses. He could touch her in a way that would ignite the flames that simmered inside her. They'd have a night to remember, because the one thing he'd never had to doubt about himself was that women enjoyed him in bed. But outside of bed...

There was a reason he'd never come home. As one of the top football players in the nation, the city of Austin had known his name. The whole town had been disappointed in him, their native son. He hadn't wanted to face that, so he'd waited a decade for the city to forget him. He couldn't drag Rebecca into a life with a man that cowardly.

He hadn't been good enough for any other girlfriend in his own estimation. Not good enough for Elaine, who'd passed the bar while he'd only passed high school.

Not good enough for Bonnie, who'd loved to throw a party, always bringing in new people, new faces, too many for him to learn, too confusing for him to mingle with. Not good enough for Robin, who'd been able to teach anyone to read piano music. Anyone but him. He'd pretended he wasn't even trying when she'd pulled him over to the piano bench to show him how to play.

What made him think he'd ever be good enough for Rebecca Cargill, whose life lay before her, pure potential?

But God above, he could make her happy for one night.

The temptation was too much. He dropped one last kiss on her bare, delicious shoulder, unzipped the sleeping bag and left.

"Where are you going?"

Becky was mortified. Trey was leaving her, going into the dangerous, freezing outdoors. What had she done? What had she said?

"I need to make you a fire," he said, blanket wrapped around him as he stomped into his boots. "I have to gather the wood before it storms again."

"It's too dark. What if you get hurt? How would I help you?" She sat up in the sleeping bag, her face filling the circular opening, tracking his every move as if she could jump up and stop him.

"I won't get hurt. I've got a flashlight, and we've got mesquite trees right here. I'm just going to pick up what wood is already on the ground."

She felt like a child who was being left alone to face the monsters under the bed. Her monster was the cold wind, and it was forcing its way into the cabin, driving through the walls. Without Trey to keep it at bay, it would get her.

"I'll be right outside the door," he said, bending to scoop his sheepskin coat off the floor.

"Don't go, please. We're plenty warm. We don't need a fire." She sounded like a child, petulant and pleading.

He smacked the coat against the cabin wall, sending ice crystals showering to the floor. "We need a god-damned fire. Our clothes are frozen." He picked up a smaller item from the pile of clothes, and closed his fist around it. It made a slight noise, like a piece of tissue paper crumpling.

He hurled it at the wall, the blanket falling from his shoulder. In the moonlight, she saw his arm muscles flex in chiseled relief, the power in his throw impressive and intimidating.

But he didn't leave. One by one, he smacked each item of clothing against the wall to shake off its ice, then hung it on a peg or nail. There was a neat row of wooden pegs to the right of the fireplace, but there were also random nails driven in various places, no doubt hammered there over the years to serve as hooks for hunting or fishing gear.

The item he'd hurled against the wall, she saw, was plaid boxer shorts. Her bra, pink and plain, hung on the nail next to them. The sight should have made her blush.

She bit her lip. The sleeping bag was already less warm without Trey by her side.

"I thought it was strictly survival," she said, "and no clothing was the best way to stay warm."

"It is. It was." He crouched by the hearth and twisted to look up the chimney, checking that it was clear. The blanket shifted with his moves, and she knew it wasn't keeping his body heat in very well. She could hardly stand to watch. He would freeze.

She didn't want him to freeze. It was painful, the way the muscles shook. It was scary, the way feet and hands lost all sensation. She didn't want him to go through it.

"Get back in the sleeping bag," she pleaded. "We don't need our clothes."

"Yes, damn it all to hell, we do." He glared at her in the patchy moonlight. "This closeness is killing me, Rebecca, because it's not close enough. I want to touch you. I want to be inside you. Damn it, if we had clothes, a frigging pair of boxer shorts, anything—" He cut himself off.

She stared at him. His breaths came loudly, harsh in the cold air, puffs of vapor disappearing as quickly as he breathed each one out. He closed his eyes and dropped his head.

"I didn't mean to say that." He grit the words out through his clenched jaw.

He didn't want to have sex with her. Her touch had driven him out into the cold.

"I'm sorry," she said, in a small voice. "I won't touch you. I'll try not to move at all. Please, don't freeze to death because of me. I'll be good."

"You'll be good?" He looked away from her and laughed, a short sound with no humor. "Rebecca, it takes two. You'll be good, but I'll try to change your mind. I'll succeed. We'll make love."

Yes, let's make love.

The thought was immediate, and true. Now she was the one who breathed harshly into the cabin.

Trey took one look at her face and left the cabin, slamming the door behind him.

Chapter Eight

The wood was too wet too burn.

Rebecca watched Trey spread the sticks and branches out on the floor, much as he'd spread their clothes on the wall. He'd said it might dry enough for them to get a fire started in the morning.

When he finished, he stayed crouched before the fireplace in the Navajo blanket, brooding at the cold hearth as if it had dancing flames to ponder.

She'd had enough time to ponder things herself after he'd stomped out the door, and she'd reached two conclusions. First, after hours of holding her nude body, he'd apparently felt some sexual urges toward her, and they'd horrified him so much, he was risking hypothermia to avoid her touch.

Second, she'd realized that when he was out of her sight for more than a minute, she was irrationally petrified that she would die. She knew that wasn't healthy, but the bottom line was that she'd been close to dying before he'd found her. Now that Trey was here, she was alive. It was unfortunate for him that he found her so repulsive, because she was going to stick to him like glue, anyway.

"Are you going to come back in the sleeping bag now?" she asked.

"In a minute."

"Come in now, and we'll trade places."

That got his attention. "You can't spend the night in this blanket, not even for a short time. It's not warm enough for me, or else I'd use it. Look, Rebecca, you don't have to be afraid of me. I say things without thinking, but I don't have any problem controlling myself. Forget that part about me trying to change your mind. I won't try to seduce you, and I'd never force you to do anything."

"Okay, fine." He didn't need to keep telling her how much he didn't want to touch her. "I need to use the blanket for something else, if you know what I mean."

He frowned at her for a moment, until understanding dawned. "I don't think it's a good idea for you to go outside on your own."

"You made me drink a canteen and a bottle of water. I don't have an option."

He sighed and got to his feet. She wriggled to sit up in the sleeping bag. He was so darned tall, that only put her face above his knee.

He announced his plan. "We'll stay as warm as we can under this blanket together. We'll just step onto the porch. Half the boards are missing, so you can find a spot—"

"No way. I'm not that fragile."

"I'm not risking it."

"You think you're going to stand next to me?" The idea was outrageous.

"I won't look." He had the nerve to act like she was the one being unreasonable.

"Trey! I'm not going to be able to go if you're standing there."

"This is survival. You can't stay warm in the sleeping bag by yourself. I'm not sending you out there alone in a blanket."

This was it, a new all-time low in her life of being obedient. She would have to pee where she was told.

To heck with being good; she let herself get mad. "Actually, I've been staying warm in this sleeping bag all by myself while you've been out there gathering wood to get away from my repulsive, non-teenager-like body. I've had a lot to drink and eat, and I'm feeling much stronger. This entire debate is ridiculous. Maybe little Becky would put up with this, but Rebecca won't." She unzipped the sleeping bag and stood tall.

Okay, it was the first time she'd actually ever stood next to him, and she hadn't realized just how huge the guy was. Still, she had righteous indignation on her side. She yanked the blanket from around his body and wrapped it around herself. Head high, she opened the cabin door.

"Your boots!" he hollered at her.

"Keep the sleeping bag warm." She slammed the door behind her.

Holy moly, it was cold outside. She two steps to the nearest gaping hole in the porch and quickly took care of business. Thirty seconds, max, was all she was outside, but that was long enough to know he'd been right about the boots. Her feet were freezing on the planks of the porch, so she ran inside.

He was holding the flap of the sleeping bag open. She

ditched the blanket and dove inside, plastering every square inch of her body to his. All thoughts of sex and modesty were irrelevant.

"Oh, my gosh, it's cold out there."

"Told you so." He sounded grumpy and just a little bit arrogant, but the fact that he was holding her made her heart hurt less.

"Fine," she said generously. "You were right. My feet are frozen."

He didn't laugh at that, but slid her up his body until he could reach her foot with his hand. He squeezed gently. "I'm afraid you might have frostbite."

"They're warming up already. All of me is warming up. I think I'm just normal cold, not cold cold."

"I think you're right."

"It's a relief to just be normal cold." She owed it all to him, and she'd never, ever forget that. "Thank you."

Because he'd slid her high enough to reach her feet, her head was above his. She could have tucked the top of his head under her chin the way he'd been tucking hers, so she kissed his forehead gratefully, and she did.

The new position placed his mouth just above her breasts.

"Are we back to the thank-yous? You really need to get those out of your system." He said it lightly, with mock grumpiness, but his breath fanned across the top of her breasts as he spoke, and she couldn't laugh.

"Rebecca," he said, so quietly she might have imagined it, but she felt his breath with each syllable. He put his hands on her hips and drew her back down until they were once more face-to-face, the way they'd started.

This time, Rebecca paid attention to where and how they touched. Nose to nose, they were nearly shoulder to shoulder, and her arm wrapped around him naturally. Her feet tangled with his calves, but the lower half of his body did not touch her. She realized he'd been keeping their distance with a hand on her hip, or on her knee, or by rolling away, the entire time. She wriggled forward, and although his hand was on her hip, he did not stop her from getting too close.

Against her thigh, she felt him. She was no expert, none at all, but she'd read the educational books, and knew men got erections. She'd read novels and knew about velvet over steel. That was surely what she was feeling, heavy against her thigh, warmer than all the other warm skin on his body.

Her lower belly reacted with something very like a shiver, and she nestled closer to him, the tips of her breasts flattening against his chest. In the dim light, she saw his eyelids close halfway, as if they were heavy with sleep, but otherwise, he stayed very, very still.

"I thought you didn't want to have sex with me," she whispered.

"I didn't say that. I know I didn't say that, because I've never had that thought."

Confusion warred with the sweet sensation of being desirable. "Then are you committed to someone? Do you have a girlfriend?"

"No. It just wouldn't be a good idea. You're about to start a whole new chapter in your life. Starting tomorrow, you've got a lot of thinking to do. You have to decide where you're going from here."

"Maybe I've decided the first thing I want to do is have sex with you." She couldn't believe how easily she said those words. The darkness gave her courage, perhaps, although she wished she could see his face better.

"You don't know me."

"I know so much about you. You saved me."

"I think there might be a little bit of that syndrome—what is it called?"

"Stockholm syndrome?"

He chuckled, breaking the tension, and gave her hip a playful push. "No, that's when you fall in love with your kidnapper. Nightingale, that's the one."

She wrinkled her nose. "Florence Nightingale? Falling in love with your nurse?"

"With whatever person saved you." He spoke kindly, tucking her hair behind her ear. "I don't need sex from a woman who'd really just be saying thank you. You'd regret it in the morning."

She let that sink in. It sounded so reasonable. She *was* grateful to him for saving her.

Into the silence, Trey spoke with authority. "Get some sleep. You're exhausted."

Frowning, she didn't object when he rolled her away with a gentle push. She turned her back to him, so they were spooning in the sleeping bag—except, of course, he kept his hand at her waist and he scooted his hips back, away from the curve of her backside. It wasn't what she wanted.

Tomorrow, they'd build a fire and dry their clothes. They'd drive the ATV back to the house. She wondered if his family would still be there, the aunt and the uncle. And then the lightbulb went off in her head.

"You're wrong, Trey." She propped herself awkwardly on her elbow and twisted her face toward his, although it was dark. "What if your uncle had found me? Do you think I'd be so grateful that I'd want to have sex with him? What about your cousin Emily? Do you think if she'd come riding up on that ATV, I'd suddenly have a thing for her? That Nightingale syndrome is an insult. You're saying I'd want to be with any person who found me."

He rubbed his jaw, so heavy with stubble that she could hear the abrasion in the dark. "What if another cowboy found you? A guy your age, blond, good-looking?"

He had no clue, this man she'd gotten to know so well. She frowned at him and hoped he could see it. "That all depends. When I tell him about my life, does he listen, or does he interrupt? When I'm mad at my own stupidity, does he tell me I'm a good survivor, or does he warn me not to do it again? Look, I'm not going to beg you to have sex with me, but don't insult me. I know what I want, and I want you, Trey Waterson, not just any old rescuer."

Tears were blurring her eyes, not that there was much to see in the night, but then one plopped on Trey's arm, so she knew he was aware. "And just so you know, I'm not crying because I'm sad. I'm so *damned* frustrated with you. I couldn't have sex with you now if I wanted to, I'm so mad. So good night."

And then she turned her back to him once more, and dropped her head onto his arm to use as a pillow.

She was determined not to cry in the arms of the man who refused to be her lover.

Trey was stunned.

Rebecca was furious with him, lying against him with a tension he could feel humming along the length of her body.

But he felt a different emotion entirely. She'd slayed him. She'd hovered over him in the dark and shown him what a fool he was with a few choice words. She was no innocent babe, unsure of the world. She knew herself, and she knew him, and he'd never been so wrong before.

She wanted him, and he was starving for her.

"Rebecca," he murmured, and he kissed her perfect ear. He inhaled the warmth of her neck, exposed as it was while she lay with her back to him. He tasted the skin of her shoulder, savoring it, saying her name, apology in every syllable. "Rebecca, Rebecca."

He moved his hand to cup her breast, holding its soft weight, learning her every dimension. "I didn't know how you felt until you told me. I want you, too. I know you, too."

He'd be her lover, because she'd demanded it. He wasn't surprised when she turned toward him and pressed him flat on his back. In the safety of their sleeping bag, she lay atop him, chest pressed to chest, her knees on either side of his hips.

She slid slowly up the length of him, and exhaled shakily. Sexily. Then she moved again, gliding up his length, and he sensed she was too close to the edge already. He gripped her hips to stop her motion.

As she leaned over him, she spoke in his ear, intimate words between lovers. "I've changed my mind, Trey. This isn't going to be sex. This is making love. Emotional, involved, sloppy lovemaking, where I tell you how much I love you. I know there's some hero worship in there, but I really don't care, because my heart wants you even more than my body does. We're alive, Trey, and we fit together. You know we do. Let's make love. Right. Now."

He'd already positioned her. Controlling her hips with his hands, he brought her down on him as he thrust himself into her. Her swift intake of breath was one of surprise; the small sound that escaped her throat told him the rest. The significance almost overwhelmed him, but knowing that she'd chosen him increased his passion, this driving need to make her his. *Her first, her first, her first time—*

He spent himself swiftly, not wanting to cause her more pain, and then it was his turn to speak, to murmur in her ear. With his fingers, he searched for the spot that would bring her pleasure as he held his body motionless inside her. He didn't have to censor himself or be careful about what he said, because he wanted her to hear the truth. As his fingers circled and her excitement built, he told her she was perfect and he was happy, so happy, to be with her, that she felt amazing and she *was* amazing. As she reached her peak, he told her how beautiful it was because he was still inside her and felt it all.

And then, there was silence. He held her and was held by her, and their breathing slowed. They kept each other warm.

With the side of her face pressed to his throat, he could feel the tickle of her eyelashes as she blinked. "Close your eyes, sweetheart. Go to sleep."

"I don't want to close my eyes. I knew when I was standing by that tree that if I fell asleep, I would never wake up."

He stroked her hair. "I promise you, you'll see the morning. As long as we're together, Rebecca, we'll survive. Close your eyes, and rest."

Chapter Nine

The fire was going strong, burning brightly as the early-morning light poured into the cabin along with the cold air. The wood hadn't dried much overnight, but Trey had brought an artificial fire starter that had ignited the first piece. Once that blazed, Trey had been able to carefully add one damp piece after another, building the fire steadily. The wet wood hissed steam, but it also provided the heat they needed, as long as Trey went about it methodically, carefully. He could not rush.

"Could you hurry that up a little bit? I need to use the blanket, if you know what I mean."

Trey smiled at Rebecca's words. For a woman who'd been raised to be patient and silent, she sure was eager and energetic around him.

"If you want it, come and get it," he said. The fire would keep him warm enough for a few minutes. He was rewarded with his first good look at his naked Rebecca, all smooth skin and tousled hair, as she bounded from the sleeping bag to him. The smile on her face stole his attention from her shapely legs. She snatched the blanket from around his shoulders and whisked it around her own, but she didn't turn to the door immediately.

Trey realized she was checking him out, too, getting her first look at his body in the daylight. He stayed as he was, crouched on one knee, and tossed another stick on the fire. His bent thigh, he knew, was blocking some of what she was probably curious to view, but as he slid a glance at her, she was smiling.

It turned out that his innocent porcelain angel could execute an excellent wolf whistle. "I sure did get a good-looking cowboy."

As she turned and walked out the door, he yelled, "Boots" over his shoulder.

"I know. I'm a fast learner." She stomped them on, and left.

A good-looking cowboy. Trey rubbed his forehead and fed the fire. He wasn't a damned cowboy. He was a landscaper in a medium-size town in Oklahoma. He planted trees and maintained some nice plants around office buildings.

Worse, he was a landscaper who had to hire someone else to total the checks and send out the bills, because the boy who'd once aced calculus couldn't keep a simple ledger. He was a landscaper who asked each new client to write their address for him on their contract. He rode in the passenger seat of his own trucks, and handed the written address to whichever crew member he'd put in the role of redneck chauffeur.

He was less than a landscaper.

Yet he'd taken an irreversible step with Rebecca last night. He'd seen the evidence of her virginity on his body this morning, and the emotions had hit him square in the chest. He'd felt honored. Responsible. But mostly, possessive. Insanely possessive, in the most primitive way, for she was his woman, and his alone. The idea of another man touching what only he had touched sent a fighting dose of adrenaline through his system.

That was a problem. He and Rebecca would break up one day. There would be no forever for her with a man like him. The humiliation of his handicaps was not to be shared. Given their circumstances and geography, he and Rebecca would part company sooner rather than later.

If he was any kind of decent man, he'd stop sleeping with her and start acting like the distant friend—no more—that he'd inevitably end up being.

"It's starting to snow out there," Rebecca said as she came back inside. "Do you think it will stick? We could have a white Christmas." She was all sunshine on this snowy day, an early Christmas gift wrapped in a Navajo blanket.

This break up was going to hurt when it happened. Trey knew it would hurt in a way he'd never get over.

She stayed near the door. "Would you help me with my boots?"

The temperature in the cabin was probably still at freezing, except directly in front of the fire. Her blanket dipped and slipped open as he hauled off one of her boots. Her breast was exposed for a moment, pure and luscious, before it was hidden by the colorful blanket once more.

Did his body respond in the freezing cold? With a vengeance.

Oblivious, smiling, Rebecca opened the blanket and invited him in. As she closed her arms around his neck, with the corners of the blanket tight in her fists, she kissed him as she had the first time, with a raw, openmouthed hunger. He'd broken off that kiss before, but he couldn't now. This was his woman, and she wanted him, and by God, he'd worry about tomorrow when tomorrow came.

Still kissing, he backed her toward the sleeping bag, which he'd dragged closer to the fire. When her feet touched it, she dropped the blanket, and they both slid into the familiar warmth. She snuggled her bare body up to his, as familiar with him as he was with her after their hours and hours of togetherness.

There was something so primal about it, very Adam and Eve, innocent and naked, just the two of them in this log cabin. He was male, she was female, and everything about her was a pleasure to him, from her face to her voice, from her body to her laugh.

She pushed his hair back with her fingers and looked at him with those brown doe eyes. "It only hurts the first time, right?"

"That's what I've heard."

"You don't know?" Her eyes widened, and then she started raining little kisses from one corner of his mouth to the other. "I'm your first *first*. I am, aren't I?"

"Rebecca, you're my first everything."

He stopped himself. He'd been about to say all kinds of things. The words were lined up, ready to pour out. *You're the first good reason I've had to want to face the day. You're the first woman I've wanted to love.*

It was an agony to hold it in, but he would not tell her he loved her when he knew he would leave her.

"What do you mean, your first?" she whispered, laying him back, prowling over him. She bit her lip, excited and anxious at once for what they were about to do—for they were, with a certainty, about to come together once more. It was as inevitable as breathing. It had been from the first moment he'd held her, Trey realized.

"There's never been another like you," he said, his back to the hard planks of the floor as Rebecca moved on top of him once more. "There never will be."

Together, they learned that the second time involved some physical tenderness. Rebecca had been dismayed that her body was delicate, because her desire was undeniable. Trey had led them to completion with more gentleness than he'd known he possessed, and they'd finished breathless and satisfied. The tenderness of the second time, Trey knew, had been as much in his heart as her body. It would be seared in his memory. He might forget everything else, but never that.

The silence they shared in each other's arms was broken by the chop of a helicopter's blades, coming to take them away.

The dusting of Texas snow turned into a blizzard under the helicopter's blades, flakes and ice and dirt flying in all directions, pelting them with fury.

Fury. That was what Trey was feeling. The arrival of the helicopter had made Rebecca distressed, and that made him angry. She'd rushed to get dressed, insisting on wearing her underpants, although they'd begun thawing and were now both cold and damp. The destroyed cashmere cardigan was the most wet item of them all, yet she'd put it on and tried to hold it closed.

Trey had pulled the cardigan off her arms and tossed it in the fire, then dressed her in his plaid Western shirt. The material was thinner but far more dry, and it reached nearly to her knees, which satisfied her sense of modesty. She'd worn the Navajo blanket instead of her wet coat. He'd worn his jeans and wrapped the foil-backed thermal blanket around himself, and they'd left everything else behind in the cabin.

At the first blast of dirt and ice, Trey had cursed himself for leaving the goggles. As Rebecca bent her head and shaded her eyes with her hands, Trey hated his sorry excuse of a brain, which had let him down once more—and Rebecca, too.

He should have foreseen that a helicopter would arrive. He'd told his cousin to call the sheriff, something that had completely slipped his mind until now. The ice storm had stopped, the darkness had lifted, their fire had created smoke. Therefore, the helicopter had come. Why couldn't he predict these things?

The helicopter wasn't painted with the sheriff's office colors, though. It was Texas Rescue and Relief's logo that was emblazoned on the side. Texas Rescue was the organization that his brother volunteered with as a fireman. Luke's new wife did something with them, too, but damn if Trey could remember what. He didn't care. He was angry with Texas Rescue, because they were literally taking Rebecca away.

A man had descended with a metal basket. He was dressed like an astronaut in a full helmet and orange jumpsuit, but he kept giving them hearty, thumbs-up gestures. Trey felt like returning the hand gesture with a different one of his own.

He would have gotten Rebecca home safely. If they'd only given him some time, he could have completed the rescue. The fire that he'd just doused had been going strong. Their clothes had been drying. He would have waited one more night, letting Rebecca get stronger, and then he would have refilled the ATV with the spare gas can before beginning the return drive over the land he knew like the back of his hand. Rebecca would have ridden behind him, and his own body would have blocked the cold wind for her.

But his plan took time. Like building a fire with damp wood, each piece of his plan had to be executed step-by-step. It was a pace that worked for him.

But Trey knew, as he'd known since he'd been unceremoniously booted out of Oklahoma Tech, that the world moved at a faster pace.

Rebecca had already disappeared into the helicopter, and the astronaut was holding the basket steady for Trey to climb in. Once inside the helicopter, the pace only quickened. The astronaut removed his helmet, stuck a thermometer in Rebecca's mouth and clipped a white plastic device on Trey's finger. After things beeped, he switched them around, popping fresh plastic on the thermometer for Trey, clipping the white cube on Rebecca's finger.

Then he turned to Trey and stuck his hand in front of his face. "How many fingers am I holding up?" he shouted over the relentless thumping of the rotor blades.

Alarm raced through Trey. They were going to start all this crap again, how many fingers, look up, look to the left, follow my finger with your eyes. There was nothing wrong with his eyes, there'd never been anything wrong with his eyes, just a little double vision after a hit during practice.

"How many fingers?" the man shouted again.

"Four, goddammit."

"Jeez, Trey, nice to see you, too. Don't take my head off." Then he turned to Rebecca and asked her the same.

The astronaut knew him.

That sick sweat threatened. Trey rolled his shoulders and tried to concentrate on the man's face. If he'd just hold still. If he'd just give Trey a minute to place his face—but he was shouting numbers he read off the white cube cheerfully, as if Trey would be glad to hear them, all while packing up equipment, pulling a microphone from a clip in the roof, talking to the pilot as he took Rebecca's temperature a second time. The engine roared, the helicopter banked, and instead of ranch land below them, city buildings and highways filled the window.

Somehow, Trey had assumed they were flying back to the ranch house. Foolish.

He could only focus on one thing at a time, and the only thing he gave a damn about was Rebecca. She looked at him, and smiled her strained, driver's license smile.

Trey unbuckled his seat belt and moved to her side.

"You done?" he asked the astronaut, but it wasn't really a question. He unbuckled Rebecca's seat belt and pulled her into his lap, blanket and all.

The other man shot him a look that Trey returned evenly. *This is the way it's going to be.*

The man got the message. He pulled the seat belt's webbing out another few feet, then buckled it around Trey and Rebecca, both. "You won't mind if I buckle my patients in. I just got my rescue swimmer's certification. I'm not losing it for you, Waterson. And, ma'am, since your bodyguard doesn't seem inclined to introduce us, I'm Zach Bishop. Pleased to meet you."

Zach Bishop. Of course, Trey knew Zach Bishop. Trey's senior year, Zach had been a freshman on the football team. He'd thought he was the best wide receiver in the state. He wasn't, but he was good, so Trey had thrown more than a few touchdown passes his way. Just to remind the cocky freshman who was behind those scores, Trey would unleash his full, NFL-worthy strength at him during practice, and throw the ball so hard that it would knock Zach on his ass when he caught it.

He realized now why Zach was grinning at him. They had a history, a rivalry and grudging respect, one Trey had forgotten for ten years.

He looked at Rebecca's face, still new to him, and tried to memorize it. Would she be erased from his consciousness for ten years? Would he run into her someday, and wonder why this sweet brunette acted like she knew him?

The thought made his gut churn. He couldn't allow it to happen. He wanted those memories of their first time, and their second. If he had to keep her beside him and look at her every single day to keep that memory fresh, then that was what he'd do.

Until she wanted to move in, settle down, have children. Then he'd have to let her go.

Chapter Ten

Rebecca Cargill had never been in a hospital before. She hated it.

Her entire twenty-four years had been spent wrapped in a pink puffy safety bubble. She'd never broken a bone and needed a cast, because she'd never climbed a tree. She'd never stepped on broken glass and needed stitches, because she'd never gone outside without her white lace socks and black patent Mary Janes. She'd gotten bronchitis once, the year she'd been sent to an exclusive all-girl boarding school courtesy of Papa Maynard, Mother's fourth husband. A physician had come to her dormitory and prescribed an antibiotic. The floor mistress had administered it as she plumped little Becky Cargill's precious pillows twice a day.

The helicopter had landed on the roof of the hospital, and the wind from the rotors had buffeted Rebecca every which way as she was taken out of Trey's arms and placed on an empty stretcher. She'd been swaddled in white blankets and held down with seat belts across her legs and waist and shoulders, and then six people had run along the side of her stretcher as they rushed her away like she was on a television drama, playing the patient who was about to die.

Maybe she was. Maybe she was suffering from some aftereffects of her freezing, and didn't know it. Everyone was so serious, so urgent. They rolled her into an elevator, and from there into a room with medical equipment hanging on its walls. Some of it she could identify, like oxygen masks, and some of it she could read, like "defibrillator," but most of it was an array of ominous stainless steel and black plastic, waiting for a life to be in danger.

Was it hers?

It could be. Trey was not here, and without him, she could die. In this hospital, the thought didn't seem so irrational.

A woman in scrubs informed her they were going to take some vitals, and then she unsnapped the shirt Rebecca had borrowed from Trey and stuck round electrodes on Rebecca's chest, pushing one breast aside a bit to stick a circle on her rib. The television screen over the stretcher started to display a bright green zigzag, and the telltale beep that Rebecca recognized from every medical movie started tracking her heartbeat.

Rebecca wondered if the number one hundred and twenty was her pulse, but before she could ask, another woman in scrubs wiped her elbow crease with cold alcohol and inserted a needle to start an IV. The bag of clear fluid, hanging from its silver hook, dripped steadily into the tube that disappeared into her arm. *Sodium Chloride*, it read.

Little Becky was frightened into silence, but Rebecca, who had the confidence to tell a man when he was wrong, asked the nurse a question. "What kind of medicine is that?"

"Oh, it's nothing. Just a precaution for dehydration." She stuck a wide piece of clear plastic over the crease of Rebecca's elbow. Rebecca kept her arm completely straight, afraid to move and dislodge the needle.

Trey had said she was dehydrated. He'd made her drink more than she'd wanted to. Had he known how sick she was? But she wasn't getting water now. She was getting sodium chloride, which the nurse said was nothing. She didn't trust the nurse; *nothing* wouldn't have a name.

She trusted Trey. She needed him to keep her warm and safe, but he wasn't here. The hospital wouldn't have kept him, she supposed, because there was nothing wrong with him. He hadn't frozen slowly in the cold. The helicopter had dropped her off at the hospital, but maybe it had taken Trey somewhere else, since he wasn't sick.

"My arm is cold." The panic was threatening to make itself heard in her voice. She could feel a creeping coldness in her arm, spreading deep under her skin.

The nurse patted her hand. "Yes, sometimes you can feel the IV going in. It's okay. The doctor will be in shortly."

The last two people left, and shut the door.

Rebecca lay in the bed, and stared at the door. It had one lone holiday decoration, a plastic cling in the shape of a snowflake. She stared at the imitation ice crystal as her ECG machine beeped.

Her shoulder started to hurt from holding it at a funny angle to keep her arm straight, but she didn't dare move with the needle stuck in her. They were putting a cold liquid inside her, when she never wanted to be cold again.

Trey!

No wonder people dreaded going to the hospital. She'd never felt so alone…except for the time she'd been clinging to a tree in the middle of nowhere. Her feet had frozen, minute by minute.

The ECG beeped faster. Rebecca flexed her feet. They were still there, but the seat belt kept her from moving her legs. They'd released the one across her shoulders and the one across her middle, but no one had done anything to her feet.

She held still, legs strapped in place. Needle in her arm. Wires coming out of the shirt from the stickers on her chest.

"Trey!"

She shouted his name, but he was not coming in the door this time. He was not here.

"Trey," she said quietly, more of a wish than a cry for help.

The door opened a few inches, and yet another woman in scrubs stuck her head in. This one was Rebecca's age, with brown hair in a high ponytail. "Hi. Did you need something?"

Rebecca swallowed. She couldn't think of the right sentence, only the kind of stilted phrases her mother had drilled into her head. *Would you please inform Mr. Waterson that Miss Cargill would like to see him?*

The woman glanced at the ECG and looked back at Rebecca. She came all the way into the room. "You don't look very comfortable. Is your IV bothering you?"

She flicked open the buckle on the leg seat belt as

she walked up to Rebecca's side and placed her hand on her arm.

"Careful, please," Rebecca said quickly. "I don't want to wiggle the needle."

"There's no needle in there. They slide it out and leave a flexible tube in its place. You can bend your arm. Try it."

Rebecca was so relieved, she could have kissed the woman.

Florence Nightingale syndrome, she could hear Trey say.

I don't mean kiss her like that, Trey. Get your mind out of the gutter.

Oh, yes. She was bold and spunky when she talked to Trey, but she was still good little Becky everywhere else. She missed Trey intensely.

"You're allowed to have one person in the room with you," the woman said. "Is there someone in the waiting room I could get for you?"

"Trey Waterson. Except, I don't know if he's here or not."

"Trey? Okay, I'll go see if there is a Trey in the waiting room."

The minutes ticked by, measured by the rapid beep of the ECG machine.

The ponytail lady came back into the room. "There's no one named Trey, but there's a woman out there who'd like to see you. Shall I send her in?"

Rebecca froze, and felt a new kind of cold, one she dreaded as much as any other she'd felt in Texas.

Her mother had arrived.

She lay there for a moment, obedient little Becky, and

then she sat up. If Trey was not here, then she'd go find him. He was the only person in the world she trusted.

She started peeling the round circles off her chest, tossing the offensive pieces of plastic onto the stretcher, but she remembered her manners and smiled sweetly. "Thank you, but I do not wish to see that woman. It was very kind of you to check the waiting room, but I'm afraid I must be going now."

Somewhere in the back of her mind, she knew her behavior was irrational. She wouldn't do anything dangerous this time. She wouldn't take an ATV into the wilderness in an ice storm. She'd just use her credit card to rent another car, and she'd go back to the ranch and find Trey. Hopefully, she'd get there before her mother tracked her down.

If she could just find Trey—

The woman stopped Rebecca by placing a hand over hers. "Just a minute. I'll help you take the rest of those off. But first, I want you to know that nobody will come into this room without your permission. Only hospital personnel are allowed. You're safe." True to her word, she removed the rest of the electrodes.

"Second, I want you to stay in this safe room until the doctor can see you. You were assigned to Dr. Brown, but she's got a patient from a car accident who's taking all her time. I'm going to get Dr. MacDowell to see you instead."

Trey recognized Dr. MacDowell immediately. He was Jamie, the youngest of the three MacDowell brothers who had played football for Trey's high school. The MacDowell family owned the River Mack Ranch, which bordered the James Hill Ranch to the east.

Trey had known Jamie MacDowell his entire life, but he doubted he would have remembered him if Zach Bishop hadn't been on that helicopter. It sometimes happened that way. Trey was missing a memory—without knowing it, of course—and then someone like Zach from football would come along, and suddenly, all the football memories would be unlocked. The MacDowells had played football. Trey now remembered the MacDowells.

Jamie—Dr. MacDowell—wanted him to walk in a straight line, heel toe, heel toe.

"Would you like me to tell you who the President of the United States is, too?" Trey asked. He was sick of this routine.

"Been through this before, huh?" Jamie said. "Sobriety test by a police officer, or did a doctor ask you?"

"Does it matter?"

"As a matter of fact, it does."

Trey had no patience for this. He wanted to check on Rebecca. "A doctor."

"When?"

"College. Let's get on with it."

"I'm going to give you three items, and I want you to remember them. A house, an apple, an elephant. Can you say those back to me?"

"House, apple, elephant. Got it."

"Do you know what each of those things are?"

This was the part that always made Trey the most angry. He hated being treated like he was a moron. "Give me a break, Jamie. House, apple, elephant. Let's move on."

There was a knock at the door, and an attractive

woman Rebecca's age stuck her head in the room. "Dr. MacDowell, can I interrupt you, please?"

Trey sat on the treatment table, feeling like a fool in a hospital gown. He'd give Jamie about two minutes more of this nonsense, and then he'd find Rebecca.

"Sorry about that, Trey." Jamie came back in the room, only to be yanked back out by the sleeve of his white coat. Trey heard the woman ask Jamie if his patient's name was Trey. An indistinct conversation followed.

Jamie returned, taking his stethoscope from around his neck and putting it in his ears. "Let me listen to you breathe."

It was awkward, having the pest baby brother of his neighbors listen to his heart. Not awkward like sharing a sleeping bag while naked, but awkward all the same.

Jamie put his stethoscope back around his neck. "Earlier, I asked you to remember some words. Can you repeat those items back to me?"

"House and apple."

Jamie put a plastic cone on the end of a flashlight and asked Trey to stick out his tongue to say, "Ah."

Trey wasn't fooled. "I can stick out my tongue straight."

"Say, 'Ah,' damn it, and stop being such a stubborn cuss."

"Ah."

"Great." Jamie tossed the plastic cone in the trash. "The nursing assistant was just telling me that your aunt June is in the waiting room with someone else. One of your cousins, I assume."

What the hell was everyone doing at the hospital? Trey had already been worried about getting Rebecca home. Now he had to transport Aunt June and Emily, too. That was four people. His pickup truck only held three.

"Thanks for the update," he said. "Now I've got to drive four people home in a three-man truck."

Jamie crossed his arms over his chest. His white coat flared behind him like a cattleman's duster. "You came by helicopter, Trey. You don't have a pickup truck here."

Aw, hell. It was so damned obvious when he pointed it out.

Trey tried to play it off. "I need to get some sleep. It's been a long twenty-four hours."

"You could also be dehydrated." Jamie handed him a hospital cup with ounces marked on its side. "I want you to drink all thirty-two ounces, and then I want you to fill it up and drink it again. Slam it, like you just finished football practice. I've got to see my next patient, but I'll be back. Drink up."

Trey wanted to ask where Rebecca was. Hell, he wanted to demand to be taken to her. But if he'd ever needed a reminder of why he wasn't man enough for her, he'd just gotten it.

Rebecca, Rebecca. He remembered the taste of her shoulder as he'd murmured the apology. He'd misunderstood how much she wanted him then.

How could he explain why he couldn't keep her now?

Chapter Eleven

Trey paced the treatment room after putting on his dry-enough jeans and reliable cowboy boots. He turned the hospital gown around so that it opened down the front. It felt more like a shirt that way, one he just hadn't buttoned up.

Jamie MacDowell came back into the room, tossed his clipboard on the sink counter and sank into the room's vinyl chair. He looked hard at Trey for a moment.

Trey waited. Whatever Jamie had to say, it was serious. Whatever it was, Trey truly didn't care. He didn't do serious with doctors anymore. They were always serious when they told him they'd found nothing. His problems were his to deal with.

"I just saw the woman you rescued from the ice storm. She asked about you."

Trey suddenly cared a hell of a lot more. He'd been ready to hear something serious about himself, but this was about Rebecca. The morning's memory was still achingly fresh in his mind. *Honored. Responsible. Possessive.*

"Where is she?" Trey made a move toward the door, but Jamie held up his hand.

"Not so fast. You aren't her next of kin. I'm bound by all kinds of patient privacy acts here. But I've known you my entire life, and I know you aren't going to hurt her, so I'm going to ask you a favor. You have every right to turn me down."

Trey sat slowly on the edge of the bed. Physically, he'd never hurt Rebecca, but if he didn't put some distance between them immediately, he was going to break her heart when he left.

She was Jamie MacDowell's patient now, and he was a good man. The hospital itself was well-known. Rebecca would be okay from here on out. Trey ought to bow out gracefully, right here, right now, before things got any deeper.

"You're under no obligation to say yes, and I shouldn't be asking. Let me explain that Miss Cargill is on a very high state of alert, physically."

"What does that mean?"

"It's not all that unusual, given what she's been through. The body can stay in survival mode even after a person is safe. I'm planning on sending her home with a few days of Valium, just so she can get some sleep."

"She doesn't want to close her eyes," Trey said, more to himself than Jamie. She was afraid she'd never wake up—unless Trey was there to keep her from freezing. He understood.

Jamie continued explaining. "I could give her a little something now, a sedative or anxiety med to take the edge off, but I'd rather see her heart rate and other vital signs come off high alert on their own before I discharge her.

"She's asking for you. I'd say she's fixated on you, like you're necessary to her well-being. Again, not that unusual, given the fact that you saved her life. You've done your part, so you're under no obligation at all, but I'd like to see if having you around will lower her stress levels. Would you consider waiting with her in her room? Just sit there, keep her company?"

Trey didn't like the picture Jamie painted. A future broken heart was an abstract concept in the face of Rebecca's immediate distress. He'd have to worry about tomorrow some other time.

Trey stood. "What room is she in?"

"Hold up. One more thing. Is there any reason she has to fear your aunt June?"

The question was so preposterous, Trey was certain his faulty brain had missed something.

"The nursing assistant told her there was a woman in the waiting room who'd like to see her, and Miss Cargill started trying to leave. Urgently. She wanted to find you. I checked out the waiting room myself. It's your aunt June."

"Your nursing assistant must have gotten it wrong."

"The nursing assistant is my wife," Jamie said. "I trust her judgment."

Why would Rebecca be frightened that a woman was waiting to see her? Trey was shaking his head at Jamie when the answer broke through. *Her mother.* Rebecca must have thought her mother had come to get her.

Damn it. It wasn't like Trey had forgotten about her mother: the woman controlled her, and she was trying to send Rebecca off with a man in exchange for houses or jewels or some other money-related thing. Because it hadn't been an immediate concern while they were worried about shelter, he hadn't thought about it yet. Piece by piece, one step at a time—his brain hadn't focused on that particular piece of wood, so to speak.

"I know who Rebecca is worried about. I'll handle it."

"All right, then. I'll walk you to room three."

Trey left the room, but Jamie was only a couple of inches shorter than he was, so the young doctor easily kept pace as Trey headed down the row of numbered cubicles.

"I don't need an escort," Trey said, impatient, embarrassed.

"My ER. My patient. My rules. Wait with her until radiology comes to do the CT scan."

"What is she getting a CT scan for?"

"She's not. You are."

Trey stopped short. "For a stupid comment about a pickup truck? I told you, I'm tired. You said dehydrated."

"Trey," Jamie said, his voice very low in the public hallway, "you forgot the elephants."

"What?"

"House, apple, elephants. You've been examined before. Second injuries are generally more dangerous than the first. It could be nothing, or it could be an old injury, but it's possible you hit your head during that rescue and you just don't remember it. I've had people brought in here who didn't know they'd been in a car accident ten minutes prior."

"It's not a new injury." Trey forced the words out. "Nothing old, either. I've been told I'm normal a half-dozen times."

"Maybe so, but when you exhibit the symptoms of a possible brain bleed, you don't leave my ER until I check it out."

Trey crossed his arms over his chest again and glared at Jamie. MacDowell seemed unimpressed. Little brothers, whether his own or his neighbors', had always been pests.

"You always were a pain in the neck," Trey said, speaking the thought out loud without intending to. He refused to apologize. He wouldn't mutter his usual *I didn't mean to say that*. It was better to let Jamie think it was intentional instead of another case of forgetting elephants.

"Well, now I'm a pain in the neck with an MD after my name."

"Which means what?"

"Which means you're getting a CT scan. Quit fighting it."

Trey had no intention of fighting, and every intention of leaving. Jamie could fill out the paperwork for a patient who refused treatment. Trey didn't want to hear, one more time, that everything was normal.

But they were standing outside of room three. Trey would not turn and walk out of the hospital now.

Rebecca wanted him, so he'd stay awhile longer, and he'd probably get another damned CT scan because he couldn't leave Rebecca here, not for any reason.

He turned the doorknob and left Jamie standing in the hall.

Rebecca watched the IV drip. She was sitting on the edge of the bed, toes grazing the tile floor, ready to jump up when the IV bag was empty, so she could get the tube taken out of her arm and get the heck out of this hospital.

Somehow, some way, she had to get back to the James Hill Ranch. Her rental car was already there, so she'd have to rent another one. She didn't care. She'd do whatever it took to get to Trey.

When she found him, she wanted to kill him. She imagined him in that ranch house, standing by that ginormous stone fireplace, waiting for her to show up once she was all better. She was going to show up, alright, and she was going to give him a piece of her mind. She was so angry at him for leaving her all alone, she would never speak to him again.

I couldn't have sex with you now if I wanted to, I'm so mad, she'd said last night. She meant it this time.

The door opened, and Trey walked in, denim below, bare-chested above, with the open flaps of a hospital gown trailing behind him.

He was the most beautiful sight she'd ever seen. She was standing and reaching for him without thinking about it, but he'd already reached her and was closing his arms around her. She clung to his neck, but her IV tubing stretched to its limit, so she lowered that arm and held on for dear life with the other.

"I missed you so much," she said, over and over, when what she'd planned to say was *How dare you leave me?* She wanted to kiss him, but she clung to him and buried the side of her face in his neck. "No one will tell me what's wrong with me, and my mother is waiting to take me away."

Trey stroked her hair and listened as she continued to babble on. "I know I'm supposed to be starting a new life, but this is my first time in a hospital and it's hard not to be silent after all these years, because I don't know these people, not like I know you. I didn't know where you were…"

He held her tightly against his chest. The sheer physical size of him was comforting to hang on to, and she ran out of things to say. Only then did he talk.

"Your mother isn't here. It's my aunt June in the waiting room. You won't see your mother without me." Trey pulled away from her far enough to hold her face in his hands.

He addressed only the issue of her mother, as if she hadn't gone through a list of worries. Rebecca realized that was the only issue that really had her scared. She was so relieved not to be alone. "You'll stay here? Just in case?"

"I'm not going anywhere. Hospitals like their rules, so they examined us separately, but we're together now." His gaze roamed from her eyes to her lips, and he gave her one soft kiss, but mostly, he cupped her face in his palms and looked at her.

"What is it?" she whispered, when she couldn't guess what his expression meant.

"I just want to memorize this pretty face."

And then they were kissing for real, openmouthed, hot and wet and hungry. He wanted her heat as much as she wanted his. It was a tremendous feeling, to think that she could be as important to him as he was to her.

She felt very near to tears, so she broke off the kiss to stand on tiptoe and whisper in his ear. "This probably sounds crazy, but I want to go back to the cabin."

"I know. It was easier."

There was a knock on the door, and Dr. MacDowell entered the room. Rebecca released her hold on Trey's neck. He was a little slower to release her, keeping her face in his hands, keeping his gaze on her face.

Dr. MacDowell sounded completely stunned.

"Waterson—what are you—when I asked you to wait with her—"

Another quick knock, and the door opened again. Trey let go of her then, but only to sit on her bed and pull her down beside him, very close beside him. He put his arms around her, and Rebecca savored the shelter.

The ponytailed woman beamed at Rebecca. "Good, I see you've got your Trey."

Rebecca felt proud to have him by her side. *I'm not a loser without any friends,* she wanted to say. Until a few minutes ago, that was exactly what Rebecca had been, and this cheerful woman had been the only one who'd listened to her worries. "I'm sorry I made a scene. You've been very kind."

"If I'd been left alone in the ER, I'd have been yelling for my Jamie, believe me." She smiled at the doctor while she said it.

Rebecca's surprise must have shown on her face, because the woman hiked her thumb toward him and winked. "This is my husband, Jamie."

Dr. MacDowell introduced his wife to Trey, also to Rebecca's surprise. The men clearly knew each other. Trey stood when he was introduced to Kendry, a show of manners that somehow didn't surprise Rebecca, and then he spoke easily with the couple about living on neighboring ranches and playing football.

Rebecca listened to every word. Trey had been the quarterback at a high school, and Jamie had taken over once Trey had graduated. Kendry hadn't known them then, but she loved the high school games, and she told Trey this year's season had been great.

Rebecca watched the three of them chat, fascinated by Trey's history. Until this moment, he'd been simply hers.

He'd materialized when she'd needed him most, and he'd been her exclusive property every moment since. She hadn't wondered what his life was like beyond her.

The MacDowells fascinated her, as well. They were a darling couple, the kind that Rebecca had witnessed now and then over the years. So much of her world had been spent with schoolmates whose fathers were on their third wives. Her mother's friends were women who vacationed with men they were not married to, but there had been exceptions. Rebecca had always noticed the exceptions.

She'd seen a millionaire get teary-eyed in the middle of raising a toast to his gray-haired wife. The Lexingtons' main home had been run by a married couple who'd worked together in the same mansion for decades. Rebecca knew true love existed, she just hadn't seen it up close very often, and she hadn't seen it in her own age group. The MacDowells couldn't take their eyes off each other. It was wonderful.

Kendry started to hook up Rebecca's ECG again in a far more discreet way than the first woman had done it.

"Now I see how you were able to get Dr. MacDowell to come see me when the other doctor was held up," Rebecca said.

Kendry winked. "I try not to throw my weight around, but sometimes, I just need to get things done."

Trey raised an eyebrow at Jamie. "Your ER? Your rules?"

Jamie shrugged. "Happy wife, happy life." He clapped Jamie on the shoulder and opened the door to leave. "You'll see."

All that new, friendly easiness left Trey's expression. Rebecca wondered where it went.

* * *

Sit up straight, Becky, for God's sake. Never behave like you think you are an imposition. Act like you belong here. Of course we should be included.

Her mother's advice was wrong. Wrong, wrong, wrong. Becky felt as if she was imposing—*no, not Becky; it's Rebecca now.* Rebecca felt as if she was imposing because she *was* imposing. She was an uninvited guest, no matter how gracious her hosts were being.

She had no choice but to accept their hospitality. She had absolutely nowhere to go, except the ranch house. She had nowhere she wanted to be, except with Trey, so she sat quietly, squashed in the back seat of Aunt June's car. She could do this, even without her mother. She'd done it so many times before.

Aunt June drove through the rain. Temperatures were above freezing, so the rain stayed wet and didn't turn to treacherous ice. June chatted away, pointing out a winery and raving about its gourmet olive oil as if Rebecca had come to Texas Hill Country to see the sights. At last, they passed the first of the simple crossbar gates that marked the highway that led to the James Hill Ranch.

"I don't mind telling you, young man," June began, glancing at Trey, "that it's a good thing your parents left on their own cruise after seeing Luke and Patricia off on theirs. When they check in, they'll find out you're already safe at the same time they hear you were missing overnight. You gave me enough gray hairs, charging out into that awful weather the way you did. I'm glad we'll spare your mother some."

She glanced in the rearview mirror at Rebecca. "How about you, honey? Do you need to tell your folks that you're safe now, or did they let you make a call from the hospital?"

Rebecca folded her hands in her lap. "Everything is just fine, thank you."

Trey was riding shotgun next to his aunt because he could not fit in the back seat. He was simply too large. In the cold light of day, Rebecca could see that he was at least six-four, with broad shoulders and long, strong legs that had carried her with long, strong strides across frozen ground. She loved the size of him, but it prevented him from sitting with her, so she was in the back seat, smiling politely at Emily's sincere attempts to carry on a conversation. Inside, however, her mother's warnings were relentless.

You must find out who really owns this house. Who was the last woman to stay here, and how long did she last? Why did she leave, or was she kicked out?

June and Emily had been the ones who'd insisted Rebecca come back to the house. Trey had been silent, wrapping the Navajo blanket around her before carrying her to the wheelchair so her feet wouldn't touch the ground. Her feet looked normal, but the next few days would tell how bad any frostbite had been. Her feet might blister. They might peel, and if they did, it would pass. But they might turn green or black, and if that happened, she was to return to the ER immediately.

June and Emily had practically given her the socks off their feet when they heard that. They really couldn't be nicer people. The problem was, they didn't own the house, and Trey, who hadn't said a word, lived in Oklahoma.

Rebecca felt uneasy. She and her mother had settled in with a man in Virginia once, in an area full of mansions and equestrian facilities. Rebecca had loved her new school and was looking forward to an entire semester in one place…maybe more. Maybe for a year or two, if Mother's boyfriend popped the question.

Then the boyfriend's mother had found out that he'd let them move in, and Rebecca's mother had found out that although he lived there alone, he didn't own the house. His mother did. Becky and her mother had come home in the boyfriend's car from a shopping excursion to find their bags packed and lined up in the driveway.

Her mother had kept the car and the shopping bags, but never again did they move into a house without the owner's invitation. The real owner.

They were still a long way from the James Hill Ranch. Rebecca was smiling politely and worrying silently. Emily was telling her she'd already brought her suitcases in from her rental car, so she could just jump into a warm shower when they got home. June was describing all the catered wedding food that could be heated up without any problem at all.

Trey said, "A rescue swimmer."

Silence filled the little car.

I say things without thinking, Trey had told her in the dark. She'd thought he meant something different.

"Did you say swimmer, honey?" his aunt asked.

Trey cleared his throat and made a vague gesture out the window toward a distant barn. "Texas Rescue sent a rescue swimmer to get us. All this ice and snow and rain are going to cause flash floods and drownings. That's why they sent a rescue swimmer. In case…"

In case my corpse was floating downstream somewhere.

"James Waterson the third, you ought to be ashamed

of yourself. Don't even say things like that. Look at Becky's face. She's as white as a ghost."

"I am?" Rebecca was startled to be the topic of conversation when she'd been being good, which meant being silent.

Trey turned around in his seat to see her. "I'm sorry."

She shrugged, the good guest. "I was so busy being cold, drowning never crossed my mind."

Trey shot a look at his aunt. "I was thinking about cattle, not Rebecca."

Rebecca felt a smile tug at the corner of her mouth. "I feel another cow analogy coming on."

Trey briefly smiled at her.

She fell silent again, shy because she'd teased Trey in front of the two women.

He looked back out the window at the passing ranch land. "The cattle were herded into the gullies to get out of the wind. Now they gotta get driven right back out, before the water rises, or we'll be lassoing a bunch of heifers and hauling them out of the water. This time of year, they're heavy with calves. It'll be hard on the horses."

June started to laugh. "Oh, Trey, you're such a rancher. You're as bad as my father, always tyin' every lovin' thing back to his ranch."

Rebecca kept her gaze on his profile, devouring the sight of him when she couldn't touch him, although his expression was hard, his mouth tight.

"I'm sure Gus is on it," he said. "They're probably out there right now, driving them in this rain."

That sounded like some of the hardest, coldest, most miserable work Rebecca could imagine, yet Trey sounded almost wistful.

"Not you, Trey," Aunt June said, patting his knee

after she turned on her blinker to turn into the James Hill. "You're going to eat some hot food and take a hot shower and get some sleep. You've already rescued your heifer for the day."

Rebecca liked his aunt's maternal tone, as sweetly bossy as anything she'd ever heard on a wholesome television show, but Emily slapped her palm into her forehead.

"Mom! You just called Becky a heifer."

The women chuckled, Rebecca being sure to chuckle politely, too, as the good guest who didn't take offense, but Trey said, "She goes by Rebecca."

His hard expression didn't change as they rattled over the cattle guard and headed to someone else's home.

Chapter Twelve

The house belonged to Patricia Cargill and Luke Waterson.

One look at the new master bedroom suite, and Rebecca knew whose elegance it reflected. This had to be Patricia's home.

"Gorgeous, isn't it?" Emily said. "My aunt and uncle—Luke's parents—were going to switch rooms with Luke when he got engaged. Since he lives here all the time, they were going to give him the master bedroom suite, and they were going to move into his bedroom. They're only here for roundup and Christmas and such, you know. But your sister, she insisted they keep the master, and she and Luke built this addition for themselves. That's one smart woman. I could live in here."

She's not really my sister, Rebecca almost said.

When someone has a good impression of you, for God's sake, don't correct them. Her mother had trained her too well. Letting people assume she was a Cargill was how Becky survived.

Rebecca didn't know any other way to get a free place

to stay. Rebecca had no job, no money and only a few blue suitcases. Rebecca would have to continue being Becky for a while.

She showered under a rainfall spout, blew her hair dry at a vanity that reminded her of Dr Pepper and red lipstick, and then opened her suitcase to find clean clothes.

Christmas was only a few days away, but her mother had packed her for a tropical island vacation, if entertaining Hector Ferrique was a vacation. Rebecca craved holiday chic, a sultry red sweater and black leather boots, but those clothes hung in Patricia's closet. She didn't feel right, using a woman's things without her permission. All Becky had at her disposal were white capris and a pineapple print blouse that Audrey Hepburn would have looked girlishly adorable in.

She pulled ballerina flats gingerly over her once-frozen toes, and tiptoed into the kitchen, ready to eat politely and stay invisible, so that no one would remember that she should really be looking for her own place to live.

That's how it's done, Mother, I know.

Emily had thoughtfully plugged Rebecca's phone into a bedside radio that charged it, but Rebecca didn't turn it on, and she didn't check for messages. She already knew everything her mother had to tell her.

Trey was disappointed in Rebecca.

He hadn't known it was possible to think so highly of another person and yet be so disappointed. The Rebecca he thought so highly of, the Rebecca he would have loved for his aunt and uncle and cousin to meet, was hiding herself away.

They called her Becky all day, and she never corrected them. She smiled a lot and said practically nothing, a pretty mouse of a woman, easy on the eyes, for certain, but easily overlooked.

He was furious with her. Jamie had said she was in survival mode, but Trey knew there was no possible way her pulse was still one hundred and twenty. Hell, if she took a Valium to calm down, she'd be so sedate she might as well be that porcelain Christmas angel who never moved.

She'd gone to bed hours ago in the pristine new bedroom Luke had built for himself and Patricia. Aunt June and her husband were in his parents' master suite. Emily had taken Luke's old bedroom, which meant Trey was back after a ten-year absence in the same room he'd always known.

Company had obviously been using his bedroom over the past decade. His mother had converted it into a guest bedroom, taking down the Dallas Cowboys cheerleader posters and packing away the detritus of a teenage life. It was clean and masculine and comfortable, but she'd left the trophy shelf.

Trey lay on top of the navy bedding, warm enough in a pair of loose flannel pants to go without a shirt. With his hands tucked underneath his head and his feet crossed at the ankles, he glared at the shapes of those trophies in the dark. Potential was what they'd represented. Nothing more, no guarantees. That potential was no more.

But on the other side of the house, in a room built for a new marriage, lay a woman whose potential was limitless. She was young and smart and ready to break free from a bad situation, yet she was letting that potential go to waste. Since they'd returned to the house, she'd become a silent, decorative doll who wouldn't assert herself, not even to ask people to call her by the right name.

He was baffled. She had nothing to gain from hiding herself. Confusion fed his anger. The damned trophies fed his anger. The way his body ached for contact with Rebecca, the way his palms felt restless without her soft skin to soothe, fed his anger.

The door opened, and an angel in a long white robe stepped inside. She shut the door and leaned back against it, glaring at him in the moonlight.

"I can't sleep," Rebecca said, and it sounded like an accusation. "You put me in a room all by myself on the other side of the house."

She sounded as angry as he felt, and that fed his frustration, too.

"You're a big girl, Rebecca. You didn't like the arrangements? Then you should have said something."

"I'm a guest." She practically hissed the words at him. "Guests don't refuse to sleep in the bed they're offered. Was I supposed to tell your aunt that I wanted to shack up with you?"

She had a point, but the fact that she did hardly helped Trey's mood. "Did it occur to you to tell *me* you wanted to sleep with me? You've hardly said two words to me all evening."

"I'm a stranger here."

"Not to me. You could have talked to me." Their time was limited, and Trey was mad that they'd wasted the afternoon and evening, nearly a whole day, not talking. "You barely made eye contact with me all evening, but now that you can't sleep, you sneak in to see me."

"Oh!" Rebecca literally stamped her foot, whirled

around and wrenched the door open. She was gone in a swirl of white fabric.

Trey wasn't sure he'd ever actually seen a woman mad enough to stamp her foot before. It had looked more adorable than fearsome on her, that perfect foot flashing through the fold of her robe, the foot that he'd warmed in his hands, the foot that might soon show signs of frostbite.

His anger dissolved. What an idiot he was. By the time they'd arrived at the house, he'd been rattled by the chaos of the hospital, embarrassed by his screwups, infuriated by yet another normal CT scan and a doctor's all-clear. He'd let his problems overshadow what mattered.

Rebecca mattered, yet he'd made her angry enough to stamp that fragile foot.

He headed after her, pulling on a T-shirt as he crossed the house. He was sure of where he was going, not only sure of where he was in the building, but sure that if Rebecca needed him, if she wanted him for any reason at all, he should be there for her. He burst into her room without knocking, catching her as she was about to turn off a bedside lamp by the four-poster bed.

She turned to see him and left the lamp on.

"I'm sorry," Trey said. "Again. I swear, Rebecca, I've never needed to apologize to anyone more often than you, which sucks, because you are the one woman I never want to hurt. I'm sorry. If you want to sleep with me, I'm all yours."

"Isn't that magnanimous of you?" She lifted her chin at a haughty angle that would have fit the most regal queen. "I no longer require your services."

He looked at her, hard. "I think you do. I think you

don't want to be cold, and you don't want to be alone, so we should sleep together, and that's final."

She raised one brow and tapped her foot, that fragile foot, in irritation.

Trey swallowed. "I'm not saying we have to have sex. We should share a bed to stay warm, because we're used to that now. We'd both sleep better."

After a long moment, she untied her robe's sash. "Fine, if that's the way you want it."

She dropped the robe to the floor, and Trey almost went to his knees. She was dressed in a version of a Christmas baby doll nightie, an X-rated version. The red puffed sleeves were exaggerated, the ruffle on the edge of the hip-length dress was green, but the dress itself was sheer. The tinsel that tied under her breasts hid nothing. The outfit had a cute and innocent silhouette but revealed everything that would make a man want the opposite. It worked. Too well.

"Where in the hell did you get that?" he demanded.

"It was in my suitcase."

"Take it off." It wasn't a sensual request, not a bedroom demand. It was an order, barked out in anger.

She frowned at him. "I thought you'd like it. It was meant to be an early Christmas present."

He drove his hand through his hair. "That's a fantasy outfit chosen by someone else to please a different man with different tastes. I never want to see it on you again."

For one second, she looked devastated at his words. Before he could curse himself and apologize to her, she started advancing on him, anger replacing dismay in her expression. She poked him in the shoulder.

"Listen. I've had a hard day. Make that two days. I've been scared out of my mind. I've been cold. I've been hungry. But the one bright spot has been you. I love being with you, but ever since we got to this house, you've been acting like you barely know me. Now you're mad at me for wearing something I know good and well looks sexy. If you don't want me anymore, Trey Waterson, just say so."

She'd never been more beautiful. This was sexy to him, this confidence, this will to challenge him.

"I want you," he growled. "I want you so bad it hurts, every minute."

"Then prove it." She pushed him down on the bed and clambered over him. Within seconds, they were tearing off tinsel and T-shirts, breathing hard, kissing harder.

Trey fought for clarity in the haze of desire. "Are you sure about this?"

"About what?" she asked, backing off him to yank down his pants, her expression one of fierce concentration.

"This is only your third time. You want…angry sex?"

She'd stripped him and was above him once more. She tossed her hair back. "Is there a law against it?"

Her sarcasm surprised him, but then Trey started to laugh, aware that he'd been conquered in every way by this virgin, this vixen, his Rebecca. She silenced him with her eager mouth, and their bodies took over, making demands and taking what they wanted from each other.

Afterward, in the quiet and the dark, with only starlight coming in through the picture window to light their bed, she sprawled on top of him and he smoothed her hair. He felt her eyelashes blink against his chest. She still wasn't sleeping.

"Close your eyes, sweetheart. I promise you, we'll still be here in the morning."

She sighed, and trailed her fingers down his arm.

"Well, I'll be here, but you'll be back in your bed. We can't let your aunt June catch us. What would she think of me?"

She was still anxious to be thought of as a good little girl. It bothered Trey.

"I'm thirty-one years old. You're twenty-four. We've decided to be with each other. This is my house, and there's no way in hell I'm scurrying back to a guest room when I want to be with you. Aunt June will survive." He tried to lighten the mood. "She's had three kids and just as many husbands. I don't think she'll be shocked."

But Rebecca had gone very still. "Do you really own this house?"

There was something so grave in the way she asked, Trey knew it was not an idle question. "Yes, a third of it. A third of the ranch."

"Oh," she breathed, with a little catch in the sound. She raised her head and looked at him, doe eyes in the soft light. "Then could I stay awhile?"

He shouldn't have forgotten what she needed. She had nowhere to call home. She had no idea how long this temporary visit would last. He'd failed to give his lover security.

"Not because we had sex," she whispered, and he knew she was thinking of her mother. "I don't want that to have anything to do with it. I just need a place to stay."

He'd always had a home. Not his apartment in Oklahoma, but this ranch. He hadn't been back in ten years, it was true, but it had always been here, waiting, ready to welcome him if he needed it. That was a security that Rebecca had never known, not in her childhood, not as an adult. It was one he'd not appreciated before, but it was one he wouldn't take so lightly again.

"Rebecca Cargill, you have a place on the James Hill

Ranch for as long as you want it. Whether you have sex with me or spit in my eye, you've got a roof over your head."

"I'm not really a Cargill," she whispered.

"I'm talking to you, Rebecca, not to a Cargill."

"I like the cow analogies better than spit in your eye." She wrinkled her nose and laughed a little bit, which he was glad to see. He wanted her to be happy.

Her laugh died away quickly. "I'd like to stay through Christmas, and a little beyond. Just until I can figure out what to do next. I'll get a job. I won't impose on you forever."

She didn't intend to stay with him forever.

He'd worried about leading her on, knowing they'd be parting ways sooner rather than later. She'd said she loved him in the cabin, but he hadn't said it back, and she hadn't repeated it since. It ought to be a relief to hear her say that this time together was only an interlude for her, too.

Instead, it cut him to the quick.

"Close your eyes now, sweetheart. I'll be here in the morning."

But for how many mornings?

He'd never been the kind of man to wish for a miracle, but now he knew the miracle he'd choose: a forever of mornings.

Forever, with Rebecca Cargill.

Aunt June and her family left the next day to go to their own home for Christmas. June's other daughters would be there, bringing their own young families.

Trey left Rebecca cozied up on the couch in her tropical clothing, but with her feet wrapped in one of his mother's afghans. She had three days of newspapers to devour, something he thought might be more than a hobby to her. When she started sentences with "I read an article once," Trey knew that meant she'd read dozens of articles, every single day, as a teenager and adult. It had been her way to learn about the world her mother wouldn't let her join.

He left to check on the horses, an impulse that seemed to come naturally with being back at the ranch. It had been ten years, closer to eleven, so his favorites were gone, the horses sold to be pampered pets in their old age after a life of cowboy work. He chose a few of the current ranch horses that could carry a man his size and rode them briefly, get-acquainted rides in case he needed a horse while he was here.

The foreman, Gus, stopped by the paddock and gave him a terse update on the flooding. The river hadn't risen too far. The flood hadn't lasted too long.

"Luke will be glad to hear it," Trey said.

"You planning on riding out there to bring those ATVs back? 'Cause that horse in particular don't like the noise. She won't be real cooperative if you want her to follow you back while you're riding a machine."

"It'd be faster and easier to drive my truck out there. Most of it was easy terrain. I'll take two men and a can of gas, and they can drive the ATVs back." Trey remembered that although he was James Waterson at the James Hill Ranch, he was also new around here in a way. He owed Luke's foreman certain courtesies. "If you've got two men to spare, that is."

"Like I said, water went back down quick. Tomorrow's looking pretty light."

"All right, we'll do it then." Trey turned his horse

from the fence and took her around the pasture one more time.

It all felt so familiar. He felt so *normal*.

By the time he returned to the house, Rebecca had redecorated the fireplace. She'd taken down the wedding decoration and hung an evergreen garland with red bells and ornaments in its place. She asked him if it was okay to continue going through the decorations she'd found in the detached garage.

Trey thought it was a lot of trouble to decorate a house for just two people, but he knew it was her fantasy to have an old-fashioned Christmas, so he dragged as many boxes into the house as she wanted.

Rebecca had hung the wedding swag around the full-length oval mirror in the newlyweds' bedroom. As they stood before it, Rebecca taught him how to pronounce cheval glass, emphasis on the "-val," and Trey taught her how to enjoy it for their fourth round of sex, emphasis on the visual.

Their fourth time. Not that he was counting. Not that he was trying to commit every encounter to memory.

The fifth round was a challenge inspired by newspapers. During a dinner of leftover wedding hors d'oeuvres, Rebecca began the topic as she set her fork and knife precisely on the edge of her plate. "I read an article once that said the traditional missionary position is universally rated number one in polls about sexual habits."

Trey kept chewing. He even managed to swallow, with a chaser of sweet tea.

"But I wouldn't know about that," she continued conversationally, "because I'm always the one on top."

She put her elbow on the table and her chin in her hand, and sighed heavily, looking as wholesome as a daisy in her yellow-and-white beach dress. "Oh, you don't have to get up on my account. You've still got three more miniquiche on your plate."

"I read an article once," he said, as he tugged her behind him on the way to the bedroom, "that said well-read women make the best lovers."

"You can't believe everything you read in the papers."

He looked over his shoulder and winked at her. "Darlin', you've already proven that one is true."

For two more days, Trey enjoyed each round. He relaxed into a feeling of normalcy, and stopped trying to commit every moment to memory. He knew where he was. He knew everything about this ranch. It didn't seem possible that he could forget the new memories he was making now.

Trey did a little more ranch work, Rebecca did a lot more decorating and they kept the sex lighthearted. Tomorrow would come. She'd find her job, and he'd return to Oklahoma, and there was no sense thinking about miracles like forever.

He'd already gotten the miracle of Rebecca. She'd survived an ice storm. She'd gifted him with her body. Even when Rebecca curled up next to him and made him watch movies about Christmas miracles, Trey knew better than to expect the universe to give him more than that.

Trey kept the right perspective for rounds eight and nine and ten, but it was Christmas Eve that did him in.

On the safety of the Navajo blanket, with the limestone fireplace warming them both, Rebecca was having her traditional Christmas. By the massive tree that she'd assembled from the box in the garage, she served him popcorn and hot chocolate as she hung the last ornament.

Her sweetness wasn't a matter of wardrobe, Trey already knew. Her confidence was real, too, and when mixed with her sweetness, the combination was like none other. Some of her ideas of daring adventures in bed were touching in their innocence. Tonight, she revealed a deck of cards and dared him to play blackjack for her idea of high stakes: every losing hand would require the loss of an article of clothing.

"Strip blackjack," she announced, as if she were a Roman emperor who'd just declared the start of a court-wide orgy.

Trey was so hopelessly charmed, so completely under her spell, that he agreed to the game before he remembered why he no longer played cards.

Rebecca dealt hearts and spades and clubs on the zig-zag diamonds of the Navajo blanket.

Trey tried to focus on the numbers. The suites were not part of the game. He focused on the numbers seven and two in the corners of the cards, but some of the numbers were Js and Qs. They had a value, he knew, when added to two. Trey felt the sick feeling between his shoulder blades begin, while he prayed this Christmas was not about to go to hell.

Chapter Thirteen

"Hit me."

Rebecca pouted. "C'mon, Trey. It's no fun if you try to lose. The idea is for you to get me naked. You have to try to win, so that I have to take off a piece of clothing, not so that you have to."

It was as if the man had never played blackjack in his life. She'd even stopped a few hands ago to remind him of the rules. They needed to draw cards—take a hit—until their cards totaled as close to twenty-one without going over.

"You've got eighteen. Why would you want another card?"

She was watching his face closely, so she saw him blink as if he were surprised. Saw the way his mouth tightened. Saw him squint at the cards.

"Do you wear glasses?" she asked.

That question definitely surprised him. "There's nothing wrong with my eyes. Hit me."

"Fine." She dealt the next card off the top of the deck.

A four. If he'd gotten a two or three, he would have beaten her. She smiled at him. "That was close."

"Hit me again."

She couldn't keep smiling.

"You already lost, Trey." She said it as kindly as she could, but her gentleness was lost on him as he glowered at the cards. Then he sat back and sent her a brilliant smile, too brilliant, and he pulled off his shirt.

"I know I lost. I needed to get rid of that shirt. It's too warm by the fire."

His bare chest was beautiful in the firelight. The lights were twinkling on the tree, and this Christmas Eve should have been her fantasy come true.

Instead, she felt cold.

"Trey, I think we should go to the hospital."

"Let me see your feet." He cupped her heel and slid off her sock, the warm wool one she'd borrowed from Patricia's drawer out of necessity. The soles of her feet were peeling from the frostbite, but there was nothing too awful to see, nothing black or green or dangerous.

"It's not my feet. It's you."

He kept his head down, her foot cradled in his hand.

"I read this article once about the signs of stroke. It seems to me you're having an awfully hard time counting and remembering the rules. You're young for a stroke, but it's not impossible. I read this article—"

His head snapped up. "I don't need to go to the hospital."

She was startled at his anger; her foot jerked in his hand.

He set her foot down gently and gathered up the cards.

"You know what?" she said brightly, coming to her feet. She moved over to the sofa, with its end table and the old-fashioned, corded phone that had a permanent place on it. "You shouldn't be driving if we suspect an issue, and I'm not the world's best driver, so I'm just going to call an ambulance. That's the fastest way to get there."

He stood, as well. "Don't call 911."

She was tempted to obey him. He looked so normal, so smoothly coordinated, as he dragged his shirt back over his head. If she hadn't witnessed hand after hand of failed blackjack, she'd never believe there was anything wrong. But she had seen it, and it had scared her. She picked up the phone because she loved him, and she couldn't watch him suffer from an attack that could be silent but real.

He took the phone out of her hand and placed it back in its old-fashioned cradle. "I'm not having a stroke. I just hate to play cards."

It was a laughable statement, but he looked as serious as she felt, standing before the fireplace with his hands on his hips. He didn't touch her. He couldn't quite look at her as he said, "Hate is the wrong word. It's *can't*. I can't play cards."

The simple sentence cost him so much to say, he turned away from her to face the fire.

"You got the first few hands right, but then I think something happened. Did you feel anything? Sometimes people report they felt a pop or—"

"I can get things right sometimes, but then the harder I try, the harder it gets. It's stupid, but it's not a stroke."

"How long has it been like that?"

He braced on hand on the mantel and leaned closer to the fire. The flames lit him in golds and oranges.

"Forever," he said. "It feels like forever."

It was hard for her to imagine Trey being unable to do anything. He was invincible in her eyes, a man impervious to ice storms and unimpressed by hospitals. She'd been spying on him through the windows, watching him ride horses, awed by the way he could make them change directions or gallop or stop, anything at all he wanted. Every night, he handled her as easily, making her climax with a word in her ear and the press of his body, making her sleep with the warmth of his chest as he stroked her hair.

But he could not make cards add up to twenty-one.

She clasped her hands in front of herself, trying to sort through the implications. "It must be more than card games. Do you run into other things that are hard to do?"

"Now and then."

He didn't fool her with his stoic profile and his calm answers. She knew him, and she knew the tension in his shoulders was not right. Her curiosity was burning, but she wasn't going to ask him about things he did not want to talk about, not when he bore each question as if it were a turn of the screw.

"Okay, then." She held up her palms, and shrugged. *All done. No further questions.*

"I didn't mean to ruin your Christmas Eve." He didn't turn to her as he said it. He didn't see the smile she wanted him to see.

She dropped her hands. "It's supposed to be our Christmas Eve, not just mine."

He was so remote as he stared into that fire, alone with thoughts that caused him pain. *Look at me. I'm here. I want to help. I love you.*

But she couldn't say any of that. She'd told him she loved him once, in the cabin. She wasn't brave enough to whisper it again, not when he didn't feel the same. But he loved her touch. She could offer him that.

She walked to his side and placed her palm softly on his back, between his shoulder blades. The muscles were taut. She kept her hand there, waiting for the tension to release.

"If my idea of fun isn't your idea of fun, you could just say so next time," she said.

"It's not that easy."

She kissed his shoulder. "Actually, it is. 'Hey, sweetheart. I don't like to play cards. Let's do something else.' That would work."

Finally, finally, he pushed away from the mantel and turned toward her, and she slid her arms around his waist, fitting herself to him as she had from the first.

"This is still a great Christmas Eve," she said. "We've got the tree and the fire and the hot chocolate."

He gently ran his fingertips over her cheek and returned her smile with a nearly authentic one of his own. "What other Christmas traditions are on your agenda? There's enough food in this house for a feast, but we're fresh out of plum pudding. We could go a-wassailing, but you'd have to tell me what that is, exactly."

She laughed, because he was trying to make her laugh, and she loved him for it. "We should be nestled all snug in our beds with visions of sugarplums dancing in our heads."

"I like the bed part. I might take it as a challenge to drive those thoughts of sugarplums out of your head."

"Challenge accepted."

Their mood was only light on the surface, and as they bared themselves to one another, they stopped trying to be amusing. They kissed and touched and moved in silence. He was hurting inside, and she knew it.

Rebecca wrapped her whole self around him, telling him with her body what she could not say with her words. *I've got you. Hold on to me. You're not alone.*

It was what he'd given her when she'd been cold and hopeless.

She was afraid he still felt alone even after he reached his completion in her arms, so she pulled the covers over his shoulders and tucked herself tightly in with him, as if they shared the warm cocoon of a sleeping bag once more.

"You weren't supposed to get me anything for Christmas."

Rebecca said it at nearly the same time as Trey. They'd agreed to enjoy the holiday without shopping. Neither one of them had cared to leave the ranch in the days since they'd come back from the hospital.

Rebecca had another reason to avoid shopping. She hadn't wanted to use her credit card, because somehow, she seemed to be escaping her mother's attention. It wouldn't last forever, but she wanted to delay the inevitable for as long as she could.

But here they were, sitting on the blanket under the tree on Christmas Day, holding gifts for each other. Rebecca was thrilled, because it gave her an excuse to be close to Trey. On the surface, everything seemed to be their usual smiles and friendship, but underneath, there was a distance between them that there hadn't been before.

He'd told her this morning that he needed to see to the horses, because he'd told the foreman to give everyone

the day off. He'd told her this politely as he'd stood by
the bed, already dressed. Then he'd left her there, alone.

Hours later, he'd returned, given her a quick kiss and
headed for the shower. She'd asked him if he needed help
soaping up. He'd smiled, but told her to stay and enjoy
her newspapers, he'd join her in a minute.

Maybe she was being too sensitive. Maybe it was unrealistic to expect a man to be so into her, day after day.
Maybe this distance was normal.

Normal or not, the distance hurt. The surprise Christmas gift helped. She let herself hope they would get back
to the place they'd been.

"Open mine first," she said, cozying up to him in
her white satin robe, wishing physical closeness could
bridge the gap.

She'd made him a coupon booklet, although it had
turned out less sleek and sophisticated than she'd pic-
tured. She'd included coupons for the free use of mirrors
and showers, one for each position they'd explored. It
had seemed very naughty and fun when she'd made it,
but as he read it, she worried. He meant so much more
to her than this.

The very last coupon said, "A hug and a kiss when
you need it most." Not sex, but closeness. That was what
she wanted for him, with him, for her.

He flipped through the book, that one-sided half-
smile on his face. When he finished, to her great surprise, he raised the booklet to his lips and gave it a kiss.

"It's like a memory book," he said. "A chronicle of
our time together. Every time I look at it, it will help me
to—" He stopped himself. "I'll think of you."

Her heart stopped. Memories?

Their time was up. The distance he was putting between them made sense now. She closed her eyes and laid her head on his shoulder. "You must need to get back to your company in Oklahoma."

There was a long pause. She didn't lift her head or try to see his face. Her heart felt so heavy, she didn't want to try to read his expression or guess what he was thinking.

"Not yet," he said.

It was her reprieve. Her heart, pitiful thing that it was, wanted to cry with relief that for a little while longer, he would stay. She would enjoy his warmth, and store up memories, and hope they would keep the cold away after he left.

It would be like capturing sunshine in a jar, but she would try. She had to try.

She sat up, dry-eyed, and faced him with a smile. "So, do any of those coupons remind you of anything that looks like it would be particularly jolly on this Christmas Day?"

He ran his fingers along her jaw lightly, then pulled her in for a soft Christmas kiss.

"Open your gift," he said.

Inside the box was a letter. In black ink dashed on white paper, in wording so formal he could have copied it from a wedding invitation, Trey requested the honor of her presence at a genuine, traditional Christmas dinner, to be served at the River Mack Ranch.

"It's cheating," he confessed, "but when Mrs. Mac-Dowell called to invite us, I knew it was the best way to give you a traditional Christmas. You already know Jamie and his wife—ah, what was her name?"

"Kendry."

"Right. You already know them, so you won't be

among strangers. Do you want to go? We don't have to, if you don't want to."

Did she want to spend time with him, among his friends, being a part of his life?

"I do."

Chapter Fourteen

Christmas at the River Mack Ranch made Rebecca happy, and that made it worth the effort for Trey. Nothing else would have induced him to accept the invitation. Social events were too fraught with ways for him to humiliate himself.

Yet, all the possibilities he'd braced himself to face for Rebecca's sake hadn't happened. The road between the James Hill and the River Mack was the same as it had been since his childhood. He hadn't needed to stop and think and check directions. He'd been able to get behind the wheel of his truck and drive his date to the MacDowells' house, like any man should be able to do.

Jamie's older brothers, Quinn and Braden, were closer to Trey's age, and he knew them better than he knew Jamie. They were here, instantly recognizable, part of the football memories that had been so recently unlocked. If anything, it was Quinn and Rebecca who seemed to have a memory problem. They spent a minute saying how familiar each looked, until they recalled meeting when Rebecca had last visited Patricia. Quinn and Patricia were both with Texas Rescue, that much Trey absorbed.

He turned to greet Mrs. MacDowell. She looked exactly as Trey remembered her. Since he'd so recently survived Aunt June's hugging and fussing, Mrs. MacDowell's was less alarming.

Trey managed not to blurt any random thoughts, taking a moment before speaking to be sure what he said was appropriate. At dinner, however, with the food and confusion and conversation, it happened. As he watched everyone devouring turkey and gravy, he said, "Rebecca devours newspapers."

The awkwardness passed quickly. The beat of surprise from the MacDowells at his end of the table quickly turned into more conversation about the local newspapers and their coverage of the hospital when its CEO had been arrested for embezzling.

Braden was the new CEO. As the meal went on and information and updates from a decade's absence rolled in, Trey could feel his brain shutting off. He fought it. For Rebecca, he wouldn't withdraw and turn into a silent, sullen guest.

But he could only concentrate on so many things at once. He stopped eating in order to focus on the faces around him. Half the people were familiar, which saved him, because there were also strangers. There was a baby, a newborn who slept while everyone sang her praises, and a toddler who fed himself mashed potatoes with two chubby hands. Not only was Jamie married to what-was-her-name with the ponytail, but Braden was married, as well. Quinn was engaged. Those women were all here, easy enough to talk with since Trey didn't really need to remember who went with which brother or which baby belonged to whom. They were all Mac-Dowells. That was all he needed to know.

No math of any kind came up in conversation, so all in all, Trey felt he'd managed to pull off a decent Christmas for Rebecca.

But he was exhausted, as if he'd taken final exams at school, math and history and literature, one after the other without a break. That kind of tired.

After dinner, the men pulled him into their father's old den, because there was a college bowl game on television. It was time for football. Trey dropped into the nearest armchair, too exhausted to drink the beer that Quinn pressed into his hand.

On television, a player got clobbered, the kind of hit that made everyone wince in sympathy—except Trey. He paid no attention, relieved to be sitting still and letting his mind take a break.

"You took a hit like that, senior year, against Anderson High," Braden said to Quinn.

"That was nothing compared to the one Trey took against Killeen." Quinn tapped his beer can to Trey's. "Remember that one? I think it was the only time coach let you sit out one whole play before putting you back in."

The MacDowells made all the appropriate manly noises, everyone remembering their tough coach, and glory days.

"You remember that?" Quinn asked him again.

Trey forced himself to pay attention. "A game against Killeen?"

"Yeah, senior year. Went into overtime. C'mon, you remember. You won it with a forty-yard pass to that freshman, the cocky kid, what's his name?"

"Zach Bishop." Trey wanted to say he'd just seen him

recently, in the helicopter after the ice storm, but putting together all the right words to tell the story would take too much effort.

"That's the one," Jamie agreed.

Still, Trey felt better. He'd remembered a name everyone else had forgotten. He was too hard on himself, maybe, when he spoke of someone like Jamie's wife as what's-her-name. Quinn, who was a doctor, had just done it himself.

"It was Bishop who got your brother to volunteer with the fire department," Quinn said. "They're working together for Texas Rescue now."

"No, my brother's on his honeymoon."

All three MacDowells looked at him instead of the television. Trey knew he'd said something off. He gripped the cold beer can.

"You remember that game against Killeen?" Jamie asked again, sounding more like a serious doctor than a kid brother. Either was trouble Trey didn't want.

"Not really." Trey kept his gaze on the television. They were strapping the player to a backboard, immobilizing his neck with a foam brace.

Jamie nodded at the screen and spoke to the group at large. "We don't let them back in the game anymore. They've gotta sit out at least a week of practice, and then they have to see me or their own family doctor for clearance. Coach is pretty pissed at the team doctor for enforcing the new rules."

"Let me guess," Trey said, taking a moment to be sure he was about to say something normal. "The new team doc is named MacDowell. Jamie?"

"Yep. Coach says he's in the business of winning championships. I'm in the business of preventing brain injuries. He thinks my first season as team doctor should be the last, but I told him that wasn't his call to make."

Quinn and Braden exchanged a look, brothers ready to defend their own, but Jamie laughed, breaking the tension in the room. "It's pretty satisfying to see the old man's face when I pull rank on him."

"Well, my wife's gonna pull rank on me if I hide out here much longer." Braden left first, but they all returned to the main part of the house, Trey hauling himself out of the armchair last.

The women were cooing over the babies, and before Trey's eyes, the men started cooing over the women. That's how it looked to him. Each man had a woman who smiled when he walked up to her, someone pretty in her Christmas finery to lift her face and accept a kiss on the cheek or lips.

Then Braden picked up his newborn child. Braden, older than them all in school, the first to make varsity, the first to graduate, the one they'd all looked up to, *that* Braden looked at that baby, and that baby looked at him, and Trey could've seen the love a mile away. Braden was a goner for a baby girl who fit in the palms of his hands, head over heels with no turning back.

I want that.

Trey would never have it, because no one had ever strapped him to a backboard and cradled his neck in foam.

On Christmas Day, in his neighbor's living room, James Waterson III knew, finally, what was wrong with him. It wasn't that he was lazy. It wasn't that he didn't try hard enough. He was not stupid, and he was not insane.

He had brain damage.

The doctors had said he didn't. The tests had all been normal. Ten years ago, they'd been wrong.

Millions of players had come through just fine—his own brother had played football without incident—but not Trey. He'd taken that hit, the dangerous kind, and he'd taken it more than once. More than twice. He'd been praised for his toughness and his ability to perform when his ears were ringing and his vision was blurred.

He stood in the doorway, watched the holiday scene before him and finally understood.

Then his worst nightmare came true. A young woman came in from the kitchen, cute with brown bangs yet sexy in a red sweater, and Trey thought, *Damn, she's pretty. Who is that?* Then recognition exploded in his mind, and he knew Rebecca and everything about her.

But for one millisecond, he'd lost his memory of her.

He wouldn't allow it. Nothing else mattered, not the strangers or the friends. Not the noise and the food. The women's laughter, the babies' tears—he cared for none of it. If his brain could only think of one thing at a time, then all of that had to go, because the only thing he absolutely had to be able to hold on to was Rebecca.

"We've got to leave now." He grabbed her hand and started pulling her to the door.

"Trey!" She hissed his name quietly, and tugged on his hand.

He stopped, because she wanted him to stop. She slipped her hand from his, went to pick up her purse and kissed Jamie's wife on the cheek. She thanked everyone and wished them a merry Christmas, and made a proper exit out of his botched one. Everyone smiled at them as they left.

Trey drove straight home. When Rebecca asked what the problem was, he couldn't explain.

He left the light on in the bedroom, and made love to her while holding her face in his hands. He made her look at him, so he could see her eyes and remember their exact shade of brown. With every stroke, he committed her to his memory. With every roll of his hips, he tried to make her a permanent part of him. He would not lose her. He couldn't bear to lose her, and he told her so. With his body and with his words.

He felt clumsy, his brain so tired from the holiday, and he didn't know if he was saying the right thing.

"You. It's you. You're everything."

Afterward, as she sprawled on his chest and he stroked her hair, she said, "I love you."

He was afraid to close his eyes and go to sleep, because if she wasn't there when he woke, he would die.

Chapter Fifteen

Trey stabbed the pitchfork into the hay. His brain was still tired from yesterday's dinner at the MacDowells', but his body was not. Physically, he felt strong and rested, so he'd left Rebecca in the four-poster bed and come to the barn to work off some energy. The cowboys he'd encountered—his own damned ranch hands, technically—had found work elsewhere on the ranch.

Trey forked more hay into the stall of an unappreciative horse. The mare picked up on his frustration and showed her disapproved by shaking her mane and blowing air through her soft nose.

"What are you doing, Waterson?" he muttered under his breath. He stopped and leaned on the pitchfork.

He was screwing everything up, that's what he was doing. Last night, tired and emotional, he'd crossed the line from an *interlude*, a pleasant week or two with the lovely Rebecca Cargill, and taken it to a different level.

Sex like they'd had last night wasn't just sex. It was the basis for a different kind of relationship. It was like laying a cornerstone to start a foundation for something big. It was dangerous, because it would make Rebecca think that the cornerstone had been laid for a reason, that it would support something built to last.

It wouldn't. It was just a brick, not a building. Their relationship was going nowhere.

"Brain damage." It made him sick to his stomach to say the words out loud, so he forced himself to say them, to get used to the feel of them on his tongue. He stabbed the hay again. "Brain damage."

Just because those freakish faults had a name and a cause didn't make them go away. He understood now why he'd let down every person who'd thought he had potential. The knowledge changed nothing. He was still the man who forgot to put water in the coffeepot and who got lost driving to client sites.

He was going back to Oklahoma, to run his landscaping business in his own brain-damaged way and to enjoy the occasional company of women who didn't want to get too serious. In the meantime, he needed to keep the proper perspective with Rebecca. They had a great time in bed. Their physical chemistry worked for them, for fun and friendship. He'd help her get set up in her first job and first apartment, and they'd part as friends, better for having known one another.

There'd been no Christmas miracle. Nothing had changed.

A piercing wolf whistle split the air in the barn. The horses shied and whinnied. Trey put a calming hand on the nose of the mare next to him and turned to see Rebecca, of course, standing with both hands over her mouth and her eyes wide with alarm.

"I'm so sorry," she said. "I didn't think about the horses. You just look sexy with a pitchfork."

It was too damned hard not to smile at Rebecca. Trey let himself grin as he nodded toward the aisle. The horses had gone back to their oats, only a few stamping a hoof to let them know how they felt about the interruption. "They're fine. They'd appreciate it if you didn't do that too often."

She came up to him, her pink parka unzipped to reveal a tropical blouse, her slacks formfitting. The parka and slacks were her clothes from the cabin, retrieved with the ATVs, washed and fresh now, but they reminded him how close he'd come to losing her once before.

Keep it light. Friendship. Chemistry. An interlude.

"Are we all alone in here?" Rebecca asked, running a finger along a stall door, pretending it was an idle question.

Trey kissed her lightly, a good-morning kiss. She smelled fantastic. She looked fantastic, with her hair brushed loose and her face clean and natural. "Just you, me and the horses."

"Have you ever had sex in a stable?"

His body tightened in response. He wanted her too much. He couldn't have casual sex with her. Not yet. Not this morning.

He turned away, and lifted another forkful of hay. "Having sex with your boots on is disrespectful to a woman. You don't take your boots off in a barn."

"But have you ever had sex in a barn? This barn?"

Trey's brain might not work well, but he knew better than to tell a woman about experiences with another woman.

"I wouldn't sleep with someone I didn't respect."

"I'm not talking about sleeping."

He rolled his eyes at that, but found he was grinning as he spread more hay.

Rebecca stood on her toes to look into the stall of a dappled gray mare. He was glad to see her feet caused her no pain. The frostbite was nearly healed.

Keep it light.

"If people have sex near them, do the horses whinny or kick the stalls or get mad?" she asked.

"The horses don't care."

"A-ha! You have had sex in a barn."

He didn't know whether to laugh or cry at her persistence. He stabbed the pitchfork into a tightly tied bale and left it there, upright, before he turned to face her. "No, I have not had sex in this barn. I've had my-father-would-kill-me-if-I-got-a-girl-pregnant-so-we're-sure-gonna-fool-around-but-not-go-all-the-way in this barn."

They stared each other down. He refused to admit he hadn't quite intended to say that.

"Wow," she said, first one to blink. "That sounds like it was kind of fabulous to be a teenager. Was it wonderful, growing up here?"

The expression on her face was so full of yearning, Trey looked up to the rafters to guard his heart. He could imagine her unstable childhood, stepparents and siblings and homes changing too often. As she'd become a teenager, he doubted she'd had the chance to taste love with a boy her age. Hell, she hadn't been allowed to choose her own clothes. Her mother had stolen her childhood.

Trey had lived a great life, the best of childhoods, until he'd become an adult.

He looked at Rebecca again. "Yes, I was lucky to grow up here. I'm sorry you never got to fool around in a barn."

He didn't voice the rest of his thought. *We're opposites, me with my great childhood and lousy adulthood. You had a bad childhood, but your adult life will be beautiful.*

Rebecca didn't seem to be thinking anything quite so philosophical. She'd advanced on him slowly, a woman walking in a way that was anything but childish.

She slid a finger between the pearl-button snaps of his plaid shirt. "Just how sorry are you about my lack of barn experience?"

"I can't help you with the not-go-all-the-way part." He slid his hands down the curve of her backside, then scooped her off her feet with his hands under her thighs. She wrapped her legs around his waist naturally as he pressed her against the door to a stall. That particular horse, at least, minded a little bit and moved away from them.

Rebecca kept toying with his shirt. "I'm a little worried about this being your first time. If you've never had sex in a barn before, are you going to be able to figure out how to do it with your boots on?"

"I've got some ideas. What happens if they work?"

"I'll make you a coupon, so you can do it again."

Trey watched Rebecca as she made her way back to the house. His body felt better than ever. His mind was still screwed up.

What the hell are you doing, Waterson?

Rebecca looked considerably more rumpled leaving than she had when she'd come in, but she walked with a bounce in her step, peeking back at Trey now and then with a look on her face like she was the cat that had eaten the canary.

Trey grinned back at her. She should look like that; she'd gotten her way.

He leaned against the barn's door frame, hands in his pockets when they should have been on the pitchfork, keeping an eye on her for the pleasure of it. He had to shake his head at himself and their foolishness. Anyone on the ranch could've taken a look at the two of them and known what was up.

Just keeping it light. Friendly-like, until I get back to Oklahoma.

He needed to get back to work. Not to the pitchfork, but to his real job. Winter was the slow season for a landscaper, of course, so it had been fine to leave his lead crew with the truck keys and orders to handle the basic routine. But Trey was the owner, and an owner couldn't leave a business and expect it to run itself.

Not the way this ranch got by without him. Luke had done well. Trey knew Luke hadn't had much of a choice, because Trey had pretty much skipped town and their parents had decided to retire young, but the James Hill Ranch was thriving in Luke's hands.

Rebecca disappeared into the house. Into her home, the only home she had right now. His grin faded. Trey was giving her a place to live, but he was being careful to give her nothing else. Sex in the stables had been fun. A little playtime. Nothing more.

He'd messed that up last night, making love to her with such intensity. They were back on track now. Light and breezy, not building any kind of foundation.

Trey turned back into the barn. He couldn't think, standing still. That wasn't part of any brain injury. He'd always done his best thinking while doing something physical. What he needed right now was something to throw. Hurling a football would clear his thoughts, but there wasn't one in sight, and no one around to catch it if there were.

He grabbed a lasso off the wall and headed through the barn to go out the far side. Coils in his left hand, loop in his right, he walked toward the paddock and started swinging the loop. He built up the motion, keeping the circle slow, turning his wrist with the loop, feeling muscles move in a way they hadn't for ten years. With the rope at its apex, he let go, not throwing so much as guiding its trajectory, the way he'd been doing it since middle school.

He missed.

The rope bounced off the paddock's fence post and hit the dirt.

Trey pulled it back toward himself, coiling it again. He needed to be able to do this. If he couldn't throw a decent lasso, he couldn't stay on the ranch. Regardless of how right it felt to be here, and despite the fact that it was the one place on earth he didn't feel disoriented, Trey would not stay if he could not do the work. He wouldn't be able to survive the sympathy if he was treated as the poor kid who'd gotten hit in the head. He'd rather mow lawns in Oklahoma than have his own ranch hands pity him.

He built the lasso's momentum, and let it go. It landed around the fence post. Reflexively, Trey pulled it taut. Then he fed it some slack and flicked his wrist to jump the lasso off the fence post.

He gathered it back in and threw it again.

The fence post was too easy. Trey transferred a few coils into his loop hand, enough to gain an extra ten feet or so, swung the circle over his head and let it sail to a farther post.

He snagged that post and pulled the loop taut, all reflex. This time, the post was too far away for him to flick the rope off. He walked toward it, winding up the rope as he went, thinking about what he needed to think about: Rebecca.

What the hell are you doing, Waterson?

He was laying a foundation with her, that was what he was doing. It wasn't just built out of the serious lovemaking, the kind they'd shared last night or her first time, *their* first time, in the cabin. It was all of it. Every blush in the mirror, every slippery encounter in a soapy shower. Each time they were together, they set another brick in the foundation.

He could tell himself this morning in the stables had been just for fun, but it had added to that foundation. When he hauled in a box of decorations or she handed him a section of the newspaper, they built something solid. Every stomp of her foot, every marshmallow in the cocoa, it all counted. All of it.

Closer now to the fence post, Trey flipped the lasso free. The foreman was walking toward him from the direction of the cattle sheds. They met at the paddock's fence.

"Been a while, huh?" Gus's voice matched his look. Tough, weathered cowboy to the core.

Trey nodded once. "I'll take that to mean it looks as rusty as it feels."

Gus turned and spit some tobacco juice, a nasty habit that Trey had been dying to try when he was eleven. Gus had let him. Trey had turned green and manfully announced he would be a tobacco-free cowboy. That had been before he'd decided to be an NFL quarterback. He'd ended up being neither.

"Son, your rusty is still better'n most boys' best."

Trey raised an eyebrow at that. Those were high words of praise from the foreman.

"How's landscaping treating you?"

"It's a living." Trey was mildly surprised at the personal question. It looked like Gus wanted to have a chat.

Trey rested his arm on the post and squinted against the Texas sun, bright even in winter, as he gazed across the paddock to the pasture beyond. That pasture, not too far away, was hardly ever used, because grass didn't like to grow there.

It was a landscaping nightmare, an acre or two of tough soil on a bit of a rise, but Trey knew what would grow there: olive trees. The agricultural magazines he read as part of his profession had been featuring olive oil and wine presses in Texas Hill Country for a couple of years now. Trey didn't know squat about grapevines, but trees were a different matter.

That pasture had always been underused. He should plant a couple of acres of olive trees there, sell the fruit to one of the local presses and turn a little profit on land that served no purpose.

If he were here to oversee it, that was. His brother didn't know trees. Trey couldn't plant an orchard and leave it for another ten years.

"Been meaning to ask you, son," Gus began, and Trey knew the reason Gus had sought him out was about to become clear, "about that new hand Luke wants hired. I've got someone in mind."

Luke and Trey and their father had held a three-way

conference call last month. Luke had asked them to sink some of the year's profits into hiring more ranch hands.

Trey remembered the conversation clearly now, because the memories came easier out here on the land with a lasso in his hands. He remembered the guilt he'd felt, the guilt he always felt about the ranch he mostly ignored.

Luke and his new wife intended to make the ranch house their home, but she was the director of Texas Rescue and Relief, the same organization that had sent the helicopter, and her office was in downtown Austin. They planned to keep her high-rise apartment and spend time there, as well.

I'm not expecting my wife to commute from the ranch all the way to downtown Monday through Friday, and I'm not expecting to live apart from my bride most days, either.

They'd agreed to his plan, but Trey had known it had been more of an ultimatum. Luke was done with being tied to the ranch three hundred and sixty-five days a year. If neither Trey nor their father were willing to shoulder some of the responsibility, then they'd better hire someone to do it for them.

Now Gus was asking Trey about one of those new hires. Trey was the wrong man to ask. He'd just come to the ranch for the wedding.

"Has Luke met him?"

"No." Gus spit again. "Luke's gone a month. This boy needs a job now, so I figured you could give the okay."

Trey tied off the rope into a knot every cowboy knew, an action he hadn't done since he was nineteen, but it came naturally, anyway. "We trust your judgment, Gus.

You don't need a Waterson's permission to hire a ranch hand for the James Hill. You know that."

"Well, yeah, but this'n is different. He's my nephew, so I don't want it looking like I'm giving salaries to my own family. Good boy, but can't seem to stick with a job in the city. I thought the ranch might be better for him."

This was a delicate subject. Gus wouldn't want to say someone in his family was a failure, but not being able to hold down a job was a red flag in Trey's book.

"Does he know cattle?"

"Nope."

"Horses?"

"Nope."

Trey hung the coiled rope on the fence post, letting his silence speak for itself. Gus knew better. Maybe he'd asked so that he could go back to his nephew and honestly say he'd tried.

"But he's strong. A Marine. Did his time overseas. He knows how to get up before the roosters tell him to and how to put in a full day. That's more than you can say for half these wannabe cowboys."

Trey rubbed his jaw. So that was the rest of the story. A war veteran, having a hard time adjusting to civilian life. He put his boot on the bottom rung of the fence. "A three-month contract, then. We can always use someone with a strong back. We'll see if he likes the ranch and if the ranch likes him. That's three months to learn enough horses and cattle to make himself useful. If it works out, we can add him to the roster for roundup this spring."

Gus tugged on the brim of his cowboy hat. "That's a fair deal. Thank you."

As Gus walked away, Trey studied the dead land of

the not-too-distant pasture. He could bring it back to life with a nice olive grove.

Hell, the view from over there was pretty nice. A house could sit in the middle of the grove, nothing fancy, just a straightforward, square limestone. Big porch to take advantage of the view. Modern inside, the kind of layout where the kitchen and the living room were one big space. Rebecca would like that. She could decorate the hell out of it at Christmas, hang little twinkly lights on the porch and stuff. He'd see them when he rode his horse back after a day on the range.

God, his chest hurt at the picture of it.

He stacked his fists on top of the fence post and rested his forehead on them, almost a prayerful position. What if…what if the next time Luke asked Trey to run the ranch with him, Trey dumped the guilt and said yes?

He felt like he could do it. He didn't get lost out here. He could lasso and ride. Making decisions for the ranch like the one Gus had just asked him to make came easily, the same kind of decisions he'd been making for years for his business in Oklahoma.

The specter of his last roundup loomed large in the wreckage of his memory. He could brand a cow upside down again or do something else that made him look like a drunken fool. But he was thirty-one years old now. He didn't care to tell anyone about his brain injury, but if he said something stupid the way he had in the hospital when he'd thought Aunt June needed a ride home in his truck, could he just let it slide and carry on?

And Rebecca…

Trey lifted his head again and looked at his dead pasture. Would a small house in a big olive grove be enough? Would it make up for the fact that she'd have a husband who couldn't help his kids with their elementary school homework? A husband who could forget which order to put the clothes in the washer and dryer? The shame of it made him not want to even try.

But Rebecca...

If he truly loved her, he'd let her find a better man, one without a bad brain. The idea of cutting her loose to build a life with another man caused a pain that felt like rage inside him.

He couldn't let her go. He'd found her, he'd warmed her back to life with his own body and they'd started laying a foundation together, brick by brick.

He was going to keep her.

If she'd have him.

He started walking back toward the ranch house to find out.

Chapter Sixteen

Rebecca sat in the mudroom and pulled off her boots. They were pink and designer-name and expensive, but they hadn't kept her feet warm during an ice storm. When she got her first paycheck, she was going to buy new ones. Better ones.

She hung up her ski parka. That, at least, had been as functional as it was fashionable. Her mother had accidentally outfitted her in something useful despite its childish shade of pink. Since the coat was warm, Rebecca couldn't really justify buying a new one right away, but she would, someday. Maybe something more ranch-like, natural leather with a sheepskin lining, like Trey wore. Hers would be nipped in a bit at the waist, more feminine in style.

Sorry, Mother, no more shapeless clothes to hide my figure. You're just going to have to admit you're old enough to have a grown-up daughter.

She walked through the black-and-white kitchen and into the comfy family room, where she'd decked the halls to her heart's content. There, standing by the ornament-laden Christmas tree, was her mother.

"Hello, Becky. Merry Christmas, baby girl, one day late."

It wasn't possible. Rebecca had accidentally, horribly conjured her by thinking of her in the mudroom.

Her mother had chosen the perfect place to stand. Morning sunlight came in the window behind her, making a halo effect around the edges of her dark hair, sparkling off the silver threads in her loose black blouse. Her mother hit just the right casual note by wearing it tucked into flattering black jeans. She looked, as always, fabulous.

"Come here, Becky. I've surprised you terribly, haven't I? No one answered the knock, but I knew an old-fashioned ranch like this would have the door open to visitors." Her mother laughed and held out both hands, simply delighted to see her.

Rebecca, who had been obedient for twenty-four years, automatically responded and crossed the room toward her mother. They were obviously on stage. She looked to see who the performance was for. A man in a plain navy suit stood by the front door, but his suit wasn't cut well enough to make him important. As she rounded the sofa, she saw, sitting in the winged-back armchair, the man for whom her mother was being so charming. Hector Ferrique, in crushingly expensive casual clothing, smiled at her.

Her mother took her hands and kissed her on each cheek. "How was Patricia's wedding? Did my ex-husband perform his duties adequately?" She sent a mocking look Hector's way with that comment, to let him know that she'd found the infamous Daddy Cargill's performance not up to her standards—unlike her dear Hector, no doubt.

"I didn't get to see Daddy," Rebecca murmured, obedient and vague, as she knew she should be.

Even as she followed her mother's cues, her mind raced. She could see things differently now. Surely, her mother had been sleeping with Hector in Rebecca's absence. Little Becky had flown away, and her mother must have gone to the Caribbean and done some explaining—and some apologizing. Some substituting.

Your mother is a call girl? Trey had asked Rebecca in the cabin, trying to understand her life.

Rebecca freed her hands from her mother's grasp and clasped them before herself. Her mother was not a call girl, but she had used sex or the promise of sex to keep a roof over their heads and to pay for Becky's private primary education. Rebecca found that sad and almost humbling. She ought to be grateful, but her mother had never acted like it had been a sacrifice, only a triumph.

The part of her that was still little Becky couldn't find it in herself to feel thankful for her mother's triumphs. For the past six years, because of her mother's need to keep men sexually attracted to herself, Becky had been deprived of a college education and a normal transition to adulthood. It was a sick thing, to keep another person eternally at age eighteen.

Rebecca had made that transition to adulthood now. Survival in an ice storm had a way of changing a person. Trey had never known her as Becky. Being treated by him like she was a whole and independent person affected how she saw herself.

"Your mother explained about your scheduling conflict." Hector spoke from the armchair like it was his throne. "I was very disappointed not to have your company this holiday."

Trey!

But Trey had stayed at the stables. He had things to do on the ranch. If he'd taken one of the horses out, he might not be back for hours. Rebecca was on her own.

She turned her back on Hector, unwilling to engage in even the most mundane conversation with a man who only wanted her because she looked like she was underage.

She was afraid she still looked that way. Her slacks were too long without her boots on. It was hard to look sophisticated in socks. But she was no child. She'd just seduced a cowboy. The man of her choice, handsome and strong, had been unable to resist her.

She unclasped her hands and stopped waiting for her mother's next move. "What do you need from me, Mother?"

"Need from you? Don't be silly, sweetie. I came to take you back home now that the wedding is over. Hector and I enjoyed Bimini but without you...well, it just wasn't the same. Your sister must still be on her honeymoon, so there's no reason for you to stay here. Patricia is gone, isn't she?"

Her mother was scared of Patricia Cargill. Rebecca had known that, even as a child. It was, after all, why she'd come to the James Hill Ranch: to hide behind Patricia's wedding gown skirts.

Rebecca felt Hector's gaze on her, and she hid behind those skirts again. "Patricia's out at the moment. I'm not sure when she'll return."

Her mother narrowed her eyes. "She's out?"

"Yes." Rebecca raised her chin and met her glare.

"Hmm…" Her mother moved from her picturesque spot by the tree and began strolling through the room, gliding her hand along the fireplace mantel, above the Christmas garland Rebecca had hung. Her gaze moved about the room, judging, weighing, evaluating. She paused at the far end of the mantel. "The fireplace is unique, very Texas. I'm sure Patricia will keep it when she remodels. The exposed roof beams have a rustic appeal."

She left the fireplace to sit on the arm of Hector's chair, a route that required her to pass Rebecca. As she brushed by Rebecca, she hissed in her ear. "She's on her honeymoon. Don't be an idiot."

Her mother perched on the armrest, forcing Rebecca to turn back around and face Hector, *Mr. Ferrique*, as her mother continued talking. "Patricia will keep those features, I'm sure. She's always had a good eye. The rest will have to be gutted. You're saying that's where she is? At the designer's? Well, if she's not back by the time you're packed, you'll just have to leave your sister a note. Hector's plane can't be kept waiting forever. Go pack, sweetie."

"No, thank you." Rebecca felt the significance of her stiff words. Her heart pounded, but the weight of the world seemed to lift from her shoulders. Three little words had never been so liberating. "I've decided to live here. I won't be returning to Boston. I was going to send for my things."

That had been a tactical error. From the way her mother's eyes narrowed, Rebecca knew she should have called the staff at the Cape Cod home and had them ship her belongings the day Trey had told her she could stay. She'd never get her things now. Not one thing.

It's okay. I'm going to have a job. I'll buy my own things.

In the meantime, she wouldn't starve and she wouldn't freeze, because Trey would support her.

Just as Hector supported her mother.

Something inside her protested that it wasn't the same thing, but as she looked at her mother perched beside her provider, she knew the truth. Had Trey been in the room, Rebecca would have sat with him. He provided all her material needs, and she…seduced him. Kept him happy.

She was just like her mother.

Hector pulled back the cuff of his sweater with a neat jerk and made a show of checking the time on his Rolex. Then he rested his hand on her mother's thigh and drummed his fingers impatiently. Just once.

Her mother got the message. With a quickness of mind that had always impressed Rebecca, she changed tactics.

"I should have guessed that once a Cargill returned to Texas soil, she wouldn't want to leave. There's nothing more Texan than an oil baron's daughter, is there?" She laughed her martini and diamonds laugh, letting it taper off into a sigh. "It looks like I've got a little family matter to address. We won't bore you, Hector."

Her mother stood and threaded her arm through Rebecca's. "Let's take this to the kitchen, Becky. Show me where they keep the coffee."

Rebecca had never been a match for her mother. She'd learned not to disagree so long ago, she couldn't recall ever telling her mother no. Her mother never argued with her, for Rebecca never opposed her. But she was disagreeing with Mother today, and the resulting battle was worse than she could have imagined.

Back in the cabin, Trey had said she'd been trying to break out of prison. The analogy had resonated with her. She'd always known the prison guard would be harsh if she were caught. The actual sting of the guard's baton, however, could not have been prepared for. Each verbal hit was painful, even though she'd known it was coming.

"You stupid child. Patricia Cargill got here first. There is no room for you. You would have known better, if you had half a brain in your head."

They were sitting at the kitchen table, steaming mugs in front of them. Appearances were preserved. Anyone walking in would see a mother and daughter catching up over coffee. Her mother delivered all her blows quietly, hissing her words through perfectly white teeth.

"Damn it, Becky, use your head. This is your chance. You can have everything. The house on Cape Cod. Trips around the world. You'll be able to point at anything in any store window, and it will be yours."

"I don't want that," she said quietly. Respectfully.

Her mother slapped her palm on the table, making Becky jump as the sugar bowl rattled. "You don't know what you're saying. Patricia will not want you underfoot in this house. You're younger than she is. Men are drawn to innocence. You think she's going to want her husband looking at you breakfast, lunch and dinner?"

"I'm going to get a job and move out soon."

"Oh, please." Her mother closed her eyes as if Becky's ignorance caused her pain. "This is what we're going to do. We'll return to Boston with Hector. If you've taken it into your head that you can do better, then we'll start looking. Cape Cod is too small. We'll stay in town and let you be seen at some clubs, so people will realize you're twenty-one. You'll need a new wardrobe. Nothing too dramatically different, at first."

"No." Rebecca stood up. "I don't want to start clubbing in Boston, Mother. I'm twenty-four, and I'm staying here."

The sound of the mudroom door opening made her knees go weak with relief. She turned to see Trey coming in as always, stomping the dirt from his boots, unfastening his coat. "Trey?" she said, trying to sound calm.

He looked up immediately. She must not have sounded very calm, because he came directly into the kitchen with his coat and boots on. After the briefest of glances at her mother, his attention was all for her. "Are you all right?"

He stood next to her, very close, and placed his hand in the small of her back as he removed his hat.

Her mother sat up very straight, missing nothing.

Rebecca took a deep breath. "Mother, I'd like you to meet Trey Waterson. Trey, this is my mother, Charlene Lexington Maynard."

Trey calmly tossed his hat on the table. It knocked her mother's coffee spoon sideways. He nodded, once. "Ma'am."

"Oh, call me Charlene, please."

Her mother was all gracious smiles, but Rebecca could see the wheels in her mind turning. She'd counted on Patricia and her husband being away on their honeymoon. Rebecca would perhaps be staying with some doddering old folks, relatives of the groom. She hadn't expected a man like Trey.

"*Trey* Waterson?" she confirmed. "Not Patricia's Luke?"

"James Waterson the third," Rebecca said quietly,

taking pride in the name, although it really had nothing to do with her.

"You live here, then, James. And my daughter's been living with you. Sit down, and let's get to know one another better." She patted the table to indicate an empty chair.

Rebecca began to move toward it, but Trey stopped her by sliding his hand from her back to rest on her hip. Other than that, he didn't move at all.

She wished she were more like him; it hadn't occurred to Trey to obey her mother. She stood still, waiting for a scene to unfold that she hadn't foreseen. Never had she imagined that she'd face her mother with a man like Trey by her side.

Her mother tilted her head, studying Trey with her smile still in place. "You look like a cowboy, James. Do you not think you ought to meet with a girl's parent?"

Rebecca looked at Trey nervously. He didn't look nervous at all. He had that stoic cowboy look on his face, the one he wore most of the time, unless she teased a grin out of him.

It didn't sit well with her mother. "This isn't a suggestion. Where I come from, a man sits when he's invited to talk with a lady."

"You don't strike me as a person I'd like to sit down and talk with."

Her mother's gasp was loud enough to cover her own. Rebecca bit her lip. It was possible Trey hadn't meant to say that, but he looked very cool and unruffled. Her mother wasn't going to hear an *I didn't mean to say that*.

He'd meant it, and he said more. "If there is anything particular you'd like to say to me, Charlene, I suggest you say it now. You weren't invited into my home, and you'll be leaving it soon enough."

Rebecca held her breath.

Charlene stood and crossed her arms over her chest. "You want it that way? Fine. I'll make this simple for everyone to understand. You're shagging my daughter. You took her virginity. I don't see a ring on her finger."

Marriage. Of course, her mother would demand marriage. Although Rebecca had broken the cardinal rule and Trey had gotten the milk for free, now her mother would demand that he buy the cow.

Tears stung her eyes. She didn't want a proposal wrung out of any man under duress. As she took a breath to beg her mother not to start with the marriage talk, Trey squeezed her hip, as if he wanted her to stay silent. Rebecca kept quiet and didn't beg.

Her mother kept talking. "Don't assume that I'm unhappy about that. Just the opposite. Thank God, there's no ring on her finger. She can do much better than a midcentury modern house in the middle of nowhere. But since you've felt free to enjoy her company, I want to know what you're going to do for her future. When you've had your fun, what is she going to have to show for it?"

"Mother, stop." It was so crass, Rebecca broke her silence. She felt her own blush.

"Do you think I'm going to keep that rental car on my credit card for one more day, Becky? Your boy here can pony up and buy you something decent to drive. You should have already arranged it, young lady."

"I don't want that." The discussion was making her feel cheap and tawdry, but worse, it was exposing every ugly truth about how she'd been raised. She'd told Trey about the stepfathers and the marriages, painting as positive a picture as she could of her life. With all these crass words, Trey's opinion of her had to fall. It was true she'd been raised with her mother's values. She'd never believed in them, but she felt guilty by association.

"You deserve a car, and more besides. Grow a spine, Becky Cargill. He took your virginity, for God's sake."

"Stop it." Rebecca stepped forward. "It's none of your business. I am none of your business."

"Hector was taking you to a seaside palace. He's got a rope of pearls in a velvet box ready for you, and that was just the first day's gift. There were to be treats every day. That's what I raised you for, to be treated like a princess. That's why I took you in, and made you a Cargill. I raised you with Maynards and Lexingtons. We've worked for this your whole life."

Rebecca whirled back toward Trey, who was still calm, studying her mother intently, taking in every word she said.

"Don't believe her," Rebecca said. "I don't want any of that. I never have."

Trey turned his gaze to her, studying her as he had her mother, as if he had all the time in the world. He placed his warm hand over hers; she hadn't realized she was clutching his sleeve. "You are the one I know, not her. I trust you. I'm just listening to the tale she's spinning. It's like watching a mare try to establish herself as boss of the corral. You watch her for a while to see if she's gonna calm down and fit in. If she doesn't, then you have to cut her from the herd. The rest of the horses don't want her around."

Rebecca wished her wobbly smile reflected her rock-solid heart better. She loved this man. She really did.

"I love your cowboy analogies."

He didn't grin, but he smoothed his fingertips over the back of her hand before moving away. "Some mares never learn to get along. They get trailered and taken to another ranch to become some other man's problem. Charlene, it's time for you to go."

He gestured toward the living room, but Charlene didn't move, so he took her by the arm and escorted her with the proper cowboy manners she'd accused him of lacking. Rebecca followed, so grateful the whole dreaded encounter was ending that she forgot what was waiting around the corner.

"Who the hell are you?" Trey demanded of the man in his armchair. He released Charlene's arm with an unceremonious push toward the front door and stood with his hands loose by his sides.

Hector had come to his feet. His initial reaction was a step back from Trey, but then he recollected himself and stood his ground. Rebecca knew that was a mistake.

"Becky, I have no further time for your games." Hector addressed her as if there weren't a six-foot-four man in between them. "We're leaving, packed or not. Get in the car with your mother."

Rebecca knew that was an even bigger mistake.

Trey crowded Hector's space, his words low, but the language that reached Rebecca was far stronger than anything she'd ever heard him use.

"Robert?" Hector called in a thin voice to the man in the navy suit who'd been stationed by the door.

"You don't want to do that," Trey said, his gaze boring into Hector's as Robert came over at a jog.

It's like watching a train wreck. It was so obvious what was going to happen. Rebecca couldn't turn away, and so she saw Trey's smile the instant before he threw his shoulder into the doomed Robert's chest, knocking the man to the ground. Trey grabbed Hector by the throat. He twisted the collar of Hector's sweater in his fist. "One piece of advice. Do not tell me your name."

Rebecca could only assume Hector had been the boss of his own little world too long. He'd forgotten that power in a Boston bank office didn't mean he had any other kind of power. "I'm Hector Ferrique, and you better remember that name. I'm going to—"

Trey's fist was quick and efficient. Hector hit the ground with only one blow. Unfortunately, he took the table lamp down with him.

"Hector Ferrique, you owe my mother a lamp. Now get the hell off my land."

Chapter Seventeen

The rain began after Rebecca's mother left. Trey left Rebecca, too, to bring the horses in from the winter weather. He was gone a long time. There were a lot of horses, and two more barns farther from the house. The ranch was far larger than she'd first realized. Rebecca watched Trey disappear from her spot by the window.

She made a pantry dinner, boiling water for spaghetti and opening a jar of sauce, but she served it on china by the Christmas tree. She sat with her back to the winged armchair and tried not to picture her mother's hand touching the mantel.

She felt Trey's gaze on her and set aside her plate.

"Not hungry?" he asked.

She looked up at him, prepared to shrug and smile and pretend. The care and concern in his summer blue eyes took her breath away. That was what she wanted most. That was what she'd failed to capture in her coupons.

The sex was important, though. It gave him a reason to keep her around, which kept her safe and provided for. She needed to lighten up this somber dinner. Keep it fun. Keep it sexy.

On the blanket by the tree, she drew her knees to her chest and clasped her arms around them, putting a little energy into her pose, tilting her head in a flirtatious way.

Trey was near her, sitting on the floor as well, but using the sofa as a backrest. He looked so wonderful, freshly showered, his black hair still damp. He was nearly done with an enormous portion of spaghetti. If she was going to play house with a man who worked outdoors all day, she was going to have to remember to cook for three. Maybe four.

She waited until he looked up from his plate, then she smiled as if she were perfectly delighted with life. "You were gone a long time. Did you miss me?"

"I keep you in my mind every minute."

"Oh." There was an intensity to his words that she wasn't prepared to hear. She'd been planning on steering the conversation in a different direction. "I guess there must be a lot of horses here, with all those different barns and paddocks. Is your ranch very big?"

"About seventy-five thousand acres."

"Seventy-five thousand?" The number boggled her mind and derailed her train of thought. "I never left the ranch when I ran away, did I?"

"You stayed right where I could find you."

Again, that intensity. Rebecca couldn't ignore it, so she relaxed enough to rest her chin on her knees. "You're the James in James Hill, I take it. Why didn't they call it Waterson Hill, or something like that?"

"The ranch is old. The only way to have one this size is to inherit it. Land costs too much to start a new cattle operation. Over time, the ranch got passed down through women every few generations. The last names would change. I'm the third James Waterson, but there were two James McClaines before that, and the original land grant was to James Schuler, my many-greats grandfather."

"You're the sixth James to own the James Hill Ranch. That's some old money." And then, to her mortification, she burst into tears. "My mother would be so proud of me."

He set his plate aside and moved closer to her. She shuddered when he sat a little behind her and wrapped his arms around her, because it made her feel like they were back in a sleeping bag. Fresh tears welled, but she tried not to cry too loudly. She wanted to hear every word as he called her *sweetheart* and *darlin'*.

Eventually, she mopped herself up with her dinner napkin. "It's just depressing that I turned out to be like her, after all."

"I don't see the resemblance."

"She has Hector. I have you. I keep telling myself you and I are different."

"We are."

"I had no idea who you were when I first slept with you. No idea at all. I want you to remember that."

"I'll remember." He started to do that wonderful, one-sided grin. "Although I'm not sure that's the most flattering sentiment. That doesn't make either one of us look very good."

"Don't make me laugh when I'm so miserable."

"My apologies."

She laid her head back on his familiar shoulder and turned her face into his neck. "I wanted to be with you when I thought you were a landscaper in Oklahoma. Re-

member that, too, okay? This was never a trap or a trick.
I wasn't ever trying to cut a deal with a wealthy man."

"I really am a landscaper in Oklahoma. I've had a lot
of time to think—"

A horrible thought occurred to her. She pushed away
from him so she could turn around. "You're not just a
landscaper, are you? You're probably some kind of landscaping tycoon."

His smile faltered. "I've got a few crews. Eight trucks.
That's more than some, less than others."

"James Waterson the third, do you really? This is
awful. My mother has to save face. You know she's looking you up on the internet right now, and she's probably
cackling with glee that she'll have a good answer when
she's asked about little Becky."

She sniffed again, not very sexy, and flexed her feet
in her socks. She was too comfortable with him, when
she should be a *femme fatale* to whom he was helplessly
drawn like a moth to a flame.

"If I married you, she'd turn that into her personal
triumph, like she'd auctioned off my virginity for seventy-five thousand acres."

The last of his smile died.

She tried to tease him like a fun girlfriend should.
"What else have you done? Nothing will surprise me.
Have you saved children from burning buildings? In-
vented a new gizmo? Won a major sporting event?"

He ran his fingers through her hair. "Your mother
might read that I was the highest-ranked college quarterback in the nation at one point."

He said it like he was confessing that he'd once been
a murderer. He was in such a strange mood.

"You're not kidding, are you?" Now it was her teasing

smile that faltered as she remembered the day's drama. "The way you took that bodyguard out…that was like some kind of tackle, wasn't it? Then you threw that punch… I'm so sorry you had to fight for me."

"I'm not. It was my pleasure."

She picked up his right hand and kissed his knuckles. "Does it hurt? I didn't get a chance to ask you if you needed ice or anything before you left."

"Rebecca, I mean it when I say it was a pleasure. Maybe it's a guy thing, or a cowboy thing—hell, it's probably a caveman thing—but there's nothing more satisfying than knocking down some bastard who deserves it. When you first told me his name in that sleeping bag in the cabin, I knew his time was coming."

"Did you know who he was today, before he bragged about his name?"

His hand grasped hers. "I may be slow, but even I can put two and two together. Most of the time."

The card game. How could she have forgotten about that miserable card game?

She kissed his hand one more time, anxious to steer away from anything he didn't like. Her mother would never have brought up a subject that offended her protector, and Rebecca was grateful for Trey's protection. "Do you think Hector will come back?"

"No. That was his only play. He'll move on now. You're safe on this ranch, either way."

She wanted to crawl inside his skin, just to be totally safe. She huddled against his chest instead. "I think that bodyguard was here to ensure that I got in that car. If it had started raining sooner and you had gone off to the pastures…" Fear of what might have been made her shiver the same as the cold did.

Trey ran his hands down her arms, warming her.

She forced herself to say her fear out loud. "If you'd left to work the horses just a little bit sooner, I would've been dragged away. No policeman would've arrested a mother who was flying her daughter home on a private jet. Money lets men do a lot of things they shouldn't."

"Did you notice the ranch hands who were out front when I put Ferrique in the car? There were at least two. One on horseback, one walking over from the cattle sheds. Did you notice them?"

"Kind of, now that you mention it. Did you press some kind of alarm?"

"There is a fire bell, but there was no need to use it. That limousine was out of place on the ranch. I couldn't see it from the barn, but the hands at the cattle shed could. They were coming to check it out. It's what you do on a ranch."

"Why?"

He shrugged. "It's always been that way. It probably goes back for centuries. You've got to know who is on your land, bad or good. Visitors get noticed. Those cowboys wouldn't have stood by if they saw a man forcing a woman into a car. You're safe on this ranch, sweetheart, even if I'm miles away. You can sleep well tonight."

The rain turned to ice. The sound of the drops pelting the window changed subtly to something sharper. Something less forgiving.

Trey lay on his back in the four-poster bed and cradled Rebecca to his chest. The sleet had blotted out all the starlight, but he could make out the contours of her shoulder and see her hand on the white pillow because of the faint glow from the tree lights she'd left on in the family room. They illuminated the open door of the suite in holiday colors, but Trey appreciated their light for a different reason. Every moment that his eyes were open, he liked to be able to see Rebecca. Commit her to memory. Never forget who he held, not for a millisecond.

He stopped stroking her hair and just held his hands still on her head for long minutes, keeping his own breathing carefully even. Her eyelashes blinked against his skin. She could not sleep.

"Does the sound of the storm bother you?" No matter how softly he spoke, his words seemed too brash in the darkness. "You could try wearing earplugs."

"Then I wouldn't be able to hear your heartbeat."

The sweetness was piercing. She should have been able to hear the impact of her words, so acutely did he feel it in the heart she was listening to.

"An acre of olive trees."

The escaped words hung in the air. Silently, he sent more after them, curse after curse.

"What does that mean?" she asked.

One more time, he gritted his teeth and apologized. "I didn't mean to say that."

"I know. Usually what you say is connected to the conversation, though. 'Rescue swimmer' took a little explanation, maybe, but it made sense. I don't understand olive trees."

"It's a long story."

He couldn't tell her. He couldn't ask her, not while she was torn up inside. She'd been essentially disowned by her mother today, who had shouted nasty last-minute things in the driveway as the bodyguard had tried to get his boss's mistress to sit in the car. Her contempt for Rebecca's choices had been poisonous. Nothing Trey could say would make it better.

I actually do want to marry you. That'll be seventy-five thousand acres—or a third of that, anyway. That's twenty-five thousand acres, a wedding ring and I'll throw in a new car, because you need one. Pretty good deal for your virginity, wouldn't your mother say?

"Long stories are good." Rebecca slid off his chest to lay on her stomach next to him, propped up on her arms. "I can't sleep, anyway."

"It's a hard thing, to cut off ties with your family, even if you're better off without them."

"I wish I'd never met her."

It was an odd thing to say about a parent. He never thought in terms of meeting his parents.

"That makes me sound like an awful person," Rebecca whispered when he was silent. "It's not like she ever hit me or anything."

He rolled on his side to face her. "Do you remember meeting her? She said something today like 'that's why I took you in'? Is she not your birth mother?"

He could tell his question caused her pain. Her eyes were luminous in the almost-dark.

"Trey, my love, we already talked about that."

His heart was pierced again, not with sweetness, but with dread.

"In the kitchen, while I was waiting for the water to boil to make spaghetti, you asked me that same question."

He searched his mind. Nothing.

"We joked about how a watched pot never boils, so we could talk as long as we wanted while we stared at it.

You asked me about that taking-me-in comment. She's not my birth mother."

Nothing. As far as he knew, this had never happened in his life.

"I told you my real name. I'm Rebecca Burgess, remember?"

Rebecca was not a Cargill. He'd drilled that into his head after a few mistakes. She'd never gone by Maynard or Lexington.

"Rebecca Burgess." He said it out loud, the name of the woman he loved, but he knew he'd forget it and have to be reminded.

There was one name she'd never use: Rebecca Waterson. Trey would never ask her to marry a man so unworthy of her.

He couldn't remember boiling a goddamned pot of spaghetti. Disgusted, angry, he rolled out of bed and yanked on the jeans he'd thrown over a chair.

"Where are you going?" The concern in Rebecca's voice was precariously close to pity.

"Nowhere. My life is going absolutely goddamned nowhere."

He slammed the bedroom door behind himself.

Out of habit, he forced out the usual words. "I didn't mean to say that."

There was no one around to hear.

Chapter Eighteen

Rebecca was scared out of her mind. She'd been scared of being forced to sleep with Hector Ferrique and scared that Patricia Cargill would kick her out. She was scared of ice storms and hospitals, and she was still scared she'd somehow freeze to death in this warm house. But nothing, nothing, scared her like the thought of losing Trey.

Her hands shook as she tied the sash of the white bathrobe. She fumbled with the doorknob, but she held up the long hem of her robe and did not trip as she ran after Trey. He was not by the Christmas tree, brooding into the cold hearth, and not in the kitchen, where they'd had a long talk he didn't remember. She opened the door to the room he'd been in the first night, the room full of trophies that gleamed in the dark.

He wasn't in the house at all.

"Trey!"

At a full run, her fists full of white robe, she plunged out the mudroom door and off the back deck into the icy sleet, heading for the barn. She would cut through that to reach the ATV shed. Maybe he'd needed to leave, just leave, to escape a bad situation that he couldn't change.

I'll go with you. I don't care.

She kept her head down against the sleet, but she was forced to run a little slower. The bare soles of her feet struck hard ground. Every piece of rock felt like a razor blade.

She heard the pounding of his running footsteps a second before he grabbed her around the waist and swung her into his arms, running the rest of the way to the barn. "Rebecca, damn it, what are you doing?"

It was dark but dry in the barn, cool enough that she could see the white puffs of their breaths as they stopped inside the door. Trey put her down and slid the door shut, then scowled as he looked her up and down. He cursed at her bare feet and scooped her up again to perch her on a stack of hay bales.

The hay pricked her thighs right through her thin robe. Trey grabbed a horse blanket and bent to dry her feet. His movements were brisk and the blanket was coarse as he chastised her. "Don't you ever do a thing like that again. You scared the hell out of me, running across the ranch like some kind of white ghost."

"You scared me first." She was wet and chilled, but inside she felt hot and angry and so incredibly relieved to have him in hand's reach, looking strong and healthy and furious.

Done with her feet, he stood and pitched the blanket into a corner. "I was standing on the front porch. Staying dry, like a normal person, when I heard my name. What the hell did you think you were doing?"

"I had to find you." She grabbed him by the only clothing he wore, grasping belt loops on his jeans and tugging him closer to stand between her knees. She twined her feet around the backs of his thighs as if that would keep him from running away.

She circled both arms around his neck to pull him close, but he resisted her for a second that lasted forever. When he gave in, his arms came around her and he held her too tightly against his chest. Crushed against him, she felt like she could breathe again.

"You thought I decided to walk to the barn in the sleet?" he muttered into her hair.

"I thought you went to get an ATV. Everyone goes crazy now and then. You're allowed to run away, but you have to take me with you. New rule. I have to take you with me, too."

"Rebecca."

"Do you want that? Please tell me you want that."

He was silent, although his hold on her didn't loosen.

It would have been so easy to slip into sex. With her robe open in front and his jeans easily unzipped, he could have been inside her with a single push. The physical reassurance would be a relief after the scare they'd given each other.

Instead, they stayed as they were, so close, not talking, not close enough. There was something terribly, terribly wrong. Whatever it was, he was not going to tell her.

It was harder than breaking out of her mother's prison, even harder than staying awake by an oak tree in the cold, but Rebecca had to know.

"Trey, what's wrong with you?"

Oh, he held her hard. His arms were incredibly strong, and emotion made his hold too tight. She did not try to get free.

"Why did you get a CT scan in the emergency room and I didn't?" At his continued silence, she asked the most frightening question of all. "Do you have a brain tumor?"

If you do, how am I going to live without you?

Hard on the heels of that selfish thought, she whispered, "You're not alone."

"It's not a brain tumor. It's not a stroke. I'm just… damaged."

He stopped crushing her with his arms, only to start touching her with his hands. He smoothed his palm over her cheek, his touch not entirely gentle, and buried his hand in her hair. He seemed to want to touch her everywhere at once, a desperate and emotional man. He grabbed a fistful of her bathrobe's lapel in one hand, holding it shut over her heart, but his other hand slipped inside to cup her breast.

"Don't you see?" he said over her lips, letting her go, touching her again, sliding his hands back in her hair and cupping her face. "I am alone. I've been alone for ten years." He kissed his way down her throat, pressing his hands into her back. "I want you. I want this, I want this so bad, but I don't get to keep it."

She tried to hold him steady as she smoothed his hair off his forehead. "You can keep me. You've got me."

"I forgot our conversation. God, I lost a moment with you today. What if I forget you? There are people I forget entirely."

Her heart broke for him as he took her mouth and whispered her name. He kissed her again and again, saying her name between each kiss.

"Trey," she said firmly, but he didn't hear her. The

muscles of his shoulders flexed as his hands roamed over every part of her he could reach.

"Trey, can I help you remember?"

When he bent to kiss her, she put one hand on the back of his head and pressed her forehead to his, wanting him to slow down. "If you forgot me, could I help you remember? Is there anything I could do to help you remember?"

The frantic pace slowed as he became more focused on her. The sleet pelted the roof and a horse shifted in her stall, but Rebecca still heard only silence when she wanted to hear his voice.

She tried once more. "When you forget someone, do you ever remember them again?"

"Sometimes, but only sometimes. In the helicopter, when Zach Bishop said his name, I remembered him. Before that, I didn't know who the hell he was."

"Then I'll tell you that I'm Rebecca Burgess." She kissed him on the cheek. "But you might remember me as Rebecca Cargill." She kissed his other cheek. "You can call me anything you like, as long as you call me yours."

She wrapped her arms around him as tightly as she could, and she held him as the shudders racked his body, until he was cold and lonely no more.

Rebecca Burgess Cargill stood at the top of the ladder and reached to the top of the Christmas tree to take the angel down. She looked like an angel herself.

Trey was the selfish bastard who wanted to keep her.

She came halfway down the ladder and handed him the angel. "I'm going to get these high ornaments while I'm up here, okay?"

He'd stand here all day at the bottom of the ladder, holding it steady and keeping her safe. It seemed to be the one thing he could offer her with confidence. He could keep her safe. But the rest...

For ten years, he'd worried about himself. When the world got too noisy or busy or dizzying, he'd escaped to make himself more comfortable, leaving parties and stores and any other situation that challenged him. He hadn't thought about what the party's host or hostess felt. He hadn't cared that a store employee would find his half-full shopping cart and have to painstakingly put back everything. When Trey had blurted out impolite truths, he'd hated his own embarrassment. If he'd noticed that he'd caused someone else embarrassment, he'd only been angry because it increased his own tenfold.

He'd ended up building a life that fit him, and only him.

Rebecca came halfway down the ladder again to hand him a cluster of shiny baubles. "Sorry, there are a bunch of fragile ones in there." Back up the ladder she went.

His life was limited because it had to be. Where would that leave Rebecca?

Confined to a ranch because her husband felt disoriented everywhere else. Forced to attend parties without him, or to leave suddenly and early as they had at Christmas. Required to watch movies on a television set, because the big screen gave him headaches.

Jeez, he'd forgotten that last one. This morning, with her unique combination of deference and determination, Rebecca had gotten Trey to describe his problems. She'd noticed the numbers, the spontaneous comments and that he'd forgotten their conversation, of course. He'd added some difficulty putting faces with names. Finding a new address.

"I'm going to drop all of these if I even wiggle a finger. Let me just carry this bunch all the way down, so you can take them from me." She kissed him before she went back up the ladder.

He'd forgotten to mention the movie screen thing. He'd downplayed everything this morning. He thought his life was straightforward, but he'd made so many accommodations over the years, he didn't think about them anymore. He didn't know how different he was— but Rebecca would find out the hard way.

If he married her, he'd bring her down. As surely as she kept coming halfway down this ladder, she'd always be the one lowering herself to his damaged level. Potential was a terrible thing to lose. If she gave up hers voluntarily, it might haunt them both.

"Don't come down again. You're wearing yourself out with all these trips to hand me things."

She sat on the top step of the ladder. "How do you propose we undecorate the rest of this tree, then?"

"Drop them. I'll catch them."

"They'll break when they hit your hands."

"No, they won't. I have it on good authority that I've got soft hands."

She made a face at him like he was crazy. "I don't know who told you that, cowboy, but between the ranch and the landscaping, your hands are not soft. I love to have them on me, precisely because they aren't soft. My hands are soft."

"It's a football term. It means—you know, forget all that. Drop an ornament, and I'll catch it without breaking it."

It became a little game, once he caught the first few and she realized he didn't miss. She started dropping them in rapid succession, or dropping two at once. He caught them all, right-handed or left-handed, without moving far from the base of the ladder. Had it wobbled, he would have caught that first.

"You're like a juggler." As she stood to get more ornaments, she said, "Soft hands is a football term, huh? You know, I read an article once about football players. About a lot of different sports, actually, that could cause head trauma."

Trey knew what question was coming. "Yes, that was it."

"So, what are you doing about it?" She pulled an ornament off and dropped it without looking at him.

"Whoa." He caught it, anyway. "There's nothing to do about it. I forgot to tell you, movies are tough, and— Whoa. You might want to give me a heads-up before you drop things on me."

She sat on the top step again. "That's what the doctors say? There's nothing to do about it?"

"Doctors." He wished he could spit tobacco juice like Gus every time he said the word.

"Lana called about an hour ago, while you were at the paddock. She'd really like to see you this afternoon."

Nothing. He'd never heard the name *Lana* before.

"Did she now?" The generic reply usually bought him time. If the conversation carried on and he listened hard enough, he might figure out who was being talked about.

"Well, she wouldn't see you personally, of course."

He looked up at Rebecca with his face carefully neutral, and kept listening.

"Because the baby's only four weeks old."

And kept listening.

"Oh, Trey, I'm so sorry."

She knew. She saw right through him when he could fool other people.

"Lana is Braden MacDowell's wife, the one with the brand-new baby."

Rebecca waited, and Trey remembered. He nodded, once.

"Dr. Lana MacDowell is in charge of research at the hospital, and she called this morning because they're running a study you could be part of. It includes a memory clinic. It's some kind of rehab program where they try to strengthen memories."

He'd given up on getting better a long time ago. Rebecca's enthusiasm was youthful and probably naive, but it was also contagious.

"Your MacDowell friends have got some serious connections with that hospital, because they could get you in this afternoon for an evaluation. I have to turn in that rental car, so I thought we could go into Austin together and make a day of it."

Trey wanted Rebecca as intensely this morning as he had wanted her in the barn last night. There were no guarantees that he could keep her. His disability and her pity could tear them apart. As she sat so hopefully at the top of the ladder like an angel, he remembered when she'd looked as white as porcelain with pale blue lips. He'd been determined not to lose her then. He had to try to keep her now.

"This afternoon, then. We'll see what the doctors have to say."

Rebecca came flying down the ladder and nearly threw herself into his arms.

She was easy to catch. Trey was only afraid she'd be hard to hold on to.

Chapter Nineteen

The doctors loved Trey.

He did not love them.

Ten years ago, he'd learned to hate the word *unremarkable*. Every test had been unremarkable in its results. He'd been accused of taking drugs as an explanation for his symptoms.

Now, he was an *interesting* case.

Hours of testing had cataloged and quantified all his shortcomings. The rehab had started the next day. Even ten years after the damage had been done, the medical staff seemed confident that his brain could form new connections and improve its function—but modestly. The way they emphasized *modestly*, Trey didn't know whether to have hope or not.

The math and the disorientation and the rest were all issues that had their own specialists. This clinic focused on memory, and that was fine with Trey. The reason he was there was Rebecca. His one, overriding fear was that he would forget her.

Memory was a tricky thing, and in this, he was an

interesting case, as well. Memories prior to his college days were still intact. The rhythms of the ranch, from the cycle of calving and culling to the seasonal demands of the weather, came easily to him because he'd learned it since birth.

The way he accessed those memories, like meeting Zach had opened all his high school football memories, made for an *interesting* case.

New information was harder to retain, like a new landscaping client's address—or a new person. He'd eventually remembered Aunt June, because she was an old memory. A new person, however, he could forget. Like Lana MacDowell.

Like Rebecca.

The key to putting new info into his memory, they said, included repetition. Had he met Rebecca at a party, he might have forgotten the next day that there was a woman he'd like to take out on a second date. But he'd met her in extreme circumstances, which made her more memorable, and they hadn't been apart since.

During their first day, they'd only been apart a few minutes, and they'd not only talked but touched. He'd learned the feel of her skin and the sound of her voice, without what they called environmental distractions, like phones or even other people passing them on a sidewalk.

If he and Rebecca hadn't liked one another, he would have stored the memory of an unpleasant person just as firmly.

Because sleep also impacted memory, the doctors told Trey that falling asleep with Rebecca every night and seeing her face every morning was exactly how they'd advise him to improve his memory of her, if it was needed.

They didn't think it was needed. His case was so very *interesting*. Given the unusual circumstances, they were certain she was in his memory now, just as the ranch and his parents and brother were. He'd never lost them, even if his brain hadn't transferred every conversation into long-term storage. He wouldn't lose Rebecca.

For that, Trey was grateful. If he returned to Oklahoma alone, he wanted to know exactly what his heart was missing.

For everything else, the doctors could go to hell. Their tests and their rehab were making everything worse, not better.

New Year's Eve was full of promise that the next year would be better, not worse.

Rebecca had looked forward to it every year for as long as she could remember. She'd hoped, year after year, that this would be the year she'd stay in one school. This would be the year her mother would let her choose her back-to-school outfit. This would be the year she'd meet a boy. It hadn't turned out that way, of course, but this was the year that would prove she'd been right to stay hopeful.

This was the year she'd begin a new life with Trey Waterson. He'd said so in the barn, five nights ago, on a rainy night full of raw emotion.

Kind of.

Every day since then, Trey had been at the hospital, throwing himself into rehab. It was all card games and puzzles, according to him, but Rebecca could see it made him tired in a way that ranch work did not. During their time together, he'd been too exhausted for much talking.

During their time apart, Rebecca had started reliving those moments in the barn.

He'd said he wanted her. He'd also said he couldn't have her. When she'd said *call me yours*, he hadn't said anything at all.

She rubbed her arms against the chill as Trey drove them back to the ranch in his pickup truck.

"Thank you for taking me out." Her voice was husky after shouting over the music. The honky-tonk they'd just left had been a new experience in loudness. She'd never heard anything like it at her mother's clubs.

The bar was the closest one to the ranch, and it had seemed like everyone remembered Trey from ten years ago. He'd been shaking hands with men and been kissed on the cheek by women practically nonstop. He'd gestured toward her and shouted *Rebecca Burgess* to introduce her to every person. People had shouted their own names back at her. The band had played on.

In other words, it had been a nightmare. No fun for her, because she knew it must have been a misery for him. Still, he'd stayed, looking great in his black shirt, blue jeans and black boots, every cowgirl's dream. She'd had to insist that she was ready to leave before midnight.

She wondered what he'd been trying to prove. She was afraid she was about to find out.

Trey parked in front of the house and turned off the engine. The dashboard clock gave them fifteen minutes before the new year was about to begin.

Trey spoke first. "We can get inside and put the television on for the official countdown."

"I'd rather stay in the truck, if it's okay with you. You're going to tell me something awful, and I'd like to get it over with."

It had just been a guess on her part, but his silence was an awful answer in itself.

She kept her chin up. "You're not the only one who can be blunt, you know."

He chuckled at that. "Fair enough, but you were blunt on purpose. There's a difference."

Rebecca waited. If he wanted to tell her why they couldn't be together, she wasn't going to help him out any further.

"Today was only a half day at the hospital, because of New Year's Eve."

She hadn't expected to hear that. She waited a little longer.

"I didn't make it home early, because I got lost. I drove for almost an hour, until I hit Sixth Street. The restaurants and bars were already getting full with the early-out work crowd. I recognized some of the buildings, and then I was able to get back to the ranch from there, because I'd done it so many times as a teenager."

"That was a clever solution."

"No, it was an accident. I got out of a jam this time, but I'm guaranteed to have that kind of thing happen again. I took you to the bar tonight because I thought you'd enjoy it, but also because I wanted to see how much I could handle. I haven't pushed myself out of my comfort zone in a long time. How did I do?"

"I don't think you recognized half of those people, but I don't think they realized it."

"I did all right, then. That's good, because I got bad news at the clinic today."

She couldn't stay cool at that announcement and turned toward him anxiously. "Like what?"

He picked up her hand and kissed the back of it. "I'm

fine, first of all. Please don't go all pale on me like that. They thought it was good news at the hospital. I've been doing this intensive training, and after eighteen total hours of work, they told me my test score had improved."

"How is that not good news?"

"Out of a possible ten points, my score went from five to five-point-three. That was it. Three-tenths of a point. They call that a victory, but it was a reality check for me. There won't be any big leaps at this stage of the game."

"And because you're damaged, you don't want to marry me, do you? That's what you said in the barn. I just didn't want to hear it."

"Rebecca." Trey put his head back on the seat and rubbed his chest, as if she'd caused him some pain there. "That was prize-winningly blunt."

"*Damaged* was your word. I would never describe you as damaged. It's the last thing I think of around you."

"All right, let's cut to the chase. I want the best for you. If you were married to me, don't you see how it would be? You'd see a new place to eat in Austin. You'd call and say, 'Honey, meet me after work.' There's a good chance I wouldn't be able to find it. I'd be lost in town. You might have to leave your friends and come to find me. What kind of husband can't meet his wife after work?"

This was it, then. He was telling her that she would always have to deal with his brain injury. It wasn't going to improve dramatically, and he thought that made him a bad husband. She chose her words with care.

"You're asking the wrong question. My question is, why do you think I'd be such a terrible wife? Why would I ask you to find a new place you'd never been to before? Instead of telling you to meet me at a restaurant, I'd say,

'Tell one of the hands to feed the horses tonight. I'll be home soon, and I want you to go with me to a great new place everyone at work is raving about.'"

He was quiet for a long moment.

"Trey?"

"You can do so much better than me."

Her mother's words. She started to protest, but he cut her off.

"You can do so much better, but that doesn't mean I'm going to let you. What I was trying to say in the barn was that you are imprinted in my heart and on my soul. I was afraid my mind would forget you. It would be agony, because my heart and soul would know you were missing. At the clinic today, they told me what I already knew. You're already a part of me, like this land. That's not ever going to change. It's almost midnight. Can I take you for a little drive?"

Don't you want to kiss me? Don't you want to tell me you love me? How about ask me to marry you?

"Sure, we can go for a drive," she said.

He backed out of the driveway and took the dirt roads that went past the paddocks and the shed where the ATVs were kept. When he stopped the truck, he pulled the Navajo blanket out from behind the seat.

"First of all, happy new year."

Rebecca looked at the dashboard clock. "Oh, we missed it."

"No, we didn't. We've got the whole year. This is only day one, sweetheart. Promise one on day one is that I will never let you get cold. Will you come do some star-gazing with me? There's something I have to show you."

Wrapped in Trey's arms inside the familiar warmth of the Navajo blanket, Rebecca sat on a little patch of land on the James Hill Ranch and waited. Anticipated. Savored the feeling of good things about to happen in her life.

She leaned back against Trey as he pointed in the dark. "Do you see that hill over there? It looks plain tonight, but this is its year. Let me tell you what I see when I look at that hill. I see potential."

Nestled into her lover's arms, Rebecca smiled as she listened. She was kissed, she was told she was loved and she was asked to become his bride.

This was the year that would start a lifetime of happiness. Throughout that long life, whenever her husband walked up behind her and whispered *an acre of olive trees*, she would know that what he was really saying was *I love you*.

Epilogue

The first year of the rest of their lives flew by. Trey sold his landscaping business and returned to run the ranch with his brother. Rebecca earned her first paycheck with Texas Rescue as an administrative assistant to her former stepsister and future sister-in-law. As winter arrived, the main house of the James Hill Ranch saw wedding preparations once again.

The new house on the hill that wasn't too far away was nearly built. The olive trees surrounding it were putting down their roots. And inside, Trey Waterson was bracing himself for a honeymoon trip.

He'd continued to make progress in his memory. He would never have the same abilities he'd had when he was nineteen, but someday he'd be able to quiz his kids on their multiplication tables. Someday.

First, he had to marry his bride, and then he had to take her on a honeymoon. It was no secret that he was more comfortable on the ranch than anywhere else in the world, but he and Rebecca made a good team and worked around his limitations, so Mr. and Mrs. Waterson were going to take a honeymoon trip...somewhere. Rebecca had planned it. Today was the big reveal.

He took a seat on the floor in front of the fireplace they hadn't used yet. Its first use was going to be as an easel, apparently.

"This is an artist's rendering, namely Patricia's. She's really good at interior design. Without further ado, may I reveal the Waterson honeymoon retreat? Ta-da!"

She set the sketchbook on the limestone hearth and sat next to Trey, scooting close. "It's our cabin. I want you to know that I spent a good portion of the budget having the walls rechinked. No cold air is going to come inside. There will be no need to borrow the blanket for certain necessities—ahem—because they make these cute little prefab cabin bathrooms that have water tanks and heaters. That was the first thing I had shipped in. The porch has been repaired, and there will be a giant pile of wood already chopped and dried and ready to go."

"You want to stay on the ranch?" He would be so much more comfortable here. That she was willing to sacrifice a trip to anywhere in the world for his sake made his chest hurt—nothing new when it came to Rebecca.

"Don't get all sappy on me. This is going to be a real honeymoon, where the couple get in bed and stay in bed." She looked at the sketch and sighed as only a girl looking at a flower fantasy could. "The bed in question will have the world's most plush mattress. We could only fit a double, but that's okay because I always sleep on top of you, anyway, and it's a lot bigger than a sleeping bag, no matter what. There will be a down comforter and pillows. Wouldn't pillows have been so great last time?

"Everything is going to be white. All the bedding, all

the flowers. And yes, there's going to be a garland over the fireplace that looks as pretty as a wedding gown, just like Patricia drew. She knows the florist who can do it.

"Best of all, we'll have baskets of food, easy stuff like wine and cheese, and champagne and strawberries. There will be a little propane stove in this corner, though, so we can make coffee. We can live on coffee and chocolate croissants. I've ordered an entire cheesecake, too."

He tried not to be sappy, and put a little fake disgruntlement into his voice. "For a sexual fantasy, you seem to have put an awful lot of thought into eating."

"I don't want to be cold or hungry. I'm taking care of the hungry part. You're taking care of the cold."

"How am I doing that?"

"Oh, I've got a whole book of coupons you're just going to love."

When James Waterson III married Rebecca Burgess and carried her over the threshold of their honeymoon cabin, he fed her a chocolate croissant, read the first coupon and they both started living happily ever after.

* * * * *

We hope you enjoyed reading

MY DEAREST CAL

by #1 *New York Times* bestselling author
SHERRYL WOODS

and

A TEXAS RESCUE CHRISTMAS

by *USA TODAY* bestselling author
CARO CARSON

Both were originally
Harlequin® Special Edition
stories!

SPECIAL EXCERPT FROM

HARLEQUIN®

SPECIAL EDITION

*When his best friend's little sister shows up with her son,
Nathan Fortune's past won't stay buried...and threatens
to snuff out the future Nate and Bianca now hope to
build with each other.*

Read on for a sneak preview of
HER SOLDIER OF FORTUNE,
the first book in the newest Fortunes continuity,
**THE FORTUNES OF TEXAS:
THE RULEBREAKERS.**

"He's an idiot," Nate offered automatically.

One side of her mouth kicked up. "You sound like Eddie. He never liked Brett, even when we were first dating. He said he wasn't good enough for me."

"Obviously that's true." Nate took a step closer but stopped himself before he reached for her. Bianca didn't belong to him, and he had no claim on her. But one morning with EJ and he already felt a connection to the boy. A connection he also wanted to explore with the beautiful woman in front of him. "Any man who would walk away from you needs to have his—" He paused, feeling the unfamiliar sensation of color rising to his face. His mother had certainly raised him better than to swear in front of a lady, yet the thought of Bianca being hurt by her ex made his blood boil. "He needs a swift kick in the pants."

"Agreed," she said with a bright smile. A smile that

made him weak in the knees. He wanted to give her a reason to smile like that every day. "I'm better off without him, but it still makes me sad for EJ. I do my best, but it's hard with only the two of us. There are so many things we've had to sacrifice." She wrapped her arms around her waist and turned to gaze out of the barn, as if she couldn't bear to make eye contact with Nate any longer. "Sometimes I wish I could give him more."

"You're enough," he said, reaching out a hand to brush away the lone tear that tracked down her cheek. "Don't doubt for one second that you're enough."

As he'd imagined, her skin felt like velvet under his callused fingertip. Her eyes drifted shut and she tipped up her face, as if she craved his touch as much as he wanted to give it to her.

He wanted more from this woman—this moment—than he'd dreamed possible. A loose strand of hair brushed the back of his hand, sending shivers across his skin.

She glanced at him from beneath her lashes, but there was no hesitation in her gaze. Her liquid brown eyes held only invitation, and his entire world narrowed to the thought of kissing Bianca.

"I finished with the hay, Mommy," EJ called from behind him.

Don't miss
HER SOLDIER OF FORTUNE by Michelle Major,
available January 2018 wherever
Harlequin® Special Edition books and ebooks are sold.

www.Harlequin.com

⊕ HARLEQUIN®

SPECIAL EDITION

Life, Love and Family

Save **$1.00**

on the purchase of ANY
Harlequin® Special Edition book.

Available wherever books are sold, including
most bookstores, supermarkets, drugstores
and discount stores.

Save $1.00

on the purchase of any Harlequin Special Edition book.

Coupon valid until February 28, 2018.
Redeemable at participating outlets in the U.S. and Canada only.
Not redeemable at Barnes & Noble stores. Limit one coupon per customer.

52615317

5 65373 00076 2   (8100)0 12324

NYTCOUP1217

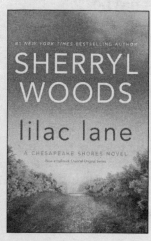

"Caro Carson writes books that touch the heart; they're witty, wise, emotional and filled with intricately layered, fascinating characters!" — *New York Times* bestselling author RaeAnne Thayne

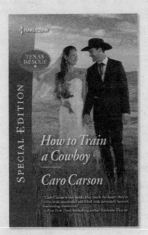

Benjamin Graham is a former marine, not a cowboy. So when he gets a job as a ranch hand, he has a lot to learn. Luckily, Emily Davis is willing to teach him everything he needs to know. But as the attraction between them grows, Benjamin and Emily will both have to face their pasts and learn to embrace the future.

Don't miss
HOW TO TRAIN A COWBOY
by Caro Carson,
available now from
Harlequin® Special Edition.